FIRES OF MEMORY

ISBN: 978-1-4392-0802-1
ISBN-10: 1-4392-0802-6

Stellar Phoenix Books
Philadelphia, Toronto

Printed and bound by BookSurge in the USA

Cover design and art by Jonathan Cresswell-Jones
Proofreading by Jennifer Loehlin

FIRES OF MEMORY

Scott Washburn

Stellar Phoenix Books

Philadelphia, USA

Toronto, Canada

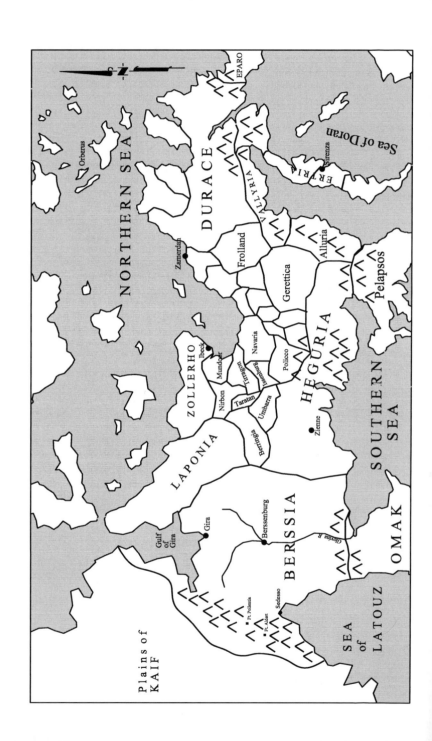

PROLOGUE

"I think there is something ahead," said Thelena. "Is that what you seek, Father?"

Atark, her father, shaded his eyes and peered past the ears of his trotting pony, but after a moment lowered his hand. "My old eyes aren't so sharp anymore, daughter. What do you see and where?"

"Just to the right of the direction we ride. It looks like a small mound or hillock." He looked again. The plain, covered with rippling waves of grass, was not nearly so flat here close to the mountains as it was farther west, but the irregular bump seemed very obvious to her. She glanced at her father. There was some gray in his dun hair and beard and lines on his sun-baked face, but he certainly wasn't old!

"Ah, I think I see it now. The wanderer wasn't too clear about what he had seen, but this might be it—although I wasn't really expecting a structure..." He trailed off into silence.

"Is there treasure there, Father?" Ardan asked excitedly. Thelena looked over her shoulder at where her younger brother bounced on his pony next to their mother. "Gold and jewels and fine armor?"

"Perhaps. We shall see."

"Your father does not seek gold or jewelry," said Mother. "He hopes for other treasure. But have no fear: the *practical* ones in this family will not turn up our noses should any gold be found!"

"Aye, your mother is always the practical one, Ardan. Listen to her wisdom instead of the foolish ranting of your crazy father." He smiled as he said it and Mother smiled back at him. But Ardan was properly scandalized.

"You are not crazy! You are the best shaman in all the clans! And that is what I tell the other boys when they...when they..." The lad stuttered to a halt, but no one had to ask what the other boys said: *Fake. Trickster. Charlatan.* Thelena had heard the taunts and seen Ardan coming home to their tent with face and fists bloodied from trying to silence them.

The sad part was that Ardan was probably correct: their father *was* one of the best shamen to be found among the clans of the Kaifeng, modest though his powers were. He could start a campfire, using spoken words like another man might use flint and steel. He could cure some of the lesser diseases that afflicted men and beasts and, on occasion, he could predict the weather with amazing accuracy. Thelena looked closely at her father's face. He took pride in being able to serve his clan, but she knew that he longed to discover the secrets of the great shamen of legend. Privately, she thought those tales of mighty spells and wonders were more whimsy than fact, but her father took them seriously and was always eager for anything remaining from the Old Days.

Which was why they were here.

The tales said that over three hundred summers ago a great battle had been fought here between the Kaifeng and the armies of the Easterners. That the battle had been fought—and lost—there was no doubt: every loremaster in every clan knew those stories and told them to the people. Thelena's own eyes were confirming it as she rode: rusted weapons and bits of armor were scattered all around. But the tales of wizards and sorcerers and shamen hurling balls of fire and cracking the earth open to swallow men and horses seemed less likely to her.

Still, terrible things had happened here: she could feel it. Father had told her that as she reached adulthood the Talent might manifest itself in her, just as it had in him. She was barely sixteen summers now, but in the past few months she had started feeling things she had never felt before. Things like she was feeling now.

"I… I don't like this place, Father. There is a…wrongness here."

Her father looked at her with interest, his eyebrows rising. "You feel it, do you? Yes, you are right. Great pain and suffering soaked into the land. It will still cry out to those who can hear."

"I wish I could not." It almost seemed like she could hear faint voices, like people screaming from leagues away over the plains. No words she could understand, just pain and fear. They had nearly reached the mound now and the closer they drew, the stronger was her feeling of unease.

"Is it a tomb, father?" Ardan asked eagerly. "Some old king's tomb, filled with heaps of gold and swords of power? Like in the old legends?"

"Do not let your imagination run away with you, boy," said her father. "This has been here a long time. Like as not it has been stripped of anything valuable." But even as he said the words, Thelena doubted them. As they walked their ponies around the mound they saw no obvious signs of digging or disturbance. It was a grass-covered lump perhaps thirty feet across and ten feet high. On the far side there was an archway of sorts and steps leading down to a vertical stone slab. The archway and the slab were covered with graven runes, nearly worn away by wind and the infrequent rainfalls. Her father dismounted and looked closely at them.

"So, husband, was it worth all the ride?" Mother asked. "We'll never make it back to the main camp before dark. Luckily, I insisted on bringing blankets and the little tent—and food and water. You would have ridden off in your small clothes had I not stopped you."

Father smiled and nodded. "True, my wife. I had not thought it would be quite so far. But we will not camp here tonight. Not so close to...to this. I shall indulge my curiosity until two hours before sunset and then we shall move away. I know I can trust you to tell me how the sun stands."

"I shall indeed. But are you not hungry? The hour for the noon meal is long past."

"Prepare your meal, woman. I shall explore for a bit and then eat."

"Can I help you, Father?" Ardan asked.

Father hesitated, Thelena could see that he did not need an eager boy looking over his shoulder just now. "Son, I need some time to think." Her brother's face fell. "But I promise you will see whatever there might be to see. In the meanwhile, perhaps you can find some treasure on your own. I saw a lance point sticking from the ground not far away. Surely there must be more."

Ardan's enthusiasm quickly returned. "I shall find a treasure, Father! Maybe even before you do!"

"I do not doubt it. But keep a watch, too. There could be...wolves or jackals."

"Wolves? In these desolate parts?" Mother said. "I doubt it."

Father's eyes drifted to the line of blue haze on the eastern horizon. Thelena looked in that direction, too. The borders of Berssia lay among those hills and the king of that land had fortresses to guard them. Patrols would come far onto the plains at times. The clans of the Kaifeng were not openly at war with Berssia or the other Eastern Kingdoms which lay beyond, but that did not stop the lesser raids and skirmishing. Yes, there could be wolves. And the land was not so flat here as it was farther west; enemies could not be spotted as far off. "Just keep a watch," he said and turned back to the mound.

Thelena dismounted and helped her mother unload the ponies and make the meal. She was tempted to ask her father's help with starting the fire, but he was already engrossed with the mound. She resorted to flint and steel, instead, and soon had a small blaze going. Ardan was grubbing in the ground for rusted bits of weapons and armor.

"I was talking with Jalla the other day," said Mother as she began preparing the food. "Her son, Utar, has his eye on you, Thelena. What do you think of him?"

"I've seen him watching me," admitted Thelena. "He is handsome enough, I suppose. But he seems a bit dull-witted. He talks too loudly and laughs at his own jokes."

"Yes, I've noticed that, too. But he is young and trying to attract attention. He will mature as he grows older."

"I doubt he will grow much wiser. I would prefer a smart man over a handsome one. But perhaps I shall be lucky and get one who is both—like you did."

Her mother smiled and cast a fond glance to where Father was standing. "Not everyone can be as lucky as I have been," she said. "Certainly you should choose the right man, but do not wait too long or you may end up a second wife and not a first. That is not something I would recommend, even though it often works out well enough."

"I don't know that I'd want to share my husband with another no matter if I was first or second," said Thelena.

"Yes, well, as the first, you would have far more say on whether or not there will *be* a second."

"Is that why Father never took a second wife?" She looked at her mother and was rewarded by seeing the flicker of a smile.

"I thought I heard the call of a partridge a moment ago, girl. Why don't you take a bow and see if you can provide some fresh meat for your father's meal?"

Thelena's smile was far more than a flicker as she got up from the fire. Her parents were very close and had made a fine home for their children. Thelena hoped that she might do as well someday. She went over to one of the ponies and got out and strung the small hunting bow as she had been told. She paused and listened and heard the call that her mother had mentioned. Yes, it did sound like a partridge. Off in the tall grass to the left. She slowly moved in that direction.

She was an indifferent hunter and archer, but she heard the call again and it was quite close now. If she could catch the bird on its nest, she would have a good chance to make a kill—and perhaps find eggs as well. She crouched down so that the grass was over her head and carefully moved forward, trying to make as little noise as possible. One step... two steps...

She saw a dark shape through the grass just ahead of her and instantly realized that it was too large to be a partridge. Far too large. She turned to dash away. But a second shape rose up from her right. A huge man was only a few paces off. She screamed and tried to run, but a strong grip seized her arm. The bow flew out of her grasp and an instant later impossibly powerful arms wrapped around her, lifting her off her feet.

She screamed again and struggled wildly, but could not break loose. She could see her mother springing up from the fire, Ardan dropping some bit of armor he'd found, and her father rushing up the steps from the mound. But there were other men appearing out of the grass. She recognized them as Varags, mercenary horsemen who served the King of Berssia. Terror coursed through her. She'd heard the stories about them. There were at least a dozen of them and they all had drawn swords and were closing in on her family.

Her father was shouting something in the Varag tongue and for a moment they all paused, but then a man grabbed her mother by the arm and young Ardan began throwing rocks at him. A stone dealt him a painful blow in the face. He snarled something and flung Mother aside and drew one of the short gunpowder weapons as the Easterners used and before anyone could do anything fired it at Ardan.

There was a small puff of smoke at one end of the weapon and a much larger one at the other, along with a loud crack like thunder. The back of Ardan's head blossomed out like a red flower and the boy tumbled backwards to the ground and did not move.

Thelena screamed again. Mother was screaming, too, but she

drew her knife and lunged at one of the Varags. The man easily evaded her blow and the counterstoke with his sword took off her head.

Thelena was sobbing hysterically now. She tried to reach her own knife, but her arms were pinned. Suddenly she stiffened. Her father was reaching for the power. She could feel it like the sun against her skin. She could see him, his face twisted in rage, and she could sense the power swirling around him.

But then a Varag came up behind him and thrust a dagger into his side.

The sensation of power vanished as quickly as it had come, the cold iron of the dagger snuffing it out like a bucket of water on a campfire. Her father slumped to the ground.

She screamed once more. She was still screaming as they tied her to a horse and galloped off.

Jarren Carabello picked a few bits of lint off his black-and-white student's robe and tried to make out his reflection in the tiny, cracked mirror that hung from the equally cracked plaster wall of his cramped apartment. Not good. He had forgotten to ask his landlady to clean and press the robe and it was badly wrinkled from being piled under other laundry and some heavy books for several months since the last time he had reason to wear it. Nothing could be done about that now. He took his hat, which was a nearly shapeless bag of black felt, and fit it on his head. Except for the wilted white feather and tiny brass cockade, it looked like a huge mushroom that had been in the sun too long. He gathered up his papers into a leather portfolio and went out of his room, pausing to lock the door behind him. There was little of interest to any thief in his room, but after being ransacked once and nearly losing his precious cello, Jarren had invested some of his scanty funds in a good lock and had not regretted it.

He trudged down the four flights of narrow wooden steps. As he passed his landlady's flat she stuck her head out to remind him that the rent was due in just five days. It was a daily ritual and he reflected that with her there, he hardly even needed a calendar. He assured her she would get it and then stepped out onto the streets of Sirenza. The heat and the stench hit him simultaneously. His dismal financial condition had forced him to take an apartment down by the docks and at this time of year the winds came from the South. They brought the heat, but somehow never managed to carry away the stink. All the sewers emptied into the bay, where the effluvia simply stayed. It would not be until the Fall when the east winds blew the heat and the stink out to sea that it would become bearable. Fortunately, he was heading to the upper parts of the city now. The heat would not be much less, but at least he would escape the smell.

He walked along the brick and cobblestone streets as quickly as the crowds—and the heat—would allow. Rather than follow the slow back and forth switchbacks of the main boulevards, he took one of the many sets of stairs that led upward. He was soon above the tops of the masts of the many ships that lined the quays and piers of the great harbor. This got him above the worst of the smell, too, and he slowed his pace. He could feel the sweat trickling down his back under the robe and his shirt.

He entered the Great Plaza and paused in the shade of one of the colonnaded buildings that surrounded it. He looked across at the Tower of Domitian and the fine new clock that had recently been installed. He saw that it was only a little after one o'clock. He had nearly an hour before he was to meet with his mentor, Hano Beredane. In his nervousness he had left himself far more time than he really needed. He could just find a bench in the shade and wait, he supposed. Many fine ladies were moving through the plaza and it would certainly be pleasant to watch them. Frustrating, too, of course. No lady, fine or otherwise, would waste a glance on a poor university student.

I have time to visit old Porfino. Maybe he's gotten in something new. The thought led to action and Jarren walked across the plaza and into one of the side streets. A hundred paces brought him to a smaller alley and then to Porfino's shop. The door was open and he walked in. It took a moment to adjust his eyes to the dimness after the bright sunshine outdoors. When he could see again, he noted that there was no sign of Porfino. This time of day he was probably taking a nap in the back room. Jarren did not bother to call for him, but instead wandered around the tiny, cluttered shop. It was filled with all manner of strange and exotic items. Nearly all were damaged or broken or simply worn to some degree. Porcelain and statues, paintings and candelabras, stuffed animals and knickknacks of all descriptions. And toys. Lots of toys.

Jarren had seen them all before and insisted that Porfino tell him everything he knew about each of the more interesting ones. He frowned. If there was anything new he did not see it immediately. He was going to need Porfino's help. Well, one way to rouse him... He went over to a small toy monkey, missing one arm, and picked it up. Instantly it cried out *"Stop! Thief! Help!"* Jarren set it down and looked to the curtained doorway that led to the back room. Only three heartbeats later an old man came barging through with a club in his hand, looking about with wild eyes. He stopped and frowned when he saw Jarren.

"Oh! It's only you! You miserable pup! You should not wake an old man in such a fashion!"

"I knew it would be the easiest way to rouse you, Porfino. Do you have anything new today?"

"Hmmpf! If I did, I shouldn't show it to you anyway!"

"Does that mean you do have something?"

"Well, yes. But I don't think I'll let you see it. And what's the point? You never have any money to buy."

"You show things to me because you love to talk about them—and I'm the only one who will listen to you."

"Not the only one. But you are the only one in the shop at this moment, so I suppose I'll have to talk to you. But why are you all dressed up? I haven't seen you in your robes in months."

"I meet with Hano in an hour. I'm not looking forward to it."

"An hour, eh? Then I best show you my new acquisition now."

"Exactly. What have you got?"

"Oh, something splendid. Hardly damaged at all!" The old man went through the curtain and disappeared into the back room for a moment, talking all the while. In a moment he reemerged with a lacquered wooden box. He shoved a few things aside on a table and set the box down. He opened it and triumphantly withdrew his new treasure. Jarren raised his eyebrows when he saw it. An exquisitely crafted dancing girl, perhaps six inches tall, stood on a marble pedestal half that height. The doll was dressed in a fashion that suggested the desert realms to the southwest, across the sea.

"Very nice," said Jarren. "But is it...magical?"

"Of course! I'd not be showing it to you if it was not! Here, watch." The old man touched a round gold plate set into the side of the pedestal. For a moment nothing happened, but then the tiny figure began to move and a strange but energetic music played. Jarren loved all kinds of music, but he had never heard anything quite like this before. Clearly this came from a long way off. He leaned close to get a good look. The workmanship was truly marvelous. He could barely make out the joints on the limbs and the motion was entirely natural. And it was not some clever clockwork mechanism driving it. The doll spun and twirled and leapt into the air, fully two inches above the pedestal with nothing connecting it at all. Then the doll was…what was it…?

"Oh my," said Jarren, blushing.

"Clearly the private toy of some nobleman," said Porfino with a straight face. The doll was discarding its clothes, one piece at a time. As each item was pulled off, it simply vanished. The detailing beneath the clothes was entirely… realistic. Eventually, only a red scarf was tied about its hips. Jarren blinked when the doll seemed about to tug away that last piece and was suddenly standing there, fully clothed, just like he had first seen it.

"As I said, almost entirely undamaged," said Porfino. "But the motivating spell is unraveling from the end, I fear. When I first saw this, she went a tiny bit farther in her dance than you just saw."

"A pity," said Jarren. "But Porfino, this is wonderful! Surely the finest piece in your collection!"

"Yes, it is. I'd almost hate to sell it. But I must get back what I paid for it—and a bit more. And I know someone who will be glad to pay for such a toy."

"Surely you will let me study it before you do!"

"Perhaps I could hold it for a week or so. But no longer. And I can't have it perform more than once or twice more for you. The spell is too fragile. If it unravels entirely I'll be out all that I paid."

"I understand. But where did you get this? Where do you think it was made? Are there any makers' marks on it?"

"There may be something on the underside. Here, let me show you…"

They were still discussing the possible origins of the toy when the plaza clock struck two. It took a few moments for the sound to register on Jarren's consciousness, but when it did he jerked erect.

"By all the gods! I'm late!" he cried.

"Well then, off with you!" said Porfino. "This will still be here when you get back."

Jarren rushed out of the shop and returned an instant later to grab his portfolio. Then he ran along the alley and back up the street to the plaza. He threaded his way through the crowd, jostling one old man accidentally in his haste. He called an apology over his shoulder and blanched when he noticed the man's priestly robes. But he did not stop; instead he hurried on. Hano was going to be angry—and he so needed him to be in a good mood! The university was almost a mile away and despite all his efforts, it was half past the hour before he stumbled, panting, into Master Hano Beredane's office. The scholar scowled at him through his spectacles and twitched his thick white eyebrows.

"Mister Carabello, you are a passed student and a candidate for master's training. I would have thought that somewhere during your years here at the university you would have learned to tell time."

"I'm sorry, Master Beredane. I was delayed," gasped Jarren.

"Obviously. But now that you are here, perhaps we can discuss this absurd proposal you have sent me for the future course of your study. Please sit down."

Jarren found a seat, but had to evict a large black-and-white cat to actually sit in it. There were several other chairs in the stuffy room, but all were piled with books and papers. As he sat there catching his breath, he was struck by how much Beredane's office looked like Porfino's shop. More books and papers and fewer trinkets and toys, but the same seeming lack of order.

"I'm sorry you consider my proposal 'absurd', sir," said Jarren.

"Well, I can't think of any other word for it that fits. And this is very disappointing. You were one of my best students and I had such high hopes for you. Granted that even then you wasted an inordinate amount of time on this 'hobby' of yours."

"It is not a hobby, sir! It is a legitimate—and terribly neglected—field of research. If you've read my proposal..."

"I have read it. Don't presume to be insolent with me, young Jarren!" He took up a sheaf of papers from his desk. "The Scientific Basis for Magical Spells and Devices: A proposal for Master's Study by Jarren Carabello," quoted Beredane. "I have read every word of this—much to my dismay."

"If you have read it, then I cannot understand why you don't see the merit in this, sir! A whole field of science that no one has..."

"Science!" snorted Beredane. "I've heard it called many things by many people, but never science!"

"It is a physical part of our world, sir! Magic exists! Can there be any doubt of that? If it exists it must obey the laws of science! I learned that much from you in my years here."

Beredane frowned and shoved his spectacles back up on his rather large nose. "If it does exist, it is dying, Jarren. Fading out of the world. The age of science and reason is replacing magic and superstition. I don't know why; if you listen to the priests it's because the gods have willed it to be so, but there it is. Why waste your skills on something that will soon be gone? Better study dead languages! At least there are still things to be learned from those ancient texts."

"Sir, magic is fading only because those that knew how to wield it have nearly all died out. All the greatest masters died at the Battle of Soor, three hundred years ago, and none have come forth to replace them. But that does not mean they can never be replaced. And there could be so much to learn. Look, sir." Jarren rummaged in the pocket of his robes and pulled out what looked like a small brass candlestick with a smooth glass ball on the top. He set it on Beredane's table and touched a certain spot on it. After a few moments the glass ball began to glow with a soft light. "You've seen such things before, sir. I bought this from a fresco painter. They covet them because of the pure light it gives with no soot from burning wax or oil. Touch it. There is no heat, but there is light. How? Magic, you say, and so it is. But *how* does it work? I am convinced that whatever creates this light obeys the same rules as everything else in our world. The same rules as Darvanor has divined for planetary motion, the same rules as Letour's theory on the differentiation of plant species, and the same rules as your new mathematics. The same! We just have not learned what those rules are. Please, sir. All I ask is a chance to prove it."

Beredane's frown became even deeper and he removed his spectacles and rubbed the side of his nose. "Botheration. You could argue a leopard into giving up its spots. All right. I suppose every young man is due his measure of folly. I suppose it could be worse. You could be wasting yourself on women or gambling. Very well. I will give you a year. One year, mind you! After that—once you see how fruitless this all is—I'll expect you to give up on this nonsense and apply yourself as I direct."

"One year, sir? I'll need to travel a great deal. Three would be a fairer test."

"Travel, is it? And I suppose you expect the university to pay for your travel?"

"It is customary for scholars, sir."

"For scholars doing something useful! Very well, two years. And don't ask for anything else or I'll change my mind!"

Jarren's face broke into a smile. This had gone far better than he had expected. "Thank you, sir. I promise you won't regret it."

Lieutenant Mattin Krasner shifted in his saddle and tried to find some spot on his posterior that had not been chaffed raw on which to rest his weight. Failing at that, he stood up in his stirrups for a few minutes until his legs began to ache and he had to sit again. Maybe he should get down and walk for awhile even though the blisters from his riding boots hurt as much as his ass. Twenty days! Twenty days of this agony. He'd never made a ride like this in all his short life. Hell, neither had any of the other men in the regiment even though some were over three times his age. And that after a two-week sea voyage and another ten days by river barge!

The column of cavalry stretched out of sight in both directions as it wound its way through the hills on the dirt road. The dust was thick in the air. And on him. His white uniform coat was looking rather pink with the reddish dust. The blue facings were looking purple. He did not want to think about how much dust had settled into the folds of his tricorn hat. Only his buff breeches looked anything like normal. And there seemed to be no end to the journey. The mountains marched away on each side. They went on and on...

"Riding to the edge of the world and beyond," he muttered. "How'd I ever get into this mess?"

"What was that, Matt, old boy? Some word of discouragement? Don't tell me you're getting tired already? Haven't you been told that the Sixth Dragoons never tire?" Matt turned in the saddle and saw that Lieutenant Phell Gerowst had come up behind him. Gerowst was his senior and three years older and was always infuriatingly cheerful.

"But we're not the Sixth anymore," growled Matt.

"Don't let the Captain hear you say that! He'll tear the skin right off you."

"Too late. This blasted saddle has already done it for him."

Gerowst chuckled and Matt frowned. "I don't see how you can take this all so calmly! Here we are: *traded* to the King of Berssia! The whole regiment! Traded for a damn bunch of *tapestries!* Like we are slaves that can be bought and sold."

"Well, the Elector liked the tapestries a lot, I suppose. And I hear they really are excellent work—not that we'll ever see them."

"That's not the point! We are soldiers, not slaves, nor mercenaries. And we were sworn to the Elector of Naravia..."

"And now we're sworn to the King of Berssia," said Gerowst. "What difference does it make?"

"What difference! Look around you!" Matt swung his hand in an arc. "Exiled to the edge of creation! Mountains and desert and snakes and scorpions! Not even a sign of civilization. I can't understand why you aren't as angry as the rest of us."

"Civilization was getting a little uncomfortable for me," said Gerowst with a grin. "My bloody creditors had the gall to actually expect me to pay them. The nerve! They were even making threats about going to the magistrate. The peasants! Imagine them trying to haul a Gerowst up before a damn magistrate. Well! That wouldn't do at all, so this little relocation is not at all inconvenient. I doubt very much that those bastards will try to follow me all the way out here!"

Matt digested this and revised his plan to ask Gerowst for a loan. "But I thought you had a girl back home."

"I did. Several of them, actually. But they'll find other lovers—and I'll find other girls."

"Out here? Where?"

"Oh, I'm quite sure there will be plenty around. The girls always seem to find out where the men are staying. And I understand there's a considerable town attached to this fort we're heading for. Anyway, there are always alternatives. Speaking of which, how's that cute little sister of yours doing on this trip?"

Matt jerked his head around to look at Gerowst. "She's doing fine—and she's only fourteen!" he blurted. He opened his mouth to add: *So you keep your hands off of her!* But snapped it shut when he recalled that Gerowst outranked him. The man threw back his head and laughed.

"Don't worry, Matt! I'm not going to seduce her or ravish her. My tastes run to more mature women. But not everyone is as principled as I am. You are going to have to post a guard on her—and then guard the guard."

Gerowst was still laughing as he spurred his horse and pulled ahead of Matt. The younger man was still frowning. He had noticed some of the other officers—and even a few enlisted men—staring at his sister when they thought that she—and he—weren't looking.

And she was awfully cute. She would be beautiful when she got older—just like Mother had been. She was already starting to blossom. Maybe he should have a word with her. He had not talked to her at all since morning. He got permission from the Captain to go back to the tail of the column and turned his horse around.

The regiment made a long column. Five hundred troopers and then a huge baggage train took up nearly two miles of the road. They had been even longer when they had started. Over a hundred men had contrived to desert once they realized where they were really heading. Two had gone just yesterday, although without their horses. Matt could not imagine where they would run to in this wilderness. But the march discipline was very strict and the officers and NCOs hard pressed to keep it so.

He drifted back to the baggage train and looked for the one with his sister and all their belongings. Eventually he spotted it, although his sister was not in sight. The driver—an old veteran missing a hand—nodded when he saw him.

"Where is my sister?"

The man jerked his head toward the enclosed rear of the wagon. "Sleepin', I think, sir."

"Kareen? Are you in there?" shouted Matt above the creak and clatter of the wagons. Immediately, the canvas flap flipped open and his sister's head popped out.

"Yes, I am, and no, I was not sleeping, Cofo!" She stuck her tongue out at the driver, who took no notice. "I was just trying to get away from some of the dust. It has gotten into everything!"

"I know. Better get used to it."

"But I thought we were supposed to arrive at the fort today."

"We are, but with the prevailing west wind off the plains, I imagine it will be as dusty there as it is here."

"Pooh! I was hoping for an exotic western city with an oasis all around it. Green grass and flowing water."

"Sorry, sis. I don't think it will be like that." He hesitated for a moment. "And I'm sorry dragging you all the way out here."

"We've discussed this before, brother dear. There was no choice for either of us. Father used almost everything he had buying your commission. Once he died, you were stuck with the army. Just bad luck that your regiment got sent here."

"But I should not have brought you along. I should have..."

"What? Left me with Granduncle Fervus? There was no chance

he was going to provide a dowry for me, so what sort of future would I have had? And that old lecher was staring down my dress before I had anything for him to see."

"Kareen!" cried Matt in embarrassment.

"See? I'm adapting to army life. I'm already talking like Cofo."

Matt turned to stare at the old soldier and was rewarded by seeing his face slowly turn red. After a moment Matt turned back to his sister. "Actually, that was something I wanted to talk to you about."

"About men staring down my dress? Well, a lot more have been doing that lately. Or do you mean about some dashing young soldier sweeping me off my feet and then making passionate love to me?"

"Kareen! Stop that!"

"Small chance of that," muttered Cofo, "I've had to put up with it for three weeks."

"You will behave like a lady, Kareen!" said Matt, glaring at Cofo in turn.

"Oh, very well. But, Matt, who else am I going to marry if not a soldier? I know it's not going to happen for a few years yet, but it will happen."

"To the right man! An officer!"

"Well of course! I would not settle for less. Maybe someone like your friend Phell..."

"What! That rake? You stay away from him."

"But he's so handsome. I think he'd make a fine husband." Kareen tilted her head and clasped her hands next to her cheek and looked off in to the distance with an expression of stupid contentment.

"Kareen..."

"All right, all right. He's a pompous twit and I'll stay away from him. But there's bound to be—oh! Look there!"

Matt turned in his saddle and followed his sister's pointing finger. The column had topped a rise and a sudden breeze had pulled away the curtain of dust. Spread out below them was a small town of adobe buildings and on a hill to the south was their destination: Fort Pollentia, westernmost possession of King Edgarn IV of Berssia. The fort was a large sprawling structure whose guns could command the entire pass through the mountains.

"Home sweet home," said Cofo.

It took another two hours for the lumbering column to reach the fort and the sun was dipping behind the peaks as they clattered through one of the gates. The fort was even bigger than Matt had first thought and it was of an older style than he was used to. Rather than the mathematically precise *Trace_Ertriane,* which was being used throughout most of the East, this fort had stone walls twenty feet high and many feet thick. Not very good against artillery, but the nomadic tribes it was built to stop had no artillery. The fort, on the other hand, had plenty. There were wide platforms at intervals along the walls and a heavy gun on each. Old guns, to be sure, but more than enough to deal with the savages. As far as Matt knew, the fort had never been attacked.

There were barracks and stables built all along the inner walls and a cluster of buildings at the far end, which had to be the officers' and family quarters. The fact that he had Kareen with him would entitle him to a small family apartment.

The Colonel called the regiment into formation and after a short wait the garrison commander came out to welcome him. Matt's place in line put him too far away to see or hear much, but he was not really interested. It had been a very long march and all he wanted to do was get off this miserable nag and sleep. Finally they were dismissed and the regiment dispersed to find its quarters. Matt spotted their wagon outside one of the smaller buildings. He walked his horse over there.

"Cofo, find a stall for my horse and rub him down will you?"

"Certainly, sir, and after that I'll unload the wagon and after that I'll bed down these two tired beasts and after that I'll…" the old man walked off with Matt's horse, still muttering to himself. Matt shrugged his shoulders and went into the building. Kareen was there with a broom.

"It's not too bad," she said brightly. "Whoever was here before us took decent care of the place." She paused and looked puzzled. "Just who *was* here before us? And why aren't they here now?"

"One of the King's other regiments. The 9th Hussars, I believe. They were ordered south to fight against the Sultan of Omak."

"So we are the only regiment here?"

Matt smiled at the way his sister had included herself as part of the Regiment. Well, in a way she was a part of it, he supposed. "No, there is a regiment of infantry and some gunners here, too. Plus some local irregulars."

"Can we look around the fort before it gets dark?"

"I guess so. Although you'll have years and years with nothing to do but look at the fort."

"Spoilsport! Let's go!"

"And leave the unloading for Cofo? Good idea. Let's." He offered her his arm and she smiled broadly as she took it. They strolled outside into the gathering dusk. Lights were glowing in many windows and there were large lanterns placed along the walls. They had walked two-thirds of the way around and were passing one of the gates when a small party of horsemen cantered in. Ten men, leading four empty mounts—scruffy ponies like those used on the plains. They were some of the irregulars Matt had spoken of and they certainly looked it. Nothing resembling a uniform and no precision or discipline at all. The sentries—Berssian regulars—called out to them.

"What have you got there? Good hunting?"

The man who appeared to be the leader dismounted and grinned. "Oh yes! Fine hunting! Three of the damnable Kaifs dead and this little one to keep us warm on the way back!" He walked to one of the empty horses and grabbed what Matt had thought was a bit of animal pelt and yanked it back. He was shocked to see that it was the hair on the head of a woman. Her blonde hair was matted with dirt and blood. The man untied her from the horse she had been slung over and tossed her to the ground. She was battered and bruised from head to foot. Most of her clothes had been torn away. Matt stared; she was naked above the waist. She lay on the ground and did not move.

Then he remembered Kareen and tried to turn her away but she refused to budge. Instead, she took three paces forward. The leader of the irregulars finally saw her and looked about in confusion. "My lady?" he said hesitantly.

"What are you going to do with this woman?" asked Kareen sternly. Her Berssian wasn't very good and it clearly wasn't the irregular's mother tongue, either. Matt wasn't sure if the man even understood the question.

"I...we...that is... My Lady?"

"Are you done raping her or do you have more planned?" Matt was shocked. So was the man when he finally understood.

"I will give her to the rest of my company. It is traditional."

"She will die!"

"Probably. What of it?" The man was regaining his composure. Kareen was silent for a moment and the man shrugged and grabbed the woman by her bound wrists.

"I will buy this woman from you," said Kareen suddenly.

"What?" said the man.

"Kareen!" exclaimed Matt.

"I shall need a servant here and clearly Cofo cannot attend to all my needs. I wish to buy this woman. How much?"

The man hesitated. He looked to Matt, but Matt just shrugged. He knew there was no stopping Kareen when she got into a mood like this.

"Thirty silver marks," said the man with a grin.

"Outrageous! I'll give you five." Matt was suddenly tense again. Thirty marks was nearly all the money they had until the next time they were paid—which might not be for months.

"Twenty-five," countered the man.

"Look at her: she's at Death's door. Six marks."

"She's strong. She'll get well again. Twenty marks."

"And she's a savage. I'll have to teach her to speak and how to do what I want. Eight marks."

"I can get fifteen for her at the brothel in town. Fifteen marks."

"You won't get anything for her after your company is through with her. Ten marks."

The man looked over at his companions. One by one they nodded their heads. "Very well! Done!"

"Good. Mattin, please pay the gentleman. Then help me carry her home."

Atark opened his eyes and saw only blackness. *Am I dead?* No, he hurt far too much to be dead. Unless he was in one of the hells the gods maintained for evil-doers. He did not think he had done any great evil in his life. At least nothing that deserved to be rewarded with the sort of pain he was feeling now. And he had done a great deal of good, he thought. He had healed the sick and predicted the weather (or tried to) and done as much as he could to help the people of his clan. And he had tried to be a good husband and father. The thought of his family brought a terrible groan to his dry lips. *Shelena! Ardan! Thelena!* They were dead, his family was dead. The raging anger that blazed up inside him forced him to move. Rubbing at his eyes, his vision slowly returned.

He put his hand to the wound in his side and then looked at it. It had nearly stopped bleeding, but he knew that was only on the outside. It would still be bleeding inside. The dagger had pierced his bowels. His shit was mingling with his blood and poisoning him. He could feel the fever growing in him. He would not last much longer without help. He could not heal himself, but another shaman with some healing skills might still be able to save him. But the chance of finding one in time was growing slim. He was his own clan's only shaman. He did not know if another clan was close by. But he had to try and reach one. He would try until he died. They had killed his family. The Varags had killed his family. The King of Berssia had killed his family. Pain and a need for vengeance were the only things left inside him. It had driven him on and on.

He thought that two days had passed but he wasn't sure. After that first long fall into darkness he had slowly awakened just as the sun was coming up. He had staggered away in the direction of camp. Another night had come. He thought it was only one other night. Surely only one more. The Varags had taken the horses and the food and the water. Atark had licked the dew off the grass the next morning, but he was terribly thirsty. Surely it had only been one more night. Without water he could not have lasted longer than that.

For now, however, he still lived. And while he lived he could not give up. Painfully, he got to his feet and went on. It was getting dark again. He wasn't sure if this was the end of his second day of torment or if his sight was just fading. It might have been his eyes. The sun had finally broken through the heavy clouds that had covered the sky all day and it didn't seem to be in the right place…

He fell again. It took him longer to get up this time. But he did get up and shuffled along. He vision was getting blurry, but suddenly he thought he saw a low shape in front of him. A tent? One of the tents of the camp? Had he truly made it? He saw some shapes moving and a flutter of wings. Hens, perhaps?

"Help," he croaked. He could hardly make a sound. "Help. Someone, help me." He tripped over something and fell heavily into the long grass. He waited. He waited for someone to come and help him. But no one came. He seemed to be lying with his legs propped up on something. He heard the flutter of wings again and a strange noise, unlike any hen. He turned his head and saw that it was not a hen. It was a large buzzard. And its beak was crusted with blood.

A feeling like panic flowed through him. He pulled himself forward, off whatever he had been lying on and sat up. The buzzards, and now he could see that there were more than one, hopped back a few paces and stared at him. He looked down.

The thing he had been lying on was the body of his wife, Shelena. He recognized the dress. And the missing head.

"No," he groaned. "By all the gods, no." He twisted around and saw that the low shape he had hoped was a tent was really that cursed mound. The mound that had brought he and his family to their doom.

He had been walking in circles.

The two days of endless effort and pain had only brought him back to his starting point. The despair that filled him was only tempered by the knowledge that he could die with his family now. The last hope left him.

The buzzards were edging closer, but a wave of his arm drove them back. He looked around and spotted something a few paces away. It would be Shelena's head. He crawled over to it to close her eyes, but the buzzards had already removed them. He tried to weep, but no tears came to his own crusted eyes. Where was Ardan? Over there, he thought. He crawled in that direction, but found nothing. He circled wearily on hands and knees but could not find the body of his son. Thelena? Where was Thelena? But no, the Varags took her, didn't they? He would not find her, either. He crouched there and wept tearlessly again. He could not even bury them.

The sun was nearly on the horizon now but he felt very, very hot. Fever. Perhaps there would be some shade on the other side of the mound. Shade to die in. He crawled toward it. The stone archway was directly facing the setting sun and it seemed to draw him to it. It looked like a gaping mouth. *The Jaws of Death.* He reached the steps leading down and carefully lowered himself down them. He collapsed at the bottom and leaned against the cool stone slab that sealed the way. He closed his eyes and waited for Death.

After a while the light faded, but it was just the setting sun, not yet Death come for him. Something was digging into his hip. It was only a minor pain compared to the others, but unlike them, he could do something about this one. He shifted himself slightly and looked down. It was a rock the size of his fist. A few faint lines had been inscribed in it. Some part of the stone arch which had crumbled away perhaps. Some part of this damned mound

"Damn you," he whispered. "Damn you all." He took a deep breath and seized the rock. "Damn you!" he screamed. He reared back and struck the cursed slab that sealed the cursed mound with what little strength he had left.

To his amazement the slab cracked. A large black crack appeared right where the rock had struck it. Quickly a spider's web of smaller cracks ran through the stone. With a rumble and a clatter the slab fell to pieces and collapsed into the interior of the mound. Atark nearly fell after it.

He sat there, clutching the door frame and breathing hard. The glow from the vanished sun streamed into the room. He gathered his waning strength and pulled himself to his feet. If he was going to die, he was going to have a look at what he was dying for. He shuffled into the chamber under the mound, his shadow stretching out before him.

It was empty. It was a stone-lined chamber six paces across and three high. The floor was simple dirt. There was a small pile of bones and rotted cloth in the center of it. That was all. Nothing more. Atark stood over the bones and looked down at them.

"Nothing."

"All this for nothing."

He did not know whether to laugh or weep, but he suddenly could not stand anymore. He collapsed onto the pile of bones. Before, he had managed to shield his wound each time he fell, but not this time. As he struck the ground he felt a sharp pain and knew that he had torn the wound open again. He did not care. It had all been for nothing. He lay there and felt his life drip away.

Blood...

Atark thought he heard a voice. It was completely dark now and he did not know if night had come or if his eyes had failed at last.

Blood!

The voice was louder now. It seemed to be coming from close by.

BLOOD!

The voice roared in his ears and he jerked where he lay. He opened his eyes and now there was light. A faint light, but not sunlight or moonlight or torchlight.

A man was standing over him. A man made of light. Atark pushed himself away and collapsed on his back. The ghostly image hovered over him.

"Who...? What are you?" he managed to gasp.

"Blood! I could smell the blood. And now I can feel and taste it! Blood! Life's blood!"

"Who are you?" Atark stared in wonder. Was he hallucinating? Was this Death coming to claim him?

"I am Ransurr of the Kaifeng!"

The name sounded familiar to Atark, somehow, but he could not place it. But the ghost was clearer now. He could see that the man was dressed in rich robes with many chains and bits of jewelry. And charms. Lots of charms. A miniature skull hung on a chain about his neck. He was a shaman. Had been a shaman. But now he was a ghost—just like Atark would soon be.

"Why are you here?" Atark did not really care, but he had spoken to no one for two days and the question came of its own accord. The ghost ignored him.

"How long?" it demanded instead.

"I don't understand."

"How long!?!" roared the ghost.

"I have been dying for two days," said Atark.

"How long since the great battle, you worm?"

"Oh. It has been…it has been three hundred summers since the great battle was fought here." The ghost seemed to shrink in on itself and the light dimmed.

"So long? So long. I never thought it would be so long," said the ghost faintly. *"And now it is too late."*

"Yes, it is surely too late." The ghost was staring past him into the dark.

"We fought. All day and into the night we fought. The warriors died by the thousands. Our shamen and their wizards died, too. By ones and by twos, but we died. Finally, only I was left upon our side. I slew the only master wizard remaining with the enemy, but then I was spent. The remaining underlings, weaklings though they were, overwhelmed me. They could not slay me so they sealed me in here. I waited. I waited to be freed, but no one came. And now it is too late."

"But you are free now."

"Too late. The spells guarding my body have failed and it has crumbled into dust. My powers are dwindling away and even at my peak I could not create a new body for myself. I cannot leave this place as I am and soon I will be gone."

"Then you will die at last. I die, too." The ghost seemed to come closer.

"Yes. The end draws near for both of us. But before that, tell me of the Kaifeng. How fare our people? Do we rule all the world?"

Atark snorted. "We rule the plains as we have always done, but no more. The Easterners have the passes sealed against us and we cannot take them. Our people grow in numbers, but so do the enemy. And they have new tools and new weapons we cannot match."

"Cannot our magic open the passes?" The ghost seemed dismayed.

"Our magic has dwindled. When you all died here the secrets of the great magic were lost. I was a shaman myself..."

"You!?!"

"Yes, and you see how weak I am. All the others are the same. Our magic cannot help us. Lost, all lost." Atark was getting very weak. He did not think he could keep talking much longer. The ghost was fading and he was quite sure it was his own eyesight that was failing. Not much longer now. *Wait for me, Shelena. I am coming.*

"And what of the enemy? Are their wizards in the same wretched condition?"

"I suppose. I don't know. Yes. Perhaps. The tales I hear say it is so. Lost. All lost. None remember the magic now."

"Except for me! I remember!" thundered the ghost and there was a note of triumph in its voice.

"It matters not. You are dying. I am dying. Lost. All lost. I am tired now. Good-bye." Atark shut his eyes.

"Worm! My powers are failing but they are still more than enough to mend your trifling wounds!"

Atark's eyes snapped open again and the ghost was rushing toward him.

"Be healed!"

Something touched him and it seemed to stab right through him like the Varag's dagger had done. Pain and more pain, but an incredible power began to flow through him, too. His arms and legs twitched and flopped about helplessly. It went on for a long time but then the ghost was back where it had been and he was...

He was...

He was healed.

The pain in his side was gone. The fever was gone. All the scratches and bruises of his long trek were gone. He felt terribly tired. Tired and weak. And thirsty and hungry. But he was healed. He stared at the ghost in awe.

"What? Why...?" he stammered.

"You! You are weak in body and spirit. But I can feel the hate in you. You hate the Easterners just as I did. You! You shall be the instrument of our people's revenge! Now, strengthen yourself." The ghost waved its hand and there was a sudden blast of wind through the chamber. One of the buzzards was swept inside with a squawk. It hung in the air for a moment and then its head was twisted round and it dropped to the ground. More wind blew in twigs and dry brush. They swirled into a pile and the wind stopped and the wood burst into flames making a small fire. The ghost gestured again and water bubbled up out of the ground.

"Eat. Drink."

Atark crawled to the water and scooped it into his mouth. Nothing had ever tasted better. He drank and drank until he had enough. Then he went to the dead bird. He still had his little knife and he set about butchering it. He looked up at the ghost. In the light of the fire it was barely to be seen.

"Thank you," he said to it. "How can I repay you?"

"By becoming great! I am doomed, but you can lead the Kaifeng to victory! Eat and strengthen yourself. Then I will teach you to be great. But learn well!" The ghost gestured again and two shimmering images appeared. Shelena! Ardan! His wife and son floated there. *"By the souls of your dead you shall learn well!"* thundered the ghost. *"If you value them, you will not fail!"*

A shudder of fear went through him. Just what was he making a bargain with? But it did not matter. He knew what he had to do. "I shall learn well, Lord. I shall become great, as you command." He stood up, the bloody knife still in his fist.

"And I shall bring vengeance to our enemies!"

CHAPTER ONE

"Trooper, you are an absolute disgrace!" snapped Lieutenant Mattin Krasner. The soldier he was addressing looked straight ahead with no emotion at all on his face. "Hell, I've seen bloody Varags that look better than you!" Ah, now he was getting through. The soldier's face slowly reddened and Matt could see the man was angry. No real soldier wanted to be compared to the scruffy irregulars they shared the fort with. Good. Four years of service at Fort Pollentia had taught him that a soldier who was angry at being dressed down by an officer was of far more value than one who simply did not give a damn. "Your tunic is filthy, your brass looks like you left it in the rain, and I don't even want to know what the bore of your musketoon looks like! Sergeant!"

"Sir?" said Sergeant Chenik.

"Four extra hours stable duty for this one. And make damn sure he doesn't present himself to me like this again!"

"Yes, sir."

"You can dismiss the rest of them, Sergeant."

"Yes, sir." Matt walked away before the Sergeant could begin *his own* evaluation of the troop. He was quite sure it would be far harsher than his had been. It was so hard to maintain any sort of discipline in an isolated post like this. It had taken Matt awhile, but he had finally learned how to be an effective officer. Not too harsh, not too easy-going. Always fair. Well, almost always. Phell Gerowst had helped him quite a bit, but he took his lead from Captain Vargos. Unlike most of the other officers in the regiment, the Captain had not purchased his commission. He had worked his way up through the ranks. A rarity. Of course, he was stuck as a captain forever now. He had neither the money nor the influence to ever rise farther. Majors and colonels had to have influence or money, or both. Matt was pretty much in the same situation, come to think of it. He'd never have the money to purchase a captaincy, so unless he really distinguished himself somehow, he was a lieutenant for life.

There were worse things, of course—like being a private.

He went over to one of the stairs leading up onto the fort's walls. It was nearly the end of the day and he liked to watch the light on the mountains. It was one of the place's few charms. He went past a batch of gunners, lounging by their cannon. They did not get up or salute. The 'real' Berssian troops had still not entirely accepted these foreigners of the Tapestry Regiment. The name was very nearly official now. On the King's roster of regiments they were the Eighteenth Dragoons, but no one ever called them that. The die-hards within the regiment still referred to themselves as the Sixth, and to everyone else they were the Tapestry Regiment.

Matt climbed up on the parapet and found a spot along the wall where he could sit and dangle his legs over the edge. "The edge of the wall on the edge of the world," he murmured to himself. The sun had gone behind the western mountains and the shadows stretched out toward him, but the peaks were silhouetted by the dazzling glow. Beyond those peaks the mountains went on for another ten leagues and then abruptly dropped away into the endless Plains of Kaif. Legend had it that those plains went on into the West forever. There was a story he remembered from childhood about some legendary hero who, on a boast, set out to run across those plains. According to the tale, he was still running even to this day.

They weren't true, of course, neither the legend nor the tale. In the last few decades exploring ships had returned from the lands on the other side of the Plains of Kaif. They did have another side, there were even other countries there, but they were three thousand leagues away. Matt could scarcely imagine such a distance. From where he sat to the farthest bit of land in the East was not even a quarter that far. It was a huge, nearly unknown land.

And the Kaifeng were out there. Tribes of nomads and wander-ing herdsmen filled those plains. They called themselves the Kaifeng and they could be fierce warriors. Three hundred years earlier their vast hordes had invaded the eastern lands. According to the histo-ries and legends, the massed knights and wizards of the kingdoms had driven them back across these mountains and a mighty battle had been fought somewhere west of here. The Kaifeng were smashed and they had little troubled the East since then. But the Kings of Berssia took no chances and strong forts made sure the nomads remained on their side of the mountains.

Strong forts, manned by bored men like Matt.

He could hardly believe he had been here for four years. Sometimes it seemed infinitely longer and at other times it seemed like he had only arrived the day before. The unending routine had a timelessness that sapped the mind and the heart. The nearest real town was a five-day ride to the east and then it was another three weeks to the capital. Matt had only made one trip there in those four years. It seemed like a dream.

A bugle call roused him from his thoughts. It was the end of the day in the fort. Those unlucky enough to have sentry duty were reporting to their posts. The rest were heading for their barracks and messes. Those with passes were swaggering out the gates for the fleshpots and taverns of the town below. Matt got up from his perch and headed for his home.

The parade ground seemed very dark after staring at the sunset, but Matt crossed it with the ease of long familiarity. The apartment he shared with Kareen and their servant was on the ground floor of a two-story brick and plaster building set against the eastern wall of the fort. Light shown around the edges of the curtains in the windows and spilled out through the open door. He stepped inside and their serving girl was there almost immediately to take his hat and coat.

"Thank you, Thelena," he said. The woman bobbed her head.

"Lieutenant Gerowst is here, sir," she said in her heavily accented voice. Then she went to hang up his things.

Matt stepped through the vestibule into the parlor. As Thelena had said, Phell Gerowst was there and, naturally, so was Kareen. "Evening, every...whoa, what have you got there?" Matt stopped short. His sister was wearing an amazingly elaborate white dress. The full skirt had multiple layers of lace and there was a tight bodice and a top that displayed a shocking amount of Kareen's bosom. Her long brown hair spilled down to her bare shoulders. She was absolutely beautiful. Her delicate, oval face lighted up in a smile when she saw him. She spun around and made the skirt flare out.

"It's my wedding dress! Phell ordered it all the way from Berssenburg! Isn't it beautiful?"

"It's lovely," he said sincerely. "A little...daring, isn't it?"

"Nonsense! All the Berssian ladies dress like this on formal occasions."

"Oh. Well it really is beautiful. But isn't it supposed to be unlucky for the groom to see the bride in her wedding dress before the wedding?"

"That's just a silly superstition," said Kareen. "I had to try it on to make sure it fits and it just would not have been fair not to let Phell see me in it."

"All right. It's on your heads. But you're not going to try and eat dinner in that, are you? Wouldn't do to have stains on it beforehand."

"Of course not! Thelena! Come and help me get this off."

The servant girl appeared immediately and the two women went into Kareen's bedroom. Matt found a chair and looked over at Gerowst. "I can't believe you are going to marry my sister. Actually, I can't believe she is going to marry you."

"Your sister is a woman of impeccable taste, high intelligence, and..."

"...and the most beautiful woman within a hundred miles."

"A thousand. But you are certainly correct. And I love her."

"You had better. If you treat her like your other girls, I'll break your neck—even if you do outrank me."

"No worries, soon to be brother-in-law," said Gerowst, laughing. "My wandering days are over. No man could ask for more than Kareen. And if her other talents are as good as how well she kisses..."

"Phell!" cried Kareen, coming back into the room wearing a more modest camp dress. "You'll shock Matt."

"I'm beyond shocking." He said it lightly and the other laughed, but inside he wasn't smiling. His father had charged him with taking care of Kareen and he had taken the job very seriously. There was no doubt that Kareen was the most beautiful woman in the fort and many a man had set their sights on her. Matt had his hands full protecting her. And this marriage with Gerowst did not entirely please him, either. Phell seemed to have changed, but you could never tell. Even Kareen seemed to have her doubts. She had postponed the wedding twice already....

"So are you still set for next month?" he asked.

"Yes!" said Kareen. "We'll have all three chaplains to do the services and even the Colonel will be coming."

"Really?" Matt was surprised. Colonel Fezdoorf spent almost all his time in Berssenburg and left running the regiment to Major Macador.

"Oh yes! Isn't it exciting?"

"Actually, that brings up a bit of a problem, Matt," said Phell. "Traditionally, you ought to be giving Kareen away, but the Colonel said something in his letter about wanting to do that himself. Would you settle for being my best man?"

"Uh…"

Matt was saved from having to respond by Thelena coming in to announce that dinner was ready. They got up and went into the cozy dining area off the equally cozy kitchen. The meal was plain, as most of them were. The choice of foodstuffs was not exactly great in this isolated spot. But Thelena was a good cook and made the most of what they had. She sat at a small table off to one side and ate her own meal. She would spring up from time to time to serve them. At least the wine wasn't too bad.

Kareen and Phell spent most of the meal holding hands and making ridiculous statements and little cooing noises to each other. Matt found himself staring at Thelena. The Kaifeng woman was a mystery to him. After she had recovered from her injuries, she had been almost uncontrollable. Matt had nearly despaired of ever being able to trust her or let her loose. She had run off again and again. Each time she was caught and returned. Matt had to reward the ones who caught her, but he knew full well that they had taken their own rewards out of the girl's body. Finally, after about a year, she had stopped running. By that time Kareen had managed to teach her to speak and do her chores. Kareen had far more patience than Matt. He could only guess why she had stopped trying to get away. Maybe it was the small hope of actually making it out onto the steppes. Maybe it was the abuse she received when she was caught. Maybe she finally realized how lucky she was to have been bought by Kareen. Other Kaifeng women had been captured by the Varags. Aside from two who were virtual slaves in a brothel in town, the rest were dead.

Thelena would have been an attractive woman if she had not gotten a broken nose and lost several teeth in her escape attempts. Her cheekbones were more prominent than was common in eastern women and her eyes had a tiny slant to them. It gave her an exotic look that Matt found appealing. She dressed in eastern clothing, but kept her long blonde hair braided in Kaifeng fashion. Once she stopped trying to run she became a good servant. She cleaned and cooked and washed and mended. From time to time Matt gave her a few coins from his own meager salary. He suspected that she made more money by selling herself to the soldiers on occasion, but he had never actually caught her at it. Not that he would have tried to stop her; what else could she really do? He felt sorry for her. She was as much an exile in a strange land as he was—and she didn't even have the comfort of a sister or a regiment.

He stirred uneasily in his chair when he remembered that after Kareen was married, Phell would be moving into this cozy apartment and he would be moving out. He was not happy about that prospect, but there was nothing for it. Kareen would marry and he supposed he would, too, someday. There weren't any real prospects at the moment, but a few of the older officers had daughters who were growing up. Maybe in a few years….

"Matt, you are woolgathering," said Kareen, jogging him out of his thoughts. "Have you decided about being Phell's best man? I'd love for you to give me away, of course, but we don't want to disappoint the Colonel now, do we?"

It didn't really matter to him, but for some reason the whole thing rankled. Still, no point in getting the Colonel annoyed with him. A knock on the door saved him from having to decide just then. Thelena hurried to answer it and returned in a moment with Major Macador's orderly.

"Lieutenant Krasner? The Major would like to see you in his office right away." Matt jumped up in surprise He had assumed it would be a message for Phell. Thelena already had his coat and hat waiting for him. He put them on and hurried out. The parade ground was completely dark by now and the stars were blazing overhead. It only took a minute to reach Macador's office. Matt stepped inside, removed his hat and came to attention.

"Ah, yes, Krasner," said Macador from behind his desk. "Sorry to interrupt your dinner, but I wanted to catch you before you were asleep."

"Sir?"

"One of the Varag patrols is two days overdue. Normally I wouldn't make anything of it—the Varags rarely ever keep to any sort of schedule, you know. But one of our scouts who just came back reported seeing an unusually large number of buzzards in the direction of Hessley Well, which is in the area the Varags were supposed to be patrolling. It's probably nothing, but I want you to take your troop there tomorrow and look it over."

"Yes, sir," said Matt, feeling excited. This would only be the third time he had been put in command of an expedition. "I'll alert my men."

"Good. I want you on the road by first light."

"Yes, sir."

"Now in order to give you a real example of what I'm talking about, I'll need the curtains drawn," said Jarren Carabello. He stood by the speaker's podium and watched as several of the students carried out his request. He really hoped this would work. He'd tested it, of course, but things did tend to go wrong at times.

"Good. Now, Mister Kafallen, would you open the right-hand section just a tiny crack? No, that's too much, try to get just a narrow beam of sunlight. Hmmm, would you mind standing there and holding it? Thank you." A thin sliver of morning sunshine was now falling on a table next to the podium. He'd have to hurry before the sun moved too far.

"I'm sure you are all familiar with Slarnaroff's experiments in optics and the refraction of light. Well, I will now use this glass prism to break the sunlight Mr. Kafallen is providing into its component colors. You can see it over there on the wall." Jarren adjusted the prism so that a broad rainbow of color appeared on a blank section of the lecture room's plaster walls.

"Very good. Now I am going to take this object here and activate it." Jarren had a magical candle, similar to the one he had shown old Hano years before. This one's spell was still quite powerful and when he set it to work, the light was very bright. "This is producing a light which is magical in origin. To get a beam I'll place it in this box which has only a narrow slit in it." He did so and then placed a second prism in the beam of light that came through the slit. A second rainbow appeared on the wall. Jarren adjusted the box and both prisms until the rainbows were side by side.

"Now, gentlemen, look closely. Observe how the light from the sun has been broken into a smooth gradation of color ranging from red to violet. There are no gaps or sudden changes in color. Then look at the light from the magical source." Jarren walked over to the chalkboard and grabbed a pointer and then went over to the second rainbow. "Notice that there are some dark areas in the prismatic display. Here in the yellow and again here in the green region, there are dark areas. You can also see how the entire spectrum is shifted and compressed slightly toward the red end." He pointed them out and then looked to his audience. Most of the students did not look terribly interested, but there were also a number of masters and aspirant masters among them who looked far more interested. He saw several of them whispering to each other.

"Just to prove that this is not some flaw in the second prism, let me switch the two." He did so and after some fumbling managed to produce the same display. There were a few more whispers now.

"Now what does this display tell us? It—oh, Mr. Kafallen, you can open the drapes now, thank you—it tells us that the results of a magic spell, the product, if you will, obeys the same physical laws as the rest of nature. But it also tells us that the way it produces that product operates in some different way from what we are used to. Clearly, the light from this device is not sunlight that has been transposed somehow—or if it is, it has been subtly changed during the transposition."

"Sir?" a hand raised among the students. "How can you tell which?"

"An excellent question. As you are aware, I am still in the early stages of my research. Right now I am working to collect the basic information from which conclusions can be drawn. I have examined a number of magical devices and I have attempted to measure quantitatively what they do. For example, I have several devices that are used to produce heat for warming rooms or carriages. Using Dr. Alpronzo's new mercury thermal measuring instrument I have calculated just how much heat the devices produce. Also, it is well known that magical spells are not infinite in nature, and thus I am attempting to discover if the amount of heat produced lessens with time."

Jarren looked at the student who had spoken up. "I know that this does not exactly answer your question, Mr. Ulnar, but I'm afraid I have no exact answer at present. Eventually, I expect my studies to take me to meet with those practitioners of magic who still exist. I hope they will be able to answer some of my questions. But at this stage I am doing the very necessary groundwork to enable me to know what questions to ask."

Jarren tugged at his robes slightly, silently admiring the red trim of a probationary master scholar and continued. "Now, let me demonstrate another example of my research..."

An hour later the lecture and the question and answer period concluded. Jarren felt drained, but elated. It appeared to have gone very well. At least none of the other masters had shouted denunciations at him, nor had the students made rude noises or catcalls. He had been to lectures where such things had happened.

As he walked back to the tiny office he had been assigned, Dr. Mirtas emerged from a side corridor and grabbed him by the arm.

"Jarren! I sat in on your lecture just now and I was very impressed!"

"Thank, you, sir,"

"I must admit that I had been rather skeptical when Hano told me what you were up to. What was it? Two, three years ago?"

"Four, sir."

"That long? My. How time flies. But in any case, I think you are making some real progress—and making a few converts as well."

"That is good to know, sir." Jarren spoke in a level tone, but he was really quite flattered by what he was hearing. Vindication! Well, some, anyway.

"If you have a moment, I'd like to show you something and ask a few questions of you."

"Certainly, sir." The diminutive Mirtas led Jarren through the maze of narrow passages that cris-crossed Toldorf Hall and finally into his small workshop that was in a shed built on to the rear. It was filled with tools and stacks of metal sheets and wood planks. As they entered, Mirtas shouted for his assistant.

"Quors! Are you ready?"

"Yes, sir," answered the young man from the rear of the shed. "Just coming to a boil now."

"Good! Here, Jarren, you've seen this before haven't you?" Jarren moved closer and saw what Mirtas was talking about. There was a small copper boiler standing over a fire. A pipe ran from it to another pipe that was bent at both ends and mounted on an axle in the center. As Jarren watched, steam began to spurt out of the two open ends and the pipe revolved around the axle; slowly at first, but faster and faster as the steam pressure built up.

"Yes, sir, I saw this when you demonstrated it for the faculty last month. Very impressive, sir."

"Yes, isn't it? I've been trying to think of possible applications for this. Perhaps to push a carriage. The first problem is the fire. Rather awkward trying to stoke a fire in a moving carriage. But today when you mentioned those magical heating devices it gave me an idea. Do you think one of those would be strong enough to boil water? If so, we could dispense with the fire entirely!"

"That's very interesting, sir," said Jarren, "I never would have thought of such a thing myself."

"That's because you have your head up in the clouds, boy! Just like most of the so-called masters around here. Theoretical knowledge is fine, but I say it should be put to work! Now, if we did away with the fire, would it make the most sense to put your magical heater underneath, where the fire was, or actually place it *inside* the boiler so no heat at all is lost? Are they proof against water?"

"I'm not really sure, sir," said Jarren awkwardly. "I've had to borrow the items I study for the most part. I'd not be able to do anything risky with them without getting permission."

"Ah, I see. Well do you think…"

Mirtas bent his ear for an hour before Jarren managed to break away. It was wonderful to have your opinion sought out, but Jarren was finding out that it could be a bother as well. Still, Mirtas' project looked to be very interesting. He put that out of his head as he hurriedly climbed the stairs to reach Hano Beredane's office. Jarren was scheduled to play with the University's chamber orchestra next week and there was a rehearsal later this afternoon. He needed to see Beredane, go back his room to get his cello and his music, and get over to the concert hall, and he had not realized it was so late. He knocked and went in. His old master looked a little older, but was as irascible as ever

"Good afternoon, sir."

"Quite a little performance you put on this afternoon."

"You saw it, sir?"

"Oh yes. I was in the back where you obviously didn't notice me. Very impressive."

"You thought so?" asked Jarren eagerly.

"Indeed. But what do you have planned for an encore?"

"I…I'm not sure I understand, sir."

"Well, it is just that you have become one of the best-known people in the university. I've even heard that you've had some offers to speak in Duma."

"Yes, that's true. In Nivenza, too. I was going to mention it to you."

"Hmmm," grunted Beredane. "Jarren, you are making a name for yourself. Normally that's a good thing, but are you aware the Church is taking interest in your activities?"

"The Church?" said Jarren in surprise. "What does the Church have to do with me?"

"In the end, nothing, hopefully. But I've received a letter from the Archdeacon of the city reminding me—politely—that the official Church position on magic is that its practitioners are heretics. He doesn't name you specifically, but the implication was plain."

"But...but that's absurd!" protested Jarren. Beredane's frown got deeper.

"Jarren, the Church doesn't have the sort of power in the city it did a hundred years ago, but you can't go around dismissing them like that! At least not in public."

"Are you suggesting I should curtail my research—or modify my findings—to please that superstitious gang of..."

"Jarren!"

"I'm sorry, sir, but I can't forget how they nearly burned Darvanor when he first proposed his theory that the earth was not the center of the universe. Am I going to be persecuted the same way?"

"Jarren, calm down. I doubt very much it will ever come to that. It's not like you are practicing magic yourself—and the University would stand by you on an issue like this if it ever did come to it—but you need to keep in mind the sensibilities of these people. I've listened to your lectures, and it seems as though reports of them have gotten back to the Church. Now, it is rather evident when you speak that you are keenly interested in magic and would welcome an open return of magic-users to the world. While I can't blame you for that, a bit more restraint on your part might be in order. A good researcher needs to be unbiased in any case."

Jarren considered this. It was true that he did get a bit enthusiastic in his lectures... "All right, sir. I can see what you are saying. I'll try to be more...sedate—but I won't stop my research!"

"No one is asking you to. Just use a little common sense, eh? Let's consider the matter closed—for now. But as for your research, you have succeeded in creating a lot of interest in magic, Jarren. But to this point your research has been entirely observational. While there is nothing wrong with that, people are going to soon start to demand more. I noticed how you sidestepped all the questions about *how* it is done this afternoon."

"I don't know how it's done, sir."

"Exactly! You have a series of phenomena—and I am willing to concede your initial proposition that these are phenomena that somehow fit into the natural order—but your information about them is strictly quantitative. You have faithfully recorded everything, but you have an explanation for nothing. People want to know more. *I* want to know more. How do you plan to give us all what we want?"

"I will have to start researching the actual process by which spells are cast and magical devices created."

"Indeed you will! How and when do you plan to start?"

"I…I'm not sure, sir. I will need to travel—and so far you have not approved any of my requests to do so."

Beredane growled. "There is nothing you can do here in the city? Surely there must have been some records left by the old wizards. Have you checked? And what about the local practitioners who still exist? Can nothing be learned from them?"

"Oh there are many records, sir. Tomes and tomes of them. Many right here in the university archives—I was amazed at how much. Some of it has been useful, but most is not. I have found nothing that gives a clue on how the spells are done."

"Nothing? That seems rather strange, don't you think?"

"Yes, sir, I do. There are countless descriptions of the effects of spells, but not a single instruction on how to bring them about. I am coming to suspect that the records have been deliberately hidden or destroyed."

"Perhaps. Perhaps the few magic users who were left after Soor hid the records because they worried that they would be too dangerous for untrained people to use."

"Yes, sir, that is a real possibility. I've consulted with some of our historians, Doctor Liegly, especially, and he tells me that after Soor there were many incidents where uncontrolled magic did damage or caused injuries. It was about that time that the Keridian Revelation was adopted by the Church and most cities began to drive the practitioners out. Perhaps they took all the records with them—those their persecutors didn't destroy."

"There are some practitioners left," said Beredane. "Even in Sirenza."

"They are hard to find because of our dear churchmen, but I've talked to some. Most are fakes. But even those who are real had little to tell me. They have spells that were passed down to them and learned entirely by rote. They have no more clue how they make those things happen than I do."

"Indeed? So how do you plan to proceed? You could just make your study an exercise in antiquarianism, a recording of devices and deeds. Certainly there is some value even in that, but hardly the task for a top scholar."

It took a moment for Beredane's statement to sink in. *Top scholar? Me?* When it did he got rather flustered for a few heartbeats and lost his train of thought. "I…I'm going to have to widen my search, sir. Travel."

"Yes, I'm forced to agree with you now. I believe I can squeeze some funds out of the Chancellor. He's been quite impressed with your progress, too, by the way."

"That's wonderful, sir!"

"Don't let your head swell up too big for your hat, Jarren!" said Beredane gruffly. He took off his spectacles and stared at him.

"Where will you go first?"

Matt stood up in his saddle and looked back at the column. No straggling. Good. The thirty men of his troop were closed up nicely. Which was more than could be said for the Varag scouts. He had no clue where half of them had gotten to, and the rest seemed to be ranging aimlessly about. But with any luck, he would not need their services. The well was only a few miles ahead and there was definitely *something* there. A huge cloud of birds could be seen circling the area. There was something dead there; perhaps many somethings.

"We are going to have to be on the alert, Sergeant," said Matt to Sergeant Chenik. "If this is as bad as it looks, the whole patrol may have been wiped out. It is possible that they—whoever 'they' might be—could be waiting in ambush for any search party. Meaning us. Have the men check their flints and their priming."

"Right, sir." Chenick turned his horse and went back down the column, passing on Matt's orders. While he did so, Matt followed the order himself. He took his pair of flintlock pistols out of their saddle holsters and checked them. The flints were new and tightly fixed in the hammers. The priming in the pans seemed fine, too. There was no way to check the actual loads, but he'd had Cofo pull them and reload them only two days ago. They ought to be all right. He gave his carbine a similar looking over. Some of the other officers made fun of him for carrying the shortened musketoon, but he was glad he had it. A pistol wasn't accurate beyond a dozen yards. He wanted to be able to hit something at greater distances, if necessary.

Of course he knew what Captain Vargos—or even Phell for that matter—would say: "It's not your business to be shooting at things, Mister Krasner. Your job is to *command!* Let your troopers do the shooting." They were right, too. If Matt did his job and his men did theirs then *in theory* he should never need to shoot at anything, except, perhaps, during a melee on horseback, in which case, his pistols would do better, anyway.

That was all true, but he still carried his carbine. He just liked having it. And since he was an officer he could do so and no one could tell him not to. He put the weapon back into its holder just as Chenik came back up beside him.

"We need to get the scouts back, sir. No point in havin' the buggers if they don't do their job now."

"Very well. Have the bugler sound the rally. I'm sure they know the call. Whether they'll obey it is another matter entirely, of course." A moment later the bugle rang out and echoed off the low hills. They were at the very edge of the plains. He did not worry about alerting any possible enemy. In these barren lands there was almost no concealment. Anyone waiting up ahead would have spotted their white uniforms and dust cloud hours ago. The call was sounded twice and after a while several of the scouts reappeared and headed back for the column. One of them appeared to have already been at the well. At least he was coming from that direction. When the Varag got closer Matt waved him over to them. The man did not seem at all happy.

"Well? What did you see?"

"Very bad, master, very bad," stuttered the man and then added a rapid string of something else in his own tongue. Most of the Varags spoke some form of Berssian and Matt had learned a few words of their language, but his own Berssian wasn't all that good, either.

"What was that? What did he say, Sergeant?"

"Not sure, sir. But I think he found the patrol and they're all dead."

"Is there any sign of who did it? Is there anyone else up there? Did you scout the area? We don't want to run into an ambush." The man babbled something else and shook his head.

"Sounds like it's clear, sir," said Chenik.

"All right. We'll go ahead. Deploy the first section as

skirmishers."

"Right, sir." The orders were given and eight men spread out in a very thin line in front of the column. Matt put the rest of them men into a single rank. Once the skirmishers were a hundred yards ahead, they all went forward at a walk. The well was only a mile away and the buzzards were thick on the ground and overhead. As they got closer, Matt could see the birds grouped in tight clusters on the ground. He did not have the slightest doubt about what they were doing.

Closer still and Matt gave the order to break into a trot. If there were any ambushers waiting up there, no sense in giving them an easy target. The skirmishers reached the outskirts of the well and a black cloud of buzzards rose into the air with a chorus of angry squawks. They pushed right on through to the other side and fanned out. No shots were fired. Matt led the rest of the troop up in support. He halted them when they reached the well.

They had driven off the buzzards, but the flies had completely ignored their gallant charge. Matt looked about and his stomach heaved. He had seen dead men before, but never quite like this... Chenik came up beside him.

"I'll get a burial detail together, sir."

CHAPTER TWO

"All of them were dead?" asked Brigadier Gerressan.

"Yes, sir," replied Matt. "We counted twenty-eight bodies. The Hetman tells me that there were thirty men who had gone out, but all those we found were dead." Matt had already given Major Macador all the details upon his return to the fort, and he was quite sure he had passed them on to the fort's commander, but he was going over it all again for the benefit of the other officers. They were all sitting around a large table in the officers' mess. The officers from his own regiment were there as well as those of the 52nd Musketeers, the artillery and the leader of the local Varags.

"Was there any sign as to who did this?" asked Gerressan.

"No, sir. We found no trace of anything at all. The bodies had been completely stripped, which is not unusual, but there was nothing else either. No broken arrows or lances, no bodies of any attackers, not even any discarded papers from cartridges. It would appear that they were taken by surprise and were unable to fight back. Perhaps at night. We did find some tracks, sir. They led west."

"Surely there is no doubt who did this!" snarled the Hetman. "Those miserable Kaifeng shall pay!"

"Could you tell how they were killed, Lieutenant?" asked Colonel Piskanan of the musketeers, eyeing the Hetman warily. The long-haired and mustached horseman made a sharp contrast to the officers. His clothing was rich and gaudy compared to most of the Varags, but he still looked far more like the savage Kaifeng than he did the soldiers he served.

"It seemed like mostly sword strokes, sir. You must understand that the bodies had been dead for at least four days. Between the scavengers and the natural putrefaction, it was not always easy to tell what had killed them."

"Yes, I can imagine."

"We did find burn marks on some of the bodies, sir," said Matt with a grimace of distaste. "That might indicate they were tortured before they were killed." The Varag commander snarled again.

"Thank you, Lieutenant," said Gerressan. The Brigadier leaned back in his chair and frowned. "Well, nothing like this has happened in almost ten years. We've had some word recently that more of the Kaifeng tribes are moving eastward again. Apparently those near the border are growing more audacious. Assuming it is the Kaifeng, of course."

"Who else?" demanded the Hetman.

No one answered. The man was probably correct, of course. The Kaifeng were the only people in any numbers out on the plains. There were a few bands of traders and caravan people who crossed the Kaif, and somehow they had safe passage from the Kaifeng—most of the time. But it seemed unlikely that any of them would slaughter the Varags. Not totally unlikely, though. The Varags would sometimes raid an isolated caravan themselves. Perhaps some batch of traders out for revenge instead of profits? There was even the possibility that it had been done by another band of Varags. Blood feuds within the Varag tribes were not unknown, either. Still, it was most likely the Kaifeng.

"All right then," said Gerressan. "We might not know all the particulars, but our response is quite clear. Major Macador, I'd like you to send a substantial force, assisted by whatever men the Hetman can provide and make a sweep of the area beyond the pass. Take supplies for at least two weeks. You are to… chastise… any Kaifeng you may encounter."

"Yes, sir," said Macador. He immediately turned to his own officers. "Captain Vargos, Captain Deerin, I want your companies for this mission. Captain Vargos, you are the senior, so you will command the force as a squadron." Both the men nodded. Matt contained a sigh. He had just gotten back after a hard three days in the saddle and now he'd have to go out again for another two weeks. And he did not look forward to the 'chastisement' they would have to deal out. It wasn't a license for indiscriminant slaughter, but controlling the Varags would be difficult. Major Macador was talking with the Hetman now.

"How many men will you bring?"

"My people are angry—just as I am. On such short notice? Perhaps a hundred. Maybe more."

"That should be more than enough," said the Brigadier. "Between the two of you there will be well over two hundred. Very good. Get your supplies organized tomorrow and you can set out the next day. Terribly sorry about asking you to do this, but you all know the situation. If we don't punish these scoundrels, it will only encourage them all the more. But perhaps I can make it up to you a bit. Sergeant, have the stewards bring wine for all the gentlemen."

"You're leaving again already? But you just got back!" exclaimed Kareen.

"I know, but that's the army. Go where you are ordered, when you are ordered. Just be thankful Phell's not in my company anymore or we'd both be gone." Matt's expression darkened. "And no funny business while I'm away! You two have been getting far too...bold. You're not married yet."

"Yes, big brother," said Kareen with false meekness. Then she smiled and quirked up her eyebrow. "I promise you I'll still be a virgin when I come down the aisle. Although why you want me to be so different from all the other brides I can't..."

"Kareen!"

Kareen just rolled her eyes and shook her head. "Men! But you will be gone two weeks? That means you'll only get back two weeks before the wedding!"

"It might be less than two weeks depending on what we find out there. If we... accomplish our mission sooner than that, we'll be back sooner. Believe me, I have no desire to be out there any longer than I have to."

"Hmmpf! You're just trying to get out of all the work there is to be done beforehand!"

"What work? You've got your dress, you've got the chaplains, you've got the Colonel, and you've got Phell. What more do you need?"

"What more? There are all the invitations, the food, the flowers, the music, why the list goes on and on!"

Matt blanched. "Uh, sis, just who's paying for all this? We have exactly forty-seven marks in our savings by my last count."

"Relax, Matt. Most of it will be donated. The wives of the other officers have pitched in to help us out."

"Well that's a relief. And it sounds like you have plenty of help without me. Now if you'll excuse me, I need to get some sleep."

Kareen watched her brother go into his room and shut the door. Men! They just had no idea of what went into something like this. The wedding was going to be the social event of the year at the fort. Not that that meant a great deal, of course. Fort Pollentia was hardly the social center of the world. She sighed. She would really like to get away from here. It had been all right when she was younger; it had been new and a bit exotic and there had been things that were fun for a child. But she wasn't a child anymore. She was a woman, soon to marry, and a dusty frontier fort was not where she wanted to raise her children or spend the rest of her life. But there wasn't much hope of getting away. She sighed again. Louder.

"Is something wrong, Kareen?"

She looked up from her moping and saw Thelena standing in the door to the kitchen. "Oh, just the usual. Wishing we were somewhere else. Anywhere else."

"Be careful wishing for such things. Sometimes they come true and we find that we did not really mean them." Karen looked closely at the Kaifeng woman. She had been their servant for four years. Sometimes Karen thought she understood her, and sometimes not. There were times when she would smile and laugh like any of her other friends, but then a curtain would draw across her smile and it would be gone. Kareen did consider her a friend. Once Thelena had gotten used to being here they had done a lot of things together. They had fun together. Granted, they had to keep up the appearance of servant and mistress when others were around—that was only proper—but Kareen thought of Thelena as more of a sister than anything else.

Certainly not as a slave! She could not believe that one of the Varags had called Thelena a slave the other day when they went down to the market. It was true that she had bought her and it was also true that slavery was not entirely unknown in Berssia. But Thelena was no slave! Was she?

"If…if you could go anywhere you wanted, Thelena, where would you go?" The Kaifeng woman looked started.

"Go, K…Milady?"

"Don't 'milady' me, Thelena. There's no one else around. Yes, go. If you could leave here and travel anywhere you want, where would it be?"

"I… I don't know. There really isn't anywhere I could go."

"Of course there is! This fort isn't the whole world. Berssenburg isn't that far and then there is the whole East! Navaria, where I come from, is just one of a dozen kingdoms and duchies. And then there are the cites of Ertria and… Oh! How I wish we—all of us, you, me, Phell and

Matt—could all go somewhere far away. Somewhere near the ocean. It's been four years since I've seen the ocean and I miss it terribly."

"I have never seen the ocean. I suppose I could go somewhere as your servant. There is nowhere I could go alone."

"Well, ladies should never travel alone anyway..."

"I am no lady." Thelena's blue eyes glinted and Kareen was startled at the stern tone in the woman's voice. A new thought struck Kareen.

"After... after Phell and I are married. Maybe... maybe we could find a husband for you."

"What man would ever want me as a wife? As a slave, perhaps, but never as a wife."

"You are not a slave!"

"No? You bought me. The law says I am your slave. I suppose if you bought a man-slave you could force him to be my husband."

"Thelena! What a terrible thought! We need to find someone you can love and who will love you back."

"Love is something for the masters. Now please excuse me, Milady; I have to get your brother's shirts washed and packed."

The squadron rode out just after dawn. A hundred and twenty dragoons, followed by forty pack mules and their drivers. The Varags swarmed around the column. Matt guessed that there were at least a hundred, but they kept no order and it was hard to count them. It was an impressive force, all in all. No artillery, but the guns could not hope to keep up on the roadless paths they would be following. Still, it was more than enough to handle any Kaifeng they were likely to encounter. They usually traveled in groups with fewer than a hundred warriors. Lots of horses and cattle and women and children, but not many warriors.

It promised to be a warm day. It was early summer and the winds blowing off the plains were hot and dry. This land only seemed to have the two seasons, summer and winter, separated from each other by two shorter periods of rain and mud. It got very hot in summer and bitterly cold in winter. It was a hard climate on men and animals. Matt noticed how almost all of the troopers had adapted their dress to the harsh realities of where they served. The tunics and breeches and tricorns had nearly vanished, packed away for dress formations. Most men wore pantaloons and short cotton jackets and straw hats to keep the sun off. It was all practical, but very unmilitary in Matt's opinion. He was still wearing the regulation uniform, although it was an old and worn set, much patched and mended over the years.

The column went down the road from the gate and splashed across the river, no more than a muddy creek this time of year, then up the other bank and onto the dirt track that led west. An hour later a turn of the road concealed the fort from view. The Plains of Kaif lay ahead. Captain Vargos set a demanding pace and the column reached Hessley Well just before dark. There was little trace of the horror they had found here only a few days before. The troopers of the regiment made their camp, while the Varags performed some sort of ritual over the graves of their fallen comrades. It seemed to involve a lot of wailing and chanting that went on far too long for Matt's tastes. He could see that most of the men wished they would just shut up so everyone could sleep, but no one, not even Captain Vargos, made the suggestion to them. Matt was paying one of the troopers to act as his servant during the expedition. The man could not cook worth a damn. Matt rolled himself in his blankets with a grumbling stomach and the Varags' wailing in his ears.

The next morning dawned much as the previous one had. The men broke their fast and then packed up for the day's march. After refilling their canteens and water skins, they mounted their horses and moved off. Some of the Varags were skilled trackers and they managed to find the traces of the ambushers' trail in the tall grass. It was very faint and the Varags doubted they would be able to follow it for long. But it did give them a direction to start their search. The Captain gave the commands and the hunt began.

An hour of riding brought them down off the last foothill and onto the plain proper. The grass rippled off to the horizon. It was a land without boundaries or landmarks. Only the sun and the stars and the hills behind them served as guides. Matt suspected that the hills would soon be left far behind.

And so they were. Day after day went by and they were swallowed up in an endless and featureless sea of grass. By day they saw nothing except a few circling hawks and eagles. By night, the vast, star-flecked dome of the sky looked down on them. The immensity of it all made their force of soldiers seem like a trifle. Matt had been out here before, of course, and for longer rides. Once a year the Major took the bulk of the Regiment on a long sweep through the plains, all the way to one of the other forts guarding one of the other passes and then back again. Those rides, though strenuous, were always a treat. A chance to visit another fort, see another pass. There would be balls and dances, too. A break in the routine.

This ride was routine. In spite of the serious nature of their mission, it was like the dozens of other patrols Matt had made. He would be glad to get back to the fort. The only good thing about it was that there was a loosening of the normal formality of the fort. At night the officers would sit around a fire, drink and talk.

"Captain, is there any chance we'll ever get transferred away from that damn fort?" asked Matt one evening.

"Wassamatter, lad?" said Captain Deerin, who, as usual, had already had a bit too much to drink. "Ya don't like our bloody damn fort?"

"Not enough to want to stay there the rest of my life, no, sir."

"Well! I don' blame you! I hate the stinkin' place, too."

"As for our chances," said Captain Vargos, carefully, "I can't really say, Matt." Vargos had probably had as much to drink as Deerin, but you would never have known it. "There's no real reason for them to send us anywhere else. No wars with the eastern kingdoms at the moment. And from what I hear, they can't supply the troops they already have facing those heathen monotheists down south. No place to send us except another garrison. No reason for them to bother."

"They should send those bleedin' worthless Royal Guard regiments out here and let *us* spend a few years in the capital drinkin' and whorin'!" exclaimed Deerin, getting a round of laughter.

"But can't the Colonel do something?" asked Matt after the laughs had died down. "Can't he use his influence to...?"

"Influence!" snorted Deerin. "If the bas...er, if our esteemed commander had any influence d'ya think we ever would have been traded out here in exchange for a buncha tapestries in the first place? Yer dreamin', lad!"

Matt nodded and took a drink from his own mug. Captain Vargos was sharing some of his wine and it was a lot better than the stuff he had brought along. As he thought about Deerin's words he got more and more depressed. Could they really be stuck out here forever? Stuck out here until the Regiment crumbled away like soft stone exposed to years of sandstorms? Desertion, sickness and the rare battle casualties would slowly bleed them away. They had gotten a few new recruits from the locals, but only a few. There were only about 450 men left now. What would it be like in ten years?

He had always hoped to become a soldier. Back in Navaria he had hung around the barracks, skipped school to watch the guards change at the Elector's Palace. His father had despaired of making him a cleric or a barrister. Finally, on his death bed, his father had purchased a commission for Matt. It had seemed like a dream come true. A month later his father was dead. Two months after that he was shipped off to the edge of the world. And now he was a soldier. A professional soldier. *Be careful what you wish for.* After a while he excused himself and went to sleep.

On the next day they reached the far point of their patrol. They had seen no one. Captain Vargos turned them around and headed back east, toward home. Around midday Matt saw one of the Varag scouts galloping toward the column. He urged his horse up to where the Captain was so he could hear the report. It was obvious the man had seen something or he would not be in such a hurry. Vargos halted the column as the man rode up.

"Lord! Kaifeng! To the south! Four, maybe five leagues south!"

"Well, at last," snarled Deerin, who had his usual hangover. "Let's go kill some of the bastards and get this done with!"

"No! No! Lord," said the scout. "Too many! Many, many Kaifeng!"

"How many?" demanded Vargos.

"Ten tens-of-ten, at the least, Lord. Maybe more. I could not get too close…"

"I'll bet you couldn't!" snorted Deerin, who obviously thought little of the report and less of the scout.

"Truth, Lord!" said the scout with a trace of anger. "They have many times our strength." The Captain scowled. If this was true then at least a dozen clans had gathered together. Not an unprecedented thing, but very unusual.

"Which way are they riding?" asked Vargos.

"East, Lord. They are… are…" The man held up both hands with the palms facing each other. "Like this! They move as we do."

"Paralleling us," said Vargos.

"So what do we do?" asked Deerin. "If we go at them they'll break, Var. They've got no stomach for a real fight."

"I don't know…" Vargos paused for a moment to think. "They have to know we are here. I don't like this. It smells." Another moment and he had made his decision. "We'll keep going the way we are. As long as they follow, we can choose our own time to fight. Against a force that size, I'd prefer to do it a bit closer to home."

"They'll run off in the night and we'll lose our chance, Var. Mark my words."

"All right, I do. But those are my orders. Let's get moving."

The bugle blew the advance and the column was in motion again. Matt went back to his place. He ordered his men to keep closed up.

They rode all day and Matt's eyes were constantly drawn to the south. There was never anything to see, but he wondered what was just beyond that horizon.

"They have made their camp a half day's ride to the north, My Lord," said the scout. "Six score of the Whitecoats and five of the Varags. They keep a careful watch."

"Well done. You may go. Eat and rest for tomorrow," said Zarruk, the Noyan of the Gettai Tribe. The man left the tent and Zarruk turned to the man sitting by his side.

"Are you sure of this, Atark? An attack by night would be safer. We could do as we did with the Varag scum."

"No. It will not do, Zarruk. It must be in the daylight. The other Noyen must see exactly what happens. There must be no doubts left in their minds. Then they will spread the word. It will spread and spread like a wildfire before the wind."

"It is not that I doubt your power, my old friend. I do not claim to understand what it is that happened to you. I hear your words, but it sounds more like one of the Great Tales from long past. But still it is a mystery and men fear the unknown. The path that you would lead us on is a new one."

"It is not new at all. Our sires long gone tread it just as we do now. To the East."

"But it is new to us. We are not our sires."

"Do you doubt that we can defeat this band that lies north of us?"

"No. We could destroy them with our arrows and our numbers alone if the will was there. But...but these are not mere Varags. These are the King of Berssia's own men. These Whitecoats have the gunpowder weapons and the courage to stand and use them. They could slay many of our young men if you fail to do what you have promised, Atark."

"I will not fail. The fire is in me and straining to be let loose."

"And what then? Even if we prevail here, the King will send more soldiers to take his vengeance. Can your powers stop them all?"

"Perhaps it can. You have seen what I can do. Soon you shall see more."

He paused as one of Zarruk's wives brought them food and drink. Atark looked at the woman and thought of his own wife. His beloved

Shelena. He closed his eyes and clenched his fists. The rage threatened to loose the fires even now. Too soon. Too soon.

"We will strike when the time is right."

"How far?" demanded Captain Vargos.

"A full day's ride behind us, Lord," said the Varag scout. "But they come fast. Two, three days and they catch up."

"How many?"

"Five hundreds. Maybe more."

"By the gods," muttered Captain Deerin. "Where are they all coming from?"

"More important: what are they doing here?"

"It's not just some raiding party, that's for damn sure."

"No. Over two thousand of them in three separate groups. This is not just a raid," said Vargos nodding grimly. Matt looked nervously over his shoulder. Another group of Kaifeng. Somewhere off to the west. Behind them, but getting closer fast. The first group had been bad enough. The column had pressed on the day after they spotted it and he was relieved that they did not get any closer. They just paced them, twenty miles to the south. But then the second group was spotted. It was nearly as large and it was off to their north. Now this. They were boxed on three sides and the safety of the pass and the fort was still four days' ride away.

"They've got us ten-to-one, Var," said Deerin. "I like a good fight as much as the next man, but this ain't quite fair."

"No. But so far they don't seem inclined to fight."

"Probably just waiting until all their friends show up."

"Maybe. Well, I don't intend to wait for all of them. We are going to make camp tonight as usual. Then, two hours after dark we are going to quietly saddle up and ride like hell. Leave the campfires burning and ride like hell."

Deerin nodded. "They'll spot it quick enough, but it should gain us four or five hours. Hard on the horses, though."

"It's going to get a lot harder. But we have to reach some defensible ground. If we can get to the hills and find a decent spot we should be able to hold off these bastards until we can get help from the fort."

"Right. You going to send off a messenger?"

"Not yet. We're too far out. There are probably Kaifeng scouts all between us and the hills. A single man would not get through. When we get closer to the hills, then I'll send one. Or three."

"All right. I'll spread the word."

The sun went down and they made their camp. Captain Vargos laid the fires out carefully so that when they moved no one would be silhouetted against them. Matt ate a skimpy dinner and then lay there in the dark waiting for the order to move. He wasn't too nervous. The enemy was still miles away. They might be spotted, but they weren't going to run into swarms of Kaifeng tonight. It had been a long day and he had almost dozed off when Vargos came by and shook him. "Time to go," he hissed. Matt sprang up and quickly saddled his horse. The mare's head came around to look at him as though he was crazy. Matt fastened on his sword belt and he was ready.

The word was passed and the column set out on foot with the men leading their horses. It seemed like there was an awful lot of noise, but hopefully it would not carry too far. They trudged along for about a mile and then they were given the order to mount up. Matt gratefully climbed on his horse. There was no moon, but the sky was clear and the stars gave enough light to see a bit.

They walked the horses for an hour, then trotted for an hour, got down and led the horses on foot for half an hour and then trotted again. Alternating in this fashion they rode through the night. Finally, just as dawn was breaking in the east, Vargos let them stop and rest. Matt immediately collapsed in an exhausted sleep. But only for an hour. The Captain had them up again and back in the saddle before the day was old.

Matt scanned the horizon for any sign of pursuit, but saw nothing. Maybe they had given the enemy the slip. But by the noonday halt, the Varag scouts were coming in to report. They had managed to steal a march on the Kaifeng, which was good. But the enemy was now riding hard to make up the distance.

"All those bastards have their own remounts, too," snarled Deerin. "They can ride four miles to our three and always have a fresh horse."

"But we've gained half a day on them," insisted Vargos. "If we can keep moving tonight they won't be able to catch us until afternoon tomorrow at the earliest. By then we will have reached the foothills."

"Can't do it, Var. The horses will never stand that pace. We'll end up on foot—still thirty miles short of the hills."

"We have to try, dammit! If we don't keep moving they'll surround us. And as you pointed out earlier: they have us by ten-to-one."

"All right, all right. But you'll have to let them rest some."

"Yes. Then let's rest now, in the heat of the day. Two hours."

The day that followed was the toughest Matt had ever experienced. They would ride until the horses were stumbling and the men nodding and then after an all too brief rest, they were in the saddle once more. Another night came and it became difficult to keep the men and horses from wandering off. By morning, four of the Varags and two of the troopers were missing. No one knew if they had collapsed, unseen, or drifted off in the wrong direction while asleep in the saddle. And there was no possibility of going back to find them.

After the morning rest, a dozen of the horses refused to move any farther. Some of the pack horses were unloaded and used as mounts. But it got worse once they were moving again. Horse after horse began to collapse. Soon only a few of the pack horses remained. But then, just before noon, a hazy line of blue appeared on the eastern horizon.

"The hills! We might make it yet," said Vargos.

"Maybe," said Deerin, always the pessimist. "Look."

They all looked where he had pointed and for the first time, Matt could see their pursuers. Far to the south he could just make out a dark blur on the plains. Vargos took out his small telescope and confirmed what they had feared. The Kaifeng were closing in on them at last.

"They still have a long way to go. If we push on, we can still get to the hills first."

So they did push on. The blue line of haze became actual hills that could be seen, with mountains beyond. The men's spirits rose. If they could find some rocks to take cover in, they could stand off any number of these savages! Soon after, however, a second party of Kaifeng was spotted to the north. They were a little ahead of the column and angling to cut them off. Vargos hurried their pace and changed their line of march slightly to the south. The horses dropped faster. The last pack horse was pressed into service. Then, men had to ride double. Two small men on a big horse. Ration bags and blankets were dumped to lighten the load. Only water and weapons were retained. A line of abandoned gear littered their trail. The hills drew closer, but so did the Kaifeng. They could be clearly seen a few miles to their north and south now. And in their rear, the following group was no more than five miles behind them.

Matt was so intent on watching their pursuers that he was startled when his horse's hooves clattered on rock for a moment. He looked ahead in surprise and saw that they had reached the first of the hills. It wasn't much of a hill, just a rocky rise that dipped back down into the grass after a hundred yards, but the real hills were just beyond. And the mountains after that. Captain Vargos ordered the three Varags with the strongest horses to head for the fort to seek help. The men quickened their pace and drew ahead.

"Come on, lads!" cried the Captain. "Not much farther now and then we can rest. Close it up! Close it up! Don't let those bastards catch you now when we're almost there!"

But the Kaifeng were closing in fast. A few galloped in and loosed some arrows. They did no harm, but they were a warning of what was to come. Another group came closer. They fired their arrows and then a few scattered shots from the troopers' musketoons drove them away again, yelping in high-pitched voices.

The ground was rising and the last of the tall grass was left behind. Vargos halted the column on a hillock to let the stragglers catch up. At the same time he conferred with the officers.

"We can't make the pass, Var," said Deerin. "Look. The bastards are in front of us." It was true, the northern band had beaten them to the hills. They were about a mile to their east and could easily block any move toward the pass. Matt had no clue if the messengers had gotten past in time. The southern batch of Kaifeng was closing on them.

"All right! That way!" said Vargos. He pointed and Matt saw a jumble of rocks at the base of a substantial hill about a half-mile away. "We can make a stand there. Come on! One last rush!"

The tired men whipped their exhausted horses into motion again and they trotted toward the hoped-for refuge. Strangely, the Kaifeng did not dash after them. They could have made a race of it, but they did not. Matt gasped in relief when they reached the rocks.

"Dismount! Get the horses back up the hill! Then start piling up those rocks. Make some cover!"

It was as good a spot to defend as they had any reason to expect. The hill behind them was quite steep, almost a cliff, and it rose up and up and joined with even higher hills farther on. It would take the Kaifeng hours to get anyone up there. So their rear was secure. They could form themselves in a half-circle with their flanks anchored on the hill. The horses were pushed back against the cliff and a few men left with them. The rest began piling up rocks and the odd bit of wood they could find. The Varags were not too happy about fighting on foot, but the men of the Regiment were dragoons, trained to fight on horseback or afoot with equal confidence.

"We need to get some cover built up," said Vargos. "Without it the damn Kaifeng can just circle around and shower us with arrows until we're all dead. Their bloody bows can fire farther than our musketoons—faster, too."

"But they are afraid of the guns," said the Varag Hetman. "They think they are cowards' weapons and it is a disgrace to be killed by one. They will fear to get too close."

"All the more reason to build up some cover. Deerin, you take the left of the line, and I'll take the right." He looked to Matt. "Lieutenant, I want you and half your platoon to stay with the horses."

"But, sir!" protested, Matt.

"Don't 'but, sir' me, soldier! I want you to be our reserve. Keep your horses saddled and be ready to make a counter-charge if they break through somewhere. And have someone standing ready with the spare ammunition. It's important, Matt."

Slightly mollified, Matt nodded. "Yes, sir."

"Good, get going."

Matt grabbed Sergeant Chenik and he helped him round up the men. All the rest of the horses were unsaddled and the saddles and any surviving gear were added to the breastworks. Unfortunately, those breastworks were not terribly impressive. There were a few large boulders and some medium-sized rocks that were too heavy to move, but not all that much that could be readily piled up. There was no real wood at all, just some brush and bushes that were uprooted and added to the defenses. Still, in a remarkably short time there was the semblance of a defense line. If the men crouched down they would have some cover against distant arrows. Any fired on a higher trajectory that would fall straight down on them would require the Kaifeng to get close enough for the musketoons to be effective. There were a few unfortunate gaps in the line, but they were not large and could be covered by gunfire.

Matt looked out from his position and could see that the Kaifeng had all united in a large group on a hill about a mile to the northwest. There seemed like an awful lot of them. But they weren't doing anything except standing there. Resting their horses, perhaps? Matt couldn't tell. Down below him, the defenses were as complete as they could make them. Captain Vargos called the men to attention and then distributed them along the line.

"Fix, bayonets!" he commanded. The rattle of iron on iron had a comforting sound to it. The dragoon's musketoons were about six inches shorter than a proper musket, but they could still mount a bayonet. If the Kaifeng got close, they could come in very handy. The Varags had no bayonets and looked far less confident than the dragoons. Still, they could be counted on to fight bravely since there was no possibility of flight. And some of them were superb marksmen.

Then they waited. The Kaifeng were still just sitting there. Matt shook his canteen and considered taking a drink. It felt like it was about a third full. His mouth was parched. Better save it. There was no water here at all. If it became a siege, things were going to get nasty. The sun was dropping into the West and still nothing happened. If night came, perhaps they could slip off and make it through the pass after all.

A sudden blast of horns from across the small valley told him that the Kaifeng were not going to lay siege to them. There was a flurry of activity and they seemed to be forming a battle line. Matt wished they had some artillery. A few three-pounders would make them think twice!

"All right, men!" shouted Vargos. "Wait for the command to fire! Don't waste your ammunition! Hold steady, listen to your officers, and we'll all come through this."

Matt hoped that he was right. He looked to his own small command. "Everyone be ready to mount up. Listen for my order. Or just watch me if you can't hear. If they need us down there, they'll need us in a hurry."

"Looks like they're going to come straight at us, sir," said Chenik. "Silly buggers."

The Kaifeng were in motion. A solid mass of horsemen was trotting down the hill into the little valley. They were packed in tight. Not a good formation to fire bows from and then wheel away. An excellent target for musketry. Matt could hear their shrill war cries and the brazen blaring of their horns. They did not seem to be coming very fast, but Matt knew that was an illusion. He'd been in many a drill and he knew that an enemy making a charge always appeared to be a safe distance away until suddenly they were *here.*

"Hold your fire. Check your priming. Wait for the order." Matt could hear the sergeants down behind the line, riding herd on their men.

"Silly buggers," said Chenik again, referring to the Kaifeng who were about four hundred yards away. "They're going to pay a stiff price to…what the bloody hell is *that*?" Matt's head jerked up at his sergeant's cry of astonishment. What was he…?

Then he saw it. Off on the far hill. There was still a crowd of dismounted Kaifeng there and something was happening. A red smoke was rising up and then there was a flash of light bright enough to be seen in the afternoon sun. But the flash did not dissipate. It hung there, a ball of golden fire. Then it seemed to explode, to shatter, into a cloud of smaller lights. A swarm of tiny fireflies. Fireflies that came straight toward them at an incredible speed.

"What are those?" cried one of Matt's men. Others along the defense line were shouting and pointing. The Varags were starting to fall back in confusion.

"Stand fast! Stand fast!" snarled Captain Vargos. He swatted a Varag with the flat of his sword and shoved him back into line. The men steadied, but their eyes were on the fireflies as much as the charging Kaifeng. The enemy horsemen were three hundred yards away when the cloud of sparkling lights swept past them. They came on with a terrible speed. Matt instinctively held up his sword as if to ward them off. The fireflies reached the defenders and…

Bang! Boom! Pow!

The line was wrapped in a cloud of billowing smoke and flashes of fire. Muskets and pistols were going off in a ragged volley, but there was far more smoke and flame than… Matt had only an instant more before another batch of the sparkling fireflies swarmed at him and his men.

Wham!

Something punched him hard in his back and he fell to the ground, swathed in smoke. There was a rippling pop of pistols and musketoons firing all around him. Bullets bounced off rocks and zipped past his head. Men shouted, screamed and cursed. There was a large explosion behind him and then all the horses were screaming, too. He lost the grip on the bridle of his own horse as it yanked away. Then he was in the mist of two hundred panicked horses, bolting in all directions. He threw himself next to a large boulder and hung on. The smoke was thick in his eyes and his nose. Shouts and screams rang in his ears. What had happened?

After a moment most of the horses seemed to have left his immediate vicinity. He pulled himself up and looked to the defense line. >From what he could see through the billowing smoke, it was a shambles. Men were rolling on the ground in pain. Some lay there and didn't move. One Varag actually seemed to be on fire.

Then, through the white cloud of powder smoke, Matt saw the first Kaifeng. A large man on a small horse, wielding a sword. He leaped his horse over the barricade and cut down a trooper who was standing there dumbfounded. Another Kaifeng followed. And another and another.

Matt snatched his pistol out of his belt and cocked it. It was only then that he realized that it had already gone off. Smoke drifted out of the muzzle and the pan. It hadn't been cocked, but it must have gone off somehow when he fell. He reached back to his cartridge pouch—and snatched his hand away again. Something had burned him. He looked back and understood what had hit him and knocked him down.

His cartridge pouch had exploded. It was small and only contained ten rounds. That, and the heavy leather back had saved him from more serious injury. He looked around and slowly began to understand. There were men all around him, some on the ground, others standing, but each and every one had a blackened patch on their coat where their cartridge box had been.

They had all exploded.

And all the guns had fired themselves off.

The fireflies. Somehow those fireflies had…

"Sir! Sir!" someone was shouting in his ear. He turned and saw Sergeant Chenik. He was hatless and wild-eyed, but he had a saber in his hand. "We gotta get out of here, sir!"

Matt looked around in confusion. The line had completely collapsed. There were mounted Kaifeng everywhere and they were killing at will. The troopers and Varags, suddenly stripped of their firepower, were too stunned to fight back with bayonet and sword.

They were being butchered.

"We can't just run!" screamed Matt. The fear and panic was rising in him, but he knew his duty, too.

"It's all gone to hell, sir," said Chenik dragging him back. "We can't do no good except to get killed with the rest!"

"But we can't…!"

"Someone's gotta warn the fort, sir!" screamed Chenik, half-dragging him. That seemed to get through Matt's befuddled brain. Warn the fort. This fight was lost, but the people in the fort needed to know what had happened here! Chenik pulled on him again and he turned to follow. He screamed at those men near him to retreat.

Retreat? Hell, to run like rabbits.

There were still loose horses bolting all over the place and a few writhing on the ground. The one which had been carrying the spare ammunition was horribly burned. Matt dodged around them all and ran back to where the cliff began. It wasn't quite a cliff, but it was steep and difficult going. A good thing right now: not even a Kaifeng could get a horse up it. He scrambled and hauled himself up the rocks. He looked back and was shocked to see only two other men following him. Farther down there was a swirling mass of horsemen where the line had been.

Where the squadron had been.

Where his comrades had been.

He almost stopped. Almost turned back. But Chenik shouted at him again and he kept going. Up and up. A hundred feet. Two hundred feet. An arrow bounced off a rock near him. Then another one. They had finally been spotted. Matt climbed faster. More arrows fell and then there was a cry. He looked back to see one of the other troopers tumbling and sliding down with an arrow in him. "Come on!" shouted Chenik.

Matt forced himself to keep moving. Up and up and after a while the arrows stopped. He looked back and saw that they were far above the Kaifeng now. A few were still shouting and shaking fists at them, but far more were whooping and celebrating.

Chenik had stopped just up ahead. Matt wearily climbed up next to him and sat down. The other trooper just stopped where he was. They all stared back.

"What...what happened?" gasped Matt between breaths.

"Dunno, sir. Never saw anything like it. The damn willow-wisps came at us and then everything blew up like a Gar Wolfe's Day celebration."

"Are you hurt? All the cartridge boxes went up."

"A little singed on my back, sir. Nothing bad."

"What are we going to do?" said the trooper, Matt now saw that it was Private Regari. A solid man, but now near panic. Well, he was pretty damn near panic himself. "They killed everyone! What are we going to do?"

"Stay alive," said Chenik.

Matt nodded. "Stay alive..." his eyes drifted eastward.

"...and warn the fort."

CHAPTER THREE

The Kaifeng were in motion. After four long years of learning and striving and planning, Atark, shaman of the Gettai-Tatau Clan, had finally put the Kaifeng in motion. Or at least a tiny part of them. Seven tribes and two score of clans, six score of scores of warriors were on the move. It was only a fragment, a sliver, of the race who called themselves the People of the Kaif. Their total numbers were uncounted. Once as numerous as the stars in the sky or the blades of grass on the plains, the People had been reduced, after the Great Battle, to a few bands of fugitives. But now they had grown strong again. The memory of the Dark Years, when nine women out of ten were left widows, was fading into legend. The fears of those times had faded, too. The tribes were beginning to quarrel with each other again as grazing land became scarce. Rather than fight each other, many chose to move and they moved in the only direction possible: East.

The Dark Years may have become legend, but all remembered the enemies who had brought them about: the Easterners, the people beyond the mountains. Powerful warriors, clad in iron and with wizards of great power. They had fought the Kaifeng to a standstill on these very lands. No, not just to a standstill. No matter what pride might want to say, the fact was that the Easterners had routed the Kaifeng, driven them like sheep back into the endless reaches of the Kaif. Then they had built mighty fortresses to keep them at bay.

The People remembered.

They remembered the loss, they remembered the shame, they remembered the humiliation. And they remembered the hurts heaped upon them since then. The Berssian raids out onto the plains, onto the lands of the Kaifeng. The burnt tents and the slaughtered and stolen women. The dead flocks and herds. The dead children. They remembered.

Atark remembered, too.

The pain of his own loss had driven him. Driven him to learn what the Ghost had to teach him. Driven him to master those skills. Driven him to convince his own clan to risk the wrath of the Berssians. Driven him to convince others, too. It had taken four years to make all ready. But he had succeeded.

At least so far.

The men in the column were laughing and singing, holding plunder over their heads and shouting. No one had won such a victory in a generation. Two hundred new horses had been added to the herds. A dozen dazed captives were whipped along by the younger boys. The men laughed and sang.

"Look at the fools," muttered Atark. "Two hundred enemy dead and they act like the King of Berssia's head was stuck atop our standard."

"Let them celebrate," said Zarruk. "They have earned it."

"Earned? It was a hard ride, yes. The Whitecoats moved faster and longer than I would ever have expected, but it was an easy fight. Not a single man killed and only a dozen slight wounds."

"Thanks to you and your magic, my friend. I bow to you and your power. You were right. Forgive my doubts."

"There is nothing to forgive. I had doubts myself until the deed was actually done. And this is still but a trifle. The real tests are yet to come."

"Then you are determined to go on with this?"

"Is there any choice? You know what promises were made to gather so many clans together: loot, women, victory. So far the loot has been a handful of horses and some trinkets. No women, and a 'victory' that our sires would sneer at. The men expect much more and it is up to you and me to give it to them."

"You are the one who can give us victory, Atark."

"Not alone. I can but strip the enemy of their cowards' weapons. I am no warrior, no general. Someone must command the men in battle. That is you, Zarruk."

The Noyen of the tribe looked uneasy. "You expect much. Perhaps more than I have to give. Not my heart, you understand, but my skills. Only twice have we ever gathered the whole Gettai tribe together, and that was but a score of scores. Already there are six times as many warriors gathered. Not all the other Noyens will follow my lead."

Atark nodded. "Holding the tribes to the task will not be easy.

But you must be the warlord, Zarruk. I have insisted the trophies go to you. The others will follow your banner." Both men looked to where a warrior was carrying the modest standard of Zarruk of the Gettai. Two other men flanked him carrying the small pennants they had taken from the Whitecoats. The warriors had brought them back to give to Atark, but he had commanded them to be given to the Noyen. "The others will follow you," said Atark again. "I will insist upon it."

"Be wary, my friend," said Zarruk. "While most stand in awe of you and your powers, others are jealous of you. Watch your back."

Atark nodded and frowned. What Zarruk said was true. Others, especially the other shamen, had given him trouble. They feared his new powers. Instead of rejoicing in what those powers could do to their enemies, they feared for their own paltry status within the tribes. Shamen who had used their puny powers to dominate their Noyens for years were suddenly shown to be mere charlatans compared to Atark. A few, all too few, had come to him hoping to learn. They could see what he offered the Kaifeng. The rest schemed and plotted behind his back.

Of course, that was before this latest fight. Up until now, he had only been able to demonstrate his powers in limited ways. There had been many who doubted he could do what he promised. The initial massacre of the small Varag party had silenced a few of the doubters and given even the skeptics hope. Now, there were few skeptics left. They had all seen what he could do. At a stroke he had disarmed the enemy and left them stunned and ripe for slaughter. If he could do it once he could do it again. Couldn't he?

Zarruk rode forward to look at the campsite that had been selected for tonight and Atark slumped in his saddle as soon as he was alone. He'd never felt this weary. Not even when he was dying by the mound had he felt so drained. No pain, fortunately, just a fatigue that reached to his bones. The long ride to catch the Whitecoats was a part of it, but only a small part. It was the casting of the spell that had nearly done him in. He had pulled in the Power as the Ghost had taught him, focused it, formed it and shaped it and sent it against the enemy. And when it left him, it took a great deal of his own strength with it. He had nearly swooned right there on the hill.

Could he do it again? And not as he had just done, but a much greater spell? They were riding against the Berssian fort now. Many more men and those huge guns, those cannons. Gunpowder in enormous amounts. How was he to destroy it all?

As he pondered, the tribes filed into the camp site. Some of the women and many of the older children had followed the warriors and now they were helping set up the tents and to tend the animals. The rest were still back with the herds. He halted his horse and sat, too tired to even dismount. The sun had disappeared long since and the sky was filled with stars. Except to the East. There, the mountains blocked off part of the sky. The mountains made him uneasy. The plains were open; nothing marred the horizons. Here, they were closed in. Secrets could be hidden beyond every turn. And the enemy fort was ahead....

"There you are, Uncle!" A voice came out of the dark and startled him. He looked down and saw Dari, a boy of ten summers. After Shelena was killed, one of his female cousins had taken Atark in. Dari was her oldest boy. "Your tent is set up and the meal is ready, Uncle. Won't you come and eat?"

"Yes, I will come." His muscles had stiffened while he sat and he groaned as he swung down out of the saddle. The boy led him to his tent, babbling away about the battle all the while. Atark looked at him sadly. Ardan would have been just about his age now. Dari took the horse to tend it and Atark ducked through the tent flap. The tent was nearly empty, but his meal was waiting there and a tiny oil lamp provided light. He slumped down onto the rug which made the floor of the tent and after a while began to eat. The food brought back some of his strength, but he needed sleep. He finished the food and then rolled himself in a blanket and lay down.

Sleep would not come. As much as he wanted to drown his weariness in the oblivion of sleep, it would not come. It was not the songs and laughs of the men that kept him awake, nor the cries of a prisoner they were evidently sporting with, it was his fear for the morrow. Tomorrow they would ride against the fort and the men would expect him to work his miracle again. He was not sure if he could do it.

After tossing and turning for a long time, Atark sat up. The lamp had gone out and it was completely dark in the tent. By touch he explored his few belongings until he found what he sought: a wooden box. He pulled it out from under a pile of blankets and set it before him. He fumbled the latch open and then lifted the lid and reached inside. Carefully wrapped in cloth was a human skull. Atark closed the box and then unwrapped the skull and set it on the lid.

Swallowing nervously, he slowly passed his hands over the skull and whispered the words he had been taught. He could feel the Power flowing through him. He could feel something else, too. Slowly, a faint light began to glow. Or so it seemed, since it illuminated nothing but the skull. Bit by bit the light grew and took shape until the Ghost's face was floating there, directly in front of him.

They stared at each other for quite a while. Atark was not sure exactly what he was staring at. He had been puzzling over it for four years. The ghost of the shaman Ransurr had kept him in the mound for over a month, feeding him when needed, and teaching him every waking hour. Day by day, the ghost had faded as the spell binding him to the living world unraveled. Atark was not sure which of them was more frantic that they would not have the time they needed.

They did have the time--barely. Ransurr had taught him the absolutely necessary things, how to grasp the Great Power, how to control it, but by then the Ghost was nearly spent. Then he had taught Atark one more spell, a spell that allowed him to renew the binding of the Ghost's spirit and thus keep him in this world. So he had bound Ransurr to his own skull and there he remained. As far as Atark could tell, the Ghost's powers had faded entirely. It could no longer cast the spells it had taught and only Atark could summon it as he had now. It could talk to Atark and listen, but that was all.

"You have won a victory," whispered the Ghost at last. *"I can see it in your face, feel the exaltation in you heart. Tell me, tell me of our victory."*

Atark told him, recounting each detail. As he did so, the thrill of it returned to him. "All but three fell to us," he concluded. The face of the Ghost seemed to swell in power.

"Good. It is good. Worry not about those that escaped. They will serve to spread the fear of us. Where are we now? What do you plan next?"

"We are at the mouth of the pass. A half-day's ride from the fort that guards it. Tomorrow we will ride against it and take it—I hope."

"They will fall before us just as these others did. Do not fear their large war machines. Their own power will be their undoing."

"I do not fear the enemy's strength," said Atark. "I fear my own weakness. The spell I cast today was harder than anything I have attempted so far. It near to overwhelmed me. What if I cannot do what is needed tomorrow?"

The floating head seemed to nod. *"Yes it is hard and you are yet a novice. The Great Magic demands much strength, though the spell you use is simple compared to some. But there are ways to find the strength. Places you can draw the strength from."*

"I do not understand."

"You shall." The Ghost appeared to smile.

"How many captives did you take today?"

Kareen knew there was something wrong even before the bugler sounded the Officers' Call. Thelena and she were just coming through the south gate, up from visiting the market in the town, when a rider came galloping through the west gate, shouting something in the Varag tongue. He was immediately surrounded by other men and then they rushed off toward the headquarters building. Soon after, the bugle rang out summoning the officers.

"What can be happening?" wondered Thelena.

"I don't know," answered Kareen, "but I'm worried about Matt."

"I am sure he will be fine."

"I don't know. Something important must be going on. What could it be except that the patrol ran into trouble?" The other woman had no answer to that. But since no answers to their questions were forthcoming, after a while they went back to their home. It seemed rather empty with Matt away for so long. She missed her brother-- although she never would have admitted it. Phell was not there, either, of course. He had been summoned with all the other officers.

"Will Phell be coming to dinner?" asked Thelena as if reading her mind.

"I'm not sure."

"Have you two quarreled, Kareen? He was not here yesterday, either."

"He's been busy," said Kareen curtly. Thelena just smiled and nodded, which made Kareen even angrier. They *had* quarreled. The other evening Phell had gotten especially... bold and when Kareen had protested and forced him to stop, he had gotten angry. Men! In only a few more weeks he would have her heart and soul and body forever. She had promised Matt and she wasn't gong to break it now! The thought of Matt brought back her anxiety. Where was he? What was going on? She was still trying to decide how many places to set for dinner when the bugles blew again. Immediately afterwards she heard the infantry drummers begin to play. It was the General Assembly for the entire garrison. The only time that was ever played was for the Sunday Parade or...

"What's happening?" she exclaimed. She went to the door and looked out. Soldiers were running here and there all over the parade ground. The infantry were scrambling out of the barracks and falling into ranks near the drummers. The troopers of the Regiment were taking somewhat longer to get their horses saddled and ready. The gunners were up on the walls doing things with their cannons. Kareen looked about in alarm, trying to spot someone who could tell her what was going on. She sighed in relief when she saw Phell trotting toward her.

"Phell! What is it? What's going on?"

"Kareen! Calm down, everything is all right."

"All right? Then why is the whole garrison turning out? We saw that rider come in. Something's happening!"

"Yes, but there's no reason to worry. A fairly large band of Kaifeng are coming this way through the pass."

"Oh, gods!" gasped Kareen.

"It will be all right," insisted Phell. "They can't possibly get into the fort. You are perfectly safe. The Kaifeng might just be coming to parley for all we know. We're falling in just to be on the safe side."

"But what about Matt? He's out there somewhere!" Phell hesitated for the merest instant, but it was enough for Kareen. "The rider brought some word, didn't he? You know something, Phell!"

"All right. The column was in some trouble, but the rider thinks they found a place to defend. Once we deal with this batch we'll go look for the column." This did nothing to reassure Kareen. She clutched Phell's hand.

"Look, I have to go," he said. "You stay indoors until this is settled."

"Phell!"

"I love you." He leaned over and kissed her on the lips. "I'll see you later." He turned and ran off toward the stables.

"I love you," she whispered after him.

Kareen stayed on the porch but she did not go inside. It was a quarter of an hour before all the troops were in place and things settled down. Or at least all the regular troops were in place; there were still many of the Varags running about without any apparent purpose. Thelena was with her and she had a strange, unreadable expression on her face.

"Some of the ladies have gone up on to the roof over there," she said, pointing. "Perhaps we can see better from there."

Kareen looked and saw that Thelena was right. The main barracks was three stories high and had a flat roof with a parapet. A number of women had gathered there. She wanted to go but she hesitated. Those were probably the women of some of the enlisted men. She really should not be mingling with them...

The hell with that, I want to see!

"All right, let's go," she said.

"Let me take the kettles off the fire first," said Thelena. She went inside and then reappeared a few moments later. She took out her key to lock the door. Kareen nearly told her to forget about that in her impatience, but Thelena looked over to her. "With all the excitement, the Varags might get some ideas." Kareen suddenly realized that she was right. The irregulars would steal anything, given half a chance. Thelena locked the door and then they walked over toward the barracks, trying to look as though they knew what they were doing.

Fortunately, the barracks building had an external stair, so they could reach the roof without going inside. The two women hurried up the steps and were puffing by the time they reached the top. There were already a number of women and children there, but it was a large building so they were able to find a spot along the parapet without difficulty. Kareen looked down and saw that none of the troops had moved. The officers had all gone up onto the walls and were looking through telescopes and appeared to be talking excitedly. Kareen looked out beyond the walls to the far side of the valley, but she could not see anything out of the ordinary. The Kaifeng must be fairly close if they had called all the soldiers into ranks...

"Can you see anything?" she asked.

"No. I cannot..."

"Look!" A cry from farther down the roof made them jerk their heads around. A young boy was jumping up and down and pointing.

"There they are!"

"We've got to keep moving," groaned Matt. "We've got to warn the fort!"

"Not much of a chance for that, sir," said Sergeant Chenik, between breaths. "Those bastards are on horses and going by the fastest route. The rate we're going, we won't get there before tomorrow afternoon. They could be there by... well, they could be there by now, sir."

"I know, I know, but we've got to try. Maybe they won't attack immediately. Maybe we can still get there before they do."

"Maybe," grunted Chenik as he scrambled over another boulder. "Not sure what good our warning's gonna do, sir. If they can do to the fort what they did to us..." Chenik stopped talking. Whether he had run out of breath or simply didn't want to finish the thought, Matt didn't know. He scrambled after the sergeant. After a while he looked back, but Private Regari was not in sight. The trooper could not keep up and Matt could not afford to wait for him.

After the disaster of yesterday—*was it only yesterday?*—they had moved as far and as fast as they could until darkness and exhaustion had forced them to stop. By chance, they could see the enemy camp from the hill they were on. They stared down at the campfires for a while, but soon fell asleep. Sergeant Chenik woke him before dawn and they moved on. They were hungry and thirsty and worn, but they had to move. Several hours later they saw the first of the Kaifeng moving through the pass. They tried to hurry, but they knew they were being left behind. By midday, their parched throats forced them down into one of the valleys to find a spring to refill their canteens. It was costing them time, but they could not keep going without water.

The afternoon was drawing on now. Matt guessed they were about six miles from the fort in a straight line, a lot farther by the paths they would have to follow. And then, they would probably have to make a wide detour to get around the Kaifeng and into the fort. There was no hope of doing it today.

"Have to try!" he gasped out loud. "Have to keep moving! Have to..."

Boom!

Matt and Chenik froze in their tracks as the faint report echoed among the hills. A cannon shot from the fort. There was no doubt about what it was. The two men looked at each other.

"They're there," said Chenik.

Matt nodded. "Keep moving."

The cannon shot made all the horses jump. Most of the riders jumped, as well. Atark and all the gathered Noyens looked to the fort to see a puff of smoke blossoming on the wall. Several men cried out and pointed when the smoke formed into a perfect ring that drifted across the valley. Atark hardly noticed the cannon ball splintering against the rocks five hundred paces short of them, he was so enthralled by the smoke ring. It was so perfect it almost seemed... magical. The thought chilled him. *What if we are wrong about the Easterners' magic?* But no, he was not wrong.

"Well, Shaman Atark of the Gettai-Tatua," said one of the men sitting his horse near him. "Do we attack now, before night, or do we wait until the morning?"

"That will be decided by Ka-Noyen Zarruk," said Atark. He said it with a perfectly level voice, but there was an immediate stir among the group.

"Zarruk is not a Ka!" cried one of them, angrily. "Only the voices of the Noyens can name a Ka! Not a shaman--no matter how powerful he claims to be!" Many of the others growled and nodded in agreement. Zarruk looked uneasy. Atark had fully expected this.

"Then let the voices of the glorious Noyens be raised!" he said. "Let Zarruk of the Gettai be named Ka. Let him order the attack. Let us win a mighty victory this day!"

"And why should it be Zarruk we name Ka?" demanded the same one. He swept his arm around to the others "Why not Muskar of the Yattu or Larrak of the Hyami or..."

"Or Teskat of the Kuttari," interrupted Atark, staring straight at Teskat of the Kuttari.

"Yes, why not?" said Teskat, not quailing before Atark's stare. "Why not Teskat of the Kuttari?"

"Why not, indeed," said Atark. "But let the Noyens decide now. I wish to know whether to prepare my magic... or to pack my horses and return to the plains."

It took a moment for his statement to sink in, but when it did there was a stir. "What do you mean, Atark of the Gettai-Tatua? Surely, you will work your magic!"

"I followed Ka-Noyen Zarruk here to work my magic. I will work it for no other Ka."

"But...but we cannot attack the fort without your magic!" spluttered Teskat.

"If you say so, Noyen Teskat of the Kuttari."

"You would use your new powers for the aggrandizement of your Noyen instead of the good of all the tribes, Atark of the Gettai-

Tatua?" asked a man. This was Gerrik, the shaman of Teskat's tribe. A jealous and unscrupulous man, in Atark's opinion.

"Just as you would use them for your own glory, Gerrik of the Kuttari? Believe what you will, but my statement stands."

The silence that followed was like the aftermath of the enemy cannon shot: a hollow, ringing silence, with a held-breath anticipation of what was to come. But there was no sudden impact as from a cannon ball. Instead, the other Noyens began muttering among themselves. Teskat looked about with growing anger. "It was agreed!" he snarled. Several heads jerked up.

"Agreed? By who, Teskat? Not by me!" said Darnar of the Retayi.

"Nor by me!" shouted several others at once. Teskat's face turned red. In a moment all the Noyens except for Zarruk were shouting at each other. Several drew their swords and shook them over their heads. Zarruk leaned over to Atark.

"What have you done?"

"What I had to do. Wait. Have patience."

The argument went on for some time. Atark looked to the sun. Another two hours of light. Perhaps the attack would not happen today after all. But then there was a sudden pause in the babble of voices. He looked back to see all the Noyens staring at him. Noyen Darnar came forward.

"We will name Zarruk of the Gettai Ka for today and for the next moon. Then we must decide anew. Is this acceptable, Oh Mighty Shaman?"

Atark looked to Zarruk. He nodded. "It is all you dare ask of them," he whispered. "Please, Atark, do not push them farther!"

"I will prepare my magic, if the Ka-Noyen so commands," said Atark bowing in his saddle to Zarruk.

"Let it be so," said Zarruk uneasily. He looked to the others. "Let the warriors be marshaled. We will attack at once." The Noyens jerked their heads in acknowledgment and then turned their horses and rode toward their men, shouting. Zarruk took one long look at Atark and then followed. Atark stood there for a moment before turning to one of the warriors who had been tasked with assisting him.

"Bring the captives forward."

Kareen was getting tired of watching. She had been standing on the roof for over an hour and it seemed like nothing was going to happen after all. A terrible anxiety had shot through her when she first saw the huge mass of horsemen appear in the pass. It looked like there were many thousands of them. If Matt had been caught out in the plains by that host...!

But the invaders had not done much after they arrived. The fort had fired a single cannon as a warning and the Kaifeng had halted and not come forward. Perhaps they would not attack. Certainly, it seemed a foolish thing for them to attack. Kareen knew little of tactics, but even she could see that horsemen alone had little chance against a fort with stone walls twenty feet high and bristling with cannons and muskets.

And those walls were indeed bristling. The musketeers were now up there, lining the parapets, bayonets gleaming in the afternoon sun. The gunners were by their cannons, smoke from the slow matches curling lazily upward. Half of the dragoons, including Phell, were still standing on the parade ground while the rest had gone down to the town. A much less substantial wall stretched from the fort, through the town and all the way to the other side of the pass. The dragoons were manning that to deny the enemy easy passage, but they could quickly withdraw back to the fort if necessary. The defenses seemed very strong to Kareen. Her fear was for her brother, not for herself.

Most of the other women, the wives of the enlisted men, had already left the roof. They would be carrying the dinner meal out to their men on the walls. Perhaps they should do the same thing for Phell?

"Thelena? Maybe you should go back home and get the meal prepared. We can take something out to Phell. Thelena?" The other woman did not appear to have heard her. She was staring out at the enemy with a strange look on her face. "Thelena?" Kareen said her name louder and the woman jerked in surprise.

"My...my lady?"

"Dinner. We must get dinner ready. You go ahead, I will follow in a little while."

"Yes. Yes, my lady." Thelena took one more look at the horsemen and then went down the steps. Kareen stayed behind, uncertain what to do. If nothing was going to happen then there was no point in staying. But she did not want to miss anything. As frightened as she was, she was also excited. Nothing like this had ever happened before! Still, she could always come back. She turned to follow

Thelena.

"Hey! It looks like they are doing something!" A boy shouted. It might have been the same sharp-eyed one who had first spotted the Kaifeng earlier. Kareen wheeled about and went back to her spot on the parapet. Something was happening? What? She couldn't... Oh, over there. The horsemen seemed to be spreading out on the far side of the pass, forming into a thick line facing the fort. Why would they be doing that if they were not going to attack? The soldiers on the walls were getting up, getting ready. A thrill of anticipation coursed through her. Was she about to see a battle? She had been a part of the army for over four years, but somehow it never occurred to her that she might actually see a battle.

But perhaps she wouldn't. It seemed to be taking an awfully long time for anything to happen. She had little notion of how long it took to form an army for an attack. The day was waning; if nothing happened soon, it would be dark.

A horn rang across the valley. It sounded very different from the soldiers' bugles. Kareen stared hard. More horns. Dozens of them, it seemed. A moment later she could see movement among the horsemen. Were they...? Yes, they were coming forward! The lines of riders seemed to ripple. Where they started was in the shadow of the western hills, but in a moment they emerged into the sunlight, which sparkled off swords and spear points. She drew in her breath. The men on the walls near the cannons were moving around. They would probably fire their guns soon. Twenty cannons could bear on the attackers and she could scarcely imagine what effect the cannon balls would have on the massed horsemen.

Then there was another exclamation from the rooftop and this time it was not the boy. Someone else was crying out and pointing at something. It only took Kareen an instant to see what it was. A bright, golden light had appeared on the far side of the pass, back behind where the horsemen had massed. It was in the shadow of the hill and it gleamed like the sun. What was it? No torch or lantern could be that bright.

She gasped when the ball of golden light exploded into a cloud of smaller lights that rose up like a mass of sparks from a bonfire. Cries of astonishment—and alarm—came from the rooftop and the walls. The cloud of sparks was rushing toward them! Far faster than any wind could have borne them! They were beautiful, but Kareen was filled with fear at what they might be.

The sparks swept past the enemy horsemen, who were moving at a slow trot, and across the valley and up the slope toward the fort. Closer and closer. The men on the walls were shouting and pointing. Officers roared out for silence. The sparks were spreading out, spacing themselves along the whole front of the fort. Kareen gasped as they reached the walls.

In an instant, the entire western wall of the fort was enveloped in smoke. A moment later a vast roar of sound hit her as all of the cannons and all of the muskets went off in a long, ragged volley. This was joined by countless other explosions as cartridge boxes and stacked artillery ammunition ignited. The sounds of screaming men was added to the din. Some had been burned by the exploding powder while others had been crushed by the recoil of the unexpectedly firing cannons. Through the smoke came more of the golden sparks. They collected over the parade ground like a swarm of bees and then darted out in all directions.

Some of them flashed toward the waiting dragoons. The troopers' formation was already coming apart because of what was happening on the walls, but now it disintegrated completely. Kareen watched in frozen shock as the dragoons' weapons all discharged and their own cartridge boxes exploded. Horses reared and fell, adding their screams to the other horrible noises. Troopers were thrown to the ground or carried off by their terrified mounts.

Suddenly a roar that outdid all the other sounds slammed into Kareen, nearly knocking her down. The whole southwest bastion disappeared in an enormous boiling cloud of smoke. Blocks of stone, cannons, men--and bits of men--were hurled skyward. An instant later the northwest bastion exploded just like the first.

Magazines. There were magazines under each of the...

She had not even completed the thought when the two eastern bastions exploded and this time she was thrown off her feet. She fell onto the sandy roof and covered her ears. Smaller explosions shook the building as small arms ammunitions stores blew up. A large block of stone from one of the bastions came hurtling down and smashed through the roof not twenty feet away. Other, smaller, bits of debris came pattering down all around her. She lay there trying to muffle the screams all around her until she realized that she was one of the ones who was screaming. She forced herself to stop and pushed herself up from the roof.

Smoke was everywhere. The sharp, bitter taste and smell of gunpowder was in her mouth and her nose. Her eyes watered with it. She stumbled over to the parapet and tried to see. The explosions had stopped, but the screams and shouts had not. More smoke drifted past her and she could smell burning wood along with the burning powder. The wind pulled the veil of smoke away for a moment and she looked down onto bedlam. Men and horses were running everywhere. Others lay writhing on the ground or were still, dead or stunned. Wreckage was strewn all about. Then the smoke concealed it all again.

She moved down the parapet, tripping over prone women and children, as she tried to find a spot to see. What was happening? Where was Phell? The smoke parted again.

The Kaifeng were in the fort.

She saw the enemy horsemen on the parade ground. How had they...? She looked to where the southwest bastion had been. It was a jumble of stone and wreckage, but there were Kaifeng picking their way across. The explosion had filled the dry ditch with rubble and the enemy was coming in.

"Oh gods!" she cried. "They're getting in! Phell! Phell, look out!" She had no idea where her fiancée was in all this mess—if he was even still alive. The thought of Phell pierced the horror that had wrapped her and she was running for the stairway. She went down as quickly as she could, pushing her way past women who were clinging to the railing, frozen in shock.

She burst out onto the parade ground, screaming for Phell. Her cries were swallowed up by the screams and groans of the wounded men and horses, the shouts of officers and sergeants trying to rally their men...

...and the high-pitched war-cries of the Kaifeng.

One of the nomads appeared right in front of her on his horse. He seemed incredibly large. Clad in leather, his long blonde hair was braided and fell around his shoulders. He carried a curved sword that was stained red with blood. He was only a few yards away.

She cried out and darted back toward the barracks. The Kaifeng came after her, but the colonnaded porch frustrated his efforts to catch her and he turned away. Kareen dashed along the porch toward her home. She didn't know where else to go. She reached the end of the porch and looked around wildly. She saw running men, but no Kaifeng were close by. She darted away from her cover...and tripped.

She fell heavily, but scrambled to her feet. Then she screamed when she saw what she had tripped over. It was the upper half of a man, literally blown to bits by the exploding magazines. Crying and gasping, she tore her eyes away and stumbled toward the officers' quarters. She wanted to find her own house and go inside and lock the door behind her. All this could be shut out behind the door of her home. Then she would crawl into her bed and wake up and this would be all right again.

There! There was her house! And Thelena was standing in front of it! If she could just get inside everything would be all right. She dodged around a screaming musketeer sergeant who had a useless musket in one hand and the collar of a terrified private in his other, and then she was on the porch next to Thelena. The woman glanced at her for a moment and then stared past her, back to the parade ground.

"Thelena! We have to get inside! We have to..."

Involuntarily, her eyes followed Thelena's gaze. The smoke was mostly gone, although several buildings were gushing flames. There were many, many Kaifeng on the parade ground now. She could see that the gate had been opened and hundreds of horsemen were galloping in.

And they were killing everyone.

White-coated dragoon and green-coated musketeer bodies littered the ground. Hundreds of them. Kaifeng rode where they would, sabering the dazed soldiers. As she watched, a horseman drove his lance through the back of a fleeing musketeer and pinned the screaming man to the ground. Fifty yards away a cluster of soldiers had gathered and they stood with their bayoneted muskets pointing out in all directions, trying to keep the attackers at bay. But the Kaifeng laughed and drew their bows. A shower of arrows felled a dozen men and the rest broke and fled--only to be ridden down by the lancers. Blood was everywhere. They were killing and killing and killing.

But no, not everyone.

There was a higher-pitched screaming now and Kareen saw women on the parade ground. Some were running, but many were already in the grip of Kaifeng warriors. She shrieked in horror when she saw Henja Wenning, a girl about her own age, struggling in the arms of one of the nomads. He had pulled her up onto his horse. Her skirt was gone and her blouse was torn open. She scratched at the face of her captor and he responded with a blow to her jaw that left her limp in his grasp.

"Gods!" cried Kareen. "We have to get away!"

"There is nowhere to run," said Thelena with a terrible calm.

She was about to grab and shake the woman when four of the Kaifeng rode toward them. Kareen cried out and then turned to flee into her house.

The door was locked. Insanely, she whirled about to get the key from Thelena. But Thelena had already been seized by one of the Kaifeng. She didn't resist at all as she was slung over the saddle in front of him.

"Thelena!" screamed Kareen. But then another man was coming at her. She dodged aside and ran. There were coarse shouts behind her and the sound of hooves pounding. She ran and ran. If she could get out of the east gate she could get away. She could run all the way to Berssenburg. She could find help and come back to save Matt and Phell and Thelena. She ran.

Something pulled tight around her waist and her arms were pinned to her sides as she was stopped short in mid-stride. A rope! There was a rope around her! An instant later she shrieked again as she was hauled off her feet. Impossibly strong hands grabbed her and she was slung across a saddle just as Thelena had been. She kicked and screamed, but her hands were caught and tied together behind her. She tried to twist around but only caught a glimpse of a grinning face.

Then she was squealing in outrage. The man had his hands on her! In a fashion far more bold than anything Phell had ever done the man was touching her! She kicked and cried with renewed panic.

She was going to be raped. Suddenly all the generalized fears crystallized into that single thought. This man was going to rape her. All of her screams, all of her struggling would not prevent him from ripping her clothes off and raping her. She gave one last convulsive jerk and then lay limply. Sobbing, while her captor's hands continued their exploration.

But she wasn't raped just that moment. The sounds of fighting and slaughtered had died down. There was still much noise: the moans of the wounded, the crackle of burning buildings and the cries of the women, but it was quieter than it had been since the nightmare had started.

Suddenly a great shout went up. All the Kaifeng were cheering. In fear she looked around. There was a man up on an undamaged section of the walls. He was too far away to see clearly in the fading light, but all the Kaifeng were cheering him.

"Atark! Atark! Atark!" the men were all shouting. This must be their leader, Kareen thought numbly. The man responsible for all this horror. She was grateful that the man had distracted her captor from what he had been doing, but she knew it would not last long. She sobbed in shame.

A few yards away, she saw Thelena in the clutches of another Kaifeng. Her dress was already in shreds and except for the lack of blood and bruises, she looked much as she had when Kareen had first seen her.

Except this time she was smiling.

Kareen looked at the woman she considered her friend in bewilderment. How could anyone smile at a time like this? But she was smiling and the cheers went on and on.

"Atark! Atark! Atark!"

CHAPTER FOUR

Atark, shaman of the Gettai-Tatua clan, strode through the camp, surrounded by cheering warriors. The heady exultation that filled him was as intoxicating as honey-wine. Victory! Such a victory as had not been won since before the Dark Times. Men cheered and women trilled and the boys capered about. He had worked the magic and its effects had exceeded all his hopes. Not only had the enemy weapons been rendered useless, but huge explosions had torn open the walls and let the warriors inside. Zarruk and he had feared that actually gaining entry to the fort could prove difficult and costly even with the enemy guns destroyed. But it had not been so. Bold riders had leaped over the rubble and then opened the main gate. The defenders had been too dazed and disorganized to resist. From then it had been a slaughter. Not just in the fort, but in the town as well. Once the garrison had been taken care of, hundreds of warriors had swept down into the town. There were still screams coming from that direction.

There were fewer screams in the camp. Moans and whimpers and sobs, yes, but few screams. There were a great many prisoners and these had been dragged and carried from the burning fort to the Kaifeng camp. The men, only a few hundred, had been tightly bound and tossed into a crude enclosure. More secure arrangements could wait until morning. A great many more women had been taken. Most of them were already in the tents with their new masters. Their screams had subsided to sobs by now. The Kaifeng women had taken charge of the children who had been captured, the small boys and the younger girls and the older women. Their fate would be decided later. Most would become slaves if they survived. A few of the youngest might be adopted into families and become Kaifeng.

The crowd of cheering people was escorting him toward the large tent of Ka-Noyen Zarruk. It was a modest structure for one who had such a victory to his credit. A bigger one would have to be made. Dozens of torches lit his path, for night had fallen. Atark only had to duck his head slightly to pass into the tent. Inside, lamps lit the space with a dim, pleasant glow. All six of the tribe leaders, the Noyens, were there, along with some of the more humble Buyantas, the clan leaders. They were all seated on cushions, but upon seeing Atark they sprang to their feet and greeted him with loud voices.

"Hail to Atark! Bringer of victory! Hail to Atark! Master of fire! Hail!"

He acknowledged them with a bow, hand upon his chest. "Hail the mighty Noyens!" he said. "Leaders of our brave warriors! And hail Ka-Noyen Zarruk! Leader of us all!" Most of the men cheered his words, but he noted that a few did not. The dispute from this afternoon was far from over and they all knew it.

Atark was escorted to a cushion at Zarruk's right hand. It was the place of honor and he was moved. The reality of the accomplishment was only beginning to sink in. The enemy fort was taken, its garrison slain or captured. The way east lay open. A grinning Kaifeng woman handed him a goblet of wine. He drank deeply. He was very tired.

But not as tired as he had been after the first battle. Today's magic had been vastly greater than the other, but it had not been as hard, thanks to the Ghost's advice. He was still a little shocked by what he had ordered done. He had been shocked when the Ghost had told him what needed to be done. But he had done it. The dozen captives taken in the last fight had been brought to him, bound like hogs and terrified. Well, not all had been terrified: the Whitecoat officer had glared defiance at him until the last. Atark admired his courage, but he had died with the others just the same. As he had begun the spell and reached for the Power, one by one the blades had fallen and the captives' heads had followed. As each man died, his own native power had flowed out. The first had slipped away from Atark and gone wherever it was destined to go. But he had seized the next and all of the others. He had added their strength to his own. At the height of the spell he had felt...what? He could not describe it. Bursting with power. He had felt like he was going to explode as the fort did soon after. The spell was cast. He was tired, but not spent. He still had the strength to enjoy this night.

A great deal of shouting from outside the tent caught his attention. The flaps were opened and a dozen warriors crowded through and then bowed. "Mighty Shaman! Mighty Ka! Mighty Noyens! We hail you all!" they cried. "Let us present the trophies of this great victory!" The assembled leaders laughed and returned the salute. The warriors formed an aisle and several more entered carrying the captured banners of the Berssian soldiers. Two of the flags were quite large and beautifully made of silk, although one had an ugly hole burned through it and the other was torn. There was also a bundle of smaller pennants of various colors. These were all presented to Zarruk and he directed that they be displayed around the already crowded tent. On his command, the side flaps of the tent were raised up. This not only provided more room, but let the crowd outside see in.

More trophies were brought forth. Fine crystal goblets were given to all. Zarruk and the Noyens received the swords of the highest Berssian officers. They were not terribly useful weapons, but most had golden hilts and scabbards and some had gems set into them. Then there was a cheer and a roar of laughter from outside and some much larger trophies were brought in. One by one, some of the captive women were presented. Each was tightly bound and gagged so that their weeping might not disturb the celebration. They were all completely naked and they were very beautiful. One was set down at the feet of each of the Noyens. They writhed and squirmed, their eyes wide with terror. As each woman was presented, the Noyen bowed and accepted the gift. Another, woman, very young, slender and with lovely dark red hair, easily the most beautiful of the seven, was placed before Zarruk. The Ka bowed in place and thanked the men for the gift.

Atark looked up in surprise, and no small bit of dismay, as an eighth woman was carried in. He bit back a cry of protest when she was laid at his feet. She was the most beautiful yet and he could not help but stare. She was taller and darker and...rounder than most Kaifeng women. Rarely had he ever seen so fine a girl. The feelings she roused in him were very... disturbing. He had not lain with a woman since Shelena was murdered. And as much as he might desire to, he would not lay with this woman now.

"Hail, Oh Mighty Shaman!" said the men. "Accept this gift from us in thanks and reverence!"

Atark reddened slightly, but then he bowed. He looked back up. "I thank you kindly for this great honor," he said. "This is a fine gift indeed. But I beg to be allowed not to accept it." The faces of the men fell and he felt like a churl. He should have just taken her and then given her away. Stupid. But it was too late now. "The...the discipline of my magic cannot suffer such a distracting... distraction." There was a burst of laughter and the men looked slightly mollified. "Please give her back to the men who took her. Let them enjoy her to the fullest. They have earned it." He looked at the men who had brought her in and a thought struck him; something that might please them. "But, if you do not object, leave her here until the feast is ended. She is a most pleasant sight and I can allow myself such a distraction for one evening." There was more laughter now and the men were grinning. They bowed and left him.

Now the women brought in the meal. A great feast had been prepared and course after course of food and drink were served. He ate and talked with those around him and listened as the men recounted their feats in the battle. But his eyes kept drifting back to the woman. She was truly beautiful. Terrified, of course, and much shamed. Several times she tried to roll onto her stomach to hide at least part of herself, but each time she was turned back over amid much laughter. After a while he noticed the woman staring at him. He glared back at her. He had no idea how to react. Even if he knew her language, what could he say to her? *Don't worry, I will not rape you this night. But many other men will. Perhaps you will die from the ordeal as my own daughter did. And if you survive you can only expect the same again for as long as you live.* He wished she would roll over again so she could not stare at him.

"So! Atark of the Gettai-Tatua!" shouted one of the Noyen. "What shall we do next? A great victory, to be sure, but what next?"

"Next, Muskar of the Yattu? It seems to me that that is a question for the Ka." All eyes turned to Zarruk, who frowned at Atark. The Ka was silent for a time and the tent grew quiet.

"We have three choices," he said, at last. "We can return to the plains. We have won a great victory and the other tribes will honor our feats. We had collected much fine booty." He leaned forward and gave the red-haired girl a firm pinch to a gale of laughter. "So, we can go back in honor. The Berssians will send soldiers to pursue us, but with the powers of Atark to aid us, they will only be riding to their own deaths." The men cheered at this, but many did not look pleased otherwise. "Another choice would be to remain here," he continued. "There is still much booty to be collected. And there are the other forts guarding the other passes. We could smash each as we have done this one. More booty from each and once they are gone, the Berssians will find it far harder to send their murdering raiders into our land!" More cheers. Zarruk paused and glanced at Atark. The two of them had discussed this very issue several days ago. Zarruk knew Atark's opinion, but would he act upon it?

"Or...," said Zarruk slowly, "...we have a third choice: We can go on from here--to the East."

"To the East?" squawked Teskat of the Kuttari. "Against the Berssian Army? Madness!"

"Only a short time ago it was madness to attack this fort," said Zarruk. "But we did it."

"That was different! A garrison smaller than our own numbers, taken totally by surprise by Atark's magic. Next time there will be no surprise! Some of the Whitecoats who were defending the town escaped. They will spread the word in Berssia. They will come against us in huge numbers. A score of score of scores. Even more. Such a host could overwhelm us with just swords and their gun-spears, even if Atark strips them of their gunpowder. It is madness!" A few men nodded in agreement.

Zarruk was silent again for a moment and his eyes darted to Atark. "What you say is true, Teskat. With the numbers we have here, to challenge the Berssians would indeed be madness." Teskat leaned back with a smile of satisfaction, but Zarruk went on. "So we must increase our numbers! We here are but one nail on one finger of the fist that is the Kaifeng. We will send for the other tribes! Send word to our friends and our kin. Tell them what we have done here. Invite them to join in our next triumph! There are a score of other tribes within a week's ride of here. Many, many more within a month. If we wait here for a bit, rest and enjoy our victory, then our numbers will grow and grow. Soon we will have ten times and more than ten times our present strength. Then we will ride! We will ride to the East!"

The Noyens sprang to their feet and cheered. The men watching from outside cheered as well and the cheering spread through the camp, though most of those cheering could not possibly know the reason. Atark himself joined in. Zarruk had made a good speech. Atark knew that his friend doubted his abilities to lead, but he underestimated himself. He would make a great Ka. And if enough of the tribes gathered, he would make a great Re-Ka, as well. And as the word spread on the Plains of Kaif enough tribes would gather.

Berssia would fall. Then the next kingdom and the next. The Dark Years would be avenged. His family would be avenged. And the Kaifeng would rule all the way to the fabled eastern sea.

The cheering subsided. Zarruk directed that in the morning fast riders would head west. Each one would carry one of the captured banners and other bits of booty. They should ride from tribe to tribe, spreading the news and giving Zarruk's invitation. Atark nodded in approval. It was good. Soon they would have the strength. He glanced down at the captive girl. She could have no clue that the end of her world had just been ordained. *Fear, little slave, fear. Soon all that you have known, everyone and everything you held dear, will lie at the feet of the Kaifeng!*

The feasting continued. The Noyens and Buyantas talked and joked among themselves. Except for Teskat. He did not laugh. He glared at Zarruk and Atark from time to time and drank a great deal. Teskat was ambitious and more than a bit cruel. Things had not gone his way today. Atark suspected that the slave woman beside him would have a hard night. He also knew that he and Zarruk would have to watch Teskat closely.

A motion caught his eye and he noticed another one they would have to watch closely: Gerrik, the shaman of Teskat's tribe. Those two were made for each other. Gerrik was as jealous of Atark as Teskat was of Zarruk. The Kuttari shaman had more than once demanded to be told the secret of the great magic and had each time rejected the notion that it could not be taught in a day or a month. He had accused Atark of keeping the secrets for himself and refusing to share. It had not been true. At least not at first. Now it was: Atark had no intention of ever giving Gerrik the power. Others, perhaps, but not him.

Gerrik slowly made his way to Teskat's side and whispered into his ear. After a moment Teskat's eyes darted to Atark. What is this? Some new scheme being hatched? Atark became more alert. A few moments later there was a commotion outside the tent. A group of men had appeared and there was a great deal of talking. A higher-pitched woman's voice cut through the babble. Someone demanding to see him. Was this what Gerrik was telling Teskat about?

After a while longer the men crowded into the tent. There was a woman in their midst. Atark looked on in sudden interest. She was dressed in Berssian fashion—or at least she had been; her clothes were in shreds and she was barely maintaining her modesty by clutching bits of the fabric to her. But her hair was blonde and braided in the way of the Kaifeng. He grimaced. A woman of the tribes, taken by the Easterners. It happened far too often. Usually the women did not survive long, but this one apparently had. Too bad for her. There would be no mercy for her now, not here in front of everyone.

But this one did not look to accept her fate quietly. She pulled herself out of the grasp of the man holding her and stepped proudly forward. There was something about her, though...

She came right up before him and threw back her shoulders. She let her hands fall to her sides and the rags of her dress fell with them. She looked him straight in the eyes.

"Hello, Father."

There was a roaring in his head that had nothing to do with the wine he had drunk. A red haze formed around the edge of his vision, blotting out everything except the face of the woman in front of him. *Thelena!*

He had no memory of having stood up. No memory of having stepped over the bound girl on the carpet of the tent. He simply had his daughter in his arms. He crushed her to him and he felt her arms clutching his back. "Thelena! Thelena!" he cried. All thoughts of conquest and revenge fled from his mind. Plots and plans and schemes were banished. All that was left was the soaring joy of seeing his daughter alive. He held her and wept.

They stood there for a very long time, locked in a thoughtless bliss. He pulled away slightly to look at her face. It was older than his memory of it and it bore the marks of her ordeal. Her lovely nose was bent and crooked. Her tearful smile was missing teeth. But it was his daughter! She lived! She was here with him and...

"Atark of the Gettai-Tatua," said a harsh voice. He scarcely noticed, but it repeated his name more loudly and he turned his head. Everyone in the tent was silently looking at him. It was Gerrik who had spoken.

"Atark of the Gettai-Tatua, you know the law," said Gerrik. His voice was cold, but there was a tiny smile on his lips. "This woman, your daughter though she might be, must die. She has shamed you and your family, your clan and your tribe. She has lived with and submitted to our enemies and now she must die! Let the women stone her to death!"

A cold lance of fear went through Atark. It was followed by a hot rage. Gerrik had known! Somehow he had learned of Thelena's presence here. What he said was true: it was the law. But it was a law that was rarely ever invoked. On the rare times that a captive woman did escape and return home, she would usually be taken back by her family and all would pretend that she had never been gone. The law was only invoked when the woman had fled her family on her own. Thelena should have been restored to him in private. All would have known, but none would have objected. But Gerrik had arranged otherwise. He had told the men to bring her here, in front of all the Noyens, where the law could be invoked. The swine! That he would take his revenge like this! Atark's fury grew.

"Stand aside, Atark," demanded Gerrik. "Let the law be carried out." The other shaman waved a few men forward to take Thelena.

"No."

Atark put himself between his daughter and the men. They halted and looked about nervously.

"No," said Atark again, "You may not have my daughter."

"It is the law!" cried Gerrik. "If you break the law you will be punished, too!"

"And who will be the one to punish me, Gerrik? You?" Atark turned to face the other shaman. His rage was coming to a peak and he instinctively reached for the power. Gerrik went pale. Perhaps he realized just what he was dealing with, the danger he was courting.

"It is the law!" cried Gerrik again. He looked wildly to the Noyens for support. But the tribal leaders sat there frozen in shock. Even Teskat was silent. Atark took a step forward. He could let it drop now, he knew. There would be grumbling and whispering behind his back, but no one would actually challenge him or try to harm his daughter. But Atark had no intention of letting it drop. Gerrik had troubled him one too many times!

"Teskat! You promised to stand by me!"

Atark had the power now. He grasped it and drew it to him. The Ghost had mostly taught him fire magic. It was the magic he used against the Berssians' gunpowder. But there were other uses for fire magic, other things he could do. He raised his arms and a ball of flame appeared in each hand. The people in the tent all cried out and Gerrik screamed in terror. He jumped over a pile of cushions and ran, trying to escape.

But there was no escape. The flame leapt from Atark's hands and struck Gerrik in the back. Immediately all his clothing burst into flames and he was wrapped in fire from head to foot. His scream rose to a shriek. He fell and rolled on the ground trying to put out the fire. But he could not. The carpet he lay on flared up and everyone scrambled to get away from the flames. Gerrik thrashed about for a few moments but then his screams and his struggles ceased. Atark waited for a few heartbeats longer and then waved his hands. The flames were snuffed out and only a blackened, smoldering husk remained. Silence filled the tent. Every eye turned from the remains of Gerrik to rest on Atark.

He returned their stares without flinching, in spite of the fact he could barely stand. The strength it had taken to cast the spell had drained him, even more than the great spell of today. With no prisoners to take strength from he had only himself to draw upon. He swayed slightly but Thelena was at his side now and he put his arm around her to steady himself.

"This is my daughter," he rasped. "This is Thelena, my daughter. She will be welcome in my tent. Let anyone raise a hand against her at their peril!"

The silence dragged on and on, but at last Zarruk stirred. "So be it," he said. "Let nothing more be said by anyone." Slowly the people in the tent relaxed. Several men wrapped the scorched carpet around the remains of Gerrik and dragged it off. Women scurried in with more wine. Atark guided Thelena over to the cushions and sat down with her at his side. A robe was produced and Thelena wrapped it around herself, covering her nudity. She leaned against him and he hugged her close. The rage in him faded and the joy returned. His daughter lived! He looked at her and smiled. She smiled back at him. He gave her food and drink, but he had no clue what to say to her. Words seemed totally inadequate. He just held her and felt the joy.

Kareen lay on the carpet and stared at Thelena and the man holding her. She was more frightened than she had ever been in her life. But this day had already taught her that there were no limits to fear. A dozen times already she had been more frightened than ever before, but each time something else had happened to make it worse. The arrival of the messenger and her worry about Matt. The appearance of the Kaifeng in the pass. The mass charge across the valley. The ball of golden light and the flying sparks. The terrible, earth-shaking explosions which tore the fort and its defenders apart. Her flight across the parade ground. The slaughter of the troops. The Kaifeng warriors chasing her. Her capture. It all ran together in an ever-increasing storm of fear.

And it only got worse.

She had lain over the saddle of the Kaif who had caught her with her heart pounding as they cheered the man on the wall. It had gone on for quite a while. But not all the Kaifeng had stopped to cheer. Even from her limited viewpoint, Kareen had seen the women and children of the fort being routed from their hiding places and caught. There were some male prisoners, too, and Kareen had tried to spot Phell, hoping against hope that he was still alive. Even then she had some crazy idea that if he were alive he could somehow make everything right. But she had not seen him. The captive soldiers were beaten and whipped, stripped of their weapons and most of their clothing and then tightly bound and driven off like cattle. The children were treated with surprising gentleness. They were simply roped together and led away, most wailing piteously for their mothers. Their mothers were with the other women and older girls...

There had been a great many women in the fort. It was a permanent garrison and the soldiers were all allowed to marry. Most of them had a wife or a lover and many of them had families. Few, if any, of them had been caught in the explosions or the slaughter on the parade ground. They had survived to be caught by the Kaifeng. Dozens of them, older women or those with infants had been herded together where they wept for slain husbands or stolen children. The rest, the younger ones, were in the hands of the Kaifeng warriors. Some struggled wildly, others, like Kareen, had been bound and could do nothing. Still others seemed too stunned to react at all. And some were already being raped. Kareen could hear the screams. They had a different tone from the earlier screams of terror. She had no doubt what was happening.

Or what was going to happen to her.

Finally, the cheering had stopped and the man on the wall came down to mingle with a crowd of other Kaifeng. The man who had Kareen laughed loudly and called out to some of the others. Then he had slapped her hard on the backside and set his horse into motion. He had trotted out of the fort with Kareen bouncing before him. A dozen other men were close by and they all laughed and shouted. Down the hill they had gone and Kareen was surprised to see that a city of tents had sprung up. It was nearly dark and there were fires and torches everywhere.

They had ridden up to one cluster of tents and the man was met by a number of women and older boys. There had been a great deal of shouting and laughing and many of them were pointing at her. The man dismounted and dragged her down from the horse. Her legs weren't tied, but she found she could not stand and she collapsed on the ground and sobbed. The other men clustered around her and after a moment of discussion, they seized her.

She had screamed when they started to strip her, but her struggles were entirely useless. They had removed the ropes that were binding her, but someone always had hold of her arms and legs so all she could do was thrash helplessly. Item by item they had pulled her clothes off. Each piece was given to the women who were gathered about to watch. They laughed and passed them from hand to hand. Her jewelry was taken, too. She shrieked when they took the ring Phell had given her. Soon they were down to her undergarments, but they did not stop. Those were peeled away and she was naked. The men hooted and laughed and many sets of hands were already touching her. She gave one last convulsive squirm and then collapsed in tears. They were going to rape her. All of them. And nothing could stop them.

But, amazingly, something had stopped them. A man rode up on a horse and shouted to them in a commanding voice. The men and women all looked to him and made some strange gesture of salute. He had another woman slung over his saddle and he tossed her down. Kareen recognized her as the wife of one of the sergeants in Phell's company. She was bound, but she still had most of her clothes. She had looked about with a blank expression, her face streaked with tears. A great deal of talking had gone on. The man who had first caught her had not looked terribly pleased, but the man on the horse and the others seemed to be cajoling him and finally he had nodded. There was a small cheer and then Kareen was rolled onto her belly and tightly bound with her hands behind her back. A gag was fitted in her mouth and then she was carried off.

And now she was here.

She lay on the floor of a large tent filled with Kaifeng and her terror was like a living thing, pulsing inside her. She and seven other girls, girls she mostly knew, had been placed before men who had to be the leaders of the Kaifeng. She, and all the others, were naked.

She was shamed like never before in her life. No man had ever seen her naked, not since she was a baby, and now she was on display before dozens of men. She had tried to roll away and hide herself, but a Kaifeng woman had turned her back over and tugged her ears painfully and spoken to her in a scolding voice. She had not moved since then.

The man she had been placed before was not especially large, nor did he have the weapons or trappings of the other leaders, but he was clearly an important man. As time went by she heard the name 'Atark' again and again and she realized that this was the man they had been cheering. She had been given to the leader, the man responsible for all this. Her fear had increased yet again. The man had stared at her with a hard expression. The other leaders had laughed and joked. They had groped and fondled the other girls. But this one had done nothing but glare at her from time to time.

And she was his slave.

She had been given to him and he was now her master. He could do whatever he wished with her and she feared him more with every passing minute. The others, the men who had caught her, would have raped her. Somehow that did not seem so bad compared with the cold gleam in this one's eyes. Eyes that traveled over her bare flesh from time to time, noting every detail. She steeled herself for some fate she couldn't imagine.

But then something had happened. There was excitement in the tent and the man had gotten up and stepped over her. She had twisted around and was amazed to see Thelena standing there. She had lost sight of her when they left the fort and she had supposed that she was being raped as she would have been had it not been for the interruption. But here she was. And the man with the cold eyes was embracing her! Calling her by name! He knew her and she knew him! Sudden hope flared in her. Thelena knew the leader of the Kaifeng! She could help her, get him to have mercy on her. Wild visions of she and Phell and Matt being spared and turned loose danced in her head.

But then something else had happened. She did not understand what, but there were angry voices and some other man shouting and pointing at Thelena. The leader had grown angry and then he had... had...

She still could not believe what the man had done, what she had seen. Fire had leapt from his hands and the other man had been burned alive! It was impossible. It was like something out of legend. It was magic.

That realization explained all that had happened. This man, the man who owned her, was a magician, a wizard, a sorcerer. Kareen had known of magic all her life. She had seen a few magical trinkets and a few entertainers who claimed to have the power. Magic existed, but it was not something anyone gave much thought. It was a thing of the far past, not the present day.

Or she had thought it was. The events of this day had proved that she had been wrong. Everyone else in the fort had been wrong, too. It had been magic that had caused the disaster. The golden sparks, the terrible explosions, had all been caused by magic.

Had all been caused by this man. And she belonged to him.

But Thelena knew him. And she was someone special to him, too. Kareen had seen him embrace her, had seen his tears. Was he her father? An uncle? Whoever, she was important and she could help her!

But so far, she had not. She was sitting next to him, only a few feet away, but she had only glanced at her a few times. There was no doubt she recognized her, but she had done nothing. What was the matter? Kareen tried to calm herself. She did not know these people or their customs. Perhaps Thelena had a plan. Maybe when the feast was over and they were alone, maybe then she would speak for her. She had to!

And as she lay there, it became apparent that the feast was coming to an end. The fiery death of the one man had only been a brief interruption, but the festive mood was gone. And the leaders were getting drunk--and impatient. Several of them had dragged the captive girls up to them and were handling them in the most intimate fashion. Kareen blushed when she saw one of them pouring wine down the throat of Letti Jowalsa and splashing it on her breasts. Finally, one of the men stood up and hoisted his girl over his shoulder and slapped her on the bottom. There was more shouting and laughing and then he carried her out of the tent. Several of the others soon followed.

Kareen twisted around trying to see what was happening. She looked back to Thelena and was relieved to see her whispering to the man. A chill went through her when she saw him shaking his head. What did that mean? Suddenly Thelena and the man were looking past her. She turned her head and froze. The man who had first caught her was standing there in the entrance to the tent. Some of his comrades were with him. The man was talking and pointing.

He was pointing right at her.

What was going on? Did he want her back? But she had been given to the leader! To her horror the leader nodded his head and the man came forward to claim her. Kareen screamed as much as her gag would allow and thrashed about with every bit of strength she had. No! Thelena!

Thelena put her hand on the man's arm and said something to him. He put up his hand and the other man stopped. There was more talking and then he bent forward and took the gag out of her mouth.

"Thelena! Thelena!" she gasped. The woman slowly turned her head to look her in the eyes.

"Yes, Kareen?"

"Thelena! Help me! Please!"

"Help you? How?" A chill went through Kareen. There was no sympathy at all in Thelena's voice.

"Don't let them take me!"

"My father does not want you as his slave. He has promised you to these men."

"No! Thelena! Please help me! I helped you! Years ago I helped you! Please!" Panic was rising in her. What was wrong with Thelena? The man, her father, talked to her briefly and then to the man who wanted her.

"You did help me, Kareen," said Thelena. "You did save me from death. So now I shall save you."

"Thank you!" said Kareen in relief. "Oh, thank you, Thelena!"

"Do not be so quick, Kareen. I shall save you. I shall save you *exactly* as I was saved."

"What...what do you mean?"

"You saved me from death by buying me as your slave--after the Varags had used me for two days. So it shall be with you. These men shall use you as they please for two days. Then they shall return you to me and you shall be my slave."

"Thelena!" shrieked Kareen. This couldn't be true! How could she do this to her? "Please! Thelena!"

"You do not think this is just?" asked Thelena. She spoke out to all in the tent for a few moments and everyone there nodded their heads. "They all think it is just."

"It's not! It's not!" sobbed Kareen. "I was kind to you!"

"By the measure of your people, I suppose you were. And by the measure of my people I am being kind to you. Be satisfied with your lot, slave."

"Thelena! No! Thelena!"

She said something and the man scooped her up. She screamed and struggled, but it was no use. The man turned to carry her out. Kareen was staring right at Thelena.

"Thelena! Please! I'm a virgin, Thelena!"

The Kaifeng woman looked at her coldly.

"So was I," she said.

Her last plea rebuffed, all the strength flowed out of her. Kareen slumped limply against the back of the man and wept as she was carried away into the night.

CHAPTER FIVE

The smoke told them the tale long before they could see the fort. The pre-dawn glow in the east had been marred by a dozen black fingers twisting lazily up the sky. They merged into a single dark mass that was tugged away by the winds at the higher altitudes. Matt had spotted it the moment he woke and he groaned when he realized what it meant.

They were too late.

They had pushed themselves to the limits of their endurance the day before. The single cannon shot they had heard spurred them to trot and jog and scramble over the rocks and hills in a desperate race to reach the fort. But they were still far short of their goal when a much greater noise had reached them. A dozen or more cannon shots followed by several huge roars that shook the ground and echoed off the hills. They had feared they knew what it all meant. But they had kept going as long as they could, until darkness and exhaustion forced them to halt again. They had seen a red glow reflected off the clouds before they fell asleep.

Now all their fears were realized. They had reached a hill that overlooked Fort Pollentia and they could see what had happened with their own eyes. The fort had fallen. The four corner bastions had been reduced to rubble and several of the buildings had been gutted by fires. There were more fires still burning in the town. The Kaifeng were everywhere. Horsemen rode in and out of the fort at will. There was a large encampment in the valley below them. Matt fumbled out his small telescope and swept it over the fort.

"Gods!" he hissed.

"Bad as it looks?" muttered Sergeant Chenik.

"Yes. Worse. There are bodies all over the parade ground and the bastards are just stripping them and throwing them in a pile. Hundreds of them."

"They did the same thing here as they did to us, sir. Those firefly things. Blew up the magazines, they did. Took out all the guns and the muskets and the bastards just rode in."

"That must have been what happened," breathed Matt. The enormity of the disaster was only sinking in. They had been fearing the worst, without really thinking about what the worst entailed. There had been three hundred dragoons and seven hundred musketeers and two hundred gunners and a gaggle of Varags there! Surely they weren't all... He shifted the telescope and looked down at the Kaifeng camp. "They didn't kill everyone! There are a lot of prisoners in a big pen down there. A couple of hundred, at least."

"Poor bastards," muttered Chenik. "Better off dead."

"They are all men in the pen. I wonder where all the...?" His voice cracked when he realized what he was asking. *Kareen!* "Oh gods," he groaned.

"They're better off dead, too," said Chenik. "But you can bet they ain't." Matt put down the telescope and bowed his head. After a moment Chenik took his arm.

"There's nothing we can do for her, lad. Nothing at all. Not for any of them."

"We have to do something!" snarled Matt.

"Keep your voice down. They're sure to have scouts out. The only thing we can do, Lieutenant, is to stay alive and free and try to get word back to the Berssians about what's happened. Maybe we can figure out how to handle those fireflies—and then pay these bastards back."

"It's a long way to anywhere from here," said Matt.

"That it is, sir," said Chenik. "But it would be a whole lot shorter if we had some horses."

Jarren Carrabello picked up his valise and his cello case and awkwardly walked up the gangplank from the canal barge to the dock. He stopped and took a deep breath and looked around. *Zamerdan! At last!* The great merchant city on the Northern Sea sprawled around him in all its glory. The banks of the Madine River were lined with barges and small boats. They were unloading cargoes of goods from the south in exchange for loads of other goods from the north and across the seas. Books and fine glasswork were exchanged for furs and silver. Spices and tapestries for lumber and tin. Sculptures and muskets for gold and whale oil. A thousand products from a hundred lands flowed from where they were made to where they were wanted. And countless people helped it all move. The barge-men dickered with merchants for their cargoes, both, in turn, argued with the longshoremen to move the loads. Teamsters whipped their horses to haul the goods to warehouses or out to the hundreds of ships that lined the quays and filled the harbor. Jarren had thought the waterfront of Sirenza was busy, but he now realized he did not know what busy was.

"Hey! Mister! Carry your bag! Only five coppers." Jarren looked down and saw a small boy, he could not have been more than nine or ten, standing in front of him. He hardly looked bigger than his valise. Jarren hesitated. All his notes were in the bag--and he was trying to save money.

"I don't think so. Thank you anyway." He phrased it carefully in the local dialect. He doubted the boy could understand Tatni. He wasn't the least bit dissuaded.

"Four, then! I'll carry it for four!"

"Thank you, but no."

"Three then! I'll—*ow!*" Without warning, a bigger boy plowed into the lad and knocked him down.

"You never learn do you, Gez? I've told you before that this is my territory! Now get out before I break your leg!" The bigger boy kicked the smaller. Then he turned to Jarren. "Carry your bag, mas-ter? Only five coppers."

Jarren frowned. He'd been bullied often enough as a boy and the memories still hurt. "I'm afraid not," he said icily. "I've already hired Master Gez to carry my bag--for five coppers." The larger boy looked outraged.

"But...but, you can't do that!"

"Can't I? It is my bag and my money. Or should we ask the con-stable to decide?" Jarren wasn't even sure there were anything like constables around here, but the boy turned red. He shook his fist at the younger lad who was standing there with a broad grin.

"I'll get you, Gez! Don't think that I won't!" Then he stalked off. Gez skipped over and picked up Jarren's valise.

"Not too heavy for you, is it?" asked Jarren.

"Nah! I'm strong."

The boy did seem strong for his size, but he still struggled with the weight of the bag. Jarren felt that was a good thing--the imp couldn't run off with it. "Where we goin'?" he asked.

"I am going to the University. Do you know where that is?"

"Gods! That's clear the other side of the city! All uphill, too! I'm gonna need another copper for that!"

"And I think that five coppers is twice what you normally get and it will serve you very nicely."

"Well, yeah, I guess it will."

"I do hope the other boy won't carry out his threat."

"Vak? Oh, he'll beat me up for sure. But I'll have the money hid by then so it won't matter."

"I think you are smarter than Vak. Shall we go?"

"Sure, I know the way."

Unfortunately, the lad did know the way. And since he was carrying a heavy bag, he made sure they took the shortest route possible. It was not a route Jarren would have taken by choice. Instead of following the grand boulevards through the city and seeing the palaces of the Princes, they wound their way through alleys and among the stalls of small merchants--which looked little different from the ones back in Sirenza. Some of the people in those alleys and among the stalls eyed him suspiciously. Jarren was glad he was in his rather shabby traveling clothes. He kept a very tight grip on his purse.

Jarren was a bit disappointed at not seeing the things he had read about, but he supposed he would have the chance later. After all, he had only been on his journey for a few weeks. If he was careful, he had the funds for a year or more of travel and study. He had decided to come to Zamerdan directly rather than make a lot of stops along the way. Some of the clues he had learned in Sirenza and Duma had indicated that the great northern port would be a good place to start his search. So he had traveled to Ertria's western coast and taken ship across the narrow Sea of Doran to the rocky shores of Vallyria. A bouncing, jolting carriage had carried him up the winding roads and through the mountain passes until he reached a village near the headwaters of the Madine. The amazing engineering feat of the Madine Canal had allowed him to travel in far greater comfort all the rest of the way to Zamerdan. He had marveled at the ingenious lock system that gently lowered--and raised!-- the barges and allowed them to bypass the falls and rapids of the upper river. There were many villages and towns along the river and Jarren had made short stops in some of them, but the canal ride was so delightful he took it all the way to the river's mouth. The evenings he had spent on the roof of the barge, playing his cello with the countryside slipping past, had been among the most pleasant he had ever had.

He and the boy finally left the rather squalid workers' quarter and Gez led him over a splendid bridge into a much richer part of the city. There was a watchman at the other end of the bridge who eyed them both closely.

"You have business here...sir?" he asked.

"Ah, yes, I am traveling to the University," said Jarren, very aware of his less than perfect command of the local tongue. "I have an invitation from Master Weibelan." The watchman looked him over and frowned, but waved him past.

"Just make sure that urchin of yours gets back across the bridge before night," he called after them.

"Why must you be across the bridge before night?" he asked Gez.

"Ah, don't pay attention to the old fart, Mister. The lords 'n ladies don't want the likes of me in their part of town. But they won't do nothing."

"I see."

"Where you're going is up the hill, there," panted Gez. Jarren looked and saw a cluster of regal buildings on a slight rise. It was no hill at all compared to what he was used to in Sirenza, but the rest of the low-lying city of Zamerdan was as flat as a table top, so he supposed it must seem a hill to the locals. The boy was sweating and dragging his valise along the ground now, so Jarren took a turn carrying it. A short while later they reached the gates of the university. There was a guard at the gate who would not let him in until he showed him the letter he had received from Master Weibelan. He would not let Gez in at all. Jarren paid the boy and thanked him and watched him run off.

The guard gave him directions to find Weibelan and Jarren hoisted his valise and started off. The university was larger than it had looked from the outside. Jarren was under no particular schedule, so he took his time and admired the gardens and statuary. There was a beautiful fountain and Jarren wondered how the water pressure was maintained with no high ground to locate the cisterns on. He was also rather surprised to see a small barracks with soldiers lounging outside it. They were dressed the same as the guard at the gate. Did the university really need such a formidable defense? Eventually he reached his destination, a large, four-story building constructed in the northern fashion: exposed wood beams and very steeply pitched roofs. In winter the city would get heavy snowfalls and Jarren supposed the roof was designed so it would slide off. It never snowed in Sirenza. He had seen snow up in the mountains, but never up close. He would have to make sure he was still in the north come winter so he could experience snow.

He went inside the building but was disappointed to learn that Master Weibelan was gone for the day. Fortunately, the University had its own guest quarters and he was directed there. They were quite comfortable and far larger than the small cabin he had on the barge. Jarren unpacked his modest belongings and then spent the rest of the day in the library. During the night he was awakened by the sounds of gunfire in the city. He looked out the window, but could see nothing. It soon stopped and he went back to sleep.

He woke up the next morning when someone knocked loudly on his door. He sleepily opened it and was surprised to see an elderly man in scholar's robes come bustling into his room.

"Master Carabello!" he boomed. "I just learned you had arrived! Forgive me for not meeting you yesterday, but I had no idea when to expect you!" The man was a head shorter than Jarren and twice as wide, with a full gray beard.

"Master Weibelan?" asked Jarren.

"Yes, yes! Oto Weibelan, at your service!" He seized Jarren's hand and pumped it vigorously. "Welcome to Zamerdan!"

"Thank you, sir. I look forward to my visit."

"Excellent! I have read several of your papers and they were first rate, absolutely first rate! So when old Beredane wrote me that you were coming I was thrilled! Have you had breakfast yet? No, of course you haven't! Come along and we'll get some!"

"Er, well, I really should get dressed first, sir."

"What? Oh yes, I suppose you should. I'm an early riser myself, but carry on, sir, carry on!"

Jarren dressed himself while Weibelan babbled on and on. It appeared that the old man was half-deaf and as a result spoke in a virtual shout at all times. But he was friendly and enthusiastic and Jarren decided that he liked him. His liking grew when Weilbelan noticed his cello and began talking about music. The old man told him about the local orchestras while Jarren laced up his shoes. As soon as he was dressed they went out onto the campus. As they headed for the refectory, they passed a squad of the guards Jarren had noticed yesterday and he commented on them.

"Oh, don't mind them!" said Weibelan. "The Princes are at it again. Fighting for control of a block here or a square there. Nothing new in that, of course. And it's just a skirmish compared to Prince Evard's War back in '32, but they've been hiring soldiers who are no better than thugs and they won't stay where they belong! We've had to hire these guards just to maintain the University's independence. Blasted waste of money, but I suppose we have no choice. The undergraduates refuse to drill like we did in the old days, so we have to use hirelings. Not like the old days, I can tell you! Ah, here we are!"

The refectory served a good breakfast, although Jarren never dreamed you could do such things with eggs and herring. Weibelan chatted away between mouthfuls the whole while.

"So! I have a good idea why you are here, young Jarren, but I'm not sure how much help I can be to you. I'm an historian, after all, not a physical scientist. Still, it's damn refreshing to see someone taking a new look at magic. Long overdue. Long overdue!"

"You've been helpful already, sir. I was in the library yesterday afternoon reading some of your 'Downfall of the Wizards'. I wasn't able to get a copy back home and I learned a great deal from just the first few chapters."

"Good to know that someone's read it! I think I have a few copies left lying about and I'd be glad to give you one."

"Thank you, sir! That would be extremely kind!"

"Not at all, not at all! Still, it's an account of the doings of three hundred years past. You are dealing with the present."

"That's true, sir, but the present was shaped by the past. If I can understand what happened back then, perhaps it will give me a better understanding of what I find now."

"And what have you found now?"

"Very little, sir! It is terribly frustrating. It almost seems like the information I need has been deliberately concealed."

Weilbelan pursued the last bit of his herring quiche around the plate and captured it. Once it had vanished he paused and scratched at his beard. "I'm not so sure there has been a deliberate attempt to hide anything, Jarren. You haven't gotten to the later chapters of my book, but the disaster at Soor was more than just the death of all the master wizards."

"Sir?"

"I can't claim to understand it all myself. I think you'd have to be a wizard to understand. But from the fragments I was able to find, it appears that the battle did not just kill the wizards, but it did something to magic itself. Something bad."

"Bad, sir?" Jarren held his excitement in check. He had obviously come to the right place—assuming Weilbelan knew what he was talking about.

"Well, 'unfortunate' might be a better term. Not 'bad' as in evil or anything like that. I've got a few letters written by the lesser magicians who were still alive after Soor and they write of unexpected dangers they were finding in casting even simple spells. Something seemed to be interfering with their powers. Not just blocking them, but making them dangerous to use."

"Well, magic could be very dangerous if used by the untrained— or so I understand."

"True. But these letters indicate that spells these men had easily used hundreds of times before were now too difficult to try. One even spoke of a friend who had been killed in the attempt."

"That's amazing, sir!" said Jarren. "Some of the stories I've found speak of the magic users all being killed by their own magic during that time. I never thought there was any truth to that before now."

"Well, you can't put too much trust in the old stories, but there may be some grain of truth in that one. In addition to those old letters, there are some accounts of strange calamities happening in cities of that period. Unexplained fires or lightning that burn whole blocks. Strange sicknesses that strike man and beast. It's hard to make much of them; that was a superstitious time and few people could write, but I've found similar accounts from all through the East."

"Perhaps there is something to it, then, sir. Maybe the remaining wizards could no longer control their magic. I wonder why?"

"You'd have to ask a wizard for that, I'm afraid," said Weilbelan, chuckling.

"I'd like that very much, sir. Do you know any?"

Weilbelan choked on his tea and grabbed for a napkin. "Ach! Don't do that!"

"I'm sorry, sir."

The old scholar looked at Jarren from under his thick eyebrows and then stood up. "Come on, let's go for a walk." They left the refectory and strolled through the campus. A cool breeze was blowing off the ocean and Jarren breathed in the salt air. It was so much more pleasant than the sea air back in Sirenza this time of year. Weilbelan was silent for quite a while—the first time he'd stopped talking since Jarren had met him. They paused by that wonderful fountain he had seen earlier.

"It's magical, you know," said Weilbelan, pointing at it.

"Really?" asked Jarren in surprise.

"Yes, one of the university's prize possessions."

"Do you suppose I might have a chance to examine the workings? Measure the water flow? It would be useful to add to my findings."

"I'll try to arrange it." Jarren thanked him and then stared at the fountain for a while. At last he frowned and turned to Weilbelan.

"You know, sir, I'm rather surprised to see this. I've studied a great many magical devices since I started my studies. They were all small and simple—well, not simple, really, the actual function of this pump is more simple than some I've seen—but certainly small. They did not move a great deal of weight or produce much light or heat. This one is moving many hundreds of pounds of water each hour. The spell must be quite strong."

"Yes, I've sometimes wondered about that myself," said the old man, nodding his head and waggling his beard. "My studies have indicated that before Soor there were many marvelous devices in the world. Fountains greater than this, devices to open gates and raise drawbridges, carriages that moved without horses. Swords and armor of great power. Where are they now?"

"Perhaps lost in the battle?"

"The weapons, perhaps, but I can see little point in dragging magical fountains halfway across the world. No, I believe that most of the great magical devices stopped working—or sometimes destroyed themselves—soon after Soor. Their demise is somehow tied to the end of the wizards themselves."

"Then how did this one survive?"

"An excellent question, my young friend. The university purchased this only a few dozen years ago—I remember it being installed when I was a new professor here. I had always assumed it was some relic that had been dug up intact. But now I'm not so sure."

"You think it was newly made? By whom?" Jarren asked excitedly.

"I don't know. But there should be records of who it was purchased from. That might give us a clue." Wielbelan paused and scratched his beard again. "Jarren, I don't think the wizards all destroyed themselves after Soor. There are many stories of towns and cities driving out the magic users after too many of those 'unexplained' fires and lightning bolts occurred. Even village healers and soothsayers were persecuted. We had a rather nasty period of witch-burnings right here in Zamerdan."

"Yes," agreed Jarren, "and in those places where the Churches were particularly powerful, there were organized campaigns to root them out and destroy them."

"True. An ugly period that was. From what I hear, there are still a few places where they treat anyone with the talent like that. Still, they can't possibly all have been killed."

"So you think, perhaps, the remaining wizards fled somewhere?"

"It is a possibility. Before Soor there were a number of wizard training schools here in the east..."

"I know, sir. There was one in Sirenza, but there's not a trace left of it now."

"Yes, and that will be the case with almost all of them that were in or near cities. But there were some that were more isolated. Maybe one or more of them have survived."

"After all these years, sir?"

"Who knows? That fountain pump came from somewhere."

"True. So where do we look?"

Wielbelan smiled and took Jarren by the arm. "Why, in the proper place to begin any inquiry: the Archives!"

"So we will continue?" whispered the Ghost. *"You convinced them to ride to the east?"*

"I believe so," said Atark. "Some of them are afraid, but the majority are willing. Some dispute Zarruk's place as Ka. I was forced to destroy one of the... troublemakers."

"So much the better. Make them fear your powers." The image of the Ghost's head floated above the skull in the darkened tent. It was difficult for Atark to see clearly, but it seemed as though it smiled.

"Even my friends begin to fear my powers."

"Friends are useful, but never let a friend's fear guide your policy." The Ghost was silent for a few moments. *"But I can sense something new in you. A joy that has nothing to do with victory or revenge. It saps your anger. What is it?"*

Atark hesitated. The Ghost knew so much already he worried to let it know more. Still, this seemed harmless enough. "My daughter, who I thought was lost, has been returned to me. That is the joy I feel."

The Ghost was silent for a long time. *"She has lived with the Enemy? Served their men for all these years? And yet you let her live? Welcomed her back into..."*

"Enough!" roared Atark. "The one I destroyed said those same words! I would not hesitate to destroy *you* if you persist! If you can look into my heart then do so and tell me what I say is not true!"

The image of the Ghost wavered, turned red and then vanished. All light in the tent was gone. Atark sat and stared at nothing for a long time. He had never quarreled with the Ghost before. Part of him was glad that he had stood up to it. Part was glad that the Ghost appeared to, indeed, have no real power. Part of him worried that the Ghost might never return. There was so much that he still needed to learn from it! He continued to sit there until the dawn's light seeped under the tent flaps.

He rose slowly and went outside. He was still using this small tent when he needed to talk with the Ghost, but he had been given a larger tent that he and Thelena could share the rest of the time. He looked toward it now and felt a deep warmth inside him. His daughter was safe and asleep inside his tent! When he started his quest for revenge he never dreamed he would find such a treasure. He had always loved Thelena so very much. She had been a wonderful child and was growing into a wonderful young woman when he lost her. He hated to think of what those years as a slave must have done to her. So far she had not spoken of it and he had not asked.

But it had changed her, and not just physically. She was quieter, although she had always been quiet. And she was stronger, too. Some women might have cowered in shame under the eyes of the other Kaifeng people, but she did not. She returned their stares boldly and went where she would without hesitation. And her dealings with the eastern slave woman who had lain at his feet the whole night of the victory; she had been strong but just then. He was proud of her. Still, he worried, too. She had been hurt badly for many years. He had no doubt that the wounds inside her were as deep and as painful as the ones he bore. And she was well past the usual age at which women married; how would she find a husband now? The knowledge of who she was and what had happened to her—and who her father was—would turn away most suitors. The only ones who might not turn away would be men seeking some advantage over him by marrying his daughter. It was a dilemma he was ill-equipped to deal with. Perhaps he should speak with his cousin about Thelena.

His feet had carried him near the pen where the captive men were kept. They were mostly asleep, but a few were moving and moaning. The wind blew some of the stench in his direction and he winced. He would have to ask Zarruk to order that proper care be given to them. He would need new sacrifices for his magic in the future and he did not want them to die before he could use them. He was slightly appalled with himself for even thinking such a thing, but he ruthlessly pushed the thought away. He was doing it for the good of the People. The lives of these men were forfeit anyway, so why not put them to good use? Still, it troubled him. He had wanted to ask the Ghost if the power he stole from the dying men was their souls. And if so, what did his using it mean to them? Were they destroyed? Condemned to Limbo or some hell? It was a disturbing question. If the Ghost was not gone forever then he would ask it the next time.

He turned away from the prisoners and continued his walk. It was still very early and the victory celebrations had been going on for days, so there were few people up and about. He spotted one of the new slave women hauling a leather bucket of water up from the river. She quickly scurried away when she spotted him. That one seemed to be adapting and would probably survive. The Kaifeng always had far more women than men; the harshness of the plains and the fighting between tribes saw to that. Many men took more than one wife. The new slaves who adapted and submitted would soon be little different from the junior wives in many marriages. Those who resisted would have a harder time of it. Atark thought of Thelena's new 'servant'. He wasn't sure about that one. Thelena clearly had some affection for the woman and that made him uneasy.

The Easterners were the enemy and they could never forget it. Anger swelled up in him at the memory of the Ghost's words and what they implied. Did it think his resolve was faltering just because he had his daughter back? The memory of his murdered son and wife never left him. Not for a day, not for an hour. Perhaps Thelena's return was a sign from the gods; a sign that they approved of his quest. The East would fall and no Kaifeng's daughter would ever be stolen again!

"I see you are up early, too, my friend."

The voice made him jump and he turned to see Zarruk standing a few feet away. The Ka looked very tired. "Hail, Ka-Noyen Zarruk," said Atark, bowing and putting his fist to his chest.

"Oh stop that, Atark. I'm getting sick of it already. Why did I ever let you talk me into this?"

"Because you believe in our cause, just as I do. The road we must follow is clear—and you must lead the way."

Zarruk sighed. "I suppose. But I must admit that I am worried. What if the other tribes don't come? What if they are not convinced of your powers and refuse to dare the Berssians' wrath? It could happen, my friend. For all the words and cheers of the other night, it could still happen, and what then?"

"We could still stay here..."

"Yes, we probably could. With the narrow pass to defend and your magic we could probably beat off every attack. The enemy would still have their swords and gun-spears, but against our arrows they would have a very difficult time. But what then? In time they would bring bows of their own. And as the seasons pass, our warriors will leave these rocky hills to return to the plains. Defending a mountain pass will bring us little loot. The men will tire and leave. Then what?"

"They will come, Zarruk. Have faith. The tribes will come. You only sent out the riders four days ago. It will be at least a week more before even the closest could come here—even if they rode the moment the messenger arrived. I would guess two weeks before we see the first new tribe. Have faith."

"Two weeks. The Berssians could come against us sooner than that if they move quickly."

"They will not. They have no clue of the danger they are in. It will take them weeks to even decide to send their army here. By then we will be ready to meet them."

"So we wait."

Atark nodded and he put out his hand to grip the arm of his Ka. "Yes, we wait. Let us rest and enjoy our victory. And when the tribes come we will sweep out of these mountains and nothing will stop us!"

CHAPTER SIX

Mattin Krasner, one time lieutenant in the 18th Berssian Dragoons (the "Tapestry Dragoons", late of Naravia) rode toward the town in the distance as quickly as his tired pony could go. Sergeant Chenik rode beside him on an equally tired mount.

"We shoulda stolen a few more horses, sir," muttered Chenik. "Have fresh mounts just like the Kaifeng bastards."

"Wouldn't make any difference in how tired *we* are, Sergeant. Frankly, I hate being dead tired on a fresh horse. The damn things always seem to know it and give you all the trouble they can."

"But it would get us there faster."

"Water over the dam now. We're here."

"Wherever here is."

"It's Havverdor...I think. Rode through here on the way to the capital. Not much of a place, but there's a Royal Post station and ought to be a magistrate. We can get word to Berssenburg from here."

"Well, thank the gods for that. We've been too damn long getting here as it is. Those bastards could be anywhere by now—including just over the horizon behind us."

"An ugly thought, Sergeant. If you get any more like that, please keep them to yourself."

"Yes, sir."

They both shut up to save their breath for riding. The town was still a few miles away and they had to get there as quickly as they could. Matt had no idea if anyone else had escaped the destruction of Fort Pollentia, but they were going to make sure that someone heard about it and soon. It had been over a week since they saw the disaster at the fort. Nearly two weeks since the squadron had been slaughtered. Matt was more tired and more dirty and more depressed than he had ever been in his life.

But he was more determined, too.

The Kaifeng had destroyed his home, killed his friends and probably—hopefully?—killed his sister. They had to be stopped. They had to be punished. Matt was determined to see that they were. He wasn't sure how yet; he had no answer to those firefly things. But someone surely did. And when they had it, they would gather the army and go pay those bastards back!

He sighed in relief as they drew near to the town. He could see people in the streets. The only people he and Chenik had seen for the last week had been Kaifeng. Stealing the horses had been easier than he had expected. Almost all the Kaifeng had been celebrating— the scum!—and not keeping a close watch. They had grabbed the horses—they even got the saddles and tack—during the night and by dawn they were many miles away. But they still weren't safe. The Kaifeng had scouts out already and they had nearly walked right into one batch of them. They had barely escaped. They were more careful after that. They had stayed off the roads and avoided villages. That had slowed them down, but it had allowed them to make it to safety.

They were passing by the outlying farms now and people were staring at them from the fields. Their faces did not look terribly friendly. Matt could hardly blame them: He and Chenik didn't look much like soldiers anymore. Their white coats had been far too conspicuous so they had gotten rid of them. Their shirts and trousers were caked with mud from the crawl through the field to get the horses and then coated in a thick layer of dust. They still had their sabers, but not much else. He felt a little bit ashamed. The last representatives of a dead regiment ought to look better than this. The thought made him feel sad. No matter what might come after this, the Tapestry Dragoons were gone forever. There might someday be another 18th Dragoons in the Berssian King's army, but it would be a new regiment, full of strangers.

"Sure hope they got something to eat here," said Chenik. Matt heartily agreed. They had had almost nothing for days. There had been some stale bread in the bags they took with the saddles and they had raided one deserted farmhouse along the way, but they were both terribly hungry. But that should soon be remedied. They had reached the town proper and he could see a half-dozen armed men coming out onto the street along with an official-looking person with a gold chain looped around his neck. Matt rode up to him and halted.

"Thank the gods we made it!" he cried. "You must send word to the Capital right away! Fort Pollentia has fallen! The Kaifeng are through the pass!"

"Have you got anything to eat?" added Chenik.

The man with the chain stared at them for a while and then motioned to the men with the guns. To Matt's amazement, they aimed them right at Chenik and him!

"Get down off those horses," snapped the man. He turned to the men with the guns. "They are under arrest. Put them with the other deserters."

Kareen knelt on the carpeted floor of the tent and stared blankly at the lump of bread dough on the wooden board in front of her. She was supposed to be kneading it. She *had* been kneading it, as Thelena had ordered her to, but little by little her hands had slowed down until they had stopped of their own accord and now they lay limply at her sides. Her mind was a thousand miles away from kneading bread dough. A thousand miles from here. A thousand miles from her nightmare.

It still seemed like a horrible dream and nothing could really convince her that it was all true. It was too terrible to be true. Some things just had to be too terrible to be true. Didn't they? The whole world was upside down and backwards, tumbling in crazy circles. When would it be right again? The explosions in the fort and the deaths of the soldiers and those people doing...things...to her just had no place in her world.

The tent flap opened suddenly and Atark strode in. Kareen instantly grabbed the dough and bent over the board and furiously kneaded it, praying that the man would not notice her. She was terrified of the Kaifeng sorcerer. Fortunately, so far, he had almost completely ignored her presence in his tent. This time, however, he did say a few words. She recognized the Kaifeng word for 'slave', but nothing else. She just nodded her head and kept working. To her relief he only remained for a few moments and then strode out again.

She sighed in relief and slowed her kneading. But then she was sniffling and crying helplessly. She was so afraid! She had never known what real fear was until now. She wanted to go home! She wanted Phell and Matt!

But her home was a pile of smoking rubble. Phell and Matt were probably dead. Everyone she knew or cared about was dead or a slave like her. Except for Thelena. But Thelena was a stranger to her now. The woman she had counted as a friend was like someone she had never seen before. It was like she had been wearing a mask all those years and had now taken it off.

She could have saved her. Kareen told herself again and again that Thelena could have saved her—but did not. And so she'd been raped. Many times. Her face burned with shame as she thought about it again. A part of her said that it could have been worse. At least they had not been deliberately brutal or hurt her for fun. Well, the one had, but he had been very young and very drunk. She remembered the bloody, battered condition Thelena had been in when she first saw her and part of Kareen told herself that she'd been lucky.

The rest of her found that hard to believe. It had been frightening and painful and utterly degrading. They had not even had the decency to rape her one at a time inside a tent. They had done it right out in the open with everyone watching and commenting. And the Kaifeng women had even joined in! They had thrown off their clothes, just as the men had done, and joined in the 'fun'. Her blush deepened.

She remembered the whispered, giggling conversations she had had with her friends about the different kinds of love-making they had heard of and how wonderful it would be when they had a husband and could try them out. What fools they had all been! They all knew better now. Kareen was quite sure that all of her friends knew better now.

She looked up as the tent flap opened again, but it was Thelena instead of Atark. Kareen was a bit relieved, but only a little. Thelena stood over her. "You should have been done with that by now. You have been slacking off."

"I'm sorry, Thelena. I'm just so... so tired."

"You will get used to it. Some real work will do you good."

"Thelena! I always helped around the house!" exclaimed Kareen indignantly.

Thelena squatted down right next to her and looked in her eyes for a moment. Then she suddenly seized Kareen's ears in both hands. "Don't you ever talk to me in that tone again—slave! And any time someone might hear, you will call me 'mistress'. I've taught you the word for that—use it!" She let go of her ears. Kareen stared at her wide-eyed.

"Y-yes, *Q-Qoyen*," she stuttered.

"Good." Thelena stood up and then went over and sat on some cushions. Kareen went back to kneading the dough, but kept glancing at Thelena.

"Oh yes, you helped out around the house—when it suited you," said Thelena with a snort. "But never any of the unpleasant jobs. Who emptied the chamber pots? I did! Who scrubbed the pans? I did! Who did all the heavy carrying? I did! You would make the table arrangements and bake the pastries and spend hours fiddling with your clothes. Well, we don't bother with table arrangements here! You'll learn your tasks and you'll do them well. Or you'll be punished! I'll take a switch to you, Kareen! Don't doubt me!"

"No, *Qoyen*," whispered Kareen. Tears rolled down her cheeks and she was sniffling again.

"What are you crying about?"

"I...I thought we were friends. You were my friend, Thelena."

"I was your slave! You never let me forget that. Oh, you would talk to me and even play with me—as long as none of your *real* friends were around. Your Eastern friends. Your proper friends. But as soon as they were there it was: 'Thelena, go to the kitchen and make us some tea. Thelena, could you run down to the village for a fruit pie for all the girls? Thelena, I'm too busy for you now!'" Kareen stared at the woman in surprise. She could not believe the anger in her voice.

"I-I'm sorry, Thelena. I never..."

"No, you never! You never thought of me as anything at all! And now you expect me to feel differently about *you*? Wake up! That world is gone! You are in *my* world now and *you* are the slave! And so are all your precious friends! Maybe we should go and visit them and see just how they are making out!"

"No! Oh, please don't do that, Thelena! I couldn't bear it!"

Thelena stared at her with a furious expression and Kareen trembled in fear. More tears dripped down her face. Finally, the Kaifeng woman seemed to calm down.

"Enough of this!" she grumbled. "You've kneaded that dough long enough! Go fetch some more firewood!"

"Yes, *Qoyen*!" sobbed Kareen. She got to her feet and started to leave and then stopped. She looked down at herself.

"Now what's the matter?" snapped Thelena.

"The... the clothes you gave me. They...they're too small." Kareen held her arms apart to show Thelena. They really *were* too small. None of Kareen's clothes had been returned when she was delivered to Thelena and she'd been given a rough woolen smock to wear. It was clearly made for a much younger girl. She was spilling out of the top and the bottom didn't even come halfway to her knees. And she had no undergarments at all. "I can't go out like this. Please." Thelena frowned.

"You'll do as you are told or I'll send you out naked! Now go!" Sobbing, Kareen fled from the tent. She stopped a few yards away and scrubbed away her tears and looked around. The world outside the tent seemed very strange and threatening now. The remains of the fort and the town still smoldered on the far hill but the whole valley was filled with tents. The Kaifeng herds were grazing in the farmers' fields. Nothing was as she remembered it. She felt like she wanted to run. Just run and run and run. Somewhere beyond those hills was the world she remembered and she only had to run fast enough to find it. But she knew she could never run fast enough to get away from the Kaifeng horsemen. They would catch her and bring her back.

There were people looking at her now. She had better find the firewood and get back as quickly as she could. Unfortunately, there wasn't any near at hand. She spotted a pile by another tent, but there was a Kaifeng woman right there and she didn't dare take any. She started walking along the rows of tents, staring back at where she had come from frequently so she could find her way back. The warm breeze touched far too much bare flesh and the rocky ground stung her unshod feet. Wood, she had to find wood and get back to the tent. It seemed like she could sense dozens of pairs of eyes watching her.

She neared a very large tent which had several guards outside and stopped in shock. She saw Teela Desseter struggling up the hill with a bucket of water, her red hair unmistakable. Kareen now realized that Thelena had been far more generous with the too-small smock than she might have been. Teela had nothing but a scrap of cloth knotted about her waist. Two small boys were hitting her with switches and laughing. Teela's face was streaked with tears. Kareen quickly turned away before Teela could see her. Shaking her head, she hurried in the other direction. Wood, she had to find some firewood. She stumbled down the hill and looked for wood. There!

She spotted a pile of wood just ahead and she hurried toward it—and stopped short.

The pieces of wood were leftovers from building a large pen near the center of the camp. The pen was filled with the male prisoners from the fort. Kareen stared at it in shock. Several hundred dejected men stood or sat or lay inside a circle perhaps fifty feet in diameter. They had been stripped to the waist and their shoes were missing. Their hands were tied behind their backs. As she watched, one of them knelt down at the edge of the pen to drink water out of a bowl like a dog. A dozen of the Kaifeng warriors were on guard and there were some small Kaifeng children around the perimeter taunting the prisoners or throwing pebbles at them. Kareen almost turned and ran off, but she really needed the wood lying there. As she nerved herself to take it, another thought struck her.

Could Phell be in there? Or Matt?

She had given up all hope for her fiancé or her brother. For herself, too, for that matter. But could they be alive after all? She stood on tip-toe and tried to see into the pen. The prisoners were all filthy and unshaven and they all tended to look alike. She moved around to get a look from another direction. No good. She did not recognize any of them. But so many of them were sitting or lying down and they were crammed in so tightly she might never see Phell or Matt even if they were right there. Her heart was pounding with a sudden need to know. She glanced around nervously. None of the guards were close by and the children seemed to have lost interest in their game. Perhaps she could…

She made her decision and walked right up to the pen. A few of the prisoners looked at her without much interest.

"Please!" she hissed. "Is Phell Gerowst in here? Matt Krasner? Have any of you seen them?" A few more eyes turned her way, but no one answered. "Lieutenant Gerowst! Lieutenant Krasner! Has anyone seen them?" One of the guards was looking her way now. She didn't have much time. "Please!" Finally someone was pushing through the crowd toward her. He looked familiar…

"Miss Krasner?" said the man in near-disbelief, staring at her. One of Phell's men!

"Yes! Yes! Have you seen Lieutenant Gerowst?"

"Gods," he said, his face twisted in pain. "He's dead, Miss. I'm sorry. I saw him killed. I'm sorry."

Kareen stepped away from the pen, shaking her head. She had

thought that he was dead for days, but the fragile hope that perhaps she was wrong had filled her so suddenly and so completely that having it dashed was impossibly hard. She kept shaking her head and backing up...

...right into the arms of one of the guards.

She squealed and tried to twist away, but two more of them were right there. They grabbed her and she could not get loose. One stepped up in front of her and took hold of the neckline of her too-small smock. He gave a pull and it tore right down the middle, exposing her completely.

She had time for one scream before they dragged her down to the ground.

Thelena sat on the cushions in the middle of the tent and looked around her with mixed satisfaction and uneasiness. This was her father's tent. She was safe here. Her father was powerful beyond her dreams; not just his magical power, but in the influence he held over the Ka-Noyen and the tribal leaders. She could scarcely believe how much had changed in the four years since she had been carried off by the Varags. Her last glimpse of her father had shown him collapsed on the ground, dripping blood from a belly wound. She never expected to see him again.

But she had seen him again. Up on the wall of that hated fort. The fort that had been her prison and her hell for four long years. He had smashed its walls and come to set her free. Seeing him, victorious and adored by the men, was the most glorious moment of her life. It seemed a miracle and perhaps it was. Perhaps she had done something to please the gods and they had rewarded her beyond her wildest dreams. Free! Home!

And loved. She and her father had loved each other very much, but for four years Thelena had been convinced she would never love or be loved again. But she had been wrong—oh, so wonderfully wrong! She and her father had spent an entire night holding each other and weeping for joy until they fell asleep in each others arms, neither one daring to let go in case it was all just some wonderful dream.

But it wasn't a dream. It was real. This was her father's tent and she was the *Qoyen* of it. She would make sure he had food and drink when he wanted it, clean clothes when he needed them, a soft bed when he was tired. She would make this tent his home—and hers.

What greater bliss could she ask for?

And yet, she was uneasy. Even though she had dreamed vivid dreams of being home almost every night of her bondage, now that it was no longer a dream it still seemed strange and unfamiliar. She stared at the lump of dough that Kareen had left. She wasn't sure she remembered how to make the thin, crusty bread of her people. And the *Yetchi*, was it two parts mare's milk and one part blood, or the other way round? She couldn't remember. She'd have to ask…

…who? Who could she ask? Her mother was dead. There were plenty of other women around, but she had seen how they looked at her when she walked through the camp. None of them had said anything, but she knew what they were thinking: *You should be dead. We should have stoned you to death for disgracing your clan and your tribe. You should have fought your captors to the death and died with honor. Only your powerful father has saved you from our rightful wrath. You can live with us, but you will never be one of us again.*

Her anger swelled up in her. What did they know? Had any of them ever been raped and beaten by the Varags? Had any of them ever been a slave in a Berssian fort? What right did they have to pass judgment on her? She sat with her fists clenched.

She jerked her head around when the tent flap opened and Kareen stumbled in. Where had she been? She went for the wood at least an hour ago. A quick glance told Thelena exactly why Kareen had not come back—and why she did not have any wood with her. The woman was filthy and her dress had been ripped open. She clutched it together with her arms. She fell on the carpet and sobbed. Thelena knew exactly what had happened, but she was still angry and she felt not the slightest pity.

"Where have you been?" she snapped. "Where is the firewood I sent you to get?" Kareen looked up at her with a dazed expression.

"I…I was raped!" she gasped. "They grabbed me and they raped me!"

"I can see that. Why didn't you bring some wood on the way back here?"

"Thelena!" shrieked Kareen, clutching herself. "How can you say such a thing?"

"You are a slave. These things happen to a slave. You must get used to it—and still do your work."

Kareen shook her head and sobbed. "You're so cruel, you are all so cruel! Phell is dead and I was raped and you don't care!"

Thelena blinked. The news that Phell Gerowst was dead was not unexpected, but it was not something she had considered either. Kareen had lost someone she had loved. Thelena's emotions swirled in confusion. A feeling like sorrow or pity floated to the top for an instant, but then was gone again. Kareen was blubbering on the ground and Thelena was suddenly furious.

"Care? Care! Why should anyone care about you, slave? Did anyone care about me? They murdered my mother and my brother and I thought they had killed my father, too. They raped me and beat me for two days! Then they sold me to you. Maybe you didn't rape me, but plenty of other people did! Do you think that when I was late getting back from the well I was off counting daisies? Half the men in the fort had me at one time or another—including your precious Phell!"

Kareen's head jerked up in shock. Shock gave way to disbelief and disbelief to anger. "You...you're lying! That's not true! Liar! Liar!"

"Bitch!" snarled Thelena. "How dare you speak to me like that?" She sprang up from the cushions and grabbed her father's riding crop from where it hung. Kareen reared back in fear. Thelena leaned over and struck. She was aiming for Kareen's shoulder, but the woman tried to duck and instead was hit full in the face. A bright red line appeared across her right cheek. Her hands went to her face and came away bloody. She screamed in pain and surprise.

Thelena was shocked, too. She had not meant to do that. But her anger was still burning in her. Not just the anger at Kareen's words or the anger at the other women's sneers. No, this was four long years of frustration and anger, pent up in her captivity, that was finally breaking loose. She needed to strike back at someone, anyone, but Kareen was the only one in reach.

Thelena kicked Kareen in the ribs and then grabbed her arm. She dragged her over to the central pole of the tent and tied her wrists to it with a piece of rope. Kareen had been too shocked to resist at first, but now she struggled frantically. "Thelena! What are you doing? I'm sorry. I'm sorry! Please stop!"

But Thelana reached down and ripped open what was left of Kareen's smock, exposing her bare back. She took the crop and brought it down with all her strength. Kareen shrieked.

"No! Stop! Please stop! Thelena, no!"

Thelena hit her again.

"Please! I never beat you, Thelena! Never! Not once! Please, Thelena, I never beat you!"

It was true: Kareen had never beaten her. Others had, but never her. Right now that made no difference at all. The crop came down again and again and again.

Atark was just about to enter the tent when he heard the shouts and the screams of the new slave woman. He stopped, waited, and then slowly walked away, nodding his head. Good, very good. Thelena had said a few things to him about the slave and he had been worried. Apparently this woman had owned Thelena in the fort and had been unusually kind to his daughter. While he might feel some gratitude, he had been worried that Thelena might be too grateful, show too much kindness. She was going to be under enough suspicion because of his breaking the law for her, and to have her pampering a Berssian slave would have just been too much. But from the sound of things he had nothing to worry about. Very good. A darker part of him hoped his daughter would leave the woman so badly scarred that she would no longer be a temptation to him. There was no reason, either ethical or practical, why he shouldn't make full use of the beautiful slave, but he simply could not. She was the enemy and he would not lie with her.

He took a deep breath. Well, one problem solved. His next immediate challenge was to decide where to go now. He had been on his way to the tent to get something to eat, but he had no intention of interrupting his daughter while she was disciplining the slave. After hesitating for a moment he turned and walked up the hill overlooking the camp.

It was a much bigger camp now. All of the tribes' herds had caught up to the warriors along with the women and boys who had been looking after them. This had meant many a reunion, but it also meant that the little valley was filled. So far, only one new tribe had heeded the Ka-Noyen's summons, but there was word that more would follow. The grazing lands would soon be exhausted here. They could not stay here much longer. They had to move.

Prudence might suggest moving back into the plains for a few leagues. There was plenty of grass there and they could wait as long as necessary for the other tribes. But Atark's heart spoke against that plan, against any backward step. They had come this far and they needed to keep going. Onward! Eastward!

The Noyens were wary. They still had less than eight score of scores of warriors. If they were caught in the open lands beyond the mountains by a much larger force, then even Atark's magic might not be enough to save them. And they would have their herds and families with them, too, which limited their mobility. The news the scouts brought back said there were no threats within many days' ride, but it was still a risk. Zarruk would do as Atark suggested, he knew that. But he did not want to force the Ka into actions he would not normally take. He had to work with Zarruk, not ride roughshod over him.

Atark found a spot to sit down. He was tired. His new role as shaman and advisor to the Ka took far more time and energy than he had expected. Someone always wanted to talk to him, always wanted his opinion on some issue or his blessing on a course of action. He worried that before long no one would dare breathe without his say-so and he would wake one morning to find the entire army suffocated.

It was growing dark and the stars were coming out. Surely Thelena was done beating the slave by now. He stood up to return to his tent. As he did so a streak of light went across the indigo sky. A shooting star. He had often seen them out on the plains. Some said they were messages from the gods. This one had been going from the west to the east.

To the East.

He found that his doubts were entirely gone. He knew what had to be done. Instead of walking to his own tent, he went to the tent of Ka-Noyen Zarruk.

"This isn't exactly the kind of greeting I had been hoping for," growled Sergeant Chenik. It was about the tenth time he had said it and Matt was getting ready to belt him. Instead, he turned and grabbed the bars on the door of the cramped jail cell and yelled out.

"I demand to see the Magistrate! I am an officer in the Berssian Army! Gods damn it, someone come and talk to me!"

"Shut your mouth before I stick my musket butt in it!" snarled back a voice. "I got no love for deserters, so be warned!"

"We are not deserters! For the dozenth time, Fort Pollentia has fallen and the Kaifeng are through the pass! If you idiots don't warn the capital they'll be here cutting your damn throats any day now!"

"Right, and I'm the Archduke of Gira!" came a different voice. "Now shut up if you expect to get anything to eat tonight."

Matt was about to continue yelling when he caught sight of the anxious faces of his men. The threat about not feeding them was a serious one. They had been stuck in this hole for three days and they had only had four meals during the entire time. Well, he and Chenik had been stuck here for three days, the others had been here longer. They were all men from his regiment. Different companies, of course, but all Tapestry Dragoons. Twelve of them, not including himself. The sole survivors.

Each one had a heartbreaking tale to tell of the death of the regiment. They had been part of the squadron sent to guard the walls protecting the town. When the fort had been destroyed their gunpowder had all gone up, too, but fortunately there had been no magazines to blow holes in the town's walls and they had had the chance to make a run for it. Twenty or thirty of them had gotten clear. A dozen had made it to Havverdor. The Kaifeng scouts had caught some. No one knew where the rest were. They had drifted into town in ones and twos—and been arrested.

Matt told himself that he should not be all that surprised. His regiment did have a lot of deserters. Men who wanted to get back to Navaria or who just could not stand their lonely fort any longer. The local authorities were always on the lookout for fleeing Whitecoats. One or two a month were returned to the fort for their forty lashes and then returned to the ranks.

But damn it, they weren't deserters!

"I should have kept my coat," muttered Matt, slumping to the floor.

"If you had, you never would have made it here to be arrested, sir," said Chenik.

"What are we going to do, sir?" asked one of the troopers. "Nobody wants to believe us about the damn fireflies!"

"And if somebody don't do something there's going to be the nine hells to pay!" added another.

Matt looked from one man to the next. He was the only officer here and they looked to him for leadership. Sadly, none of his little leadership tricks were designed to work from inside a jail cell.

"Well, they're going to find it a might difficult to send us back to the fort to be flogged," said Chenik.

"Always looking at the bright side of things, aren't you,

Sergeant?"

"I try, sir. We're still a damn sight better off than we were a week ago."

"Only until the Kaifeng come trotting into this town. We'd have a harder time getting away this time."

"True."

Conversation came to a halt and each of them sank into gloom. Eventually a meal was served and the thirteen of them spent another very uncomfortable night in a cell designed for four.

The next morning there was no breakfast, but shortly before noon a squad of the police came and unlocked their cell and prodded them outside the jail. They were surprised to see an enclosed wagon waiting for them.

"What is this?" demanded Matt.

"You are being sent to Berssenburg," replied the chief. "For trial."

"Trial!" exclaimed Matt and several others.

"Yes, your mass desertion has made some important people in the capital angry. I believe they wish to make an example of you."

The prisoners all looked around in consternation. Matt saw one of their guards grinning hugely. He put one hand up to his throat and stuck out his tongue and rolled his eyes. Then he laughed. The chief pointed to the wagon.

"Put them in and make sure they are secure."

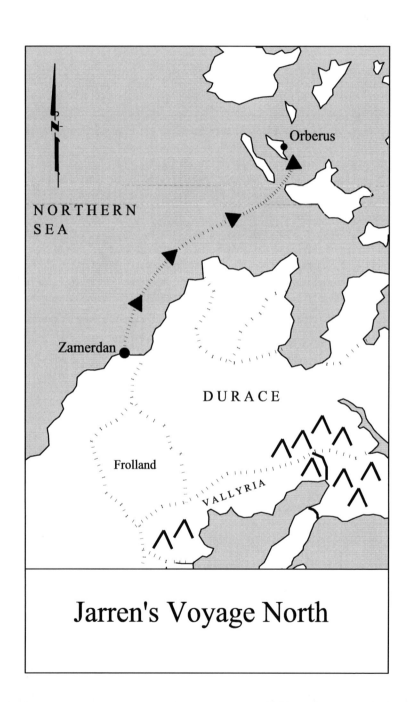

Jarren's Voyage North

CHAPTER SEVEN

"I'm going to miss you, Jarren. I've enjoyed your stay here immensely," boomed Oto Weibelan. "I wish you all luck on your voyage."

"Thank you, sir," said Jarren. "You've been extremely kind and I hope to return here in a few months to share my findings with you. If I find anything to share, of course."

"Oh, I'm sure you will find something. Maybe not what you expect, but something for sure."

Jarren smiled and nodded and then grabbed the side of the carriage as it lurched over some bump in the road. Then they turned the corner onto Dock Street, the wide avenue that bordered Zamerdan's great harbor. It was even busier than normal with the summer drawing to a close. The autumn storms would start in a few months and the merchants were eager to get one last voyage in before they did. Wagons filled the street and the side alleys; longshoremen passed seemingly endless numbers of crates and bags and bales onto the ships. The masts of hundreds of vessels made a floating forest of timber. Jarren could see a half dozen under sail being warped out of the harbor.

Their carriage maneuvered through the mass of wagons and people that filled the quays. Jarren was grateful for the ride Weibelan was providing. It was a long walk from the University and Jarren had quite a bit more baggage now than when he had started his journey. Weibelan's wife had supplemented his rather paltry wardrobe with numerous pieces of additional clothing. Jarren was grateful since he had brought little warm clothing and it might be quite cold where he was going. Oto had given him some books and a wonderful portable desk with places for paper and ink. Weibelan appeared to be quite wealthy. Jarren now owned a small trunk to go with his valise and cello case.

He looked out again at the ships. He would soon be aboard one of them. The long hours he had spent in the archives had finally paid off. The University's archives had led to the merchant who sold them the magical pump. The merchant's records led to the trading house he had gotten it from and the trading house's records had led to the ship that brought it into Zamerdan. They had been lucky that it was one of the independent houses rather than one of the Princes' or they never would have gotten access to the records.

The Princes of the City tended to be a touchy and jealous lot. Jarren looked out the side of the carriage and saw they were passing one of the fortified naval arsenals that studded the harbor. A half-dozen warships floated at anchor there. Only one had all the spars and sails and things that it needed to move about. The others only had stumpy masts with no sails and Jarren suspected they were not ready for sea. Each of the other princes had their own arsenals, too. Weibelan had tried to explain the complex and convoluted political system of the city, but it had eluded Jarren. There was some sort of strange balance of power between the five princely houses, the guilds, the churches, and even the University. He could not see how it could work, but apparently it did. Zamerdan had managed to remain a free city for half a millenium, although Jarren suspected the wide bands of marshes that surrounded the city on the landward side had more to do with that than the city's leadership.

Once they discovered which ship had brought the pump to Zamerdan, they had been lucky enough to find her captain, now living in retirement in the city. Some friendly persuasion (and, Jarren suspected, a sizeable bribe by Weibelan) had gotten the old man to reveal where he had acquired the pump: a town on an island in the Northern Sea. More research had revealed that a small but steady trickle of magical objects seemed to be imported from that unlikely source. The University archives gave hints that there once had been a wizards' school in the far north. The inevitable conclusion was that there might be a hidden enclave of magic users still there or nearby.

So now Jarren was going there to see for himself.

The carriage slowed to a halt opposite a medium-sized merchant ship, which was tied to the stone quay. A net-full of cargo was being swayed down into its hold by a gang of sailors and longshoremen. The guilds were incredibly strict about who could do what in the city. While the cargo was on the dock no sailor dared touch it. But once on the ship, it was just the opposite. Jarren wasn't sure who—if anyone—was allowed to touch the net itself. He got out of the carriage and helped Weibelan down. Then he started unloading his bags, expecting at every moment to have someone tell him he was violating guild policy by doing so.

"Carry your bags, Mister?" said a familiar voice. Jarren turned to see the same young urchin he had met on his first day here.

"Well, Master Gez, you do seem to get around."

"Huh? Oh! It's you again! What are you doin' here?" The boy seemed as surprised as Jarren, so apparently he was just another random customer rather than a deliberate target. Jarren frowned when he took a closer look. The boy's face was a mass of old bruises, turned yellow with time. And his two front teeth were missing.

"It would seem that Vak finally caught up with you."

"Oh yeah. He was madder'n I thought. Brought a couple of friends and beat the livin' crap outta me."

"I'm sorry about that."

"It happens. But he didn't get the money," said Gez with a broad grin. "Can I carry your bags again, Mister?"

"Well, I am going aboard that ship, there, so I don't really need them carried far, I'm afraid." Gez goggled at the ship Jarren had pointed at.

"You're goin' on the *Unicorn*? Wow! I'd give my eye-teeth to go somewhere on her!"

"It looks as though you already have," said Weibelan gesturing to Gez's missing teeth. "But perhaps something can be arranged."

"What d'ya mean, mister?" asked Gez.

"Uh, yes, what do you mean, sir?" asked Jarren.

"Just that you really could do with a servant on this journey, Jarren. I've been aboard a few of these ships and they do precious little to make their passengers comfortable. And there's no telling what sort of accommodations you'll have at your destination. Having someone who can fetch your meals and wash your clothes would let you concentrate on your studies. What do you say, Gez? Would you like to go on a trip with Master Jarren?"

"Would I? Yes! Yes! Yes! And I can cook n' clean and all that. And I'll only charge…uh…three coppers a day."

"One copper," said Weibelan firmly. He twitched his bushy eyebrows at the lad and he relented. "Good." He pulled out a gold dollar and passed it to Jarren. "Here, this will pay his wages for the whole trip."

"Thank you, sir—I think."

"Oh don't worry, he'll pull his weight, I'm sure."

"Actually, I was a bit concerned about what his family might make of his sudden …disappearance."

"Eh? Well, that is a point." He looked at Gez. "You have a family, boy?"

"Just my gramma. And she won't care if I go."

"We should at least let her know," said Jarren. "Can we send a message?"

"Yes, we can certainly do that," said Weibelan. "Where do you live, boy?" Gez told him and he wrote it down. "There! That's settled. Now I suppose you ought to be getting aboard. I understand sailors are very particular about tides and wind and such."

"All right, Gez, will you get my valise? I'll take the trunk and if you could get my cello, sir, we can do it all in one trip."

They trundled over to the gangway leading onto the ship. There was a harried-looking man at the bottom of it with a sheaf of papers. He looked at them suspiciously as they came up to him. They explained who they were and the man flipped through the papers until he found the one he wanted. His frown deepened.

"You bought passage for only one person," he growled, looking down at Gez.

"Master Carabello *is* only one person," said Weibelan. "That," he nodded at Gez, "is a servant."

The man shrugged and grunted and waved them aboard. Jarren made his way up the precarious gangplank and sighed in relief when he reached the main deck. It was cluttered with ropes and casks and all manner of objects whose function he could only guess at. The boat he had taken across the narrow and calm Sea of Doran had only been a third this size and far simpler in construction. He looked about in uncertainty as to where he belonged in all this.

"I believe the passengers are usually kept in the stern castle," said Weibelan, pointing towards the rear. This part of the vessel reared up like a small house. A pair of steep ladders led up to a railed balcony with a door that Jarren guessed would lead to the captain's cabin, but the lower story, the one on the level with where they stood, might be what Weibelan meant. They tried the doors and soon found a tiny room—cabin—with a bed and a small window. Inquiries with a passing sailor confirmed that this was where he belonged. Apparently he was the only passenger. They stowed Jarren's belongings and then he let Gez go out to explore the ship.

"Well, you will soon be off," said Weibelan, "and I must leave before I become an accidental passenger."

"Thank you once again, sir. You and your wife have been so kind."

"Glad to do it. Oh! I nearly forgot. Here's a little gift from Madame Weibelan. She says it might make your voyage a little less tedious." The elderly professor produced a large envelope from the folds of his robes. Jarren took it and opened it. It was sheet music.

"Flaretti's latest cello concerto," explained Weilbelan. "Perhaps you'll have a chance to practice it while you are gone and you can give us a private performance when you return."

"Thank you, sir!" exclaimed Jarren, who was deeply touched. He had a modest collection of music, but it was all older works. "Please give your wife my thanks as well."

"You are quite welcome, I assure you. But now, I must be getting ashore, and you must get settled in."

They returned to the main deck and already it seemed less disorderly than it had moments before. The last of the cargo had been put below and the covers put over the openings in the deck. Jarren escorted Weibelan to the gangway, said good-bye and watched him walk back to his carriage. They exchanged waves and then the old man was gone. Jarren sincerely hoped to see him again.

The man Jarren assumed was the captain was bawling orders at the men and urging them to hurry, for the tide was about to do something and he did not want to miss it. Jarren had only the sketchiest notions about seamanship, but he was determined to learn as much as he could about it.

After a great deal of shouting by several different men, all the amazingly thick ropes that had been holding the ship in place were untied and hauled on board and neatly coiled. Meanwhile, other men had produced some long wooden poles and were using them to push the ship away from the dock. It was a very slow process to set such a large mass in motion using nothing but muscle power. But the current seemed to be helping them and in a quarter of an hour they were a hundred yards from the shore and clear of the other immediate ships.

Now almost all the crew assembled and Jarren saw that the long poles they had been using were actually enormous oars. They fitted them into the locks set along the rail and began to row. Five men were working on each of the four oars. With these oars, or sweeps as he later learned they were called, the crew managed to slowly turn the ship so it was facing the harbor's mouth and creep toward it, assisted by the outgoing tide. The men were sweating and cursing and Jarren was tempted to lend a hand, but just then a puff of wind came by and the captain ordered the men to take in the sweeps and unfurl several of the sails. They did so in a very efficient manner, scrambling up the ropes and out onto the precarious horizontals that held the sails. Jarren cringed at the thought of being up that high with so little to hold onto. The sailors did not seem to mind it at all.

The breeze hardly seemed enough to move the ship, but the sails quickly filled and the vessel was soon sliding through the water at the rate of a slow walk on land. Jarren tried to calculate the amount of force being applied to the sails, but could not seem to do the figures in his head. He was too excited about being on the way.

The captain skillfully guided his ship out of the harbor and came so close to one of the huge towers guarding the entrance that Jarren could actually see some of the mechanism that raised and lowered the great chain that could bar the entrance. Once past the harbor mouth, the wind freshened considerably and more sails were unfurled. The waves were much bigger, too, and the ship rose and fell in a gentle rhythm. >From time to time a wave would hit the bow in such a manner as to throw spray on the deck. Jarren found it exhilarating. He could see Gez scrambling around the ship like a squirrel, obviously enjoying himself even more than Jarren.

Eventually, there was a call for dinner. Gez went to find the galley and get them their meal while Jarren returned to his cabin. Gez appeared shortly with two bowls of some sort of stew, bread and mugs of a watery ale. The boy gulped his food down and then went out on deck again. Jarren took a bit more time, but was soon finished, too. He leaned back on his bunk feeling quite content. Then he remembered the gift from Weibelan's wife and took it out. He scanned over the music and tried to imagine what it would sound like. While he was doing so, the ship took on a slightly different motion. Jarren did not notice immediately, but rather suddenly he found his head spinning and the notes on the paper impossible to read, He looked up and noticed the lamp hanging from the ceiling and how it swayed to and fro, to and fro... He was sweating rivers...

His stomach heaved and he grabbed the empty bowl his stew had been in and quickly refilled it. More than filled it. He was scrambling to find another container when Gez returned.

"Do you need any...oh gods! I'm gonna want another copper to clean *that* up, Mister!"

The wagon took another nasty bump and Matt was thrown against Sergeant Chenik again. The man was quite a bit larger than Matt and the impact scarcely moved him. He arched a bushy eyebrow and helped Matt sit upright again. The shackles they all wore made movement difficult. Matt squirmed around to try to find a more comfortable position, but there just weren't any. A week in the prison wagon had rubbed him raw in several spots. And it stank. They were not let out nearly often enough. Or fed often enough. Nearly all of them had sunk into despondency. Including Matt.

He still could not believe this was happening. No one had listened to their pleas or their warnings about the Kaifeng. The authorities were convinced they were just deserters making up wild tales. It was enough to drive a person mad—and it nearly had.

"Hey! I think I see something!" said one of the troopers, suddenly. The man had his face pressed to the small, barred window on the side of the wagon.

"What?" asked several troopers simultaneously.

"Buildings, a church steeple. A pretty big one. Lots of buildings! A city!"

"Has to be Berssenburg," said Matt.

"About bloody time," said Chenik.

"Yes!" said Matt. "Now we can finally get someone to listen to us."

"Assuming they don't just hang us first," said another trooper.

"They won't," said Matt. "Don't worry, men, we'll get out of this soon enough." Matt wished he felt as confident as he tried to sound. Surely someone would come and talk to them. And sooner or later they would find out the truth about Fort Pollentia. He just hoped they did not find out about it the hard way.

The wagon rattled on and soon everyone could see buildings lining the streets. There was no doubt they were in a sizable town. After a week in the wagon, it seemed as though it took forever to cover the last few miles to their destination. But finally they turned through a gate in a stone wall and lurched to a halt. After another agonizing delay, the door was unlocked and swung open.

"All right you scum!" snarled the leader of the gendarmes. "Get your asses out here and be quick about it!"

They were not quick about it, but they did get out, glad to breathe some free air. Matt looked around and concluded they were in one of the forts that ringed the capital. A squad of musketeers commanded by a sergeant waited to take charge of the prisoners. The sergeant seemed to be cut from the same cloth as the leader of the gendarmes had been.

"Right this way, gentlemen," he bellowed. "We have a nice comfy cell waiting for you and a very efficient gallows. We'll have your heads up on pikes in no time." He and his men laughed most unpleasantly. Matt and his men shuffled in the direction indicated. As he got close to the sergeant, Matt tried to talk to him.

"Sergeant..."

"Shut your trap and keep moving!"

"Sergeant..."

The man shoved him and that was the last straw. Matt whirled around and put every ounce of strength he had into his best parade ground bellow.

"Sergeant, you will stand at attention when addressed by an officer! You and all of your misbegotten curs! Do you understand me?!"

Years of training and discipline took hold where courtesy and reason could not. The man instinctively snapped to attention for an instant. Only for an instant, however. Then his face began to turn red and he started to draw his sword. "Why, you miserable..." he began.

"Sergeant, it is going to be *your* head up on a pike if you don't shut up and listen to me! Now, you are going to go and tell your commander that Lieutenant Krasner of the 18th Dragoons has an urgent message for Colonel Fezdoorf from Major Macador! You tell him that or by all the gods I'll see the flesh flogged right off your bones!"

"And he'll do it too," added Sergeant Chenik into the ringing silence that followed.

The musketeer sergeant stood frozen for a long, long moment, staring at Matt. Matt held his eyes and refused to blink. The sergeant blinked first. "We'll see about this," he snarled. "But for right now you go in the cell! Move them out!"

"Thank you, Sergeant. I'll be sure to mention your cooperation in my report." Matt turned and marched away with all the dignity he could muster. The rest of his dragoons followed, looking proud despite their rags and their chains. Their guards all looked distinctly uneasy.

But they were still put in a cell that was much too small and none too clean and it was still hours before anyone came to see them. Matt looked up anxiously when he heard the outer door open and he sprang to his feet when he saw a familiar white coat with gold braid upon it.

It wasn't Fezdoorf, but it was his adjutant, Lieutenant Lerner. "What in all the hells is going on?" he snapped. "Why aren't you men back at the fort? I got some crazy message that Lieutenant Krasner was here, wanting to see the Colonel."

"I am here, sir," cried Matt. "And you have to let me see the Colonel!"

Lerner blinked and looked hard at Matt. They had only met a few times and Matt prayed that he would recognize him under all the dirt.

"Krasner? Is that really you?"

"Yes, sir! And none of us here are deserters! Can you get us released—and me to the Colonel? It's terribly urgent!"

Lerner looked at him with a little bit of skepticism. Matt supposed he could not blame him: it wasn't totally unheard of for an officer to desert. "What's this about a message to the Colonel from Macador?"

Matt took a deep breath. "Major Macador is dead, sir. Or maybe a prisoner. The Kaifeng have overrun the fort. These men and I only just managed to escape. We tried to get back here to give a warning, but we were arrested as deserters. No one would believe that the fort had fallen."

The way Lerner's eyes kept getting bigger and bigger, it was clear he was having a hard time believing it, either. Matt glanced nervously at the other dragoons. On the long journey in the wagon, they had finally agreed to not say anything more about the fireflies. That had always seemed to be the part of their story the listeners found the hardest to swallow. So their new story was simply that the Kaifeng had attacked in overwhelming numbers, filled the moat with their own dead, and swarmed into the fort despite a valiant resistance. Once they were out from under arrest, then—maybe— they could tell someone about the fireflies.

"Well, w-where's the rest of the regiment?" squeaked Lerner, finally.

"We're all that's left, sir. There might be a few other survivors, but I don't know where they are."

"Oh, gods," hissed Lerner. "The Colonel's going to go mad."

"Please, sir, can you get us out of here?"

"Uh, yes, yes, the Colonel will want to speak with you—once you've been cleaned up a little. Wait here and I'll go speak with the commandant."

"Wait here?" said Chenik after Lerner had gone. "As if we could do anything else."

"Patience, Sergeant," said Matt.

But the delay was severely trying even Matt's patience before they were finally released. It was nearly two hours before Lerner returned with the order to get them out. Their cell was unlocked and then more time spent finding keys that would unlock their shackles. At last it was done and they walked painfully back out into the sunshine.

"I'm not sure how I'm going to get you to the Colonel," said Lerner. "I only have my horse. And as for getting you cleaned up and properly dressed..." Matt was not too concerned about all of that, but he could see that Lerner could not be diverted from proper routine.

As they neared the gate, they saw that the prison wagon they had come in was still there. The door to the guardhouse was open and the gendarmes were drinking and exchanging tales with the muske-teers. Apparently they would not be starting back to Havverdor until the next day. One of them caught sight of the liberated prisoners and cried out in surprise. A few moments later they had all crowded out the door to gawk at them. Fortunately, Lerner's splendid uniform gave them an aura of authority they had completely lacked on the way in.

"Open the gate, Sergeant," commanded Lerner.

"Yes...yes, sir!" said the startled man. He snapped a few orders and the gate was quickly swung open. Matt and the others were thinking up witty parting remarks when a clatter of hooves seized everyone's attention. A man in a gendarme's uniform whipped a lathered horse into the fort so quickly the sergeant had to leap out of the way in a most undignified manner.

The man on the horse reined his mount to a halt and looked about wildly. He and the commander of the gendarmes recognized each other at the same moment.

"Dars! What in the name of all the gods do you think you're doing?" snapped the commander. "Why are you here?"

"Thanks the gods I found you, sir!" cried the man on the horse. "Kaifs! Kaifeng have attacked the town!" Shouts of alarm came from gendarmes. A chill went through Matt, but he felt a guilty surge of vindication, too.

"What? Are you mad?" said the gendarme leader.

"No, sir! It's true! Four days after you left hundreds and hundreds of the savages attacked without warning. The magistrate sent me for help immediately. The rest of the gendarmes were trying to organize a defense when I left, but there were hundreds of the murderous bastards! The...the town was in flames before I got over the next hill." The man's voice was breaking and Matt's satisfaction fled. Havverdor was a town of at least two thousand people.

"Gods," hissed the commander.

"I rode as fast as I could to get here...but...but..." the man trailed off. Everyone stood there in stunned silence.

"We told you so," said Chenik.

Atark glanced at his daughter and smiled. Thelena had her head tilted back and her eyes closed and was letting the wind of her horse's speed set her long braids flying. She had always loved to ride and he doubted she had been on a horse once in the four long years of her captivity. The enemy had taken so much from her. He hoped that he could give at least a little of what had been stolen back to her. Some things, sadly, were beyond his powers to restore, but he was determined to do whatever he could. Bringing her on this expedition was just a start.

Atark and Thelena and two score of scores of warriors were riding south at a hard pace. Four days ago Ka-Noyen Zarruk had moved all the tribes, including the herds, east into the plains beyond the mountains. The other Noyens had been wary and nervous, but Zarruk had insisted and they had obeyed. More clans were coming, but until they arrived, their position was precarious and all knew it. Some had urged huddling as close to the mountains as they could while still finding enough grass for the herds. If the Berssians came on in force, they could always retreat back through the pass.

Initially, Zarruk had gone along with this plan, but the very next day he gathered the Noyens and laughed out loud. He said that in the doubts and dark of the night he had realized that already they had become too dependent on Atark's powers to do their fighting for them. They had forgotten what had always been the Kaifeng's greatest weapon.

Mobility.

A Berssian army, under a demanding general, might march fifteen miles on a good day. A purely cavalry detachment might do thirty or thirty-five. A Kaifeng warrior could ride sixty miles in a day and still be fit to fight at the end of it. The Kaifeng could ride rings around the Berssians. They could baffle and confuse the enemy about their plans or intentions, appearing here on one day and then many miles away on the next. Zarruk had presented his plan and it had been a good one.

Two score of scores would ride northeast, burning any villages they found. Atark with another two score of scores would go south, skirting the mountains, to the next pass and destroy the fort guarding it. Zarruk, himself, would take the rest and ride east toward the Berssian capital. Each force would do as much damage and spread as much terror as possible. They were to make sure that many people were left alive to flee and spread panic. The Berssians would not know how many Kaifeng there were or where they were headed. By the time they had it figured out, the limbs of the army would be reassembled and the new tribes would have arrived. Some of the Noyens objected to being sent off without Atark's magic, but the magic would be needed for the fort and none could argue with that. The others were going off to raid, not fight battles. They could do without the magic for a few days.

So Atark rode south. He had brought Thelena along, although no other women were with them. No one thought to challenge him on matters concerning his daughter. He was not concerned that someone might try to harm her while he was gone—he simply wanted her company.

"We will reach the fort today, Father?" asked Thelena.

"Yes. Before dark. We will attack immediately. We have no time to lose."

"We have but eight hundred warriors," observed Thelena. "You had far more when you took the other fort. Will that be enough?"

"It is a smaller fort and a less important pass. The garrison is not nearly so large. With the magic, we shall have enough."

"I look forward to seeing you work the magic. I have seen the results, but not the working of it. Do you really think I might learn some of your magic?"

"I think it is possible. You always seemed to have the talent. I will try to teach you—but be warned: it is not a quick or easy process."

"Over the years I have learned patience, Father." A shadow passed over her face and Atark frowned.

"Good. That puts you ahead of most of the other shamen. They refuse to believe that I cannot teach them everything in a day or a month. Fools."

Thelena was silent for a while, but he could tell she wanted to ask him something. They jogged along for a few miles and finally she asked her question. "Father, you have said nothing of how you survived the Varag's dagger. Or of how you gained your powers. When I saw you on the fort's walls, being cheered by the men, I thought it was a miracle."

"Perhaps it was, daughter. I have told no one else, but you deserve to know. I found…something…in the mound there on the plains. Call it a ghost, if you like. It had once been a mighty shaman. It healed me and then taught me the magic. Not a very good explanation, I'll admit, but the only one I have."

"This ghost was very kind to you—to us."

Atark frowned. He had not spoken with the Ghost since their quarrel. Whatever else the Ghost might be, 'kind' was not a word Atark would have applied to it. "The ghost had its own ends in mind, I think. It desires revenge on the East. Perhaps it sees me as the means. I do not know. But I will use the power it has given me."

"For revenge?"

"The Easterners killed your mother and your brother, Thelena. They held you as a slave for four years. Do you not wish for revenge?" His daughter blushed and turned her head away. He had seen the blood on the back of the slave woman when he returned to their tent. Thelena had clearly taken some measure of revenge already.

"They should be punished," she said at last. "And prevented from ever hurting us or our people again."

"That is what I intend. But no simple measures will suffice. If we have to conquer and collar all of them to be safe, then that is what we shall do."

They said no more for nearly an hour as the miles sped past. A new column of smoke rose up to the southeast. Scouts were ravaging the countryside. There was no time for proper looting, but a dozen villages had already experienced the wrath of the Kaifeng. He noticed that Thelena was looking at him, again.

"I love you, father," she said. Now it was his turn to blush. But he smiled and nodded. "Many, many times in the fort I wished I had told you that more often. I never thought I would have the chance again. But now that I do—I love you, father." There were bright tears on her cheeks. He blinked back his own. "I just wish…I wish I could tell that to Mother and Ardan."

"I'm sure they know, Thelena."

They were silent all the rest of the way to the enemy fort.

It was three hours before dark when they arrived. The enemy was taken completely unawares and they had caught a great many people outside the fort's walls. Atark had been counting on this. He would be needing sacrifices to work his magic, but he had not brought any captives along. Fortunately, he now had more than enough. He chose twenty men for his needs. There were a number of women and children among the prisoners, but he did not choose any of them. He supposed they would work well enough, but he wasn't sure. Did physical size or strength affect how much power could be drawn from them? In any case, the women could serve the men this night and the male captives would be put to the sword when they left.

"Have them tightly bound and gagged and brought up to the hill over there," he commanded. The men struggled, eyes wide in terror, but they could offer no real resistance. Well, one resisted to the point that he had to be killed and another substituted, but soon twenty men were readied.

"What do you need them for?" asked Thelena.

"Their lives will help power the spell."

"Really?" Atark looked closely at his daughter. Her voice had wavered a tiny bit and she seemed upset. Well, he could hardly blame her. He had been upset the first time he had done this, too. But it was necessary. She would come to realize that. "When you worked your magic against the first fort, I thought I felt something very…odd."

"Indeed? Well, you were always sensitive to the power. Watch what I do now."

They walked up to the grassy mound opposite the fort. The warriors were assembled below them, just out of cannon shot from the fort. Noyen Muskar of the Yattu was in command of them and he told Atark that he could work his magic as soon as he was ready. Atark had a number of helpers now: a few young shamen he was trying to train and a score of warriors whom Zarruk had assigned to him. They were bodyguards as well as helpers, Atark knew. Zarruk was far more concerned about that sort of thing than he was. Still, they were useful. The warriors had the sacrifices arranged and stood ready with their swords. They were bronze swords, because iron would interfere with him seizing the power from the sacrifice. When he worked his magic at the first fort they had had to search through the whole force to find enough bronze weapons. A few of the sacrifices had simply had their brains dashed out with wooden clubs. This time, however, there would be enough. The apprentice shamen had a low table laid out with the items he would need for the spell. They were quite simple: a pair of candles, some incense and a small amount of gunpowder in a crystal jar.

"I'm afraid I will have no time for any instruction today," he said. "We are in haste. But observe what I do and try to sense me grasping the power. That is the essence of it." The others nodded and lined up behind him. He made sure Thelena had an unobstructed view and then took his own spot by the table. He could see the ranks of horsemen below him and the enemy fort a little over a mile away. It was smaller than the other one, but the approach was more difficult. He hoped the men would be able to get in as easily as they had before. Enough, that was Muskar's responsibility. He sprinkled a little incense on one of the candles and breathed in the smoke and cleared his mind.

He began to recite the incantation for the spell and reach out for the power. The words and the incense had no actual function other than to allow Atark to concentrate properly. The Ghost had told him that with more practice he would not need either anymore. Indeed, when he had destroyed Gerrik, he had not needed them. But then this spell was of much greater power and mistakes with powerful spells were to be avoided at all costs.

He had the power now and drew it to him. He shaped and molded the spell with the strength in himself. He formed it so that it was like the mold of a metalworker, ready to receive the hot metal. He knew that, in fact, he was doing nothing of the sort, but that was the image he used and it served him well. The Seekers were ready now and at his signal a helper tossed a handful of the gunpowder into the flame of one of the candles. It flashed and a puff of smoke rose up and turned red as it did so. The Seekers now knew what they were to seek. Now he needed only the raw power to multiply the Seekers and send them on their way. The signal was given and the swords began to flash down. The sacrifices were behind him and he could not see them, but he could feel what was happening with ease. The first man died and his strength flashed away like the gunpowder. Atark seized the smoke from it and added it to his spell. The next died and the next. He continued to gather and add. The spell grew stronger. The golden ball started to become visible directly in front of him. More deaths and more power and the ball grew and grew. The last man died and again Atark felt like he was stuffed almost to the bursting point. But not so much as he had the last time. It was easier this time: he knew what to expect and he could control it more easily.

He had the power now. The spell was shaped. He let it loose. The ball exploded into thousands of individual sparks which rushed away toward the enemy fort. A single Seeker dashed itself against the crystal jar containing the remaining gunpowder and vanished. Atark watched as the cloud of sparks faded into the distance. The horsemen were already in motion.

A few moments later, the cannons on the fort began to roar out. The sharper crackle of muskets joined in and then other explosions, growing to a huge roar. The fort was completely wrapped in smoke. Atark sighed in relief and smiled. He had managed to do it again.

"Lord! Lord!" shouted one of the lesser shamen suddenly.

He turned around and froze when he saw his daughter crouched on the ground with her hands clutching her head.

"Thelena!" He dashed over to her and knelt beside her. "Thelena! What's wrong?"

She was kneeling there, trembling hard, but when she saw him she slowly lowered her hands.

"Thelena, what's wrong?" She looked up at him and then her fear-filled eyes darted to where the sacrifices' bodies lay.

"The dead. I can hear them. I can hear the dead!"

CHAPTER EIGHT

"Silly buggers," muttered Sergeant Chenik. "They shoulda made you the general of this traveling circus, sir—not that we're actually traveling anywhere."

"Just be grateful they gave us a home at all, Sergeant," said Matt. "They didn't have to do even that—not after the way the Colonel behaved."

"Another silly bugger. The place is crawling with them."

"Well, it must have been a real blow to him. The regiment was all he had and to learn that it was gone…" Matt shook his head. Lieutenant Lerner's statement that the Colonel was going to go mad had been remarkably prescient. At first he had refused to believe it, then, when his commanding general had summoned all of them to report on what they knew, he had started raving and demanding a new command. The Colonel's only source of income was what he was paid for his regiment and apparently he was rather deeply in debt. It had been extremely embarrassing and eventually Colonel Fezdoorf had to be taken away. Matt and all the other survivors of the Tapestry Dragoons had been questioned and then assigned to another regiment.

"Sir, they still don't believe us about the fireflies," said Chenik.

"I know. We tried our best, but if we kept at it, they'd lock us in a mad house like the Colonel."

"If somebody don't do something about 'em, sir, we might as well just ride east right now and get a head start on the rout."

"I do wish you would stop thinking, Sergeant. It's a really bad habit for a non-commissioned officer."

"Sorry, but someone's got to do it…Captain."

Matt frowned and glanced down at the gold braid around his buttonholes. He still was not sure why he had been promoted, but he was not going to argue about it. Personally, he thought the general was so embarrassed about poor Colonel Fezdoorf that promoting Matt and calling him a hero for escaping the Kaifeng was some sort of salve to a guilty conscience. But whatever the reason, Matt was now a captain in the 14th Dragoons with his own company. This regiment wore sky-blue coats with buff breeches and black leather boots. Except for a modest bit of gold lace, Matt's uniform looked little different from his men's.

He glanced outside his tent as the bugler sounded the assembly. He heard a chorus of groans from the row of tents his men occupied. He had drilled them this morning and he was going to do it again this afternoon. Most of them were not happy.

Most of them.

He had sixty strangers in his company, native Berssians, who did not know him and he was quite sure did not like him. But the twelve men he had brought with him from the Tapestry Regiment were his men, through and through. Every one of them was itching to pay back the Kaifeng. Matt had used them as the solid core of his company and they took care of any bellyaching by the others. There had been no serious trouble so far, but he wasn't sure how long that was going to last. It had been two weeks since the word about the Kaifeng had reached the capital and things were still in a frenzy.

The army was being marshaled as quickly as possible, but far too slowly in Matt's opinion. Those regiments which had responded to the summons first, like the 14th, were being held in a rapidly expanding camp west of the city. The men were getting restless. They were tired of all the drill and eager to get into the taverns and fleshpots of the city. Matt had no intention of letting his men out of camp. He could get away with it for a while longer, but if more weeks went by it was going to get difficult.

Matt was of the opinion that the generals were making a serious mistake. Not just because no one would believe them about the fireflies, but also because of this delay. The Berssians had ten regiments of guard infantry and four of cavalry in the city and another fifteen musketeer regiments and six of cavalry close by. Nearly twenty thousand troops by the time you added in the artillery. While it was true that another ten or fifteen thousand could be assembled in a few weeks, he felt sure the Kaifeng were making better use of the time than they were. Reports from refugees and cavalry patrols indicated that the Kaifeng were raiding along a wide front. Several dozen villages had been burned. But allowing for the inevitable exaggeration by people fleeing the carnage, it did not seem as though the enemy had more than six or eight thousand men. Surely twenty thousand could handle those scattered bands even if they did have the fireflies. At the least, they should drive ahead to the pass and seal it off before more of the savages could come through.

Matt sighed. No one listened to him. He only knew what was going on because the colonel of his new regiment saw fit to keep his officers informed. He got up and buckled on his sword belt. He was wearing a standard trooper's heavy saber. His slightly more ornate one had been left back at Havverdoor and he doubted he would ever see it again. No matter, he wanted a heavy blade. He didn't even have a set of pistols anymore and he no longer carried a carbine. His small cartridge box was empty. He knew that his old troopers were only carrying them because the regulations insisted they do so. He also knew that when combat was near they wouldn't be carrying any powder at all. Twelve men he could count on. If nothing else, they would cut a swath through the enemy with cold steel.

He stepped out of his tent and looked off toward the west. The Kaifeng were out there and he would dearly like to cut a swath through them. A man was standing there with his horse. He was one of the new men. He missed old Cofo, but he had never made it out of the fort. A lot of people had not gotten out of the fort. *What has happened to Kareen?* It was a question he tried not to ask, but there was no avoiding it. He knew that the Kaifeng usually slaughtered any male captives, but rarely ever killed women. Those they would keep as slaves. If Kareen had not been killed in the explosions or the fighting in the fort, she was almost certainly some Kaifeng warrior's slave. A beautiful girl like her would be a real prize.

Matt clenched his fist. The thought of his sister being raped and forced to serve one of those savages filled him with a rage unlike anything he'd ever felt before. Perhaps the chance would come to drive his heavy cavalry saber through that man. He would like that very much. Perhaps the chance would come to rescue his sister. He had not thought about that a great deal. One part of him already considered her dead. But what if she wasn't dead? What if he did manage to find her? Some people would consider her better off dead. Too defiled to be redeemed. Sergeant Chenik certainly felt that way. Did he believe that, too? Was his sister somehow a lesser person because some man had taken her by force? Several of the gods emphasized that the spirit was more important than the flesh. Kareen had a wonderful spirit—despite how often it had vexed Matt.

Would he think less of her if she had traded her flesh to save her spirit? Did he think she was better off dead? No, of course not. He hoped she was alive. He hoped she was not suffering too much. He hoped to see her again. But to have any chance to do that...

"The company is assembled, sir," said Chenik, startling him out of musing. He saw that the men were all mounted and waiting his command. Stupid of him. One of the things soldiers hated the most was to be forced to stand in ranks in the hot sun while their commander ignored them. He quickly mounted and went to drill his company.

"So, all goes well?" whispered the Ghost.

"Yes. Our warriors have ridden far and wide over the land," said Atark. "The enemy assembles a large army near their city, but it has not moved. They are confused and uncertain about where we shall strike next. Still, their numbers are great. We grow in strength as well, but not quickly enough. It will be several weeks yet before Zarruk will be ready to move."

Atark stared at the image floating in the darkened tent. This was the first time he had summoned the Ghost since they had quarreled. He was very relieved that the Ghost had come. So far, neither of them had mentioned the incident.

"Time is our ally," said the Ghost. *"Have patience. The tribes will come to swell our strength. Fear not the growing enemy army. They simply gather all their soldiers in one spot so that we may smash them at a blow."*

"So we can hope. Each time I have cast the spell it has been easier. I can increase the strength by using more sacrifices. But the enemy army will require a spell far greater than any I have attempted. I fear I will not have the strength or the skill."

"You will have the strength. Or, at need, you could cast a lesser spell against one part of the enemy army. This would throw them into confusion and give you the time to cast a second spell to finish them."

"Many are asking that I teach the other shamen my powers. I have taken on a few helpers, but so far they have learned little."

"Your powers," hissed the Ghost, reminding Atark where those powers had come from. *"The time may come when you need to share, but not yet. Zarruk does not yet have full control over the noyens. The influence you wield is necessary to keep the Kaifeng focused on the goal. Share your power and that influence is gone. The tribes could*

splinter and the great goal be forgotten in squabbles between the noyens."

"Yes, so I thought as well. For now I shall hold the power myself." Atark paused. He had another question to ask, but he hesitated to do so.

"Ask what you will."

Atark frowned. The Ghost was far too adept at sensing his thoughts and moods. Still, there was no use denying it. "I have a question to ask about my daughter."

"Your daughter." Was there a note of disapproval in the Ghost's voice? He wasn't quite sure. But it said nothing more, so he went on.

"When I last cast the spell, I had my daughter present. She has the talent and I wanted her to learn. But when the sacrifices were killed she was filled with pain. She says she could hear the death screams of the sacrifices. She has always had a certain sensitivity, but it has never been like this. Is there anything I can do to lessen her suffering?"

The Ghost was silent for a very long time. *"There is something that could be done,"* it said, at last.

"What? What can be done?"

"You have bound my spirit to this skull. To this bit of bone. The spell could be re-cast. If you were to bind my spirit to the body of your daughter..."

"What!?" exclaimed Atark in shock.

"It can be done. If she has the talent, my spirit could live with her own. And I could shield her from the pain she feels. With her living strength my powers could be restored. I could help you and our people, I could..." There was an eagerness, a hunger, in the voice now that chilled Atark to his marrow. This...this...*thing* wanted Thelena's body so that it could live again!

"No! I will not allow it!" The image of the ghost flickered red and for an instant he expected it to disappear again, but it did not. After a moment it spoke.

"I can feel your repugnance. Your love for your daughter blinds you too much. So be it. We shall not speak of it again."

"There is nothing else that can be done for her pain?"

"Give her the juice of the poppy or fill her with wine and keep her as far from the sacrifices as possible. This is all the advice I can give."

"All right. Thank you," said Atark. He was both relieved and alarmed. Just the suggestion that what the Ghost proposed was even possible filled him with horror. He shook himself and pushed it from his mind.

"We have other things to discuss..."

Thelena knelt in the dark, outside the small tent, and tried to keep from shaking. She could hear her father's voice and she could 'hear' the Ghost as well. She was quite certain that it was not her ears that were hearing the Ghost. No, it was the same as when she heard the sacrifices' screams. It was a voice inside her head, not in her ears. She stopped her ears with her fingers. Her father's voice was muffled, but not the Ghost's.

She had not been able to keep out the screams of the sacrifices with her fingers either.

Sometimes she thought she could still hear them. It was just an echo, but she would wake up in the night with their cries ringing in her head. The echoes didn't hurt like the real screams had, but they still frightened her. She had been around death before; only a few weeks ago she had been in the middle of a fort where over a thousand men had died in a quarter hour. Then, there had been some very faint cries in her head, but they had been drowned out by the real screams around her, and they soon faded. They had not hurt and they did not echo. These other ones were different.

No, not entirely different. As she knelt there, she realized she had heard voices like these before. Fainter, infinitely fainter, but she had heard them before. Four years before.

At the mound.

Her father had told her that a great battle had been fought there. Thousands upon thousands of men had died, he had said, and she was hearing the ancient echo of their death cries. She realized now that her father had been wrong. It wasn't the screams of the warriors she had been hearing. It was the screams of the sacrifices.

Ransurr's sacrifices.

The name meant nothing to her, but she had heard her father chant it again and again as he summoned the Ghost. It was the name of the Ghost. Ransurr. It sent a chill of fear through her. The Ghost had given her father his powers. It wanted him to fulfill its desires for revenge on the East.

And now it wanted her to fulfill its desires for life.

Her father had refused it, of course, but that did not make her fear it any less. She could feel its hunger. It was an evil hunger. She shuddered. Then she silently rose to her feet. Her father and the Ghost were still talking about plans for the war and she took the opportunity to slip away. Her father would be angry to know she had been spying on him. The Ghost would be angry, too.

She walked quickly back to her own tent and went inside. She was chilled, and not just by the cool, pre-dawn air. She slid gratefully into her blankets and shivered. It was still an hour until the first light and she was tired, but she could not sleep. She was afraid of the Ghost and she was afraid of the influence it seemed to have on her father. It was not right. None of it.

But there was nothing she could do. The war was in motion now. Her father's powers—wherever they had come from—were critical to the war and he would go on. Not that she was against the war. She had as many reasons to hate the Easterners as her father did. More. They did need to be punished and her father would be the one to do it. She was proud of him. But she could still hear the echoes of the sacrifices' cries. How much could be justified by the needs of the war? It was a difficult question and she had no answer.

She heard a faint moan that was not an echo. Kareen. She looked to the lump of blankets where Kareen lay. The lump moved slightly and there was another moan.

"Are you awake, Kareen?"

"Yes, *Qoyen*," came the reply after a short pause.

Thelena frowned. Kareen had not called her by name in weeks. "Are you still hurting?"

"Yes, *Qoyen*. A little."

Thelena sat up and her frown deepened. She had done a far more thorough job on Kareen than she had intended. There was still a livid cut across her cheek and Thelena knew she would bear a scar there for the rest of her days. And her back... Dozens of welts and cuts had crisscrossed her back by the time she was done. She had not really meant to do that, but she had not been able to stop herself. Granted that Kareen had deserved some punishment. Fate had made her into a slave and a slave had to be punished when she did something wrong. But Thelena had to admit that the punishment had gone far beyond necessary discipline and had turned into... revenge. Revenge. An ugly word. She got up from her blankets and went to sit next to Kareen.

"I'm sorry I beat you, Kareen," she whispered. "I was angry. Not just with you, but with the whole world. I was angry and I took it out on you. I'm sorry." Kareen sniffled, but said nothing.

"And I lied to you." Kareen finally turned over and peered at her from under the blankets.

"I lied to you about Phell. He…he never raped me. I just said that to hurt you more. I'm sorry. I'm sorry he's dead. And I'm sorry Matt is dead. Your brother was always kind to me. I'm sorry."

"Thank you, *Qoyen*," whispered Kareen.

"Please don't call me that when we are alone."

"I'm your slave. You're my m-*Qoyen*."

"I won't try to tell you that you are not a slave. You are. We come from two different worlds, Kareen. The only way we can exist together is as *Qoyen* and slave. First I was your slave and now you are mine. It's the only way. But…but that doesn't mean we can't still be friends."

"Friends?"

"You said we were friends before."

"That was…different."

"Why? Because I was your slave? We can only be friends when I'm the slave?" A tinge of anger was creeping into her voice and she ruthlessly stamped on it.

"I don't know. This is so hard for me, Thelena," said Kareen. "I'm only beginning to realize how hard it must have been for you, too. I'm sorry I was so stupid. I tried to be good to you, but…but…oh, I don't know what to think now! This is all like a nightmare!"

"I'm sorry. I wish there was some way we could just be friends. Just friends. But there isn't. You are my slave, but I don't want to be cruel to you. If you cooperate—like I cooperated with you—I won't hurt you again. I don't want to hurt you again."

"You…you could let me go, Thelena. Just give me a horse and let me go. If I'd understood I would have done that for you, Thelena. I would have let you go!" Kareen stared up, her face pleading.

"Would you? Really? Before you understood what it means to be a slave?"

"Yes! I would have! If I had understood I would have! And you do understand, Thelena! Oh please let me go!" The girl was sobbing now.

"I can't do that, Kareen. If you had let me go, I would not have gotten far. The Varags would have captured me again and I'd be dead now. If I let you go, one of my people would catch you before you could get twenty miles. Then you'd be his slave and not mine. Do you want that?"

"No! No, but your father is important. He could give orders to the warriors to leave me alone. I could get away. Back to my own people. Oh please, Thelena! I can't bear this!"

"Yes you can. You must. My father would not let you go even if I asked him. He…he hates the East. He won't help you. And…and there is nowhere for you to run, Kareen. Even if you did get away for the moment, the Kaifeng are coming. What happened at the fort is only the beginning. Thousands and thousands more warriors are coming. With my father's magic, the eastern armies will be swept away. The cities will fall. Anywhere you might run to will eventually fall to us. You would end up a slave again in the end."

Kareen's eyes had been getting wider and wider. Now she shook her head. "No! No, that can't be true! You're… no, that can't be true!" She pulled the blanket over her and wept.

Thelena reached out and put her hand gently on Kareen's shoulder. "I'm sorry it has to be that way. The world can be very cruel. But I won't be cruel to you, Kareen. Accept your role here and we can still be friends. Please."

The eastern woman was still weeping when the dawn came.

"Land ho!" The cry came from far overhead and Jarren sprang to his feet, nearly knocking his cello case overboard. He grabbed it and then scanned the horizon, looking for the land. He could see nothing except the rolling gray seas. He felt a little better when the captain shouted to the lookout, demanding to know where the land was.

"Two points off the port bow, sir! "

"Good! Well done! Helm come a point to leeward." The captain came walking near him, rubbing his hands together and Jarren intercepted him.

"Is it the island, sir?"

"Eh? Yes, yes, a perfect landfall. We should make Orberus before night. A damn good thing, too. A tricky approach that is. Now if you'll excuse me, sir." He hurried off to yell at some of the crew. Captain Kostlan yelled a lot, Jarren had noticed, but his ship seemed to be well run. A moment later Gez came scampering on deck. He climbed halfway up the shrouds and looked around.

"I don't see any land!" he said accusingly.

"It is quite some distance off. You should be able to see it when we get closer—assuming the fog doesn't close in again."

"Blasted fog. Too damn much of it."

"The Captain told me that there is a current of warm water flowing into this area from the southeast," said Jarren. "The warm water and cold air causes the fog." Gez did not reply. Jarren had been trying to educate his young servant, but so far the lad had shown no interest at all.

"So why're we going to this island anyhow?"

"I'm looking for something."

"Treasure? Buried treasure? My share is one-tenth, remember. More if I gotta carry it."

Jarren laughed. "You shall get your share of any treasure I may find, Master Gez. But don't set your hopes too high. The type of treasure I seek won't be gold or gems."

"All right. So if we do find any gold or gems I can have it all, right?"

"We shall see. But tell me, Gez, do you ever think of anything besides money?"

"What else is there? Of course if I had *more* money, perhaps I wouldn't be thinking about it all the time."

"And perhaps if you did not play dice with the sailors, you would have more money."

"Just a run of bad luck," muttered Gez. "I'll make it up on the trip back." Jarren just shook his head. The boy often talked like a man of thirty instead of a ten-year-old.

"We shall be docked by this evening, Gez. Please make sure we are all packed and ready to get off, would you?"

"Sure. I'm getting tired of this tub anyway." The boy jumped down from the rigging and ran off to their cabin. At least he was willing to work—although he had lied about being able to cook.

Jarren took a deep breath and stared at the point on the horizon where he estimated the island lay. He had found that if he spent most of his time on deck and kept an eye on the far horizon, then he was not troubled with the awful seasickness that had struck him the first day aboard. Sleeping was not bad either. He just had to be careful of the time he spent in his cabin awake—or eating.

Still, he was anxious to get ashore. Three weeks at sea had nearly exhausted every source of amusement the ship had to offer. He had read every book aboard, including several on seamanship and navigation, He had talked to all the crew members who were willing to talk. He had mastered—well, mastered for him—the Flaretti concerto Madame Weibelan had given him. And he had stared at the ever-changing—and changeless—sea and sky for hours on end. He was ready for something new. He hoped that he would find it on the island that lay ahead.

He stared and stared and eventually he could see the island from the deck. At first it was just a fuzzy spot on the horizon, but it slowly became a mountain peak, then a whole mountain, then a mountain and surrounding hills. By mid afternoon it was an island, a fairly large island whose other end was still beyond the horizon. The island was called Gerousi and, according to the maps, it was fairly large with several small villages and towns. It was one of a cluster of islands far to the northeast of Zamerdan and the mainland. The largest island in the group, Bernahi, was farther north. There was something like a city there, ruled by someone like a king. All these islands were nominally his, but from what Captain Kostlan said, they were really independent and rarely thought about their ruler. Many of the islands only had a tiny population and were perpetually shrouded in the fog. To Jarren, it sounded like an ideal place for a wizards school that desired privacy. Or he certainly hoped it was.

The sun was dipping toward the sea by the time the *Unicorn* was anchored in the small, narrow bay that the town of Orberus nestled alongside. There were dozens of fishing boats coming in for the night, but the newly arrived merchant was the only large ship. There was no dock or wharf to tie up to, so Jarren and Gez would have to get to shore by boat. He looked on nervously as his belongings were lowered into the fragile-looking craft. But the men were experts and nothing was wetted or even bumped very much. He turned to the Captain.

"Thank you for the pleasant voyage, sir. I look forward to sailing with you on the return."

"You had better look forward, Master Carabello," replied the captain. "I will be touching at a half dozen of these islands over the next month before heading back to Zamerdan. Depending on the weather I meet, I should be back here in between six and eight weeks. Be here! The storm season will be almost on us and I will not wait. Be here, ready to go, or be prepared to spend the winter!"

"I understand, sir. I'll be ready."

"Good luck with your studies, although I still can't see why anyone would come all the way out here to look at birds!"

The old captain in Zamerdan had forced him to promise not to tell any other captain why he was coming to Orberus. Apparently he was breaking some agreement to tell Jarren and Weibelan about this place. So Jarren's official reason for travelling here was to study the birds. "Uh, there are a number of local species that are completely unique to these islands, sir. I'm quite excited about getting the chance to see them."

The captain's expression told what he thought of the whole idea. He did not offer to shake hands, but made it clear that it was time for his passengers to leave. Jarren looked down and saw that Gez was already in the boat. He gingerly let himself down the ladder and thumped into the boat beside the boy.

"This is where we are heading?" asked the boy, gesturing to the town. "What a dump! What the blazes do you expect to find here that's worth anything?"

"We shall see," said Jarren. He tried to sound confident, but his own spirits had sunk a bit. The town seemed hardly more than a fishing village. It was made of mostly wooden houses of no more than two stories. They clung to the steep hillsides or perched precariously over the water on wood pilings. There were a few larger stone structures which looked to be temples. Still, the place had a prosperous look to it. The buildings were all in good repair with fresh paint and they all seemed clean and tidy.

"Is there an inn here?" Jarren asked the sailor steering the boat.

"Yup. The big building over there. Not too bad a place. Good food, good ale and some pretty wenches. Lousy bedding, though, so be warned."

"Thank you."

The boat crunched ashore on a gravel beach and the sailors drew it up a bit. Jarren and Gez and their luggage were soon on dry land. It felt strange not to have a deck moving under them. Unfortunately, the sailors had all headed off before he could think to ask them to help with his luggage. Gez had acquired a small bag for his meager possessions, and they were now one pair of hands short to be able to carry everything at once. After some experimentation Gez ended up lugging Jarren's valise and his own bag while Jarren clutched his cello case under one arm and dragged the trunk over the rocks with the other. Eventually they reached the inn. It was a larger structure than it had seemed from the boat. Well-constructed and decorated with rich carvings in the wood. The sign showed some sort of sea monster but the text was unintelligible to Jarren. The door was standing open.

Inside, it was crowded with the fishermen returned from their day's labor. A few people looked at them with curiosity. Then more. The sailors from the *Unicorn* were known, if infrequent, guests, but Jarren and Gez were true strangers, apparently something they did not get very frequently in Orberus. Before long almost all the conversation had stopped and everyone was staring at them.

"Uh…we'd like to get a room," said Jarren.

"With clean beds," added Gez.

A man wearing an apron came around from behind the bar. He smiled warmly while eyeing them suspiciously a rather interesting accomplishment, in Jarren's opinion. "You wish a room, Master…?" He was speaking in some heavily accented dialect of the language used in Zamerdan. That was the tongue Jarren had spoken in, but he had to concentrate hard to understand what the man had said.

"Carabello, Jarren Carabello. Yes, we would like a room," he said loudly and slowly.

"With…clean…beds," said Gez, even louder and slower.

The man frowned at Gez, but nodded to Jarren. "Three coppers a day. Includes hot water and meals." The man said it almost defiantly, as if he expected Jarren to argue. But the price was half of what he'd have had to pay in Zamerdan—or Sirenza for that matter—and Jarren saw no reason to argue.

"Very well. Can you have someone help us get our luggage up to the room?" The man seemed surprised, and maybe disappointed, that Jarren did not haggle, but he accepted a silver mark for a week's lodging without quibbles and rousted out a servant to help with the bags. Soon they were in a cozy room on the second floor with a small fireplace burning cheerily and several candles keeping back the coming night. Gez poked at the bedding suspiciously, but could not find any unwanted inhabitants at first attempt.

The sailor had been right about the other things, however: the food was good, and the ale was good and the girl who delivered them was rather cute. Gez, who continued to amaze Jarren, tried to proposition the woman. She seemed interested until she realized that Gez was acting on his own behalf, rather than for Jarren. At that point the woman slapped him and then laughed and left the room. Gez rubbed his cheek and cursed.

"Gez, why are you in such a hurry to grow up? What on Earth were you planning on doing with that girl if she accepted?"

"Well, if you don't know, I can't explain, Mister! As for growing up, why the hell would I want to remain a kid? You just get paid half as much for the same work and get beaten up for good measure."

"No one's beaten you this journey."

"Nope, but that's because you're soft. If *I'd* been you I woulda beat me up a half dozen times already."

"Perhaps I'll have to start…"

"Too late. I ain't scared of you. Wouldn't do any good now. Hell, I could probably beat *you* up if I wanted."

"Go to bed, Gez."

"Don't have to tell me twice." The boy dove into the smaller bed and disappeared under the covers. Jarren was tempted to do the same in his own bed, but even though he was tired, he was not sleepy. He was too excited. Somewhere on this island, perhaps in this very town, was the next clue in his search. Unfortunately, finding it might not be easy. The old sea captain would tell them nothing more than the name of this town. No names of contacts, no address to go to, nothing. In the morning he would just have to start asking questions. He had a feeling that the locals were not going to beat a path to his door with information. He had six weeks, at least, but somehow that did not seem like nearly enough time. He sighed and then decided he really was sleepy after all. He took off his outer clothing and crawled into his bed.

The next morning he quickly discovered that his search was going to be more difficult than he had feared. He started by asking the innkeeper if he knew of anyone selling magical devices. It was a simple enough question and he figured that if anyone would know it would be the innkeeper. At first the man did not appear to understand what Jarren was talking about. He hoped it was simply a language problem, but he quickly found out otherwise. He tried showing the man his small magical lamp, but the innkeeper insisted he knew nothing about such things and no, no one in the town sold things like that. Jarren tried a small bribe, but the man firmly shook his head and would say nothing more. Discouraged, Jarren left the inn to try his luck elsewhere. Gez was eyeing him closely now.

"Magic, huh? I knew that story about the birds was a load o' dung. So you're trying to undercut one of the other merchant houses? Risky business, Mister! They guard their secrets close."

"I'm not..." said Jarren, but the boy interrupted him.

"Oh, don't worry, I'm still working for you. But I want a share of this! I know what kind of money this stuff brings on the market in Zamerdan! And that's a really good disguise you've got. Studying birds! It never fooled me, of course, but old Kostlan swallowed it whole."

"But..."

"Still, you nearly copped it with the innkeep. He'll be in the merchant house's pocket and he won't say nothing to you. You need to find someone in town who'll be willing to undercut *him*!"

Jarren was speechless. He had not thought about any of this before. He had assumed that the merchants simply came here and bought the magic items when they were available. Naturally, they would want to keep the source secret from rivals, but he wasn't a rival! He just wanted to know who was making them—not buy and sell them himself! This was getting too complicated. "Uh, do you have any ideas about where I could find someone like that, Gez?"

"Hard to say. I don't know anyone around here. And now that you've tipped off the innkeep about what you are really up to it will be harder. He'll spread the word to clam up."

Unfortunately, Gez was correct. By mid-morning few people would even talk to them and no one would say a word about magical devices. Jarren tried to make it clear that he only wanted to study them and talk to the person who made them. Even Gez did not believe him. On the one hand, it was frustrating, but on the other it seemed to prove that he was on the right track. Clearly these people were hiding *something*.

He paused outside the small temple to Donisa, the sea god, and considered going inside and asking the priest if he knew anything. The official position of most of the churches was that magic was heresy, although only a few actively tried to root it out. In a small community like this, surely the priests would know if magical items were being imported and sold. But would they be any more likely to talk to Jarren about it? It seemed unlikely, and after a moment he turned away.

"So what would you suggest now?" asked Jarren to Gez.

"There ain't no secret that can stay secret if more than one person knows it. If the whole town knows about the magic, then one of them will be willing to talk for the right price. We just have to find the person."

But they did not find the person that day or the next and the townspeople were becoming increasingly unfriendly. If Jarren went into the common room of the Inn, conversation immediately stopped until he left again. The pretty serving girl left their food outside their door—and it was usually cold.

On the third day Gez suggested Jarren stay in their room while he tried his luck alone. He said that people weren't as suspicious of a kid. That was probably true, but Jarren was worried about how Gez would represent him. Suppose he actually found someone selling magic devices and promised them some huge sum of money? Eventually, he relented and let Gez go out. He spent a long, dull day in his room. He tried to cheer himself with his cello, but his efforts were half-hearted. Why had he begun all this? Four years ago when he proposed his thesis to Beredane, he had no clue it would lead him to this. He was farther from home than he'd ever dreamed of being. On the edge of the world, it seemed. He felt very lonely. Then, around dinnertime, Gez charged into the room and seemed very excited.

"I think I found our man!" he gasped.

"What? What do you mean?"

"I found someone who will talk to you about the magic! He'll meet us down by the shore later tonight."

"Why doesn't he just come here?"

"Are you serious? He's not gonna meet us where others might see him! I can't believe your bosses sent you on this trip! You don't know nothing!"

"Uh, well, I am a bit new at this, it's true."

"The boss' nephew or something?"

"Not exactly..."

"Well, anyway. We go meet this guy in three hours. Better get dinner now."

"How did you find him?"

"Professional secret," said Gez with a wink. He would say no more and before long they heard the girl leave their dinner outside the door. At least it was still warm this time. They ate in silence and then got on each others' nerves waiting for it to be time to go.

Finally, it was the appointed hour and they went down the steps and out the front door. No one appeared to even notice them. Outside, the fog was thick and damp. Beads of water quickly gathered on the wool of Jarren's cloak. They set off with a brisk stride and

Gez guided the way. As they neared the edge of the town, they were forced onto a long wooden dock that eventually petered out and left them on a stone sea wall a few feet above the water. Gez slowed down and looked around.

"Is this the spot?" asked Jarren.

"This is where he said. Must be late."

They waited for a while and then finally heard the sound of feet coming toward them from the town. Many pairs of feet from the sound of it.

"How many men were we meeting with?"

"There was only supposed to be one," said Gez, looking nervous for the first time. "Something ain't right." He started looking around for a route of escape, but the sea wall ended against a cliff. Short of climbing the cliff or swimming, there was nowhere to go.

The footsteps got closer and a number of lanterns were suddenly uncovered. Jarren saw at least a dozen men only a few yards away. "S-stop! Who's there?" he cried. The men came closer and halted in a half circle around them, pinning them against the water. He wasn't surprised to see the innkeeper with the men. Alarmed yes, but not surprised.

"You are not welcome here," said the Innkeeper.

"We already figured that part out," muttered Gez.

"But why?" demanded Jarren. "We mean no harm. I just want to talk…"

He was interrupted by an angry outburst of several of the other men. They were talking quickly and loudly in the local language. Jarren could not understand any of it, but he was frightened to see that one of the men was waving a knife and pointing at him.

"Hey! Easy there!" squeaked Gez. "I'm just a kid! I only work for this guy! I don't know nothing!"

"Thanks a lot, Gez," said Jarren.

"Every man for himself, Mister." Gez looked over his shoulder at the cold water behind them.

The other men continued to argue. Jarren was glad that at least there was an argument. The one man clearly wanted to harm them, so apparently some of the others did not. But it was getting louder and several more men seemed to be siding with the man with the knife. Jarren glanced behind him. The water looked very cold and he could barely swim and these men could get him before he went five yards. He did not like this at all. Weibelan had given him a tiny flintlock pistol before he left Zamerdan, but it was still sitting inside the trunk in his room. It had never occurred to him that he might face a danger like this. Some of the men were edging in his direction…

"Time to go, Boss, "said Gez suddenly and he hopped off the wall into the water.

"Gez!"

Apparently the boy expected the water to be shallow like the beach they had landed on because he gave a very surprised yelp as it closed over his head. He reappeared almost instantly and began splashing and floundering. He grabbed at the stones of the sea wall, but they were wet and slippery and he could not get a grip. "H-help!" he gurgled. Jarren knelt down and extended his hand, but the boy was just out of reach.

Jarren spun around to face the men. "Well, are you going to let him drown?" he snarled.

"If that's the gods' will," said the innkeeper.

"The gods?!" spat Jarren, suddenly furious. "May the gods curse you all for cowards!" With that, he turned and jumped in after Gez.

The water was *very* cold. The shock of it made him gasp, which is not a good thing to do while under water. He popped to the surface coughing and sputtering. Gez was a few feet away and Jarren grabbed him. The boy attached himself to Jarren like a limpet. He reached out to grab the wall, but the stones were set very closely and were very smooth and wet. He could not get a real grip, either. He scrabbled at them, and although he managed to find enough of a hold to keep their heads out of the icy water, he could not haul himself out. He looked up to see a dozen faces staring down at him.

"Help us!" he shouted, but the men did not move. All he could do was cling to the stones as the water sucked the warmth out of him. Gez was already shivering uncontrollably. "Hang on, Gez."

"C-can't d-do m-much e-else r-right n-now!"

Jarren looked around desperately. He knew he did not have much time before the cold left him helpless. Could he go hand over hand back toward the town? There would be ladders somewhere, surely. Would the men try and stop him if he did? He had to make a decision. *They are not going to help. It is up to me.* He could scarcely see anything, but he felt out with his left hand along the rock, searching for a new handhold, He found one and pulled himself and Gez two feet to the left. Then he did it again. Another two feet. How far did he have to go? A few hundred yards, at least. An impossible distance.

Would it be better to try and swim? No. Reach and pull, reach and pull. His hand slipped as he tried to shift again and they were both dunked under the water. He surged to the surface and scrabbled wildly, scraping his knuckles, before he found another hold. He clung there gasping. He thought he could hear the villagers arguing, but he had no clue what about. He was getting very cold now, but he had to keep moving. He reached out again, but his hand could find no grip on the next section of wall. He would have to try and swim for a while. But Gez was just dead weight and he was so tired...

Suddenly there was a horn call. It was a piercing but very pure note. He could not tell what direction it was coming from. The fog confused the sound and it echoed off the cliffs. But the effect on the men standing over them was remarkable. They immediately stopped arguing and stared out to sea. They seemed very surprised.

Jarren turned as best he could and followed their gazes, but could see nothing but the bank of fog. He peered into the grayness and thought he could see a spot a tiny bit lighter than the rest. Moment by moment it grew stronger until there was no doubt that a boat with a lantern was approaching the shore very close to where he was hanging on.

The lantern grew brighter and a darker form began to take shape in the fog. It looked much larger than any boat he had seen aboard the *Unicorn.* And it had a mast and a sail of its own. It wasn't being rowed. The vessel was only a few yards away now and Jarren looked at it in amazement. The bow of the ship swept up and then bent over and bore the carved head of some monster. It was frighteningly realistic in spite of being wood instead of flesh. The rest of the ship was rather round and low to the water. A single square sail hung down from the central mast. Jarren had barely taken this all in when the ship gently nudged the sea wall and came to a halt. A dark shape was standing next to the amazing figurehead and then jumped down onto the shore. The circle of men backed away and he could no longer see them at all.

"Get them out," said the figure. Instantly the men came scrambling over to the wall and in a moment they were hauled out of the water and stood there dripping wet and shivering with cold and fear.

"Master Carabello?" said the figure.

"Who...who are you?" stuttered Jarren.

The figure came closer. He now saw that the person was shorter than him and his fear lessened slightly. It threw back its cloak and Jarren was amazed to see the face of a young woman.

"Jarren Carabello?" said the woman. "My name is Lyni. I've been sent here to get you."

The bugles rang through the camp. Each bugler repeated the call of the one farther up the line until dozens of them were playing the same tune, all completely out of synchronization. The drummers in the infantry camp began their own calls and soon there was a cacophony of noise in the city of tents. As soon as he heard it, Matt leapt off his cot and began grabbing his gear.

"Looks like the real thing this time, sir," said Sergeant Chenik as he stuck his head through the tent flap.

"It certainly does."

"About bloody time."

"Yes. Make sure the men know this is for real and find the teamsters if they're not drunk. Hell, find 'em even if they are."

"Right." Chenik vanished.

Matt packed his few personal belongings, leaving the bulkier items for his servant to put in the wagons. He did not have much. He had come here with nothing at all and the paymaster had been reluctant to advance him enough money to even get his uniforms, equipment and horse. He would not be seeing anything except his subsistence pay for the next six months.

Assuming there was anyone left to pay him six months from now.

He kicked himself mentally for the gloomy thought. The army was finally assembled and soon 35,000 men would be on the road marching west. To fight the Kaifeng. He was still terribly worried about the fireflies, but he told himself he was overdoing it. Berssian light cavalry had been skirmishing with Kaifeng parties for weeks now and there had been no sign of fireflies. Carbines and pistols had been used and Kaifeng had been killed and nothing unusual had been reported. Perhaps the disaster with the squadron and the fort had been some sort of fluke. A trick that could not be repeated. A mass delusion. He didn't know. He did know what his duty was, however.

He stepped out of the tent and his horse was waiting for him, held by one of the men. He threw the valise across the horse's back and tied it in place. All around him the tent city was coming down and being packed up. It would be hours yet before it was completely gone, but the army would be on the road by then.

It was nearly an hour before his own regiment was ready to move. He was pleased that his company was the first on the line. They were good men. He knew they didn't really understand the obsession he and the other survivors had for drilling and drilling, but they had accepted it and even felt some pride in knowing they were the best company in the regiment.

Finally, the call for his own brigade was sounded and they wheeled into a march column and set off. The dust was already thick in the air, but they soon turned off the dirt road and into a huge grassy field. The King had come out to see his army march off to war and there was to be a grand review. The gaudily uniformed Guards regiments were already assembled there and the rest of the army was filing in. Then they halted. And waited and waited. Matt hardly noticed. He was in the army and this was how armies did things. Eventually there was a commotion by the little pavilion which had been erected. The bugles sounded again and things began to move.

Regiment by regiment, the army passed before the King. The Guards regiments went first, of course, and it was over an hour before Matt's brigade started to move again. They were in a column by company and Matt rode in front of the center of his. As he neared the pavilion, Matt saluted with his sword. He looked in vain for someone who might be a king. There were a number of people dressed in dazzling finery, but none of them seemed terribly interested in the martial spectacle passing by. Matt shrugged. He felt no more loyalty to the King of Berssia than he did for the Elector of Navaria who had sent him out here. His only loyalty now was to the men of his company and his regiment. His only desire was to kill Kaifeng.

He and his men swept past the King's pavilion and then headed west to find the enemy.

CHAPTER NINE

The ship sailed smoothly over a calm sea. Its single square sail bellied out with the steady breeze. The sun was just rising out of the low-hanging fog but did little to warm the crisp air. Jarren was still grateful to see it. Just a few hours earlier he had been afraid he might never see another sunrise. He clutched the blanket he had been given and looked around. The ship only had four crewmen and they seemed to do very little compared to the men he had seen aboard the merchant ship. There was one man at the tiller and the other three just watched.

In the daylight he took a closer look at the woman who had saved him and Gez from the villagers and the sea. She had very short brown hair, a prominent nose and round cheeks. Her eyes were green and her lips narrow. No one would ever call her beautiful and even 'pretty' was stretching things, but she was certainly not ugly. She seemed very young to Jarren. *But if she's a wizard, maybe she's two hundred years old.* She was wearing trousers and a tunic with a cloak and boots. Since their rescue she had not said a word to him.

She had said very few words to the villagers, either. She had simply told them to bring all of Jarren's luggage to the boat. They had done so with instant obedience and great deference to the woman. When the luggage was aboard, she had 'invited' Jarren and Gez to accompany her. Under the circumstances they had not even considered refusing. He glanced over at Gez, but the boy was sprawled on top of their bags, wrapped in blankets and snoring quietly. Mustering his courage he approached her.

"I...I want to thank you for getting us out of that situation, Madame Lyni," he said.

"Just 'Lyni'. No 'madame' needed," she replied.

"Ah. And I am simply 'Jarren'. But please accept my thanks. I was afraid that those men might harm me and my servant."

"A few of them wanted to cut you into fish bait."

"Do you know why?"

"Overzealous loyalty, I would imagine."

"I don't understand."

"When you and your young friend came barging into Orberus like a beached Kraken, asking about us…"

"About you?" exclaimed Jarren.

"Well, you were asking about magic devices and the people who made them, weren't you?"

"Yes. Is that you?"

"Not me, personally, no, but some of my associates. In any case, when you started snooping around, that made the good townspeople nervous."

"Why?"

"Because they've got a good thing and are afraid of losing it, I would imagine." The woman was silent for a moment and Jarren looked at her intently. "You see, we provide them with good fishing and fair weather. We heal their sick and make sure their livestock are healthy and fruitful. In return they respect our privacy and provide us with an outlet to the outside world. It has worked for centuries and they were worried that you were going to ruin it for them."

"Would they really have hurt us?"

"Several of them seemed quite intent on chopping you up for fish-bait. I have no idea how it would have turned out."

"Well, I thank you again for intervening."

"Don't be too grateful. Had it been my decision I would have been in favor of the fish-bait solution." Jarren looked at her sharply but could not decide if she was joking or not. There was a hard look on her face that made him nervous.

"But it wasn't your decision?"

"No."

"Then whose?"

"You will find out soon enough." The woman moved away from him and he resisted the urge to follow her. He had so many questions! But it would not do to be rude or pushy. They were going somewhere and presumably there would be some answers when they got there. Instead, he went over to where Gez was sleeping and sat down beside him. He was no longer dripping wet, but still quite soggy. He took off his cloak and spread it out to dry and then wrapped another blanket around himself. In spite of not getting any sleep at all the previous night, he was wide awake.

An hour or two passed and Gez continued to sleep. No one else aboard had said a word and at last Jarren could stand it no longer. He got up and went over to where the woman was standing. "How long a voyage do we have ahead of us?"

"Only a few more hours. It is not far."

"Really? How do you maintain your privacy so close to the inhabited islands? I know that many ships pass through these waters. Do they not see your...abode?"

"It is not so difficult. The sea is much larger than most people realize and almost all of it is empty and trackless. Several of my associates have powers which affect the winds and the currents. A gentle push here, a tiny tug there is enough to guide ships safely away from our home—and they do not even realize it is being done."

"Amazing! And you have maintained your privacy in this way for centuries?"

"So I am told. I have not been here very long, so I'm afraid there is little I can tell you."

"Indeed? The...uh...wizards recruit new members and bring them to the island?"

"You are certainly the curious one. I don't think I will tell you any more. And you should keep in mind that the fish-bait option has only been deferred, not canceled."

"I...see," said Jarren nervously. He moved back to his baggage and carefully took out his journal. He really needed to record what had happened before he forgot any of the details—or was swamped with new information. He found the familiar routine of scratching away with quill and ink to be relaxing. And he had already learned a great deal. There was a hidden enclave of wizards, as he had hoped and suspected. And they did have contact with the rest of the world, although only in secret. New members were also secretly recruited and...

"So you really are a scholar?"

Jarren jumped and nearly spilled his ink. He looked to see that Lyni was standing behind him and looking over his shoulder. Gez started awake at the same moment.

"Uh, yes, yes I am."

"Birds," said Gez, "he studies birds."

"I study magic," insisted Jarren.

"Whatever you say, boss."

The woman frowned as if in thought. "I'm not sure which is worse, a real scholar or some money-grubber out to undercut his rivals. Either way, you spell trouble. If it comes to a vote, I'm all for fish-bait."

"I'm sorry you feel that way," said Jarren. "If that's so, then why did you rescue us at all?"

"I was instructed to bring you to the island."

"How did you know we were in the town?"

"Hey, they're wizards, ain't they?" said Gez. "They know everything, I bet."

"Hardly," chuckled Lyni. "And we knew you were in Orberus because some of our friends sent us a message. Nothing magical, just a homing bird. The Masters decided to bring you here and that was all there was to it."

"I…I'm hoping they will be willing to talk to me when I get there. I have a great many questions."

"I'm assuming they wish to talk," said Lyni. "I can see no other reason to bring you here. Our dungeon facilities are quite limited, and if they had anything more drastic in mind there would be no point in bringing you to the island."

"Well, that sounds hopeful," said Jarren.

"Sounds like trouble to me," muttered Gez. But then he brightened. "This island must have a lot of gold and gems lying around? I mean you folks can turn lead into gold and all that, right?"

Lyni merely laughed and walked away. After a while one of the other crewmen offered them some bread and cups of watery wine. They were both very hungry by this time and accepted gratefully— although Gez was disappointed. "I thought wizards would have cakes and brandy or something fancy. If they don't live better than regular folks then what's the point?"

"Some people don't put so much importance on material wealth, Gez."

"Some folks are damn fools."

Another hour passed and then there was some activity among the crew. Lyni seemed to be doing something, but Jarren could not understand what it was. She stood near the bow of the ship and moved her arms in odd patterns and seemed to be chanting something. The others made adjustments to the sail or helped with the tiller. The ship was heading toward a thick wall of fog. Jarren moved forward so that he could see better.

The ship got closer and closer to the fog until it formed a gray curtain across half the world only a few hundred yards away. Closer still and the monster's head on the bow touched the fog. It was so thick that the bow of the ship disappeared even though Jarren was only a few yards away. Then the fog swept over him and he could barely see his hand in front of his face. He stood there, frozen in anticipation.

Then, as quickly as it had come, the fog was behind them and the air was clear. It was like, well, it was like magic. "Wow! Look at that!" exclaimed Gez.

In the distance, perhaps three miles away, was a rocky island. It was tall and very steep, almost like a mountain crag that was sticking up from the ocean. Even from here, Jarren could see buildings clinging to the sides and a narrow tower sticking up from the very top. He stared at it for a while, trying to comprehend just what this all meant. Then, when he noticed that Lyni seemed to be finished with whatever she had been doing, he went over to her.

"This is our destination, I presume?"

"Yes, welcome to Peridoq."

"Peridoq? Is there some significance to the name?"

"None that I am aware of. But I'm sure someone here must know the origin of it. Like as not, it is just some word in the local tongue that means: 'chunk of rock sticking out of the sea.'"

Jarren laughed. "True enough." Lyni lapsed back into silence and Jarren contented himself with just watching. The ship covered the last few miles quickly and Jarren was able to see that there were actually dozens of stone buildings on the island. Or perhaps there was only one. It was hard to tell. The buildings all seemed to be connected to each other and also to be part of the island itself. Rock blended into walls, walls into stairs, stairs into bridges and then bridges back into the rock again. Parts looked to have been carved out of the rock while other parts had clearly been constructed. But it was all stone. Even the roofs appeared to be made out of thin sheets of rock. There was some variation in color, but not much. Gray, everything was a shade of gray. It was a drab and gloomy place—or at least it looked that way from the water.

As they got closer, he could see that there were a number of small waterfalls splashing down from the heights. They fell into pools at different levels and then splashed down again until they finally reached the sea. It added a bit of life to the stone island. But as he watched, Jarren suddenly thought about the magic pump in the fountain back in Zamerdan. There was no possibility of there being a natural spring at the top of this stony island, so the water had to be pumped up to the top in the same fashion as the fountain operated.

"Not a speck of gold," sighed Gez. "Nor a glint of gems. What a rotter! A den of wizards and they're paupers!"

By now the ship was nearing a stone dock that jutted out from the island in a small, sheltered cove. Several more of the monster-headed ships were tied up there, but he could see no one else about. With only a few movements of the tiller the ship slid right up next to the dock. The square sail rolled itself up all on its own and the ship slowed to a halt. Two of the men jumped out onto the dock and tied the ship to it.

"We are here," announced Lyni. "Please come with me. Your baggage will be brought." Jarren followed her eagerly, but he noticed that Gez grabbed his own small bag before coming along. There was a heavy door—also made of stone--which was the only exit from the dock. Lyni led them through it into a dark passageway. Jarren was completely blind for a moment, but then they emerged into the light again. A set of steps cut into the face of the island led upward and they followed them higher and higher. From time to time there would be doors set into the rock, or a balcony or even a small house sticking out from the cliff. It reminded Jarren of some of the steeper parts of Sirenza, except for the lack of color or decoration—and people. They met no one.

He also noticed that everything needed repair. Stonework was cracked. Balusters or entire railings were missing. Grass and vines were pushing through joints. Some windows were boarded up or had broken glass. The place had a shabby, sad feel to it.

"What a dump," said Gez.

"The lower levels are unoccupied," said Lyni, who, for the first time, looked less than totally self-assured. "Up above, things are in better shape."

"How far above?" asked Gez. "This is turning into quite a hike!"

Lyni did not bother to answer but continued up the steps. Jarren was getting tired, himself. Still, they continued, up stairways, over small bridges, through tunnels. The waterfalls splashed down around them or flowed under them. He looked out and saw that they were several hundred feet above the water now. But then he looked up and saw that they still had a long way to go—assuming they were headed all the way to the top.

As it turned out, they were not. About two-thirds of the way up, just as Jarren was sure he could not make his legs bend and straighten one more time, Lyni announced they had reached where they were going. She even let them rest a bit although she did not look the least bit tired. They were on a wide balcony with a breathtaking view of the ocean. From the balcony a bridge jumped across a cleft in the rock to what appeared to be a large hall set into the side of the cliff. It had many windows and balconies of its own. As Lyni had promised, everything here was much better maintained than it had been down below.

When they had caught their breath, Lyni led them over the bridge and through the large double doors of the hall. Inside there was a spacious foyer with two staircases curving up and away on either side. Several doors were set into the walls which opened into other rooms. The stonework here was much more elaborately carved than outside. Graceful columns and wood beams—the first wood Jarren had seen, aside from the boarded-over windows—held up the roof. Elegant brass chandeliers were suspended above them and he was excited to note that the lights in them were magical rather than oil or candles.

Their guide led them through the door to their right and they found themselves in a comfortable library with book-lined walls, a marble floor, tables and several leather chairs. Sitting in one of the chairs was an old man with a long white beard. Lyni went up to him and curtsied. "I have brought them, Lord," she said.

The man slowly got to his feet, and leaned on a walking stick. Jarren looked at him closely. The beard and his very bushy eyebrows concealed much of his face, but he had high cheekbones and a large forehead with a much-receded hairline. His nose was rather bulbous and he had twinkling blue eyes behind a pair of spectacles. He looked exactly what Jarren would have expected of a wizard. He was relieved to see that the man wore a friendly smile in addition to his long dark blue robes.

"So! Our visitors are here at last!" he said. His voice was high-pitched, but strong and steady. "I am Dauros and you must be Master Jarren Carabello and this is Gez. Welcome to Peridoq!"

"Thank you, sir," said Jarren, bowing. "I'm very pleased to be here. But you speak as though you were expecting us."

"Oh, but we were! Indeed, there have been a few among us who have been making wagers on how long it would take you. I daresay, you got here quicker than anyone anticipated. My congratulations."

"But how did you know? Did your magic...?"

"What? No, no, my dear boy, I'm afraid predicting the future isn't something we're terribly good at around here. But let's sit down! Lyni, dear, would you have the servants fetch us some refreshments? Sit, sit!" Jarren found a seat opposite Dauros, who sank back down into his own chair. Gez took a seat off to the side and Lyni left the room.

"Now where was I? Oh, yes: your coming here. No, we weren't divining your movements, it was simpler than that. You see, although we have remained in seclusion here for a long time, we have kept an eye on what has been going on on the mainland. We have...representatives, and a few friends, who pass on the news to us. In particular, anything regarding magic. So, when you started making a name for yourself in academic circles with a study of magic, it naturally sparked our interest. I've read some of your papers and heard accounts of your lectures. Very well done, young Jarren, very well done. At least for as far as you've gone."

"Thank you, sir," said Jarren, quite pleased that his fame had spread much farther than he ever imagined.

"You made it no secret that you wanted to search out any remaining practitioners of the art, so we expected that sooner or later you would be led here. I must say that I'm personally a bit alarmed at how quickly you did manage to find us. I thought we had been more careful than that. Still, one slip in three hundred years isn't too bad, I suppose."

"And I never would have actually found the island if Lyni had not come to our rescue, sir." At that moment the young woman returned with a servant bearing a tray. Conversation was interrupted while they were served. Gez was pleased that now they did, in fact, receive some delicate pastries and he insisted on having a cup of the very good wine. Jarren had already discovered that the boy could out-drink him any day. Dauros took a glass of the wine, but Lyni took nothing. She stood against one wall with folded arms. Jarren shifted in his seat. His clothes were dry by now, but they were starting to itch rather badly.

"I suppose we could have just ignored your presence in Orberus," continued Dauros, "but that would have been rather rude. Especially since the villagers were upset enough to do you harm. Besides, I was looking forward to talking with you."

"I'm glad to hear that, sir. I've a great many things I want to talk to you about, too."

"No doubt! No doubt!" chuckled the old man. "A thousand questions! Why we disappeared, why magic has nearly died out, why we remain in hiding, why we now agree to talk with you? Questions, questions! We won't have time for too many before dinner, but which one would you ask first?"

"Where do you keep all the gold?" asked Gez.

"Uh, I suppose the first question would have to be why you've consented to speak with me, and..." here he paused and glared at Gez, "...what you intend to do with us afterwards."

Dauros' expression darkened slightly. "Hmmm, I think it would be best to postpone that particular question until later. What would your second question be?"

"I suppose I'd want to know what happened after Soor. Why did the magic users who survived disappear? Master Weibelan has his own theories, but..."

"Ah yes, Oto Weibelan's *Downfall of the Wizards*, an admirable effort," interrupted Dauros. "He managed to piece together a great deal. But, of course, not being a magicker himself, he was missing several important pieces." Dauros paused for a moment and leaned back in his chair. He took off his spectacles and rubbed at his nose.

"The Battle of Soor was a disaster for magic," he said. "Not just for the magickers who were killed in the battle, but a disaster for the magical arts as a whole. So much knowledge and experience was lost there. All of the great wizards were slain. I suppose it is a point of pride that all of the great wizards were *there*, but it was a tragic loss. Still, there was no alternative. The Kaifeng had descended on the East in numbers that modern people can scarce conceive. I've seen a few recent histories of the Great War with the Kaifeng where the authors discount the numbers given by the historians of the time as exaggerations. I can assure you that they were not. One of the wizards there was able to count the enemy with a magic spell. The Kaifeng had 1,487,359 warriors at the Battle of Soor."

Jarren gasped. It was an impossibly huge number. No army of the present day had even a twentieth of that strength.

"The East could not field anywhere near as many knights and warriors. It was only the wizards who allowed us to win."

"Were you there?" asked Gez, who also looked properly

impressed.

"Me? No, of course not!" laughed Dauros. "That was three hundred years ago! How old do you think I am?"

"Pretty old. A couple hundred anyway. And you're a wizard."

"Well, I'm sorry to disappoint you, young Gez, I'm a mere stripling of eighty-five. While it is true that some of the great wizards managed to live for as much as one hundred and fifty years, the knowledge to do that was lost with so much else. Many generations of magickers have come and gone since Soor. We only have the knowledge that was passed down to us by the survivors—not personal memories."

Jarren nodded, but was secretly relieved that Gez had asked the question. He'd been wondering exactly the same thing but didn't know how to ask. "Sir? That brings up another point. You speak of all the magical knowledge that was lost. But you say you have accounts of the survivors. They were passed on, why not the magical knowledge itself?"

"Most of that knowledge—the knowledge of the spells themselves—died with the master wizards."

"I don't understand. I mean, I can see that the death of the wizards would have lost all the actual experience of the men, but why the basic knowledge? Surely the spells were written down somewhere. In my research I found many descriptions of the effects of spells, but never one book with the instructions of how to cast them. Were they intentionally destroyed? Or did you bring them all here?" Jarren waved to the rows of books lining the walls.

Dauros sighed. "No, no, you don't understand. Not being a magicker there might be no way you can truly understand. Magic is... well, it might be easier to tell you what magic is not. It's not the science you seem to think it is—I'm not saying your theories are wrong!" added Dauros hastily when he saw Jarren's expression of shock. "No, you are probably correct that magic does, somehow, fit into the physical framework of the universe, but if it does, it is in a manner different from the other physical sciences. There are no convenient equations or formulas for casting a magic spell. No magicker ever even came up with a satisfactory vocabulary to describe what we do. The truth is, Jarren, that there are no written instructions for any of the spells."

"What?" gasped Jarren. "None? How can that be?"

"It is difficult to explain. You realize, I am sure, that magickers have a special talent for magic that most people lack. Actually, some theorize that everyone has the talent to some degree, but it is simply much stronger in the magickers. In any case, you can think of it as an additional sense, like hearing or seeing. The sensations we receive from this sense are no more describable in words than what we receive from our other senses."

"But we can describe those," insisted Jarren.

"Really? Accurately? How can you describe the color blue except by saying that it is blue? A meaningless term to a blind man. Try explaining music to a deaf man. It can't be done."

"If they don't have the sense, then no, I can see that it couldn't be done. But for someone who does have the sense there must be ways. Written descriptions of color or music will make sense to those who can see or hear."

"In general terms, perhaps," admitted Dauros, "but without the masters to explain those descriptions, you are crippled. I understand you are an avid musician, Jarren."

"Just an amateur, sir, but I do enjoy it."

"Perhaps you'll favor us with a recital while you are here. But to give you an example of our difficulties, consider music. Clever men have devised a system of recording music on paper. Notes on a scale. It's a set of instructions on how to produce the music."

"Exactly, sir," said Jarren. "A unique language created for a specific purpose. Why weren't the magickers able to do the same?"

"Perhaps we just weren't clever enough," sighed Dauros. "Perhaps it is, indeed, possible to create such a thing, but no one ever succeeded. But consider our problem in the terms of music: Suppose you took a man who had a great natural skill for music, but who had never in his life heard music or played an instrument. If you handed him a musical score and your cello, would he be able to play it? Even if you explained what the notes on the page meant and described how the cello was operated, could you expect him to play the music on his own?"

"No, of course not."

"No, you would have to *show* him how to do it. You would have to demonstrate it yourself. Play the cello and let him watch. Let him see how you move your hands and listen to the music that is produced. Then he could try it himself. Even then it would take years of practice before he could play a concerto. We magickers were in the same fix: the masters were all gone, who could show us how it was done?"

"But…but not every magicker was gone!" insisted Jarren. "There were still some of the lesser ones left. Granted they might not know all the great spells, but at least they knew the basics of how to do magic. They could teach others and then new masters would arise." Jarren blushed. "Or…or at least that's the way it seems to me."

"In theory you are correct," said Dauros nodding his head. "But in practice it was much more difficult. You see, the Battle of Soor did far, far more than simply kill a lot of wizards."

"Sir?"

"I'm groping for an analogy to explain 'blue' to a blind man," sighed Dauros. "As a scientist, I think you can understand that the energy to perform magic spells has to come from somewhere."

"Yes, sir. I've measured some of the energies produced by magic items. Discovering its source was a major focus of my studies."

"Indeed. Well, imagine, if you will, that the energy is a large, calm lake. A lake of magical water. Does that make any sense?"

"I suppose so, sir. At least as far as it goes."

"All right then. When a magicker casts a spell, he must draw the energy from that lake. But this is a very special lake, Jarren. You cannot just dip in a cup or a bucket and draw the water out. No, the only way to get the water is to toss in a pebble or a stone and then catch the water that splashes up. For a small, simple spell, just a pebble is needed and you catch the splash in a thimble. For a more powerful spell, you need a larger stone, which makes a larger splash."

"I think I can visualize that, sir," said Jarren. He glanced over to Gez who had finished off all the pastries. He also noticed that all the silverware that had been on the tray was missing.

"Well," continued Dauros, "When you toss a pebble or a stone into the lake it also makes ripples in the water, just as it would in a real lake. Usually the ripples are small and quickly fade. But for the great spells, you must drop very large rocks into the lake and make very large splashes. And to catch the splashes you must venture out onto the lake, into the deeper water. Imagine the magickers in boats. Very small boats for the novices, much larger ships for the masters. It is quite dangerous for a novice to be too close when a master is making a big splash!"

"I'm following you so far, sir," said Jarren, wishing desperately that he had paper and ink to record all this.

"Good. Well, the Battle of Soor saw all the great wizards of the world—and the Kaifeng had some powerful ones too, although not so many—and they were all casting their most powerful spells at the same time. Nothing like that had ever happened before—and the results were not what anyone had expected."

"Sir?"

"The lake of magic was stirred up into a raging storm. Huge waves that threatened to swamp and drown any but the most powerful. Many of the lesser magickers were destroyed by the lake rather than by hostile spells. All the master wizards were killed by the battle and only a few of the lesser ones were able to survive this storm on the lake. A great tragedy—but worse was to follow."

"Worse?"

"Yes, much to the horror of those magickers who were left alive, the storm on the lake did not dissipate. It went on and on for years. The waves bounded and rebounded off the shores. Year by year they lessened a tiny bit, but for nearly a century the lake was far too dangerous to venture out on."

"Oto theorized that something bad had happened to the magic!" exclaimed Jarren.

"Yes, he got that exactly right. A very clever man, Master Weibelan. Sadly, the magickers of the times were not so clever. Or perhaps they were simply desperate. Again and again they tried to venture out on the lake—usually with disastrous results."

"The unexplained fires and lightning in some of the cities! The mysterious illnesses!"

"Exactly. A tragedy, as I said. Doubly so. Not only were many more magickers destroyed, but in the process they made the survivors feared and despised. The Church, who had never liked the independent magickers to begin with, used this as an excuse to persecute them. In the end, only a handful were left and they were forced to flee the cities. Most ended up coming here."

"Most?"

"There are others, Jarren, but I have no right to speak further of them. So, you can see the situation: We had a group of magic users huddled here who did not dare to use their magic. Or at least they could not use it in any meaningful way. It was still possible to grab tiny bits of power from the shores of the lake. It was at least enough to teach the next generation how to do magic at all—but barely."

"I see," said Jarren. "So to continue the musical analogy, you had a group of people who could teach their students how to hold the instrument, describe how to play, perhaps pluck a few of the strings, but never actually play it."

"Yes, exactly," said Dauros, nodding. "And by the time the magical lake had settled down enough to be usable again, all the old magic users had died off. The next generation had to begin very nearly from scratch. Ancient records from before Soor are fragmentary, but the evidence suggests that it took thousands of years of trial and error to reach the level of sophistication they had achieved. We have had to start over again, with our way made only slightly easier by those who went before us."

Jarren was trying to digest all of this when a servant entered to announce that dinner was ready.

"Splendid!" said Dauros. "The others will be very eager to meet you, too. I abused my position here to get first crack at you, but now I'm afraid you will have to be shared out. We don't get many visitors here, you know."

They all got up and Dauros took Jarren by the elbow and steered him back out into the foyer and then through another set of doors into a large dining room. There was a long wooden table nearly covered with dishes, platters, silverware and glasses. It was large enough to accommodate thirty people and very nearly that number were standing by the chairs waiting. Jarren halted for a moment and looked them over. They were mostly men, although a half-dozen women were scattered along the length of the table. They were mostly old, although a few were middle-aged. They were mostly smiling, although a number were not.

"My friends, we have a guest tonight," said Dauros. "Please let me introduce Master Jarren Carabello." There were some polite murmurs of welcome and even a small bit of applause. Jarren smiled and bowed. Then Dauros was introducing him to the assembly. Jarren made a heroic effort to remember all the names and the faces they belonged to, but failed. There were some who did stand out, however, and Jarren made sure he remembered those. Dauros' second in command, in particular caught his attention. He was a tall, thin man, named Stephanz, with black hair fading to gray. He had a neat black mustache and tiny chin-beard. His eyes were dark and he stared at Jarren without any welcome at all. Stephanz's cold manner was more than offset by a plump, jolly woman named Idira. Apparently, she was the group's master healer. She giggled when she said hello, but then said that she had so much to talk to him about. The third one was a man with iron gray hair that was quite short and he wore no beard at all. He was stout, but not so plump as Idira. His name was Hessaran and he was the alchemist. Finally, there was Prestan, who was the master artificer.

"Are you responsible for the devices which produce the waterfalls on this island?" asked Jarren.

"Why yes, I am," said Prestan. "I've been slowly rediscovering the secrets of the Ancients. Those are some of my proudest discoveries."

"Ah, then it was you who led me here," said Jarren with a smile. "The University in Zamerdan bought such a pump for a fountain. We traced it back to Erberus and thus to here."

"You don't say!" exclaimed Prestan, who was clearly delighted.

"I warned that this would happen," said Stephanz coldly. "We should never have sold any of those items to merchants operating so close to here."

"Now, now, Stephanz," said Dauros. "All's well that ends well."

"The end remains to be seen, My Lord."

"Excuse me for asking," said Jarren, "But why did you sell those items in the first place?"

"Oh, for only the noblest of motives," chuckled Dauros. "We needed the money."

"What?"

"For the money. Everyone needs money, my friend."

"You've got that right," muttered Gez.

"As you can imagine, our rocky isle has very little in the way of resources," explained Dauros. "We can get fish with no difficulty and there are a few goats on the island and birds as well. But that would be a rather monotonous diet, I'm sure you would agree. We need to import our grains, our wine and ale, beef, cheese, the list goes on and on. To say nothing of other supplies: paper and ink, chemicals for our good alchemist, iron and copper and tin for our artificer, books for old men like me. All of that requires money. The only product we can produce of easily convertible value are the devices good Prestan and his comrades create. But let's not stand here: our expensive, imported dinner is getting cold!"

Jarren was guided to a place at the right hand of Dauros who occupied the table's head. The other magickers found spots all along the length. Gez was led over to a smaller table where a number of younger people, including Lyni, were seated. The food was very good, indeed. A veritable feast with many courses brought in by servants. The first sip of wine reminded Jarren that he had not slept in a day and half. He firmly put the cup aside, determined to stay awake as long as he could. There were a dozen separate conversations going on around him and he tried to listen to them all. It was impossible, of course, but he did his best. Those seated nearest to him kept up a polite stream of inquires about his journey or compliments about his work. Several had more pointed questions.

"Master Carabello," began one man who Jarren believed was named Fretna, "Is it true that there is a dragon skeleton on display in the museum at Sirenza?"

"Just the skull, I believe, sir. And there are those who claim that it is a fake, that dragons existed only in fables."

"Fables!" exclaimed the man. "Fables! Why the very idea! I can assure you that dragons did, indeed, exist. I have researched them thoroughly. In fact, I have a theory that with even a small fragment of dragon bone I might be able to recreate living dragons again!"

"That is remarkable, sir. Although I must admit that the idea of a living dragon fills me with some bit of dismay. They were reputed to be rather…irascible creatures."

The man jerked in his chair and frowned. Then he turned to his companion and spoke in a loud whisper: "And he calls himself a scientist!"

"Uh, yes," said Dauros. "I never mentioned the dragons or the other magical creatures in my little history lesson, Jarren. There were quite a number of animals who seemed to have some sort of magical nature. Dragons, gryphons, pegassi, unicorns, a whole menagerie-full of them. The terrible aftermath of Soor destroyed almost all of them. Apparently, they could not survive the surges of magical energy."

"'Almost all' were destroyed, sir? There are some left…?"

"A few. Cats, of course, and owls. Would you believe that the common hedgehog is magical?"

"Amazing. I assume that these creatures were only mildly magical and that is how they survived?"

"Probably, although in the case of cats, I think they were just smart enough not to use their powers."

"I see."

The conversation went on and on. Jarren found himself stifling yawn after yawn, in spite of his intense interest. He cursed himself for not sleeping on the voyage here as Gez had done.

"I understand that dear Lyni saved you from possible harm at the hands of the villagers," said Stephanz, suddenly.

"Uh, yes, she did. I'm extremely grateful." Stephanz frowned and turned to Dauros.

"My Lord, surely it is time to discuss whether we should have dispatched Lyni to rescue Master Carabello."

"The deed is done, Stephanz."

"True. Then we need to discuss what is to become of him now that he is here."

"I had hoped this to be a purely social gathering tonight. Such weighty matters could be left for another..."

"We are all gathered, My Lord. I am sure Master Carabello is very interested in our intentions. It might be more rude to keep him in such suspense."

Dauros was silent and the conversation in the room came to a halt. After a long while he slowly nodded. "What Stephanz means, Master Jarren, is that there are those among us who believe the time is not yet ripe for direct contact with the mainland. I do not agree, but I am not prepared to make the decision on my own. It could be a great risk and, if we are wrong it could be the end of us."

"Surely you exaggerate the danger, sir," said Jarren, now fully awake. "You are still hidden here where no one can find you."

"Not so," said Stephanz. "We may be safe from random discovery by passing cargo ships or fishermen, but if you were to report what you know, a systematic search by many ships would almost certainly find us."

"Why would they do that if you asked to be left in peace?"

Stephanz made a rude noise. "Ha! You have separated yourself from the realities of the world more fully than we here, Master Carabello! Why would they seek us out? For wealth! For power! Or simply out of fear. The kings and princes would seek to control us for their own ends. Or, failing that, they would destroy us so that others could not succeed where they failed. There are still fanatics in the Church who would condemn us as heretics. They would never simply 'leave us in peace'!"

"They wouldn't...!" began Jarren, but then he stopped when he realized that there were people who would. Ambitious rulers who would seek any advantage over their neighbors. Greedy men who would see wealth. Zealots who would see danger. Yes, there could be men who would not leave them in peace…

"There is a danger," said Dauros nodding sadly. "But there could be great gains, too. We are cramped in this tiny place. Hindered in our research by lack of resources and lack of people. If we were welcome on the mainland again, we could accomplish a great deal."

"And think of how much good we could do for the people!" exclaimed Idira. "Thousands die every day from diseases we know how to cure! I weep to think of how much suffering is going on that we could stop."

"Ha!" said Stephanz, "Think of the suffering our magic could *cause* in the wrong hands! Their kings would think of us only as weapons—and treat us no better than the cannons in their arsenals!"

"I agree there is a danger," said Prestan, "We would need certain guarantees…"

"Guarantees? What guarantees would they honor once they had hold of us? It is not as though we are the master wizards of yore! We are not magickers to make mere mortals tremble. If we had the powers of our ancestors, it would be one thing: we could protect ourselves. But our powers are weak. They would soon realize this and reduce us to slaves."

"Stephanz, I'm hardly suggesting we simply get in a boat and sail to the mainland and declare ourselves openly!" said Dauros. "We would have to take slow steps and consider carefully at each one. My hope is that Master Jarren, here, can be that first, small step."

"What do you mean, sir?" asked Jarren. He was alarmed by Stephanz's words and his attitude. Would they actually kill or imprison him to keep their secrets safe?

"Your research has kindled a new interest in magic, Jarren. Only in very limited circles, it is true, but the interest is there and it is growing. And it is a sympathetic interest, not a fearful one. People want to know more about magic and why it has nearly disappeared. It is my hope that if you continue your work, the climate will slowly become more favorable to our return."

"I would certainly do anything I could to help, sir! Your goal seems like a very noble one."

"I am glad you see it that way. But this will be a slow process and I shall not live to see it reach fruition. For Stephanz is correct: there is a great danger. We must proceed with care. We will need your help, Jarren, and unfortunately, we will have to ask you to do something that no scholar ever wants to do."

"Sir?"

"We will have to ask you to lie, Jarren. Or at the very least to hold back information." Dauros peered at him from over his spectacles. His gaze seemed to go right through him. "Do you understand what I'm asking?"

"I...I think maybe I do, sir."

"You cannot simply return home and tell one and all what you have learned. If you tell of what you found here and where you found us, then Stephanz is quite correct: a fleet of ships would soon search us out. No, I'm afraid you must lie about where you found us. Too many people know that you sailed to Erberus to lie about that, but you must fabricate a tale of taking another ship to another island far away. Then, you must not reveal all of what you have seen and learned here—certainly not all at once! A bit here and a bit there to generate interest, but you must not allow people to think that there is some treasure trove here to be plundered."

"How can he prevent that, My Lord?" demanded Stephanz. "People would come here just to steal Brother Prestan's magical pumps! You have been away from the mainland too long. You have forgotten the limitless greed of those people!"

Dauros sighed. "Perhaps you are right, my friend. But perhaps there is a way to spark their interest and gain their trust—without inflaming their greed."

"How?"

"I think that Idira had presented us with the solution: ease their suffering. If Master Jarren were to limit his initial findings to descriptions of her healing magic, that might do the trick. No one would fear a healer, and few would see healers as a means to acquiring wealth or power. No doubt some would still try, but it would be a lesser danger. Perhaps, with time, Idira might travel to the mainland and start a school to teach healers. Once magic has been accepted in that role, it might be possible to introduce other disciplines." Idira was nodding her head eagerly and many of the others were making favorable noises.

Stephanz turned and fixed his gaze upon Jarren. "It all depends on the honesty of this man, My Lord. Can we trust him?" Everyone was looking at him now. He felt light-headed. He'd had too little sleep to face such a situation.

"Well, Master Jarren," said Dauros, "can we trust you?"

Jarren hesitated. It went against all of his instincts and training to conceal information. He tried to estimate how badly the restriction might cripple his work. What would it do to his reputation if he were found out? *What will these people do to me if I refuse?* That thought cut through the haze that was gripping him. If he did not agree, he might never get home again. And as he thought about it, he realized that he did want to help them. Bringing magic back to the world could be a very good thing, but only if it was done correctly. He could still do much of his basic research even if he restricted himself to the healing arts at first. Yes, it could be done...

"I...I would be honored to be your ambassador to the world, My Lord." Dauros seemed to relax and then smiled broadly.

"Splendid! My friends, let us drink a toast to a grand new future where magic and science exist together in peace!" The assembly raised their glasses. Even Stephanz.

"To the future!"

The Kaifeng were in motion. A huge army of horsemen swept east out of the foothills. Atark looked on in satisfaction. As he had predicted, the other tribes had come. The stories of victory and the lure of booty had drawn them. Clan after clan, tribe after tribe had ridden through the pass to join the army. Nearly four score of score of scores, thirty thousands as the Easterners would reckon it. An enormous force, far larger than any Kaifeng army since before the Dark Times. It was true that if the tales were to be believed, then this was still only a tiny force compared to the armies of old. But more warriors were coming. The word had spread far and wide on the plains. More tribes were answering the call and they would come.

More were coming, but the army would not wait for them. Scouts reported that the Berssians were finally moving. Their army, somewhat larger than the Kaifeng's if the scouts were correct, had left their capital and was marching against them. There would be a great battle very soon.

None too soon as far as Atark was concerned. The multiplication of their numbers had also multiplied the problems. Feuds and rivalries between tribes and leaders threatened to tear the army apart before the enemy was even reached. Tradition dictated that each score of score of score of warriors, or *Helar* as it was known, should have its own Ka to lead it. The army had four helars and should, thus, have four Kas--and a Re-Ka to command them.

The clans and tribes had sorted themselves out along the lines of blood-ties and after a lot of arguing and a small bit of violence had selected their Kas. Zarruk had remained Ka of the helar that had formed around the original gathering, but the position of Re-Ka was still empty. As had happened before, the newcomers would not submit to Zarruk until they had seen Atark's powers with their own eyes.

Atark looked behind him to where his guards and assistants rode. They had the implements he would need to cast the spell. They had all the remaining captives taken at the forts.

Soon, very soon, the warriors of the Kaifeng—and the army of the Berssians—would see his power with their own eyes!

CHAPTER TEN

"Well, at least it's not hot anymore," said Mattin Krasner, as the driving rain poured off his hat.

"Yes, sir," grumbled Sergeant Chenik. "But if this don't stop soon, the damn Kaifeng won't need their bloody fireflies. There won't be a working musket in the whole blamed army."

Matt nodded his head, bringing down another cascade of water. A really heavy rain could render a musket inoperable even with the covers over the pans. It had been known to happen in a few battles.

"Well, a heavy rain will muck up the Kaifs' bows, too. And the gunners can usually fire their pieces no matter how hard it rains. If it comes to rain or fireflies, I'll take the rain."

"No argument there, sir."

"Of course, if the roads get any worse, we probably won't even be able to find the Kaifs, let alone fight them."

Chenik grunted some reply that he could not catch. Matt let the conversation die and looked up at the clouds. It did not seem to be raining quite as hard as it had been earlier and the sky to the northwest did seem a bit brighter. Maybe it would stop soon. The rain had begun the second day out from Berssenburg. The summer was nearly at an end and the autumn rains were beginning.

There was some commotion on the road up ahead and the column halted. This had been happening more and more frequently. After a while the column started moving again and the brigade swung off the road into the field alongside it. Matt saw that there was an artillery battery stuck in the mud blocking the road. The cannons were sunk up to their hubs in the sticky goo. Better yet, it was one of the Guards units. The gunners' red leggings were now a chocolate brown. The dragoons all hooted and laughed at the cursing artillerymen. The regiment plodded through the fields, tramping the unharvested wheat into the mud. This might have been a disaster for the farmer who owned the land except he had already fled and abandoned his farm—assuming the Kaifeng had not killed him. Matt could see the remains of the burnt-out farmhouse a few hundred yards away. That had been happening more and more frequently, too. They were about seventy miles west of the capital and it was clear the Kaifeng had been here. They had passed hundreds of refugees on the first day or two, but there were no more now. Either they had fled—or they were dead.

They had seen a number of the dead on their march. Men, women, children, farm animals, the Kaifeng seemed to kill anything that could not get away from them. The mood of the army had become steadily grimmer. At first, for everyone except Matt and his Survivors, this had seemed like some vast picnic excursion. No one had been terribly worried. There had been the initial fright, but then the troops began massing and the fear had gone. The Kaifeng savages could never stand up to the Army of Berssia! The regiments were so splendid, the cannons so powerful, surely the enemy would be driven back across the mountains in short order.

But now they were seeing first hand what the enemy was capable of. And the old tales were being recalled. No Kaifeng might have set foot in Berssia for three hundred years, but people still remembered the last time they had. The hordes had swept over the mountains and scourged the land. Everything west of the Glovina River had been devastated. Even after the Kaifeng had been driven out, it had been generations before the wasteland they had left behind was repopulated. People were remembering those old tales. The soldiers in the army were now out for revenge—not a picnic excursion.

The confidence in the army was still high, despite their grim mood. They would win and the enemy would pay. Matt had no doubt those Guard artillerymen would soon have their cannons free and rolling again. Everyone wanted to strike a blow.

Matt's regiment rode on until mid-afternoon. The rain had stopped by then and it was getting unpleasantly warm again. He was expecting another long wait for the wagons with the tents to catch up and then another too-short night before they set out in the morning. The column halted again, but this time a swarm of mud-spattered couriers went galloping by. One stopped with Matt's brigade commander and he could see a great deal of gesticulating and pointing.

"Looks like something's happening," he said.

"The general's favorite poodle is probably missing," grumbled

Chenik. "We'll spend half the night looking for it."

But it was not the general's poodle, it was the Kaifeng.

"It looks like the bulk of them are up ahead, maybe twenty miles," explained Matt's colonel a little while later. "Considering how fast the bastards can move, the general wants to deploy the army now so we're ready for them in the morning. Our brigade will be on the right. Stay ready to move."

Matt had never seen a whole army deploy from a column of march into a line of battle before. The process was excruciatingly slow and cumbersome. The infantry battalions, marching in columns by company, wheeled off the road one by one and marched off to the right or left. Mounted orderlies carefully measured the distances between each company, between each battalion and between each brigade. If anyone wasn't in the proper position, they were ordered to adjust their distance—which often meant that everyone else had to adjust as well. Once everything was exactly right—and the sun was getting quite near the horizon by then—a single cannon shot boomed out and all the companies of all the battalions slowly swung around like doors on hinges and the battle lines were formed.

There were two lines of infantry, each 'line' being three ranks deep, with artillery and cavalry spaced along them in carefully created gaps. The bulk of the cavalry was massed on both flanks and Matt's regiment was on the right, as he had been told it would be. Once the deployment was finished, bugles sounded and the infantry stacked their weapons in neat rows and the cavalry picketed their horses. They would sleep on their arms tonight. The enemy was nearby and there was no time for tents or any of their other meager comforts. The baggage trains were still well to the rear and would not catch up for hours yet. Details were sent back to fetch rations, but nothing more. The men settled down on the soggy ground, made what fires they could, and tried to be as comfortable as possible. There would be a battle the next day, everyone was sure of it.

Matt made certain his men and their horses were properly cared for and then sought out the fire the other officers of his regiment were at. He'd much rather spend what might be his last night on earth with Sergeant Chenik and the other Survivors, but there might be useful information to be gleaned here and he owed it to his men to be as well informed as possible.

Plus there was much better wine to be had here.

The other officers had all been polite enough to Matt, in spite of his being a stranger. The fact that the general of the brigade had promoted him and assigned him here personally probably convinced them he had a powerful patron. He saw no reason to disabuse them of that notion.

"Well, the scouts report that they are coming right at us," said the Colonel. "One hell of a lot of them, too."

"Good," replied the Major, who, like in many regiments, was a real professional while the colonel was not, "it would be an awful mess if they tried to swing around us and hit the baggage train. They can move so damn fast they could have us spinning in circles if they wanted to."

"No, apparently they want to fight. But the General isn't taking any chances. You can see he's got us deployed in an arc. He's going to tuck the baggage train right up tight and if the savages go for our rear we can just bend the line around and we'll be practically in a circle."

"Like as not, it will be up to the cavalry to do most of the bending," said the Major, scratching at his chin.

"Right, so we'll have to be ready to move."

The conversation shifted to non-military matters for a few minutes and then one of the other officers turned to Matt. "Well, Captain Krasner, have any of your men seen any fireflies lately?"

There were a few laughs and then silence fell on the group. Everyone was watching him. He had not said anything to these people, but clearly the story had spread. Keeping his voice carefully level he replied: "No, sir, not a one. I'm hoping it stays that way."

The group relaxed slightly but another officer jumped into the pause. "You know we do hear the most outlandish stories, Captain. I mean about how Fort Pollentia fell. But you were there, sir. What really happened?"

"I'm afraid I can't really answer that, sir. I was out on a patrol when the fort fell. We were ambushed ourselves and only a few of us escaped. By the time we got back to the fort, it was all over."

"But what about these tales of magic fireflies that explode gunpowder? I've heard stories that you saw them yourself."

"Captain Milhar," said the Colonel, breaking in. "This must be a rather painful subject for Captain Krasner. Perhaps we should not press him for stories so soon after the tragedy. I'm sure he lost many a good friend at the fort."

"Of course, sir. My apologies, Captain. I should have been more thoughtful. Still, one does have to wonder what we might be riding into..."

"I only know what I saw," said Matt quietly.

"Indeed. And what did you see, sir?"

Before Matt could answer, there was the sound of firing in the distance. It was quite dark now and everyone stood up and looked toward the west. A few small flashes of light appeared and then, a few seconds later, the sound of a few pops.

"Those are our pickets. I think we can assume the enemy has arrived," said the Colonel. They continued to watch and after a while some horsemen came riding in. The sentries challenged them and then passed them through. A half-dozen hussars trotted past the group of officers.

"What did you see?" asked the Colonel.

"Kaifs. One bloody lot of Kaifs. Two less than there were a few minutes ago, but still a hell of a lot of 'em. We're going to be busy come morning!"

The troopers rode off, but the officers continued to stand there, sipping their wine and looking across the valley. By ones and twos and then by tens and twenties, campfires sprang up on the far ridge. In a remarkably short time there was a blazing constellation of them. Finally, the Colonel stirred.

"Yes, I believe we shall be very busy come morning."

Atark sat in Zarruk's tent and watched the angry man wave his sword.

"One of my men was killed by those cursed fire-weapons," snarled Ka-Noyen Battai. "You had promised that your shaman could steal their power!"

"As we've explained many times, my lord," said Zarruk, "Atark's magic requires preparation. He can only be in one place at a time and I, for one, do not wish him with the army's vanguard where he might be slain by some misfortune. I mourn the loss of your man, but he will be avenged when Atark works his magic tomorrow and we destroy the enemy army."

"So you keep promising! I shall believe that when I see it happen with my own eyes!"

"We saw the remains of the enemy fort when we rode through the pass," said Ka-Noyen Oliark "Was that not enough to convince you?"

"No, it was not," said Battai defiantly. "A mighty deed, to be sure, but I have no proof of how it was done."

"It was done like this, oh, mighty Ka," said Atark, growing impatient. He held up his hand and a ball of bright flame appeared in it. There were a few gasps among the onlookers and Battai drew back a pace. It was the same spell he had used to destroy Gerrik, but this time no one would be destroyed. Instead, he flung the ball into the pile of wood the women were preparing to light. The logs and sticks instantly burst into flames. The women shrieked and scrambled away in such a fashion as to make the men laugh. This was enough to break the tension in the tent. Battai finally nodded his head and sheathed his sword and sat down on some cushions.

"I too grieve the loss of your warrior," said Atark to Battai. "But surely all here realize that we are engaged in a great task. Some of our men will die in the doing. But their names will be remembered by the loremasters and sung by the bards as long as our people exist."

"Well said!" exclaimed Oliark. "And were there no danger at all, then what glory would lie in the deed, eh, Battai?"

"True enough," growled Battai. "But the men, perhaps, expect too much. They grow careless."

"That surely is our responsibility," said Oliark. "The Kas and the Noyens must see that their men act as warriors and not carrion birds. Remind them to fight as they always have. If mighty Atark can smooth the path for us, all well and good. But tell your men to put their trust in their sword and bow!"

"You speak wisely, Ka Oliark," said Atark, and he meant it. He had never met Oliark before, but the man seemed intelligent and reasonable—qualities all too often lacking in the army's leaders.

Conversation was interrupted for a moment as the women came and served the first course of the meal and poured out the wine and *yetchi*. Zarruk was entertaining all of the Ka-Noyen and their retinues in his tent. His own wives and slaves were insufficient to the task, so some of the other women were helping out, Thelena and her slave among them. Thelena poured his goblet of *yetchi* and the slave set a plate down before him, bowed, and scurried away.

The woman was dressed almost completely in Kaifeng fashion now: linen blouse, long wool skirt, split for riding, and a short leather vest. Thelena must have found the clothing for her. Her hair was braided properly, too. Except for the hair being such a dark brown and her feet being bare, she could have passed for Kaifeng. The wound on her cheek was fading, but there would definitely be a scar. Atark stirred uneasily; for some reason he found the woman more provocative now than when she had been naked. He sighed. The woman was clearly adapting to her slavery very quickly. In all likelihood she would be a fixture in his tent for many years to come. He noticed that Zarruk's slaves, on the other hand, were wearing far less than Thelena's. He suspected Zarruk was using them to remind the gathered leaders what booty awaited them when victory was won. Zarruk was becoming very shrewd and Atark approved.

"I still say I should take my *helar* around to the enemy rear at first light," said Ferache, the fourth of the Kas. "The enemy is no more agile than an ox stuck in the mud. We could be among their wagons before they realized it."

"There is no need for such a stratagem, my lord," said Zarruk "All of their wagons will be ours in any case. If we follow the plan that has been laid out, a great victory is assured."

"A moment ago we agreed not to place all of our hopes on the magic of your shaman," countered Ferache. "Now you counsel we should do exactly that."

"That is different! Atark cannot accompany every group of scouts, but once the enemy army is assembled in one spot, he can deal with all of their gunpowder at once. If we attempt to be clever, the enemy may disperse and escape Atark's spell. Is that not so, my friend?" All eyes turned back to him.

"Yes. Keep the enemy all together and I can deal with them all together." He spoke with assurance, but he was not entirely sure of the truth of his words. He had no idea what the farthest range of the seekers really was. He suspected that it was fairly short, but he did not know for sure, so perhaps it was not vital to keep the enemy all in a group. He was even less certain he could produce a spell powerful enough to deal with the entire enemy army all at once even if they remained concentrated. He would try, but he was filled with real doubts. Still, the spell he had just cast had scarcely tired him at all. He was getting stronger and stronger.

"So you ask us to charge straight against the enemy's fire weapons?" asked Battai. "It seems like madness to me. If you fail to do what you promise, we will be cut to pieces!"

"He will not fail," said Zarruk. "And to show you my confidence in him, I will be in the first line of the attack."

A low murmur filled the tent. Some nodded in approval, but the other Kas all looked put out. Zarruk had craftily claimed the post of honor for himself and considering how he had done it—in support of his own shaman—none of the others could challenge him for it. Atark forced himself not to smile.

"Well, then," growled Ferache. "When do we launch the attack? First light?" For some reason all eyes seemed to turn to Atark. He waited a moment before saying anything.

"If it is all the same to you, My Lords, I would prefer to wait until later in the morning. I've never liked getting up early. And in any case, we really should permit the enemy to make his breakfast." He paused and looked at the puzzled faces around him. He cracked a tiny smile. "After all, it is customary to allow doomed men a last meal, isn't it?"

"Rise and shine, sir," said Sergeant Chenik who was shaking Matt gently. "They've passed the word for the wake-up. No bugles this morning."

"It's still dark," grumbled Matt. "I just got to sleep. Go away."

"Sorry, sir. Orders."

Matt groaned and threw off his blankets. He saw that it wasn't quite dark anymore. The eastern horizon was a bright blue. The sun would be up very soon. Men were moving all around him and the horses were stirring and snorting. Fires were being built up and the morning meals were being scrounged. He shivered. The air had turned colder during the night and there was a heavy dew. He was still soggy, just like yesterday.

He shuffled over to the nearest fire and tried to warm himself. After a while his servant approached with a cup of hot tea which he took gratefully. The hot liquid seemed to bring him back to life. A few minutes later the man returned with breakfast: the last of the bacon along with the last of the soft bread. Somewhere he had managed to get hold of an egg. At least two eggs, Matt suspected, but only one had found its way onto his plate. He munched on the food slowly as the sun came up and his shadow stretched away in front of him. After today, it would only be hard bread and salt pork and dried beef. It was very fortunate that the Kaifeng were offering battle like this. The army could only carry a few weeks' rations in the supply wagons and there was no hope of foraging under the circumstances. If the enemy had just harried them without committing to a major fight, eventually the army would be forced to retreat for lack of supplies.

The enemy certainly knew this. So why were they so eager to fight? Matt was afraid he knew. *Fireflies.* The Kaifeng were not fools. Even though their bows could do a lot of damage, they would be pounded by musket and cannon in return if they tried a direct assault. If they were going to be so obliging as to come straight at them, it could only be for a reason. A chill passed through Matt that the tea could do nothing to dispel. He'd been clinging to his hopes during the last week of skirmishing that the Kaifeng could not do again whatever they had done at the fort. A week with lots of gunfire and no fireflies. But now he was quite sure his hope had been in vain. He looked around at the army. If the fireflies hit them the way they had the fort…

"Are you finished, sir?" Matt looked up to see his servant standing there. He handed over the empty plate and mug and then went back to where he'd left his blanket roll. What could he do? No last-minute warning about the fireflies was going to do any good. They had not believed him before and they would not believe him now. Hell, even if they *did*, what could they do about it at this late hour? Throw all the powder away and try to fight with saber and bayonet? The Kaifs would just stand off and shower them with arrows.

The word came down to get mounted, and the men dumped out the last of their tea onto the campfires and began rolling up their blankets and saddling the horses. There was very little unnecessary talk. Whether the men were tired or scared or just had nothing to say, Matt didn't know. Veteran though he was, he'd never been in a situation like this before: part of a large army preparing for battle. His servant brought him his horse and he buckled on his sword belt. He set his tricorn hat firmly on his head and then mounted.

"All right, fall them in, Sergeant," he said to Chenik, who had come up beside him. The Sergeant started bawling out orders and the company assembled itself along the lines that had been laid out the night before. The regiment was drawn up in a column by squadron. Matt's company was number two, which put them in the first squadron, which was at the head of the column. Matt was happy about that: he could see a bit better. The other regiments of their brigade were assembling as well, and Matt could see the infantry forming lines and taking their muskets from the stacks. Standards were unfurled and they fluttered bravely in the freshening breeze.

By the time the army was ready, the sun was a hand's width above the horizon. But the enemy had done very little as far as Matt could see. Smoke rose from innumerable campfires, and the Kaifeng were apparently still eating breakfast. What would happen if the Berssian cavalry suddenly charged? Could they catch the Kaifs by surprise and spoil whatever plans they might have? But no movement was made. The General was going to let the enemy begin the battle. After perhaps a quarter hour he heard the first horn calls from across the valley. As if that were a signal for his own side, fifes and drums and bands began to play along the line of the Berssian Army. It was a cheering sound that did nothing to cheer Matt.

He could finally see some motion in the enemy camp. Horsemen were coming forward. They halted about a mile away and were joined by more and more and more. Matt told himself that a man on a horse took up far more room than an infantryman in ranks. Even though the armies were nearly the same strength, the Kaifeng, all being horsemen, were going to look a lot more imposing. And they certainly were starting to look very imposing. They made no attempt to form any sort of ranks and if they had any organization more complex than a mob, he could not see it. But there certainly were a *lot* of them.

A musical chanting from close by dragged his eyes away from the enemy host. A group of men in robes carrying icons on poles and swinging incense burners were walking along the lines of troops. Chaplains. The Berssian troops worshipped a dozen different gods and there were chaplains for all of them scattered through the regiments. The soldiers were praying to the gods of their choice, some making ritual signs with their hands, some actually dismounting and abasing themselves on the ground. Matt looked back to the gathering mass of enemy horsemen.

"Pray, Sergeant," he whispered to Chenik. "Pray to every god you've ever heard of."

"I am, sir. But I don't know as any of them give protection from fireflies. What are we going to do, sir? What do we do if there are fireflies?"

Matt drew his saber and ran his finger along the blade.

"We'll keep praying—and then we'll kill as many of those bastards as we can."

The horns were ringing out through the camps. The horns were calling the People of the Kaif to battle. Atark, master shaman to Ka-Noyen Zarruk, walked from his tent and was greeted by the ringing cheers of hundreds of people. He nodded his head slightly in acknowledgment, but kept walking. This adulation embarrassed him. He was not doing this for his own glory, but for the glory of the Kaifeng and for vengeance upon the East. Unfortunately, it would only get worse once this day's work was done. Right now only the ones who had seen him do his magic at the forts were cheering. In a few hours it might be them all.

Scores upon scores upon scores of warriors were moving into position. The enemy army was on the high ground a half league away. Atark could see the rigid lines of infantry and the cannons interspersed between them. It was an imposing spectacle, but he would soon turn that order into chaos and the warriors would sweep it all away. Or so he hoped. He had spent the pre-dawn hours in meditation to clear and focus his mind for the great task. He believed he could do it. He would do it!

"Are you ready, my old friend?" asked Zarruk as he rode up with his escort.

"Yes. Let us begin." Atark mounted a horse that was being held for him. He glanced briefly back at his tent. Thelena was there, smiling and waving. He nodded to her and then followed Zarruk.

The cheers grew louder as they rode out of the camp and into the area in which the warriors were assembling. But now not all of the cheers were for Atark. In fact, probably very few were. Instead the cheers were for the Kas who were taking their places with their *helars.* As they neared the center of the army, the cheers for Zarruk increased. These were the men of his *helar* and he had proven himself in front of many of them. They also knew Atark, of course, so they cheered him as well.

Zarruk slowed and then turned his horse. "I must take my position. We will begin the attack when we see the golden ball of light."

"Very well. Stand ready, it will not be long," replied Atark. He hesitated for a moment and then extended his hand. Zarruk seized it immediately.

"Today, my friend."

"Today."

They parted. Zarruk and his escort made his way through the warriors to the front. Atark turned and went up the slight rise to where his own people were making the final preparations. They had erected a small wooden platform. He had not asked them to do this, but they had insisted it was only proper that he be elevated. The materials he would need were there. The sacrifices were in place. They were all tightly bound and gagged. Most of them knew what was to happen and their eyes stared white with fright. There were six score of them, all the remaining men taken at the first fort. This was far more than he had ever used before. He hoped he would be able to withstand the huge energies he was to unleash.

As he dismounted, one of the captives managed to wriggle free of the guard holding him and thrash around on the ground in panic. He was quickly hauled back into place. Atark wondered if drugging the sacrifices would reduce the power he got from them in any way. He would have to test that out. If it did not, then it would be easier—and more merciful—to have them all drugged in the future.

He nodded to his attendants and then stepped up onto the platform. He looked out on a mighty army. The massed horsemen of the Kaifeng were spread out before him. And they were all looking to him. Looking to him to give the signal to attack. Looking to him to give them victory. A great thrill passed though him, a mighty strength seemed to fill him. He raised both his fists and looked at the sky.

"Shelena, my wife! Ardan, my son!" he cried in a great voice. "Can you see? Can you see? Look down from the heavens! Look down and see! Your vengeance is at hand!"

Kareen huddled in the tent and listened to the cheers. Thousands and thousands of voices were cheering and chanting in the Kaifeng tongue. She was learning more and more of their language, but the only word she could make out for certain was: *death*. Death, but for who? She understood that a great battle was at hand. The Berssian Army was a few miles away and a battle would be fought today. She prayed the Berssians would win, but she feared they would not. Atark was here and he would use his magic just as before. But surely even he could not destroy an entire army! Kareen knelt on the carpet and prayed.

She looked up as Thelena entered the tent. The woman had a strange look on her face. "Is…is it starting?" asked Kareen.

"Soon. Very soon."

"You will not watch?"

"No." Thelena sat down on some cushions and took up a wine skin. She filled a cup and took a long drink and then grimaced. Kareen looked on in puzzlement. This was her second cup of wine today and she rarely ever drank at all.

"Are you all right, Thelena?"

"Yes. I'll be fine. How are you feeling?"

"I'm all right. My back is nearly healed. Thank you for giving me these clothes. I...I feel much better about going out of the tent now."

"Is anyone bothering you?"

Kareen reddened and stared down.

"Speak," commanded Thelena.

"There are three men who wait for me. Not every day. And some days I can avoid them. But other days..."

Thelena stared at her and took another long drink. "Do these men have yellow and green ribbons in their braids?"

"Yes. Yes, they all do."

Thelena nodded grimly. "Kuttari bastards. They have a feud with my father. They think that by raping you—his slave—that they dishonor him." She laughed. "He could not care less about that. But if the Kuttari even think they are winning a victory against him by grazing in his fields, it does dishonor him and will weaken his influence with the tribes. I will speak to my father. He may be able to do something."

"Thank you! Thank you, Thelena. They...they are very cruel."

"I'm sure. But my father will not be doing this to save you, Kareen. It is a matter of his honor. You are nothing to him."

"And to you? Am I anything to you?"

Thelena looked at her for a long time without answering. She opened her mouth to say something, but then she suddenly twitched and knocked the cup of wine on the ground. A sound came out of her mouth then, but it was not speech. It was a terrible moan. The woman slid off the cushions onto the ground. She grabbed her head with her hands.

"Thelena!" cried Kareen in alarm. "What's wrong?" She scrambled over to Thelena. She was lying on her back and staring straight up. She was clutching herself so tightly that her fingernails were drawing blood on her scalp.

"Thelena!"

"Looks like they are about ready," said Sergeant Chenik.

"Yes. Any time now, I would think," answered Matt.

The Kaifeng were massed across the shallow valley about a mile away. Thousands upon thousand of them. They were many, many ranks deep, although they had nothing resembling ranks. Strangely, or perhaps not so strangely, they were making no effort to move around the Berssian's flanks. They were all clumped together, opposite the center, although there were Kaifs opposite every part of the Berssian line.

The enemy had made no move forward yet, but the Berssian general was not going to wait for them to do so. Bugles rang out up and down the line. As Matt watched, the infantry battalions went from line of battle into columns and then opened out into hollow squares. Then they expertly pivoted an eighth of a circle so that one corner of each square was pointed right at the enemy.

"Why're they doing that?" asked a nearby trooper. He was a new recruit. "They've opened up gaps all along the line now. The Kaifs could ride right through!"

"That's what the general's hoping for," said Matt. "The damn Kaif bows could make real trouble for us if they just stand off and shoot. If we can lure them in by making them think they can get into our rear, so much the better. See how the squares are arranged? Each face of each square can fire straight ahead without hitting any friend—well, except for the gunners, but they'll have the sense to get out of the way. If the Kaifs try to ride through, they'll be shot to pieces."

Assuming there's anyone to shoot them.

The trooper looked satisfied and more confident. Matt envied him. The maneuver was completed flawlessly and now the army waited.

"Well, let's get on with it!" growled Chenik. "No point waiting here the whole blamed day!"

Matt agreed. Get on with it. But nothing happened for another quarter of an hour and then there was a great deal of cheering and chanting from the enemy army. Matt squinted and thought he could see small groups clustered around banners moving toward the front. "Must be their leaders. Stand ready everyone. It should not be long now."

"Sir!" hissed Chenik. Matt looked where the sergeant was pointing and his heart sank. A golden ball of light had appeared behind the enemy center. It looked just like the other one when the squadron had died—except this one was larger. Much larger. The enemy had still not moved. Before, they had already started their charge before the ball had appeared, but not this time. Why? No matter, Matt knew exactly what was going to happen—and he knew what he had to do.

"Get rid of your powder!" he screamed. "Take off your cartridge boxes! Throw away your musketoon and pistols!"

"Do it!" roared Chenik. The men looked around in confusion and then caught sight of the gold ball—just as it exploded into a million sparks.

"Fireflies!" cried a half-dozen men simultaneously.

"Get rid of your powder!" Matt was still screaming and the twelve Survivors were doing so as well. Everyone in the regiment had heard the crazy stories those men had been telling. Now, suddenly, they realized they had not been so crazy after all. Men began tearing off the slings that held their cartridge boxes. Musketoons and pistols went flying to thud down in the thick grass. A few of the other officers sat there in stunned amazement, but then started shouting the same command.

Matt was carrying no powder, so all he had to do was shout. But he was watching the fireflies, too. There were an incredible number of them and they were flying straight for the center of the army. They began to spread out, but they were clearly going to reach the middle of the line first. As soon as they were past the Kaifeng, the enemy began to trot forward.

The neat lines of Berssian troops began to fall apart as more and more men saw what was coming. Perhaps a few of them had heard the stories, but certainly most had not. The majority had no clue what the glittering fireflies were.

They soon found out.

The fireflies reached the closest troops and the men disappeared in puffs of white smoke. An artillery battery's guns fired themselves off and then a moment later the battery was blown to bits in a series of large explosions as their caissons detonated. The cloud of fireflies spread out, as if seeking new victims. More battalions were wrapped in smoke, more batteries were shattered. Matt looked on and felt ill.

Insanely, he thought of when he had been a small child. He had taken a vase off the shelf. It was very valuable and it was his mother's favorite. She had come into the room suddenly and he had dropped it. It was only a three-foot drop to the floor, but it had seemed to take forever. He watched it drop and drop and thought about how sad his mother was going to be. About how angry his father was going to be. About how much the paddling was going to hurt. There had been plenty of time to think all those thoughts—but somehow not enough time to reach down and grab the vase before it smashed to pieces on the floor.

The sparks were getting closer and a new series of small explosions tore through the air. They were louder and sharper than the cartridge boxes, and they were followed by the most horrible screams.

"Gods!" hissed Chenik. "The Grenadiers!"

A moan escaped Matt's throat. There were four regiments of grenadiers among the Guards. Big men, trained and disciplined and good with the bayonet. Matt had had some hopes that these men could do some good even without being able to fire their muskets. He had forgotten that each man carried two or three small hollow iron spheres packed with gunpowder. Dangerous weapons to friend and foe alike, but on this day it was only the friends who were in danger. Even one of those exploding right next to a person...

"There are no Grenadiers, Sergeant," said Matt.

"Shit, here they come."

The fireflies swept toward them, mangling the army as they came. Matt just sat and stared. There was nothing he could do. The vase had hit the floor. All around him men were screaming. Some tried to run, others threw themselves on the ground. It made no difference. The gunpowder blew up all the same.

The sparks were here. They zipped past him and around him and there were hundreds of pops as guns discharged and cartridges exploded, but most were yards away instead of close by. Almost all of his company had tossed away their lethal burdens. One or two had not and a few horses went down. Matt had a glimpse of the other companies and saw that fewer men had heeded his frantic shouts. Some had, but not enough. Men and horses screamed and tumbled. Then the smoke blotted everything out and he could see nothing.

"Stand fast! Hold your ground!" he shouted. "Wait!"

A series of huge explosions rocked the ground. They came from the rear and Matt guessed they were the reserve ammunition wagons. "14th Dragoons! Stand fast! Rally on me!" he cried. He had no clue if the colonel or the other officers were still in action, but he shouted anyway.

It was doubtful that anyone more than a few yards away could hear him. Even with the explosions fading, they were being replaced with the moans and screams of the wounded, the shouts of officers, sergeants and terrified men...

...and the steadily growing war cries of the Kaifeng warriors.

Matt could hear them getting closer, but the smoke was still too thick to see them. He could not just sit here and let them overrun his company!

"14th Dragoons! Forward! Forward at the trot!"

As he shouted, the smoke thinned a bit and he could see for a dozen yards. He shouted the order again and waved his sword and kneed his horse into motion. He gasped in relief as his men went forward with him. The order was repeated by NCOs farther down the line and more and more men obeyed.

Matt broke out of the smoke and nearly quailed. There was an endless line of Kaifeng horsemen stretching out of his sight in both directions. They were galloping toward him and only two hundred yards away. He glanced back and saw perhaps a hundred and fifty dragoons following him: his own company and whatever other troopers who had managed to throw away their powder and hear the command to advance.

"Close up! Close up! Forward at the canter!"

The pace picked up and the men closed in on him as they had been trained to do. In a moment they were in a solid rank, literally knee to knee with the men on either side. Sergeant Chenik was right next to him. The Kaifs were sixty yards away.

"Charge!" he cried with all the force his lungs could produce. The dragoons broke into a gallop. The Kaifs were thirty yards away and Matt could see that those immediately in front of him were not happy about it. They had charged forward without discipline, expecting an easy fight, and were now unexpectedly faced with an ordered counter-charge by men with murder in their eyes. A few of them tried to halt or turn aside, but there was no place to go with the crush of their fellows.

Matt had his saber poised and was suddenly only a yard away from a Kaif who had unwisely tried to get out his bow. Matt drove the point of his blade into the man's throat. Matt had never killed anyone before, or even seriously hurt a man. Right now he didn't give a damn. He wrenched his sword loose from the man he had slain and struck at the next one who appeared. The Kaif partially blocked his blow, but he still slashed away part of the man's face and an instant later Chenik finished him.

The dragoons had heavier horses and they were moving downhill. The Kaifeng were not in a close formation and the 14th Dragoons sliced right through them, leaving two score of dead or wounded in their wake. They broke through the first mass of Kaifs, but did not pause. They realigned their ranks, filled in the gaps left by their own dead, and pressed forward. The second line of enemy had a bit more warning, but it did them little good. The Dragoons crashed into them. Matt killed another man and then another. His horse knocked one of the smaller plains ponies right over and he trampled the rider.

Matt was screaming at the top of his lungs. His only desire was to kill Kaifs until he was killed himself. What else was there to do? They broke through the second wave and Matt rallied his men for the next charge. He only had about a hundred men left, but they had killed more Kaifs than that. There were no more enemy directly to his front—they had punched right through the enemy army—so he wheeled his troopers around to the left.

Then he saw the Berssians.

The Army of Berssia was on the ridge and it was dying where it stood. Despite his gallant little charge, he had done nothing to halt the Kaifeng attack. They had swept up the hill into the demoralized and disordered ranks of the army and they were butchering anyone they could reach. A huge mass of horsemen was milling around on the ridge, swords flashing red in the morning sun. As he watched, a Kaif horseman came galloping down the hill holding a Berssian flag. The sight froze him for a moment.

Then something zipped by his head. Another. They were arrows and he realized that the enemy they had smashed through had now turned and strung their bows. Arrows started to rain down on them. A trooper fell with a shriek. Then a horse went down.

"We can't stay here!" shouted Chenik.

"Forward! Forward, men! Forward at the canter!" The horses were getting tired, but Chenik was right: they could not stay here. They had to move. He led his men back the way they had come—back against the enemy. There was open ground off to their left now. Maybe even the possibility of escape, but not a man faltered. The enemy was in front of them and that was the direction to go!

"With me! Follow me! Forward! For...!" An arrow struck his horse in the throat and it stumbled with a gurgling scream. Matt knew he was going down and kicked his feet free of the stirrups. Then the horse toppled over on its side. Matt nearly got clear, but the beast landed on his left foot and pinned it. There was some pain, but he did not think anything was broken. He tried to drag himself free, but his foot caught on something. Maybe his spur was tangled in some bit of harness. Damn! He had to get loose!

"You all right?" shouted a voice from close by. He looked up and saw Chenik on his horse towering over him. He glanced up the hill and saw the dragoons still charging forward. Their ranks were being thinned by the Kaif arrows, but they were still going on!

"Yes! I just need to get free. You should have stayed with the men, Sergeant!"

"Gotta look after you, sir. You need help?"

"No, I think I can..."

Another equine scream cut him off. He jerked his head up to see Chenik's horse rearing with an arrow in its chest. It was going to fall...

...right on him. Matt twisted and covered his head with his arms. An instant later a crushing weight slammed down on him and everything went black.

CHAPTER ELEVEN

"Good luck and have a safe voyage home, Jarren," said Master Dauros. "A lot of our hopes are riding with you, my friend."

"Thank you, sir," said Jarren. "I'll try not to let you down."

"Do more than try, Master Jarren," said Stephanz. "We have placed our very lives in your hands. If you stumble, we shall be the ones to fall." Jarren nodded; Stephanz had been making gloomy statements like that for four weeks and he was getting a bit tired of them.

"I have given my word that I will not reveal the location of this island, nor reveal anything other than what was agreed upon, sir. I can promise no more."

"Nor do we have a right to ask any more," said Dauros, cocking an eyebrow at Stephanz. "We take the risk with open eyes and you have my trust, young Jarren."

"And mine, too," said Idira. "I'll be following your progress closely, Jarren. And I'll be making my plans for the school for healers when the time is right."

"Surely that is years away, Idira, if, indeed, it ever becomes practical!" said Stephanz.

"We cannot know for sure," said Dauros. "We can hope that it will not be too long, but Stephanz is correct that it might be many years. We shall not rush into things."

"I shall be careful, sir," said Jarren. "But how will we contact each other? I know I've asked this before, but surely we shall need to communicate."

"For now you must be content, Jarren," said Dauros. "We have means of following your progress and if it becomes necessary, we can get a message to you. For now, that will have to do."

"Very well, sir. If that's what you want."

"Yes. And you do have enough material to keep you occupied for quite a while, I would think," said Dauros, pointing to Jarren's bulging portfolio. He smiled and nodded. He had been filling paper with notes for almost four weeks without a pause. He had used up all his own paper and had been forced to beg for more from his hosts. He had spent hour after hour with Idira, listening to her talk about the type of magic she practiced. She had demonstrated her skills as much as could be done without any actual injuries to treat or serious diseases to cure. He'd spent some time with the others, too, but his agreement with Dauros precluded him making extensive studies. He especially regretted not being able to work with the artificers. They had an incredible collection of magical devices—old Porfino would have thought he was in heaven—and they actually *knew* how many of them worked!

Still, Dauros was correct: he had more than enough material for several books. The information on the aftermath of Soor would allow for an entirely revised edition of *Downfall of the Wizards*. Oto Weibelan had already hinted he would consider a co-authorship if Jarren brought back the required information. The other things he had could fill a year's worth of lectures and many papers. His future academic career was already assured. And if he could follow up by producing a live wizard or two...!

"Oh, by the way, Jarren," said Dauros, "Brother Rianzzi is extraordinarily sensitive to ripples in the 'lake' and yesterday he felt a significant one from far to the southwest. It probably is nothing: such things do happen naturally from time to time, but you might want to keep an ear and an eye open for any news from that area."

"Yes, sir, I'll do that."

"We are ready to depart, Lord," said Lyni coming up and curtsying to Dauros. "All the baggage is loaded, we only await the passengers."

"Well! Then I suppose I should let them go. Good-bye, Jarren. I sincerely hope we are able to meet again."

"Good-bye, sir. I hope so, too." Jarren bowed and then followed Lyni out the door of the library. Gez had been prowling around the foyer of the hall and now attached himself to Jarren.

"We leavin'?" he asked.

"Yes. Time to head home."

"Through that bloody town again? Erberus or whatever it was called?"

"I'm afraid so. But we have been guaranteed safe passage. There's nothing to worry about."

"Like hell. I'm gonna load that dinky pistol of yours before we get there and you bloody well carry it, mister!"

"I don't think that will be necessary."

"All right, I'll carry it then."

"Gez!"

"Alright, alright! But remember it's my neck, too."

"I've already saved your neck once. I think you owe me this."

"Aw, I was doing okay. Just needed to catch my breath and I coulda swum out of there."

"Really?"

"Well..."

The boy fell silent and they concentrated on following Lyni down the many steps that led to the dock. It was a gray and windy day. A few drops of rain were falling by the time they reached the boat. They hopped in and almost immediately the vessel was cast off from the dock. The sail unfurled itself and caught the wind and the boat surged forward sharply enough to almost throw Jarren off his feet.

"I suppose you will be glad to see the last of us," said Jarren to Lyni.

"If it is the last of you, then yes, I'll be glad."

"You don't like me," said Jarren.

"My, you *are* observant."

"Why? What have I done to anger you, so?"

"Not you personally, but what you represent."

"And what is that?"

"Danger."

"So you side with Stephanz on this issue."

"Yes. I have my own reasons to hate and distrust the mainlanders, just as they hate and distrust my kind. I do not believe that the two can live together. We are better off separated."

"I'm sorry. And I do hope you are wrong."

"I'm not."

"You could still invoke the fishbait option."

"Dauros has ordered otherwise and I will obey him."

She would say nothing more and Jarren turned to look back at the rapidly dwindling island. He did hope he could return here someday, but he feared he would never see the place again.

A few minutes later, the wall of fog swallowed them up and the island was gone.

"You don't have to carry me, Sergeant," growled Matt. "Save your strength for yourself."

"Just so you keep up, sir. Them bastards will spit you if you can't. I've seen 'em doing it."

"So have I. Don't worry, I'll keep up."

Chenik grunted and then they both stopped talking to save their breath. Matt was sweating. The weather had turned warm again, which was fortunate since the Kaifs had stripped them of everything except their trousers. Matt cursed as he stepped on a sharp stone. His boots were gone and his feet were cut and bruised. Just about all the rest of him was bruised, too. Chenik's horse had fallen on him and he was black and blue from head to foot. Everything hurt. But amazingly, nothing was broken. Or he didn't think so.

He had come back to his senses to find that Chenik had freed him from under the horse. Unfortunately, he had also come to his senses to find that there were a dozen Kaifeng warriors around them with drawn weapons. Chenik was standing there with an arrow through his arm and a bloody sleeve. His sword was on the ground.

Matt had scarcely been able to move, so there had been no hope of fighting. The Kaifs took them prisoner and herded them off to where all the other captives were being kept. There had seemed like a large number of them, but it was actually shockingly few compared to how many soldiers there had been in the army. Maybe a thousand were left alive. At least among the soldiers.

As with any army, there had been a large group of camp followers tagging along. The Kaifs had scooped them up with everything else. The first day and night of Matt's captivity had been filled with the cries of the women. The men had been too stunned, or in Matt's case too bruised, to make any trouble at all. Matt had managed to remove the arrow in Chenik's arm and bandage him as best he could. But it wasn't a good job at all and they both knew it.

They had been marched east for the last three days and all the captives were nearing the end of their endurance. They had only been fed once and not given nearly enough water. Matt's mouth was parched.

"Hell, and I thought those bloody gendarmes were bastards," gasped Chenik.

There was a commotion up ahead and Matt saw that a man had collapsed. He was still wearing the red leggings of the Guard artillery. Two of his comrades pulled him to his feet and they staggered along for another hundred paces before all three of them fell. One of the Kaif lancers rode up and shouted at them. They tried to get the man to his feet, but could not. The Kaif just shrugged and drove his lance into the man's body. The two others stared for a few moments and then shuffled along with the rest of the prisoners. Three days ago, there might have been a fight, but by now, the prisoners didn't have the strength for any resistance. Matt trudged by the body of the man. He was face down with a bloody hole in his back. Chenik was cursing beside him.

"What…what d'you think they're gonna do with us?" gasped a man at Matt's side. He looked over and saw that it was Private Teeldor, the last surviving Survivor. None of the others had made it through the battle. Matt had listened with pride when Teeldor described the dragoons' last stand.

"I don't know," said Matt. "I can't think they are going to drag us all this way just to kill us. The Kaifs will make slaves out of the women and children, but I don't know what they want with us."

"The shape we're in, we wouldn't even make much sport for torture," said Chenik. "Course I suppose they could let us rest and feed us first."

"You're thinking again, Sergeant. Stop it."

"Yes, sir."

They marched along in silence, passing several other bodies in the road. There had been a thousand or so when they started this, but Matt doubted if there were even seven hundred now. Around mid-day they were allowed to stop next to a stream. It had been muddied by those who had come by before them, but they didn't care. They drank their fill and washed the filth off themselves. Matt tried to change the bandage on Chenik's arm, but all he could do was rinse the cloth out and tie it on again. The wound looked inflamed.

"No surgeon around if it has to come off," observed Chenik, as it he was talking about a hangnail.

"It's not that bad yet."

"Not yet."

They were not given anything to eat, although a few men dug up some sort of roots and were gnawing on them. Suddenly, a large band of Kaifs rode up. Several hundred at least and they were each leading an empty horse. There was a great deal of shouting and then Matt could see that they were grabbing some of the prisoners, tying their hands behind them and then slinging them over the empty horses like sacks.

"What's this all about?" wondered Matt.

"Dunno, but at least those sods get to ride," said Chenik. "Think we ought to volunteer?"

"No. I don't like the looks of this at all. They're not picking the ones who are worst off, they're just grabbing the ones who are nearest. Let's skip this party, Sergeant."

"If you say so."

The Kaifs finished what they were doing and rode off with the men they had selected. All too soon the rest of them were on the move again. They were prodded back to their feet and the march continued. By the middle of the afternoon, Matt was almost ready to drop and wondering if not getting a ride had been the right decision. He forced his mind away from his own pain and looked around. There were more buildings along the road now. All were deserted and some of them burned.

"That mill looks familiar," muttered Chenik. Matt looked without much interest and then looked again. He *had* seen that mill before. It was not far from the camp they had been in outside of…

"Berssenburg," he hissed. "We're back."

He shook his head. They had left this place so proud and determined, 35,000 men off to rout the Kaifs. Now a mere five hundred stumbled back as miserable captives. It was almost unbelievable. Matt could believe it only because of what he had gone through earlier. He could scarcely imagine what was going through the minds of the other men. A nightmare.

Booom!

There was suddenly a low rumble from beyond the next ridge. Then another. Then a whole series that blended into each other.

"Gods! They're attacking the city!" hissed Matt.

As they continued to march, clouds of smoke began to appear. First they were white smoke, but they quickly turned to black. The column somehow instinctively quickened its pace, prisoners and guards alike. Another few hundred yards and they would be over the ridge and could see…

More rumbles. Louder now and sharper. More smoke. A white thundercloud hovered just beyond the ridge and columns of black smoke were rising up to mix with it. *Boom, boom, boom,* the explosions continued. The head of the column reached the top of the ridge and halted. Those that followed crowded up behind and then spread out on either side of the road. Their guards seemed as transfixed as the prisoners. All just stood and stared. Matt and Chenik hobbled off the road and around to the right of the crowd to get a clear view. A moment later Berssenburg was laid out before them.

"Gods!"

From the ridge, the city was like a detailed map or an exquisitely crafted model on a table. Matt could see the whole city. The Glovina River was a glittering ribbon that ran from his left to his right. The city sprawled on both banks. It was a large city of a quarter-million people and it was the capital of a very large kingdom. Churches and palaces rose up above the rooftops of the lesser houses, broad boulevards led to parks and plazas. Matt knew that there was an opera house and several museums and a university. By good fortune, most of the city lay on the east side of the river, away from the invaders, but there were still thousands of buildings on the west side. A ring of modern forts dotted the outskirts. They were in the latest, precise mathematical style, mounting hundreds of cannon. Even though the Berssians had sent the bulk of their army west, they had retained many thousands of troops to man those forts.

But the forts were in flames.

As Matt came up to look, the magazine of another fort exploded. A dirty cloud erupted upward with tiny specks that Matt knew were men or cannons flung above it. Long seconds later the noise rolled over them. Columns of black smoke rose up from the other ruined forts and a number of buildings were on fire. Smaller explosions kept puffing up here and there. He could not see any fireflies, but he knew they must be there, doing their fiendish jobs.

Then there was a bright flash down by the river itself. A huge ball of red fire climbed up into the sky and then faded into gray smoke. Across the miles an enormous roar shook the ground.

"The gunpowder works!" cried one of the onlookers.

More explosions. The river was navigable to this point and he saw a ship dissolve in flame. Then the forts on the far shore began to explode as well. Smoke rose up from a hundred points. Many of the Berssian prisoners were weeping now.

The rumbles slowly died away and then Matt heard that hated sound: the cry of Kaifeng warriors riding to the attack. From his position on the ridge he could see the waves of Kaif horsemen riding toward the city.

"By the gods," whispered Chenik. "Can anything stop these bastards?"

"I don't know," said Matt. "I just don't know."

A warrior on a blown horse trotted up the hill and halted in front of the assembled Kas. The man was covered in soot and his sweat had made muddy little tracks down the side of his face. "It is no good, my lords," he gasped. "We have tried, but we cannot break through."

"And why not?" demanded Ka Battai. "The enemy cannons and muskets have been silenced. How can they stop you?"

"Yes, lord, their fire weapons are useless, just as in the great battle. We rode past their forts with no trouble—the fools put them hundreds of paces apart with no connecting walls! We can ride many scores abreast between them!"

"Had their cannons been working, they would have filled those gaps with your broken bodies," said Zarruk.

"No doubt," said Battai, angrily, "But they were not working. So what has stopped you from taking the city?"

"Inside the city, among the houses, there is another wall, lord," said the man. "A much older wall. But it is thirty feet high and made of thick stone. There are many gates in it, but they were all closed. And we found no soldiers among the ruined forts and very few people in the outer houses. They have all fled within this inner wall."

"We gave them too much time," said Atark. "Survivors from the battle probably reached here two days ago. They abandoned the forts and the outer houses and now defend the old wall."

The other Kas frowned and Atark wished he had said nothing. After the battle he had urged speed, but there was far too much loot to be had in the Berssians' baggage train. The army had not even attempted to move for a full day. True, there had been much fine booty and many women. The Berssian general's pretty mistress now served in Zarruk's tent alongside the red-haired girl. But Atark had urged haste. He had now been proved correct-—but it was not a wise thing to remind the Kas of that.

"And you cannot get over this wall?" asked Zarruk.

"No, lord. The Berssians have no fire weapons, but they can throw rocks at us from the walls. And some of them have bows and crossbows. Many have swords. I'm sorry, lord, but this is a great city and the men outnumber us many times. The top of the wall was thick with them. We lost three score of warriors from our *helar* alone. We killed some of them with our bows, but they are difficult targets. Then some of the houses near us caught fire and we had no choice but to retreat."

"Very well," said Zarruk. "Call the men back. We shall make camp and try again tomorrow." The man bowed in his saddle and then rode off. The other Kas were grumbling, but agreed to meet later that night to decide what to do next. They rode away, leaving Atark with Zarruk and his escort.

"So what *shall* we do, my friend?" asked Zarruk.

"I shall have to think on this. I cannot burn stone, so I will need another spell—if that is the way we choose to deal with this."

"If not with your magic, how else? We have no siege engines, nor those skilled in using or making them. Our numbers are still too small for a direct assault."

"They will grow. When word of our victory spreads, our numbers will grow beyond your dreams, Ka Zarruk."

"Yes, you are probably right." Zarruk paused and chuckled. "We have already received a messenger from some of the Varag tribes to the south asking to join us."

"Varags," growled Atark. "They are…not to be trusted."

"I know. They will sell themselves to anyone. But if they try to sell themselves to us, we may find some use for them. I told them to come if they wish."

Atark kept any emotion from his face. "Yes…we'll definitely find some use for them."

"In the meantime," continued Zarruk, "we need to get our men across the river. You can see that they are already moving people east, out of the city. With most of their army destroyed we can go where we will and they can't stop us. If we could get a *helar* across to the far shore, we could pen them all up in the city until we are ready to strike. I will send north and south to seize any boats they can find."

"That sounds wise, my Ka. I shall leave all of that to your skills. For now I must go and meditate before we meet with the others tonight."

"As you will, mighty shaman." Zarruk turned and rode off with his men. Atark stayed there for a while, looking at the burning parts of the city. He felt irritated. This was the first time his magic had failed to bring total victory. The enemy still held their city. All of the best booty had been removed within the walls. Several score of warriors had been killed to no purpose. It irked him. True, he had wreaked terrible damage to the forts and some parts of the city, but other parts were undamaged and the enemy was defiant. He had hoped that the destruction of their army would leave them demoralized and ripe for conquest. But the Berssians had some steel in them yet, it seemed. He needed to think. He needed advice. He turned his horse and rode back to his tent. On his way, he passed the spot where he had worked his magic. People were still dragging the bodies of the sacrifices away. He had instructed that they be properly buried. It only seemed right somehow.

There were many people around his tent and it was obvious that it had just been set up. Men were pounding in the stakes and stretching ropes. Carpets and other goods were being unloaded from horses. He was slightly amazed at how he had acquired a retinue of his own. The small group of assistant/bodyguards provided by Zarruk had grown after each fight. He was not entirely sure who these people even were. Gettain, one of Zarruk's most trusted men, was in charge of them and Atark was willing to trust him, too. He did find it a bit disconcerting to have all these people hovering around him, but he also had to admit it was nice to have someone else set up his tent. Thelena was there and she was directing the activities. She had become the *Qoyen* of his household and was doing an excellent job. Despite their suspicions and jealousies of her, no one dared disobey her orders when it came to his property.

He looked at her closely as he dismounted. She looked very pale and drawn. The latest batch of sacrifices had certainly pained her. But she refused to go away or to take anything stronger than wine. He wished there was something he could do to ease her suffering, but he was also proud of her. She bore her pain without complaint. He smiled at her and she returned it when she saw him. He wanted to be with her and talk with her, but she was busy and he needed to do something, too. He directed one of the men to set up the small tent in a spot away from the others and then he found the wooden box and carefully took it off the horse it had been strapped to.

Unfortunately, with the army grown as much as it had, finding a secluded spot for the small tent meant making quite a walk. He was wishing he had ridden by the time he got there. But at least there was no possibility of Thelena eavesdropping this time. He knew she had done so several times. He didn't exactly object, he was simply worried to allow her to get too close to the Ghost.

Once the tent was set up, he sent the man away and then went inside and closed the flap. A short while later, the image of the Ghost was floating before him.

"*So, another victory, but not a complete one,*" said the Ghost.

"Yes. The enemy huddles behind stone walls and for the moment we cannot get at him. In time, yes, but it could be weeks."

"Or months. Winter will come sooner than you think. You cannot be caught here, still outside the walls, when the snows come."

"I see little choice but to wait. The spells I know cannot bring down stone walls."

"I know of spells which can."

"Indeed? Can you teach them to me?"

"I have given you a great deal already..."

"And I have paid you back in full! Victory after victory..."

"They are but trifles!" said the Ghost and the image flickered red. *"Three hundred years ago this Berssia was nothing! A collection of rude villages, ruled by petty knights. The true East lies farther on. You have scarcely begun to give me the revenge I have paid for! You are still in my debt."*

"You may not have my daughter!" snarled Atark.

"I did not ask for her. But perhaps another. Some young shaman with the talent might consent to the bonding. You cannot imagine what I am enduring in this existence."

"I am sorry. I could release you..."

"No! Not yet! Not while the great task lies undone!"

"I...I will consider it," said Atark after a long pause.

"Do so. But you cannot wait for the spell you need. I will teach it to you now."

"Thank you."

"But be warned: this spell's power exceeds that of the others you have used by many times. You will be tested as never before."

"I understand. I am not afraid."

"Good. But you will need many more sacrifices. Many more."

Kareen waited patiently in line to get her sack filled with flour. There was a huge stack of barrels of the stuff that had been looted from the city and it was being doled out to those that wanted it. Thelena had sent her here to get some. While she waited she stared at the city in the distance. Much of it was still smoldering, but she could just make out a Berssian flag waving defiantly from one of the taller buildings. The city had not fallen yet and that made her feel very good. The Kaifeng were not completely invincible after all!

But then she turned back to look closer by and her heart sank. No, they might not be invincible, but that was little comfort to those who had been captured by them. A great many camp followers had been with the army and they had nearly all been caught. There had been others who had not escaped across the river in time and they were being hunted down, too. A steady stream of warriors were coming into camp with the captives. The captives were mostly women, some battered, some naked and bound over saddles, others simply trudging along behind the horseman with a noose around their neck, a dazed expression on their face. There were a few men, too, and some children. The children usually were taken away by Kaifeng women. The men were taken to the large pen that had been built near one edge of the camp.

The pen for the sacrifices.

Kareen shuddered when she thought about that. She could still scarcely believe that the Kaifeng would slaughter helpless men to power Atark's magic. It was incredibly barbaric even for a barbaric people. After the great battle, Thelena had come out of her fit and then immediately left the tent. She had been so unsteady on her feet Kareen had gone with her. They had swayed and staggered toward the battleground and then she had spotted Atark standing on a wooden platform. They had gotten closer and Kareen recoiled when she saw what was lying on the ground. Over a hundred bodies and their severed heads lay there with their blood soaking into the earth. They were all bound hand and foot and she was quite certain they were all prisoners taken from the fort. She had nearly vomited on the spot. Then she turned and ran back to the tent, leaving Thelena standing there. Later, Thelena had explained what it was all for. The woman was still slightly drunk and dazed, but the explanation left Kareen more dazed still.

Is this to be our fate? she wondered numbly. *Our men to be slaughtered like hogs and the rest of us to serve in the tents and beds of our conquerors?*

But all was not yet lost. For her personally, yes, she had resigned herself to that, but the Berssians were still fighting and the other kingdoms of the East would, too. Even with Atark's terrible magic, perhaps they would not conquer all.

She reached the head of the line and the woman there shoveled the flour into her sack. She gave Kareen a startled look as she finished. She was getting a lot of that lately. Her clothes and her braids made her look like a Kaif at first glance. She supposed as more and more of the new slaves adapted to their lives that would stop, but for now she was an oddity. She closed up the sack and slung it over her back and started for the tent.

There was very little order to the Kaifeng camps. Clans and tribes all stayed in the same area, but there were no neat rows of tents as you would find in an army camp. Animals were kept in separate areas normally, but usually not too far away. Kareen had to wend her way around tents and pens to get 'home'. It was very strange: in some ways the tent really was home now. It was the only place she felt even a little bit safe. She was nervous when Atark was there, but when she and Thelena were there alone it was much better. She found that she could lose herself in simple chores and forget where she was—almost.

She rounded a tent and suddenly found herself face to face with two men. Her heart froze. They were two of the Kuttari men who had been stalking her. They grinned when they saw her. One of them said something and the other laughed. She was getting better at understanding the Kaifeng tongue. She thought the comment had been about her clothes—followed by something rude. One of them took a step toward her, but she stood her ground. She glanced around and saw that there were a dozen people within earshot. That had never stopped them before, but Thelena had taught her something to say and now she said it--loudly.

"I...I am bringing this to the tent of Atark the Great. I must not be delayed in serving him." Her pronunciation was terrible, but the men both rocked back in surprise. All the heads of the nearby people turned in her direction. "Please let me pass." The men scowled and glanced around uneasily. Finally they muttered a string of what must have been curses and then stalked away. Kareen let out a long sigh. Her legs were shaking, but she felt exhilarated, too. She smiled and then hurried home.

She reached the tent without further trouble and put the sack of flour where it belonged. Neither Thelena nor Atark were there. She looked around the tent, but there was nothing out of place or in need of cleaning that she could see. It was hours yet until she had to start working on dinner. Some of Atark's relatives tended all the animals, so for once, she had little to do. She sat down and closed her eyes and rested.

A short while later she became aware of a clamor of voices in the distance. At first she ignored it, but finally she got up and went out of the tent and listened. A lot of people seemed to be talking and laughing. She was reluctant to leave the tent—especially after her close call—but her curiosity was aroused, too. Sometimes there were groups of dancers or jugglers or tumblers who came through the camps. She had seen them several times and they were quite good. Perhaps she could risk going to see them now? The tent, for all of its reassuring safety, offered little in the way of diversion.

The guards outside the tent were glancing in her direction. As far as she could tell, they were strictly there to protect Atark and Thelena. They never interfered with her coming or going, but she must look a bit suspicious hesitating there. She made her decision and walked toward the noise.

She got closer and the laughing was louder. Perhaps it was the tumblers, they had been quite funny. But as she got closer yet, a chill went through her. She suddenly realized which part of camp she was heading for.

The pen the sacrifices were kept in.

What was going on? Were the Kaifeng tormenting those poor, doomed men? The thought made her angry. She nearly turned around and went back, but something drew her on. It was like she wanted something to fire her anger. Yes, anger, that was what she needed. For weeks she had been filled with fear and pain and shame and despair. She needed to be angry. The need drew her on.

She reached the rear of a crowd of people. They were mostly women and children. The majority of the Kaif warriors were still off collecting booty and rounding up more slaves. The women and children were all laughing and talking. Kareen slowly worked her way through the crowd to where she could see.

As she had feared, the center of attention was the pen and the men inside. But not just the men. She now saw that the real reason for the attention was the fact that the men were being fed—and the people feeding them were some of the newly captured slaves. A hundred or more of the women were bringing food and water to the men. They were all battered and undressed to some extent. A few sobbing girls were completely naked. Many were stripped to the waist. Small Kaifeng boys with switches were herding and prodding them. The prisoners looked on in shock and anger.

Kareen was furious. The swine! It wasn't bad enough that these men had been abused and would soon be murdered. No, they had to see the shame and degradation of their women, as well! The only thing worse would be if the Kaifs actually...

She froze in mid-thought when she spotted a cluster of the

guards off to one side. No, they had not spared them that either! Bastards! She choked off a scream of outrage that was building inside her. If she drew attention to herself, they might well drag her out there along with the other slaves. A part of her almost wanted for that to happen. She was tempted to grab a jug of water or a tray of bread and walk out there proudly—not ashamedly!—and serve her men. Her men! Berssians though they all were, those were her men!

She moved closer and looked at the faces of the prisoners through the wooden stakes of the enclosure. Some of them looked dazed, others looked fearful or ashamed. But most of them were angry. They accepted the food and water, but they spoke kind words to the weeping women and cast hate-filled looks at their captors. They were prisoners, but they had not been beaten. She felt a thrill of pride. She moved farther around the pen. She wanted to see all the men. Remember their faces. She could do nothing to save them, but she would remember them. Each and every one. She felt the urge to strike a laughing Kaifeng woman next to her. But she had a better idea. A strange, crazy mood was filling her. First she had stood up to the Kuttaris who wanted to rape her. Now...now... She was mustering her courage to go out there. To bring water to her men. She could not imagine what would happen to her or how severely she might be punished, but she did not care. She would do it. She would find a jug of water—no!—she would find a skin of wine! She would find it and then take it to those men. She would take it to that one, that young man right over...

Matt!

She fell to her knees.

"Matt!" She gasped out his name but it was lost in the noise around her. Her brother! Her brother was alive! He was right there! Twenty yards away! Her hands were shaking and she could not seem to catch her breath. Tears streamed down her cheeks. Her brother was alive!

But not for long.

The icy chill blasted the joy right out of her like a winter gale snuffing a candle. He was there with the other sacrifices. And as soon as Atark needed more sacrifices for his magic Matt would be bound like a hog and dragged into position and...

No!

She had to do something. She had to try and save him somehow.

He had not seen her—had not even noticed her in her Kaifeng dress. All her plans for an act of defiance evaporated. She wanted to rush to her brother and kiss him, but she could not. She must do nothing stupid yet. Nothing to draw attention to herself or get anyone angry with her. She did not know what she was going to do—but she was going to do something!

She sprang to her feet and fled.

CHAPTER TWELVE

Kareen collected the plates from dinner and began to clean them. She glanced up as Atark left the tent. He was going to a meeting of the Kaifeng leaders and would not be back for hours. Thelena helped her for a few minutes, but then stood up.

"I have to go out for a while. I'll be back later."

"Yes, Thelena. I'll finish this and prepare the beds."

The woman paused and stared at her. "Is everything all right, Kareen? You've hardly said a word. Did…did anyone bother you today?"

"No. They left me alone. I am fine. Just a little tired."

"All right. I'll be back." Thelena left and Kareen was alone in the tent. She finished her chores and then went to her little pile of blankets and began to shake.

She had been right weeks before: there were no limits to fear. She had thought she had found the limits lying there naked in front of Atark or while she was being gang-raped that same night. But she had been wrong again. She was far more frightened now than she had been then. Far more. For tonight she would not just be raped or tortured.

Tonight she would commit murder.

She had been thinking about it for hours. Ever since she had returned to the tent after seeing Matt. She had to save him. She had to. But how? No one would help her. She was nothing to Atark and Matt would be even less. Atark was the only one who could order Matt spared and he would not. Thelena, Thelena would care, but would she help? Kareen was not sure and she could not take the chance. If she refused, it would spoil any chance at all.

So she had to do it herself. But what? Help Matt escape? How? He was in a pen guarded by warriors. She could not get him out of the pen without being caught, nor overcome the guards. That was hopeless. But if she did not do something then Matt would be sacrificed to fuel Atark's magic. And probably very soon. There was no time. What could she do?

The answer had come while she was cutting up some mutton for the dinner. She had stopped and looked at the small knife she was using. *Matt would be needed as a sacrifice for Atark's magic only if Atark was alive to use the magic!* It was a wonderfully simple answer to her troubled mind. Kill Atark as he slept tonight. That would save Matt and perhaps save all the East as well. It was Atark who used the magic that let the Kaifeng win. If he was gone...

Part of her realized that it might not save Matt at all. They might still kill him anyway. And it would surely mean her death as well. And she trembled at the thought of hurting Thelena so. She knew how much she loved her father. But she had to do something and this was the only answer that she could see. She had the little knife. After Atark was asleep she would creep slowly to his side and slit his throat. Then she would flee. She would run and run until they caught her and killed her. She was afraid. She had never been so afraid, but she would do it! She took the little knife out and stared at it. She would do it. She would take the knife and...

"It won't work, Kareen."

She shrieked at the voice. Thelena! Thelena was standing in the tent. She had come back without a sound and there she was! Kareen hastily hid the knife, but it was too late.

"What...what do you mean?"

"You saw Matt in the pen today, didn't you? That's what was wrong with you. I just saw him there now. You saw him. Don't deny it."

Kareen just stared with wide eyes and fingered the knife under the blanket. If she had to, could she kill Thelena, too?

"You're planning some crazy way to rescue him and escape, aren't you? It will never work and then they will kill you, Kareen. I don't want that."

Kareen's mouth worked but no sound came out. Thelena had caught her, but she had guessed completely wrong about what her plan was! She could not let her guess the truth!

"I...I have to try and save him, Thelena. He's my brother!"

"There's nothing you can do. The guards will catch you."

"Please help me, Thelena!" All her plans were in a jumble now. She did not know what to say or do.

"There's nothing I can do, either."

"You can ask your father! He can save Matt!"

"He won't. If I even ask he will have you killed or given away. He thinks I am too soft on you as it is. If I ask something like that he will think you are manipulating me—and he might even be right."

"Please, Thelena!" Kareen began to weep. All of her hopes and resolve were crumbling away. There was no way she could kill Atark now. Thelena would be watching her like a hawk for days. She could not kill both of them. She could not bring herself to kill Thelena at all and she knew it. She would be able to do nothing and time would pass and then they would take Matt out of the pen and cut his head off.

"Help me, Thelena! Help me save him! He was always kind to you!"

"He was. And I grieve with you for him. But there is nothing we can do."

"Please!" she sobbed. "Thelena, you had a brother once, too! You have your father back, but Matt is all I have in the world!"

Thelena felt like she had been punched in the belly. Ardan. Little Ardan. He had been a nuisance at times and a rival for her father's attention. But she had loved him, too. And he had died with a Varag bullet through his brain. The shock and grief of that loss slammed into her and she nearly went to her knees. Ardan's death had been a cruel and totally pointless act; Matt Krasner's death would be...

Worse. Worse than murder.

Much worse. Or so she feared. Her father had tried to ease the pain the death cries of the sacrifices caused her, but he had not tried to understand what they really were. Thelena feared that she knew. The last time Atark had needed the sacrifices Thelena had not tried to block out the death screams. She had tried to latch onto one of them, listen to it so she could recognize the voice. It had hurt, hurt terribly, it felt like she was dying, too, but she thought she had succeeded. Then, later, she went to the site of the sacrifice and tried to find that voice again. She had found it. It was there. She could not communicate with it, but the voice was definitely there. A terrified, confused, wailing voice, echoing silently among the rocks.

She did not know what she was hearing but her only theory filled her with horror. She feared that when Atark took the power from the sacrifices he robbed those souls of the strength they needed to reach the next world. The weak and shrunken remains could only wander helplessly and scream. It was a fate so terrible to her she could scarcely bear to think about it.

But now she had to think about it, because a man she had liked would soon suffer it. Matt Krasner was a good man. He had been kind to her. He had never hurt her. He had even given her money at times. He had saved her from being raped on a number of occasions, although he had not been there to save her on countless others. Thelena had even been a little bit in love with him once. Well, not really, but she had flirted with him in hopes he would take her as his mistress and thus protect her from the others. She didn't think he ever really understood what she was doing. But he had never touched her and had offered her as much kindness and pity as anyone could. He was a good man and Kareen loved him…

…and in a few days his body would be killed and his soul damned—by her father.

Kareen was sprawled on the carpet at her feet sobbing hopelessly. Thelena suddenly found herself crying. She sank down and cradled Kareen in her arms.

"I'm sorry, I'm sorry," she whispered, rocking them back and forth.

"Please help him!" wept Kareen.

Pity and doubt and fear swirled through her. Was there anything she could do? If not to save him from death, then to at least save him from damnation? There was no one she could ask for help: she realized that immediately. Her father would not help, nor any of the other leaders. None of them liked her and they would never do anything to help in a matter like this. Her other relations were also extremely wary of her. They would neither help nor keep a secret if she asked them. No, if anything was to be done, it was up to her and Kareen. She paused with a bit of a shock when she realized she had, in fact, decided to try.

"Kareen, I want to help you. But I don't know what I can do. No one else is going to help us."

"We have to help him escape!" said Kareen, getting control of her weeping. "If we can set him loose maybe he can escape!"

"Maybe. But we would have to get him out of that pen and then get him a horse. Horses since you'll want to go with him. That will not be easy." Even as she said it she realized it would be nearly impossible. Did she really want both of them to get killed? A clean death for Matt, yes, if that was all that was possible, But the thought of Kareen dead as well was like another blow to her belly.

"Perhaps late at night…"

"There will still be guards. But night is best, yes. And it will have to be this very night, Kareen."

"Yes, tonight! But what can we do about the guards?"

"We shall have to distract them somehow. They have their fire right there by the only gate."

"Perhaps if we caused a commotion somewhere else?"

"No, that would rouse the whole camp and Matt and you would never get away. Whatever we do has to be quiet and secret."

They both fell silent to think. Kareen's face became very thoughtful. "I can distract the guards," she said suddenly.

"Kareen, if you are distracting the guards, how will you escape with Matt?"

"I won't," she said and her voice cracked slightly. "I won't, but Matt will. You can take him a knife so he can cut his ropes and then cut his way out of the pen. It isn't that sturdily built and he should be able to get out."

"Kareen," protested Thelena, "you can't do that! If anything goes wrong you'll be the first one killed! And even if it works, they are sure to kill you afterwards!"

"So what? I'm only a slave, after all."

"Kareen!" Thelena stopped and looked at the woman very closely. "I…I don't want you to die. You're more than just a slave, you're my friend."

Kareen looked back at her and then suddenly gave her a strong hug. "Thank you, Thelena, thank you. But I still need to be the one to distract the guards."

"But why?"

"Two reasons: the guards will know who you are. If Matt escapes you'll get in real trouble. If it's me, they'll just think it's another Berssian slut they can rape in the dark. The second reason is that I can't ride worth a damn. Never could. I'd just slow Matt down and then we'd both be killed."

Thelena shook her head. This was insane. How did she talk herself into doing this? And she could scarcely believe how determined Kareen was. She had always seemed so soft and weak. Now she was showing more strength than she had ever suspected was there.

"It could work, Thelena," insisted Kareen, "Will you help me?"

"So you would go and distract the guards? And then I try to find

Matt and slip him the knife?"

"Yes! And then you get out of there! We can't ask any more of you. Once Matt is out and the guards have finished with me I'll just come back to the tent."

It all sounded so simple, but so much could go wrong! But maybe it could work. And with luck no one would get killed. She could not bear the thought of some of her own people being killed in this crazy scheme. But at least this way there was a chance that no one would be killed.

"Do...do you think you'll be able to distract the guards?"

Kareen stood up with a strange expression on her face. She undid her braids and shook her hair out. She pushed a thick lock forward so it covered the scar on her cheek. Then she pulled off her skirt, shrugged off the vest and flung away her underclothes. Then she unlaced her blouse as far as it would go. The blouse was *very* short and her legs were bare almost to the hip. She took on a pose that would have done any whore in the town by the fort proud.

"Yes. And I can keep them distracted as long as necessary."

Thelena gasped. She had always envied Kareen her beautiful face and voluptuous figure, but she had never seen her flaunt them like this. The sight stirred something deep inside her.

"I...I guess you can. But put your clothes back on! It will be hours yet before we can start!"

Kareen lay in the darkened tent and tried not to shake. Soon now, they would go very soon. She listened to Atark's faint snoring from the far side of the tent. She was very glad they had come up with a plan that would not require her to kill Atark. The thought of actually slitting his throat as he slept was just too horrible. And he was a sorcerer after all, he probably had some spell protecting him while he was asleep. No, the plan they had agreed on was best. Matt would escape and no one else would be hurt.

She twitched when Thelena nudged her. She looked out from her blankets but it was so dark the woman was just a slightly darker blob. "Now?" she whispered.

"Yes," came the reply. Kareen got up from her bed, She was only wearing her blouse and there was no need to put anything else on. She felt around and found the wine skin and slung it over her shoulder. It did not contain wine. Thelena had found some brandy taken as booty and filled the skin with that. She carefully tip-toed to the back of the tent. Thelena was already there and she had lifted up part of the fabric so they could crawl out. There was a pair of guards at the front of the tent and they could not afford to be seen. Fortunately, the guards were considered more ceremonial than anything else and were not terribly alert. In fact, they usually took turns sleeping.

Kareen wriggled under the tent and Thelena followed in an instant. Then Thelena took the lead and they silently made their way between the tents. It was about three hours before dawn and it was very dark and very quiet. Cold, too. Kareen was shivering in her skimpy outfit and the dew on the grass felt like ice on her feet. They took a round-about route to the pen that Thelena had scouted the previous evening. They saw no one. There would be a few sentries around the camp's perimeter, but none inside. As long as they did not encounter anyone answering the call of nature, they should be safe.

Soon enough they reached the area the pen was built in. They stopped and peered at it for a while. It was overcast so there was no moon and most of the campfires had died down. It was very dark. The pen was not much more than a black wall in front of them. She could see the fire for the guards about two-thirds of the way around the pen. That was her goal. She was trembling hard now. She had to do this. She had to!

"Do you still want to go on?" whispered Thelena.

"Yes. I'll go now."

"Wait. Are...are you sure you don't want me to tell Matt about you?"

"No! We already talked about that. You can't tell him I'm here! He'd never leave without me. Tell him...tell him I'm dead."

"Kareen! I can't...!"

"You must! It's the only way!"

Thelena was silent but after a moment she seemed to nod. Kareen hesitated for just an instant and then she walked forward. She was not trying to hide any longer, instead she had to act completely normal. She walked along the outside of the pen and tried to see inside. There were just hundreds of pale lumps huddled on the ground. As cold as she felt, they must be freezing! Anger flared in her again. Her doubts vanished and she knew she could do what she had to do.

She neared the fire without being challenged. It appeared that all the guards were trying to stay warm, too. They surely must be tired and bored. She quailed slightly when she saw that there were twelve of them. Earlier there had only been eight. No matter. She was only a few feet away before anyone noticed her. Then one man sprang up and challenged her. The others looked up sleepily. Kareen stopped for an instant and then slinked forward as provocatively as she could manage. Thelena had taught her what to say:

"Hail, mighty warrior. The goodly Noyen Teskat of the Kuttari sends refreshments for you." She held out the wine skin and then thrust forward her bosom and smiled.

The man's look of suspicion turned to delight. He took the wine skin and drank from it. He coughed and sputtered as the brandy burned his throat. He called out something and the other men laughed. He handed the skin to one of the others and then reached out for Kareen. She playfully spun away from him and then began to dance about, smiling invitingly to all of the men. Others grabbed for her, but she eluded them for a moment and led them after her— farther from the pen. They were all in pursuit now. She peeled off her blouse and tossed it to them. They laughed loudly as she danced naked before them. She led them a few more paces away. The fire was now directly between them and the pen.

Finally, one of the men caught hold of her. Her heart was pounding so hard she was afraid she was going to faint. Instead, she leaned into the man and kissed him. He laughed and clutched her tightly as the others closed in around her.

Thelena could hear the laughter on the far side of the pen and she shook her head. Kareen was letting herself be used by a gang of men. Considering the circumstances it could not quite be called rape, but she was sacrificing her body to save her brother. *Could I have done that?* Her thoughts went back to that terrible day at the mound. The one Varag had been pawing her and she had been terrified. When he tore her dress she had struggled wildly and her family had tried to help her. Her brother and her mother and—she thought—her father had all died trying to save her from being raped. If she had known that was going to happen, if she had known beforehand that they would die, could she have done what Kareen was doing now? *Yes! Yes, I would have thrown my clothes off and done anything they wanted—anything!-- if it would have saved them! I would!* Of course it would not have saved them. They would have just raped her mother, too, and killed Ardan and her father anyway. But she would have tried to save them if she could.

She could do nothing for her brother or her mother now, but she could try to save the soul of Matt Krasner. She rose from her crouch and moved quickly toward the pen. She reached it in moments and then peered in through the stakes. Hundreds of men were huddling together for warmth. She knew that a good number of them had to be awake despite their exhaustion. It was just impossible to sleep for very long when you were this cold.

"Lieutenant Krasner!" she hissed as loudly as she dared. "I have a message for Lieutenant Matt Krasner! Is he there?" A few groans answered her, but that was all. She moved a couple of yards along the pen and tried again. Her heart sank as she realized how hopeless this probably was.

"Matt! Matt Krasner! Are you there?" Several voices answered back, far too loudly, but they were not Matt.

"Quiet!" she said urgently. "Lieutenant Matt Krasner! Is he here?" She moved again. There was a frightening amount of movement and noise in the pen. But then she heard more laughing from the far side of the pen. Perhaps the guards would think it was their play that was awakening the prisoners. She moved a dozen yards farther and called again.

"Lieutenant Krasner! I have a message!" She was about ready to give up and run when she got an answer.

"Who? Who's there?" It didn't sound like Matt.

"I have a message for Matt Krasner!"

"Wait. He's here."

There was movement among the huddled shapes and some urgent whispering. Then someone—two someones—were coming closer, stumbling over the other bodies on the ground.

"Over here!" she whispered. The smaller of the two shapes came right up to the edge of the pen and peered out at her.

"Matt?" she said. It was hard to see in the dark.

"Yes! Who are...? Thelena?"

"Yes! It's me!"

"What...? What are you doing here? Is Kareen with you?" The question froze her heart. She almost told him the truth. Almost told him that his sister was a few yards away having sex with a dozen men so he might escape. But no, Kareen was right. He'd never leave without her. He would attack those men with his bare hands to try and save her—and then they would all die.

"I'm sorry, Matt. She...she's dead." The shape in front of her seemed to shrink in on itself. She heard a groan. "She was killed when the magazines in the fort exploded. I don't think she suffered at all, Matt," she lied.

"Thank...thank you for telling me, Thelena," he said after a moment. "You better go before you get in trouble."

With a start she realized that Matt did not know why she was here! *Of course he doesn't, you idiot!* "Matt! Matt, I'm here to help you escape!"

"What? Are you crazy?"

"Probably. Turn around and I'll cut your bonds." Matt hesitated for an instant and then did as she had told him. He thrust his bound wrists toward the opening in the pen. She used her knife to slice through the ropes holding him. He pulled his hands loose and then turned around again. She held out the knife for him and he took it.

"Cut your way through the pen here. Then go that way about four hundred paces. There are horses there. Ride north as fast as you can. Go for at least three days before you try to get back to the river." She hesitated for a moment. "Whatever you do, don't let yourself be taken alive."

"Thank you, Thelena. Thank you very much." He pressed his face up to the gap in pen to stare at her

"May the gods watch over you, Mattin Krasner." She leaned forward and kissed him on the lips. Then she turned and fled.

Matt stared after the dim shape as it vanished in the darkness. Thelena! He could scarcely believe it. And Kareen was dead—he could scarcely believe that, either. Something inside him seemed to have died as well...

"Have you got a knife?" hissed a voice at his side. It was Chenik, of course. His sergeant was the one who heard Thelena and roused him. The man's voice roused him now. He could mourn his sister later—right now he had work to do!

"Yes! Turn round!" Chenik did so and he quickly cut him free. Other men were starting to cluster around. "Untie them. I'll get to work on the pen!" Chenik sternly warned the men to keep quiet and then started untying them. As each one was freed, that man would go to work on another. A steadily growing ripple of freedom began to silently sweep through the pen. Matt was already sawing at the ropes that held the pen together. The wooden stakes were all a few inches thick and had been pounded a foot or so into the ground. Then ropes had tied them together at the top and in the middle leaving about a five inch gap between each one. It was a fairly flimsy barrier, but more than sufficient to hold men with their hands tied behind their backs.

He cut through the middle ropes on either side of three of the posts. Then he called for one of the freed men to kneel down so he could stand on his back to get at the upper ropes. Two other men were already digging frantically at the base of the posts. Matt jumped up on the man and sawed as fast as he could. The prospect of getting away filled him with more energy than he'd had since they were captured.

He—and almost everyone else—had sunk into a miserable apathy. The army was destroyed, the capital was falling, the Kaifeng were catching and enslaving everyone. They had been marched into this camp, bound, and herded into this pen. The Kaifs had managed to communicate the fact that they would all be killed soon enough and there had been twenty men from the two hundred who had been taken earlier who described what had happened to the rest. All hope had faded and they had just waited for death. Even the spectacle of the captive women, stripped and whipped and forced to bring them their food and water, had not roused very many from their stupor. A few, like Matt, had been angry and a few more had nearly gone mad when they recognized a wife or lover among the slaves, but most had not had the energy for anything. Matt had scanned the women's faces, hoping to see Kareen. He had been glad then that he had not—each time one of those ghastly reunions had taken place the Kaifs had immediately seized the woman and raped her right there in front of the crazed soldier. The thought that she was dead gnawed at him now, but he refused to let it distract him.

The knife was starting to get dull, but he cut through the last rope and stepped down off the man. Immediately he went to his knees and began chopping at the ground to help uproot the posts. Where were the guards? They had all seemed bored and uninterested—except when they were tormenting the prisoners. Were they asleep? The dirt was flying away from the posts and he could sense men crowing behind him. Several men were pushing on the posts now and trying to rock them loose.

"Easy!" he hissed. "No noise! All right, try to pull it out." They had dug down nearly to the bottom of the posts on the inside of the pen.

Now a half dozen men seized the posts and the ropes still holding them and pulled. With surprising ease they tilted over and came right out of the ground. They were laid down and then men began pushing for the gap in the pen.

"Slowly! There's plenty of room! Four hundred yards west there are horses. Go!" The gap was just big enough for one man at a time and Matt and Chenik passed them through, whispering the instructions as they did so. Ten, twenty, fifty men were through. The others were crowding in. Suddenly, Chenik grabbed him and hustled both of them through the gap.

"Our turn, sir. Not right for an officer to wait 'til last." Matt nearly protested but then a fear gripped him that he might wait too long. Suddenly he *had* to get out. He ran.

Almost immediately they were in a bewildering maze of tents, It was hard to maintain a sense of direction in the dark, but he kept moving. He was aware of other dark shapes moving all around him. He stubbed his bare foot on a tent peg and nearly fell. The pain was so intense for an instant that he almost cried out. Chenik was right there and kept him moving. He hobbled for a dozen yards before the pain started to subside. He limped along, growing more afraid every second. Surely someone would give the alarm soon. They reached a dead end and had to backtrack and try another way. Where were the damn horses? They'd gone a lot farther than four hundred paces!

"Over there, sir," gasped Chenik. Matt looked and he saw a dark mass off to one side. Horses! He could smell them. They limped over to them as fast as they could. Other men had already found them and the horses were stirring and making far too much noise.

"Hope you can ride bareback, sir. No hope of finding any saddles."

They reached the horses and Matt was relieved that they at least had bridles. They were picketed to stakes in the ground. Matt grabbed one and pulled it out of the ground. "They'll chase us, Sergeant. Better take two apiece." He grabbed a second picket rope and saw that Chenik was doing the same. He could already hear the sound of pounding hooves. Some of them were getting away!

Suddenly there was a shout from close by. Someone had seen them! He tried to scramble up on the horse, but it was hard without stirrups. He was weaker than he had thought. Then Chenik was there again and he was boosted up onto the horse.

"Go!" he said urgently. Matt clutched the horse's mane with one hand and the two bridle ropes and the knife with the other. A man appeared out of the dark with a sword. Chenik turned to meet him. The Sergeant was a big, powerful man. He blocked the attacker's sword stroke and them knocked him to the ground with his fist. Left handed, too, his right was nearly useless now. He kicked the Kaif and scooped up the sword. He turned to look at Matt. "Go!" he shouted.

"Come on, Sergeant! We can both make it!"

There were more cries closing on them. Matt could see at least several Kaifs running their way.

"Will you do what I tell you just once, Matt?" shouted Chenik. Then he turned and charged the Kaifs.

"Sergeant!" There were cries and shouts and ringing steel coming out of the dark. Matt stared in frozen shock for a moment. He almost went to his friend's aid. Almost. A dozen more shapes appeared, shouting in Kaif voices. They were closing in from almost all around.

Then he turned his horse in the only open direction and kicked it into motion. He held back his sobs as he galloped north.

CHAPTER THIRTEEN

Kareen clutched the blankets to her and tried to burrow down in them even farther than she already was. Gods, she was tired! And sore, too. Not as sore as after those first two nights of her captivity, but sore enough. But unlike the aftermath of that first horror, today she had a growing exaltation inside her instead of a numbing shame.

Matt was free! He was safe!

Or at least she kept telling herself that. He had not been among the dead nor those who had been recaptured. He had gotten away from the Kaifeng camps and with any luck he might get away completely. Nearly a hundred men had managed to steal horses and escape. Some had been caught and killed, but she did not think Matt was among them. With that many men to try and track down, his chances of escaping were good.

She had to admit that the scale of the breakout had surprised her. Thelena, too, she was sure. They had simply wanted to get Matt out, but in hindsight it was obvious that the other captives were not just going to roll over and go back to sleep! Clearly, neither of them had been thinking too clearly at the time. As it turned out, almost all of the prisoners had made it out of the pen. There had been a few who were too hurt or sick to move, but anyone who could even walk had gotten out.

Kareen had been waiting and waiting for the alarm to sound. All the time the guards were using her she had waited. She halfway expected them to kill her the instant they realized anything was wrong—her guilty conscience, no doubt. But when the first shouts had come, they had simply jumped up and ran back toward the pen. Kareen, knowing exactly what was happening, had not waited one second more and she scrambled off into the darkness instantly. No one had even chased her. The camp was immediately in an uproar and no one noticed one more naked girl running through the night.

She had gotten back to the tent and sneaked in the way she had left and not even Atark had noticed. Thelena was already there. She just nodded to her and they tried to go back to sleep.

It had been impossible to sleep, of course, there was far too much commotion. But eventually the camp had quieted down and Kareen had managed to doze off. In the morning she had gotten up and done her chores and waited while Thelena gathered news. Unfortunately, a lot of the news had been bad. Of the five hundred prisoners, nearly four hundred were dead. Caught while trying to escape, they had fought like lions rather than go back to the pen. Over twenty Kaifeng had died during the fighting and many more had been hurt. She felt bad for Thelena: those were her people, enemies though they were to her. Neither of them had expected so much carnage. But Matt had gotten away. To Kareen that was all that really mattered.

She shifted in the blankets again. She really was sore. The guards had not been easy with her. Still, she did not care. It was very odd: last night she had 'willingly' done things they had scarcely been able to force her to do that first night. But this time she felt no shame. She had been there by her own choice and she had been using *them* even though they didn't know it. They had taken their pleasure from her, but in doing so, she had killed twenty of their fellows and let her own men die with honor—and saved her brother! A little soreness was a tiny price to pay for that!

Of course, she might pay a much higher price in the end, but it would be worth that, too. The camp was still stirred up and she imagined the Kaifeng were eager to find out who was to blame for the mess. If they decided to blame her...

She turned to look when she heard someone enter the tent. She was relieved to see that it was Thelena. The other woman came over and sat down near her. She looked very tired. "Is...is there any news?"

"Nothing beyond what you already know. Men are out searching for the ones who escaped, but a great many of the warriors were already out and won't know about the escape. I think Matt has a good chance."

"Thank the Gods!" She looked over at Thelena and smiled. "And thank you. I owe you so much now." Thelena looked down and shook her head.

"Save your thanks. This did not go as I had hoped. We may both have to pay a high price for your brother's life."

"I'm sorry some of your people were killed."

"I... I was stupid. I should have known this was going to happen."

"There wasn't any other choice, was there?"

"The other choice was to let your brother die. But I couldn't bear that choice, either. Sometimes there is no right choice."

"For me the choice seems right. And for that you have my thanks."

"You are welcome. I just wish..."

Thelena was cut off by the tent flap opening. Atark stormed into the tent and Kareen could see that he was furious. She cringed back as he came right up and stared down at her!

Thelena stiffened when she saw the look on her father's face. He was very angry and when he stopped in front of Kareen, there could be little doubt what he was angry about. "Get up, you Berssian whore!" he snarled. Kareen's eyes got very wide and she crouched down, clutching the blankets to herself.

"Father, what's the matter?"

"This one!" he said pointing at Kareen with one hand. "This is the one that helped the prisoners escape! Get up, you slut! You will pay for your crimes!"

"No, father! It was not her! She...she was with me last night." She stumbled over the half-lie.

"Don't try to protect her, Thelena! The fools who were on guard could only say that the woman who pulled them from their duty had dark hair and was very pretty. The blouse that was left behind could have belonged to anyone. But she forgot about this!" Atark raised something in his hand and then flung it to the ground. Thelena hissed when she saw it. The wineskin. The skin they had put the brandy in. It was like a thousand other wineskins in the camp, but none of the others were decorated quite like this one...

"Your mother made this! It hung in our tent the night you were made and the day you were born! And this bitch used it to free the captives and kill our warriors! She will die—slowly and painfully! And before she dies she will tell us who else was involved. She clearly was not acting alone."

"No! No, Father, you cannot!"

"Don't interfere, Daughter! I'll get you another slave."

Thelena was trembling. She had never defied her father before, but now she did. She stood up and put herself between him and Kareen.

"You may not have her, Father."

Atark's eyes grew wide in surprise. "Why are you defending her? She helped kill our own people! Has this slave bewitched you? She must be dragged out and flogged to death for what she has done!"

"Then you shall have to flog me to death, too, Father."

He took a pace back. "What are you saying?"

"She distracted the guards, but I am the one who gave the prisoners the knife they used to escape. If she must die for her deeds, then so must I."

"I...I don't believe you! You are just making that up!" The pain in his eyes was like a knife in her heart. She was hurting him. The last thing in the world she wanted to do was hurt him. But she had to.

"I speak the truth. And if you try to harm Kareen, I shall stand before the assembled Kas and confess my guilt. Do you think they will not believe me?"

He took another step back. "Why? For the sake of all the gods, why did you do it?"

Her shoulders slumped and her head fell. "I...I had to, Father. Kareen's brother was among the prisoners. I owed her—and him—a debt. It is paid now. And if I must pay further for this act, I will."

"They are both our enemies! You owed them nothing!" Atark cried in anger and anguish.

"I owed them my life. I could not allow her brother to be sacrificed. But I was stupid, I never thought that any of our own people would be killed. For that I beg forgiveness."

"Forgiveness! Twenty of our people are dead, Thelena!"

"They died honorable deaths—in battle. And so did the prisoners. Father, you must take no more sacrifices! It is an abomination!"

"What are you talking about? What nonsense is this?"

"When you steal the sacrifices' strength you rob them of the afterlife as well! You condemn them to wander forever in the shadows between worlds. I have heard their cries, Father. I know of what I speak! I could not allow Kareen's brother to suffer such a fate. You must take no more sacrifices!"

Her father shook his head and looked stunned. "This is madness," he muttered. "You will speak of this to no one, Thelena! No one!" He motioned to the wineskin on the ground. "I have not mentioned this to anyone and I sent the guards away before coming in. No one knows of your insanity. If you value the life of this slave—and your own—then no one must ever know. I am very angry, and very disappointed, with you, Daughter."

"I know, Father. I am sorry."

Atark turned to Kareen. "I grant you your life, slave. But give me no reason to regret my decision! If you do, you shall surely die!" He spun about and left the tent. Thelena slowly sank to her knees, her shaking legs unable to support her any longer. She jumped when Kareen reached out to touch her arm.

"Am I to die?" she asked. "I could only understand a little of what was said. But I could tell your father was very angry."

"He was. But, no, you are not to die. At least not now."

"But he knew what I had done?" She touched the wineskin.

"Yes."

"Then why is he sparing me? Surely he would have me killed. What did you say to him, Thelena? How did you save me?"

"I...I..." she couldn't say any more. She was too confused and she hurt too much inside. But suddenly Kareen clutched her.

"You told him what you had done, too, didn't you? You did! Oh, Thelena, that was foolish!"

"He would have killed you if I had not," she whispered. Kareen moved closer and put her arms around her and hugged her tight.

"Thank you. Thank you for my brother's life and for my own." She held her for a long time. Finally, she pulled away and when she did she had a strange look on her face.

"When... when I wanted to save my brother it wasn't just to save his life. It was...I guess you could call it an act of defiance on my part. Some way I could strike back at my captors. I never dreamed it would do so much damage. But now I owe you two lives: mine and Matt's. And I will repay you, Thelena. I suppose what I'm saying is that I've struck my blow and now I'm done. Back in the fort you were a good slave. I won't insult you by saying that you were a servant. You served me faithfully and now I promise to do the same for you. I won't make any more trouble. Tell your father I'll be a good slave and I'll serve you both well."

Kareen bowed down and touched her head to the ground. Thelena had no clue what to say.

Atark was still furious. He was hurt and shocked and embarrassed, too, but mostly furious. Somehow that Berssian bitch had subverted his own daughter! Every instinct told him to have the woman killed before she could do more harm. But he had seen the look in Thelena's eye. She would really do it. If he killed the slave his daughter would confess what she had done and then not even his powers could save her.

So the slave would live—for now. Perhaps later he would have her killed, but not now. Thelena was on her guard now, but if in a few months the woman simply disappeared one day, what could she do? He would not even have to kill her, so he would not have to lie to Thelena. Some of the merchant tribes were already starting to gather and they would buy slaves and ship them west. Perhaps one of them would soon have this woman as part of their merchandise. Enough! He could deal with that later.

Without thinking, he had been stalking up the little hill where his private tent was located. He had been spending almost every waking hour there for the last three days learning the new spell the Ghost was teaching him. It was a spell of immense power that would move the earth itself and bring down the walls of the Berssian city. He felt that he was very close to mastering it. The Ghost had complimented him on his ability to learn the great spells. He was nearly ready. Just a bit more work...

He stopped in mid-stride, a dozen paces from the tent. No. It would not do to go there now. He was too upset to concentrate properly. And the Ghost would immediately sense what was on his mind. He suspected that the Ghost could not reach very deeply into him to get information, but anything he had been thinking about was there like an open scroll. He did *not* want the ghost to know what Thelena had done!

He clenched and unclenched his fists and breathed deeply until he had calmed down. This was not as bad as it all seemed. His daughter had made a mistake. A very bad one, it was true, but he knew that she was truly sorry about the deaths. Clearly she felt that she had owed some debt to the slave and her brother. Perhaps she did. *And Shelena and I always taught her that debts had to be paid.* But now the debt *had* been paid and hopefully that was the end of it.

He stood there, locked in indecision. He could not go to the little tent with the Ghost and he did not want to confront Thelena again just now so he could not go to the big tent, either. So where should he go? The additional practice with the spell could wait, anyway: he would need to find more sacrifices somehow. The Ghost said that at least five hundred would be needed and there were less than a hundred in the pen right now. That was where he would go: to Zarruk's tent to talk about finding more.

As he walked there, he reflected that finding the sacrifices quickly could be a problem. All of the Berssians in the immediate area had already been found. Most of the men were just killed, so there were few male prisoners. He supposed that he could always use women, but he did not want to do that. Partly because he simply did not like the idea. Women—even enemy women—were not for killing. Slaves, yes, but not sacrifices. More importantly, all the women who had been captured were already the property of the warriors. It could cause very hard feeling to order them to give them up—even if their loss would mean the fall of the city and countless thousands of new slaves to replace those lost.

So, the warriors would have to scour the surrounding countryside to find the sacrifices he would need. That could take weeks. He sighed. The delay probably was not critical. Winter was still several months away and surely they would have the city long before then.

As he walked, he suddenly chuckled. Thelena's 'mistake' had done one good turn already. The cunning little vixen had had the slave tell the guards that Teskat had sent her! The Noyen of the Kuttari had denied it, of course, but he was still humiliated and under suspicion. All knew that he hated Atark, and the fact that the escape had hindered his magic only made people more suspicious of Teskat. He had already petitioned Zarruk to transfer his allegiance to one of the other Kas and Zarruk had granted it. One problem solved anyway! Teskat could still plot and scheme, but against some other Ka! By the time Atark reached Zarruk's tent, his good humor had returned...

...only to be lost again once he stepped inside. Zarruk was seated there, surrounded by his two wives, the red-haired girl and his new slave, the former mistress of the Berssian general—who looked neither quite as young or quite as pretty once stripped of her finery and makeup. But it was the other person seated there that destroyed Atark's good mood.

A Varag! What in the name of the gods is that animal doing here?

Zarruk sprang to his feet as soon as he saw Atark. The Varag rose a bit more slowly. Zarruk's wives greeted him warmly and the two slaves pressed their faces to the carpet.

"Mighty Atark!" cried Zarruk. "I was just now speaking of you! Let me present Hetman Reganar. He has ridden here to offer the services of his warriors."

"Indeed," said Atark his voice as flat as the Plains of Kaif.

"Yes, but please sit down. Slaves, wine for the shaman!"

Atark carefully sat down, as far away from the Varag as he could manage. In spite of Zarruk mentioning this to him days earlier, he still could not believe a Varag had actually dared come here.

"Hail Atark," said the Varag once they had their wine. "I have heard many tales of your powers. Now that our common enemy, the Berssians, have been humbled, I feel that it is time for long-sundered kindred to re-unite."

You mean that now that your former masters can no longer pay you, you hope to help pick their bones! Atark's anger was growing. The comment about 'sundered kindred' rankled especially—particularly since there was some truth in it. Long, long ago, the Varags had been kin to the Kaifeng. But the Varags had moved east across the mountains and become a different people. A mongrel and degenerate people, in Atark's opinion. For centuries they had served the Berssians and raided the Kaifeng. They had murdered his wife and son and raped his daughter and now they wanted to join them?

"I realize there may be a few difficulties to overcome, Atark," said Zarruk, eyeing him cautiously. "But Reganar tells me that there are many thousands of Varags to the south who are eager to join us. Their strength would be very welcome just now. More tribes are still arriving, but too slowly. With the forces we have gotten across the river to bottle up the Berssians effectively removed from what we can use for any assault, we could use Reganar's men."

"Yes," laughed Reganar, "my men would be most eager to help finish off the damn Berssians! Provided, of course, your powers don't also affect our own firearms." The Varag drew out one of his pistols and Atark tensed. He could burn the man to ashes in an eyeblink, if necessary. The man did not cock the weapon, but he waved it around in an unfriendly fashion, the muzzle pausing for an instant on both Zarruk and Atark. The man laughed again and put the pistol away.

"Atark has already destroyed all the gunpowder in the city," said Zarruk. "He probably won't need to use that spell again."

"I was not planning to, no," said Atark. His anger continued to grow, but then a very interesting thought struck him. "Tell me,

Hetman Reganar: how many men will you bring and how soon will you arrive?"

"I can be here with six hundred in three days—if we can reach an agreement here."

"What a wonderful coincidence," said Atark, forcing a smile. "The assault on the city will take place in four days. You and your men will be just in time."

"Four days?" said Zarruk in surprise. "Will we be ready that soon?

"I will be ready. But to be ready, I must begin my preparations at once. If you will both excuse me." Without waiting for an answer, he got up and walked out of the tent. Outside he began to tremble with anger. But he contained it and walked back toward his own tents. Once there he found Gettain.

"What do you wish, Lord?" said the commander of Atark's escort.

"How many men do you command?"

"Lord? I have about a hundred men who have been judged worthy to serve you."

"Could you find more if they were needed?"

"Oh yes, Lord! Many, many men—and women—have pleaded with me to be allowed to serve you. But you said that you wished no more than necessary. How many more do you desire?"

"I will need another five hundred," he said and Gettain's eyebrows shot up. "And I will need them in three days. Good strong men who will obey orders—any orders."

"I will have to work quickly, but I think it can be done, Lord."

"Good. And send some men out to gather up all the best brandy and wine they can lay their hands on. And a hundred pretty wenches to serve it. And some good food. Musicians. Jugglers."

"Yes, Lord." The man looked very puzzled. Atark smiled at him.

"We are going to have guests. And I want them to be treated as they deserve."

Matt crawled through the thicket and spread a few leaves so he could look out the other side. It was a cold morning and he shivered. He'd managed to find some clothes in an abandoned farm two days earlier—even some shoes, although he was certain one of his toes was broken and the shoe hurt terribly—but he was still chilled to the bone after another night where he did not dare light a fire. There was some low-lying fog so that it was hard to see very far, but he did not see anyone. Good. He turned and crawled back to where the others and the horses were waiting.

"Looks clear," he said. "Everyone ready?"

The four men who were waiting for him all nodded. "Right, Captain," said one of them. "You sure about us traveling in daylight?"

"We've been going too damn slow trying to ride at night. We're only about sixty miles in a straight line from Berssenburg. The damn Kaifs are going to be all over us unless we put some distance between us and them."

The man looked dubious, but he didn't argue. The five of them had hooked up the day after the breakout and had stuck together since then. That was three days ago. They had seen numerous parties of Kaifeng warriors since then. It wasn't certain if they were looking for them, or just looting, but it would make no difference if they were caught. Once again, Matt was the only officer in the group. Fortunately, one of the men had been from his brigade and knew who he was, so there was no question about them accepting his authority.

They mounted their horses and rode northwest. With all of the abandoned villages and farms, they had managed to find almost everything they needed, including saddles and tack for the Kaifeng ponies. Almost everything: they were basically unarmed except for some knives and small axes. Certainly nothing to let them fight the Kaifs on anything approaching equal terms. So they would not fight, they would run.

So far they had done well moving by night. The Kaifs would make fires at night and all they had to do was stay away from them. But traveling in the dark was slow going. Matt had a growing fear that if they did not get farther away, they were going to be in trouble.

Once out of the woods, they broke into a trot. The sturdy ponies could keep up that pace for hours. They rode for most of the morning and saw no one. They hugged the edges of the numerous woods and forests in the area. This would make them harder to see from a distance and give them some place to hide. It seemed as though the Kaifs did not like this closed-in land and they tended to stay in the open spaces. Around noon they saw some smoke in the direction they were riding and Matt shifted course a bit farther west to avoid it. They halted in some woods at noon and had their meal. So far, finding food had not been hard. The Kaifs had looted most of the places, but there was always something left. While they were eating they spotted a party of twenty or so Kaifs heading south. They never got closer than a few miles and eventually disappeared. They waited an extra hour and then went on. By late afternoon, Matt was feeling a lot better. They had covered at least forty miles that day. If they could do that for two or three more he might consider turning east and heading for the river. Thelena had said to ride for three days, but he was sure she was expecting them to be riding fifty miles a day or more.

As they stopped for the night he found himself thinking about the Kaifeng woman who had freed them. He surely hoped that she would not be caught or punished for what she had done. Why had she done it? Gratitude for what he and Kareen had done for her? Perhaps. The thought of his sister wiped out the satisfaction he had been feeling over the day's ride. Blown up with the fort. Quick, probably painless. Far better than what might have happened to her, he supposed, but she was still dead. He felt very lonely. Chenik's death was weighing on him, too. The sergeant had been with him since his first day in the army. There was a huge empty space at his right side that nothing could fill. Could he have done anything to save Chenik? No, if he had not ridden out when he did, they would both be dead. Well, so what? It's not like he counted for anything, really. Just one more man.

Matt shook his head. What was done was done. He was still alive and he planned to stay that way until the chance came to kill some more Kaifs. He unsaddled his horse and pulled out the bag with his food. He had some stale bread and a sausage. Tomorrow they would have to do some foraging and that would slow them down. He took out his knife to cut up some of the sausage. It was the knife that Thelena had given to him. He was glad he still had it—even though it wasn't a very good knife. The blade was too short and the handle was strangely thick.

He stopped to look at it more closely and he realized that there was a strip of rawhide that had been wound about the hilt and that was why it was so thick. One end of it had come loose and was unraveling. In the last light of the day he saw that there was something under the rawhide. A piece of paper?

His curiosity was aroused and he unwound the leather strip. Yes, there was no doubt that a small piece of paper had been wrapped around the hilt of the knife and then tied in place with the rawhide. A message? From Thelena? She had learned to write pretty well during her time in the fort, so it was possible. He put aside the knife and the rawhide and unfolded the paper. It was badly wrinkled and a bit torn and discolored with dirt and his own sweat, but he could just make out the writing on it:

Mattin,

I pray the gods that you are safe to read this. I wanted you to know that Kareen is alive and safe with me. She would not allow me to tell you, because she knew you would never leave without her. I will protect her as much as I am able. I promise. Go now. Ride to safety.

Thelena

Matt crumpled the paper and bowed his head. The other men wondered what he was weeping about.

Atark's head hurt. The previous night had been long and loud and filled with drink.

But the feast had been very successful, very successful, indeed.

He walked toward the platform his men had erected. It overlooked the Berssian city and the quickly massing *helars* of the Kaifeng. There were five *helars* now. Just in the last four days enough new tribes had arrived to create a new score of score of scores. Word had it that even more were on the way, hoping to take part in the sack of Berssia and the East.

The latecomers might still enjoy future triumphs, but they would miss the sack of Berssenburg—for the city would fall today.

The defenders had seen the Kaifeng warriors assembling and they were clustering atop the ancient walls of the city. Good. So much the better. They would all be swept away when he brought the walls down. He had worked with the Ghost almost non-stop and had mastered the new spell. In spite of his aching head, he was prepared. The army was prepared.

The sacrifices were prepared.

Six hundred men knelt behind the platform in neat rows. They were all very tightly bound. Forked sticks had been pounded securely into the ground and the neck of each sacrifice lay tied in one. One of Gettain's men stood by each one. One man in every six held a carefully sharpened bronze sword. They had not been able to find enough of the bronze weapons, so each executioner would have to dispatch six men.

Atark walked to the front of the sacrifices and stood before the first one. Hetman Reganar looked up at him in combined fury and terror. He, like all the others, was gagged, so he could only make a muffled grunting sound.

"Today you and your men will die," said Atark. "And after you are dead, I will dispatch warriors to where your village is. All of your sons will die just as you are about to and all of your women will be our slaves." The man thrashed violently but uselessly in his bonds. "And after your village, we shall go on to the next and the next and the next. Until the last Varag man is dead and the last Varag woman is the slave to a Kaifeng warrior. None will remain, Hetman Reganar, none. A year from now, the Varags will be a people known only in legends." His thrashing grew to a climax and then ceased. The man now had tears on his cheeks.

"The Berssians, at least have some honor. They fight for their homes and their families. But you, you and all your jackal kindred, have no honor. You will serve anyone who is stronger so that you may prey on those weaker. You deserve nothing but the fate I have decreed for you!"

Atark turned to go to his platform, but just then Ka-Noyen Zarruk and his escort galloped up. His face was twisted in amazement and anger. "What is this?" he demanded. "Why are these men here?"

"They are the sacrifices for my magic," said Atark.

"They are our allies!"

"It is true that they pledged us their aid, Mighty Ka," said Atark. "And they shall aid us now in a fashion far better and far truer than any other."

"I promised them safe conduct!" protested Zarruk.

"And they received it. Your honor is unblemished, my lord. I never gave them any word of any kind. But you and the other Kas promised me whatever aid I needed in carrying out my spells. I require the service of these men and they shall now give it to me."

"Atark, you cannot do this! When the word of this reaches the other Varags, they will pledge an eternal blood feud! It will be war to the knife with them forever!"

"Yes, and so it shall be. But we hold the knife, my lord, and the blood that is shed shall be theirs. We could never trust them, Zarruk, you know this. This answer is best. Now, if you will return to your troops, I will commence the magic and the city will fall. Victory today, my friend!"

Atark stood there, quivering slightly. He had never done anything so high-handed with Zarruk before. For all practical purposes he had just dismissed his own Ka and bade him return to his duty! Some would think such an affront would warrant death and in the old days they would have been right. What would Zarruk do? It was a foolish question. What could he do? Cut down the only man who could give them victory? Tell the other Kas that the war was over and they could all go home? No, he had no choice at all and the look on his face told Atark that he was well aware of those facts. The hot anger faded to be replaced with a cold mask, devoid of expression.

"Very well, Mighty Shaman! Since it seems you now command the army, it shall be so!" Zarruk savagely turned his horse about and galloped off, followed by his escort.

Atark watched him ride off and then slowly turned back to the bound hetman. "There is no hope for you or your people now. And in a few moments you shall be in hell." He looked to the nearest swordsman. "This one dies last."

He turned again and strode toward the platform.

"Let us begin!"

Matt sighed in relief. The Glovina, at last! They had ridden hard for the last three days. By yesterday they had outrun the last signs of Kaifeng depredations and he had allowed them to turn east. The previous evening he had known they were close to the river, but he was not sure how close. They had been riding only two hours so far today and the river was now in sight. His men laughed and joked. Once on the far bank they would be safe.

At least for a while. He had little doubt that Berssenburg would fall eventually—if, indeed, it had not fallen already. And once the Kaifs were done looting it, they would continue east. He was absolutely certain of that. There were a few more important Berssian cities to the east and then they would reach the other kingdoms and duchies. Would they be able to mount a defense? Was there any answer to the fireflies? Well, if not, then they would have to learn to fight with sword and lance and bow again! They would stop the damn Kaifs one way or another!

The other men with him were all Berssians. They planned to just find the nearest garrison and fall in with some other regiment. Matt had other plans. The Berssians could never stop the Kaifs on their own. This was going to take a combined effort of all the Easterners. But would they see that?

By the gods, I'll force them to see it!

Matt was not going to stop on the other side of the river. He had made up his mind to keep going. Keep going east until he reached those smug, fat kingdoms beyond Berssia. He would tell them what he had seen and what he knew. He would *make* them listen!

His horse suddenly whinnied and all the others did, too. They were frightened by something. Matt dismounted and tried to calm the animal. But then the ground quivered slightly beneath his feet and there was a low, faint rumble. Like distant thunder except there wasn't a cloud in the sky this morning. The shaking stopped and the thunder faded and the horses were calm again.

"What the hell was that?" cried one of the men.

"I don't know," said Matt, "but we are not waiting around to find out! Get mounted! We are crossing the river today!"

CHAPTER FOURTEEN

Kareen looked apprehensively down the rubble-choked street. The city had fallen a week ago, but there were still bands of Kaifeng roaming through it looking for more loot and slaves. It was unlikely that anyone would bother her considering how she was dressed and that she was Atark's slave, but you never knew. If the warriors were drunk enough, they might not care. She was carrying a basket with food and drink for Atark's mid-day meal. Thelena had sent her. She would have gone herself, but she was still feeling poorly.

The magic Atark had worked to take the city had nearly killed his daughter. She had moaned and shrieked and clawed at her face until Kareen had managed to restrain her. She had held her close and rocked her and whispered stupid things in her ear, while the earth trembled around them, until it had passed. Thelena had lain in a stupor for a day and a night. Kareen had tended her and even Atark seemed grateful to her for it. She was doing much better now, but she was still unsteady on her feet and thus Kareen had been sent into the city with the basket for Atark. There was certain to be food in plenty wherever the shaman was, but Thelena took or sent a basket each day. It was a gift of her love as well as of food.

It was the first time she had been to Berssenburg since she and Matt had ridden through here over four years ago. Had she not known where she was, she never would have recognized it. The city was a shambles. The initial explosions and fires had done a lot of damage, but that was as nothing compared to what Atark's last spell—and the sack that had followed—had done.

The terrible shaking that had brought down the walls had also destroyed a great many buildings. Collapsed houses were everywhere. The damage was greatest on the western shore, but the main part of the city on the east bank of the river was also heavily damaged. Even the great Temple of Hadron was missing its tallest spire.

The shaking had upset candles and lanterns and many fires had raged unchecked for days. More buildings had been burned when the Kaifeng had sacked the city.

They were still sacking the city.

From the stories that Kareen had heard, the bulk of the city's defenders had been crushed under falling stones when Atark brought down the walls. The Kaifeng had then been able to charge into the city virtually unopposed. They had butchered the few remaining defenders and swept across the single surviving bridge to take the eastern part of the city as well.

Despite the vast damage, there had still been unimaginable amounts of loot to be taken. The King of Berssia and his immediate family and retainers had managed to slip away, down the river on a boat, in the confusion of the assault, but he had left most of his treasures behind. The Kas occupied his palace and now lived among small mountains of gold, silver, jewels and wealth too numerous to classify, let alone count. Hundreds of lesser nobles had not been so lucky as their king. They were dead or prisoners and their more modest palaces were occupied by the noyens. Even the youngest Kaifeng warrior had more loot than he could carry.

Of course, he could always get a slave to carry it for him. Berssenburg was normally a city of around two hundred thousand. But even before the army had marched to its doom, a tide of refugees had descended on the city from the villages and towns to the west. After the word of the army's destruction reached here, even more people had fled to the city. Some had kept right on fleeing and headed east. But once the Kaifeng had gotten their horsemen across the river they had closed off any retreat and penned everyone up inside. When the city fell, most of them had been caught. Many had been killed by the earthquake, and a surprisingly large number had broken through the cordon and escaped to the east, but most had been trapped in the city. They were all slaves of the Kaifeng now. The Kas had given orders that any of the men who surrendered were to be spared. Probably not all the Kaifs had obeyed that command, but still, there had been a minimum of wholesale slaughter. The Kas wanted the slaves to help harvest the crops that were standing unattended all around the city. Many thousands of them had already been driven out of the city to do just that.

Their women had stayed behind. In all the previous battles, there had always been far more Kaifeng than there had been women to be captured. Not this time. The rape of Berssenburg had gone on for a week. It was still going on if Kareen's ears were not deceiving her. Such things did not really shock her anymore. The scale of it was rather horrifying, she supposed, but she knew full well what the individuals were going through and she knew that most would survive. The sheer number of women available probably meant that they were having an easier time of it than she and her fellows had.

She reached the river and paused to look around. It was still choked with debris. Four of the great bridges had collapsed into the river and were obstructing the flow. The dockyards had mostly burned before they had been flooded out. Parts of the city were still burning and the smell of smoke was everywhere. There were guards on the one remaining bridge, but they passed her through with scarcely a glance.

Kareen could not help but wonder what was going to happen to all the Berssian women. In the long term, she meant. Their short term fates were not in doubt. She had talked with Thelena about it, but apparently Kaifeng customs did not quite cover the current situation. When they were out on the plains, the Kaifeng tribes would fight each other at times and steal each others' women. It was customary. They would also take foreign women when they could. Kareen had been surprised to learn that there were other lands that bordered the Plains of Kaif and other people who lived in them.

If a Kaifeng warrior took a Kaif woman in a raid he would almost always take her as a wife. With common languages and customs, it was not usually a hard transition. If the man already had a wife, then the new woman would become the junior wife and be taken into the peculiar joint marriages that the Kaifeng had. It had taken a while for Thelena to get the idea across to Kareen. When a man had more than one wife, it was not as if he were marrying each woman individually. Rather, all the partners were marrying each other. The man to the women, the women to the man, and the women to each other. It seemed strange and even a bit sinful to Kareen, but it did explain some of the things she had witnessed and experienced among the Kaifeng.

If a foreign woman was taken then her status was a bit different. She would be a slave in her captor's household, serving the warrior and any wives he might have. But if she served well and adapted, she quickly became just like a junior wife, especially once she had borne a child or two. Her children would grow up as Kaifeng.

The capture of Berssenburg was presenting some real problems, it seemed. The Kaifeng customs worked just fine with the normal state of affairs which might see a few new women brought into a tribe each year. But this enormous influx was unprecedented. The new women actually outnumbered the Kaifeng women. Some of the noyens had taken five or even ten new slaves and the Kaifeng women were not happy about it. Of course, not all the captured women were being added to Kaifeng households. Just the young and pretty ones—which also did nothing to improve the mood of the Kaifeng women. Thelena speculated that a lot of the excess women would be sold to the new Kaifeng who were arriving, or possibly shipped west in slave caravans.

Kareen got the impression that Thelena was actually amused by the situation, although she could scarcely imagine why. Her amusement had vanished when she asked Thelena what exactly *her* status would end up being. Atark had yet to touch her, but was that going to last? Would he take her into his bed? What if he did? What if she bore him children? Would she then be his wife? Would that make Thelena her step-daughter? Thelena had brushed off the notion, but Kareen could see she was disturbed by the question.

She pushed the thought out of her own mind as she reached the gates of the palace. The King's former residence did not seem too badly damaged, although one section had a collapsed roof and an outbuilding had burned. There were many more guards here and they were far more alert than the ones on the bridge. But they still passed her through once she identified herself. They pointed to the great central hall and she nervously strode down the broad avenue that led to it. The carefully manicured gardens on either side were already showing signs of neglect and tethered horses were grazing on the flowers. A lot of the palace's windows were broken, although that might have been from when the gunpowder works exploded or the earthquake rather than deliberate vandalism.

She reached the grand staircase leading up to the doors of the hall. She was getting tired: this was a far longer walk than she had imagined. Atark had refused to move his quarters into the city as the rest of the Kas had done and his tent was easily four or five miles away. There were more guards at the doors, but once again, they did not stop her. The foyer of the hall was magnificent and hardly damaged at all, although there was a large mound of broken glass that had been swept into one corner. Another set of doors led to the great audience chamber. She could see and hear that a large number of people were gathered there. Atark would surely be there, too.

She came to the doors and halted. Something was going on inside and she was not sure she wanted to know what. The assembled leaders were there, as she had expected, but she had not expected to see a hundred terrified women kneeling in the center of the chamber.

"So then, we are agreed," said Ka-Noyen Zarruk. "These women, the daughters of the nobility of Berssia, shall be sent west along with fine clothes and precious jewelry. They shall be presented as gifts to the greatest noyens in the land. They shall be an invitation to them to join us in our conquest of the East!"

There was a great cheer by the assembled kas and noyens and Atark saw the women huddling against each other in fear of what it might mean. As the cries of approval died down, Ka-Noyen Ferache stepped forward.

"And when shall that conquest begin, my lords? The year is growing late. The rains are coming. Snow will follow in less than two moons. Are we to press eastward through the snow?"

"No!" cried Ka Battai. "We are warm and comfortable here. Let us spend the winter in this hospitable city and start fresh in the spring. That will allow time for the others to come and swell our numbers."

There were a number of men nodding their heads and murmuring assent. Atark was none too fond of Battai, but he had to admit that there was some wisdom in his words. He and Zarruk had discussed this very thing and had reached much the same conclusion.

"You speak wisdom, Battai," said Zarruk. "But there are still tasks to be done before the snows come."

"And what tasks do you speak of?"

"We must send at least one *helar* east to seize the towns that lie within fifty leagues of here. Right now they will be ripe for capture and holding them will ease our task in the spring. Of more importance, however, will be to send another *helar* south and west to crush the Varags. If we can burn their villages now, most will perish in the winter."

"Had it not been for your shaman's rash actions, we would not need fear the Varags," said Battai harshly. "Already the Varags sniff around the edges of our herds, looking for revenge. Instead of adding to our strength, they will take from it."

"What is done is done, Battai," said Zarruk, casting a stern glance in Atark's direction. "We must move our herds south from here for the winter. To do that, the Varags must be dealt with."

"Then send the mighty shaman to deal with them! He will be needed to silence their guns, in any case."

"He will also be needed in the east to secure those towns," said Ka Oliark. "Surely the time has come for Atark to share his skills with the other shamen. The spring will see us at war with all of the East. His magic powers will be needed in many places at once." All eyes now turned to Atark. Another well-reasoned argument from Oliark and he had been expecting this.

"Yes, you are surely right, Ka Oliark. As I have said before, the teaching is a long process. Up until now, the demands of the war have denied me the time I need to teach the other shamen. But the winter will mean months of enforced idleness. I shall be happy to teach those who wish to learn during those months." There was whispering among those in the hall now. Clearly some were not expecting this answer. Atark was not terribly happy with it, himself, but there was no way to postpone it any longer.

"And what of the immediate campaigns? The ones Ka Zarruk desires for this autumn?"

"I would suggest that we move against the towns to the east at once. We know where they are and they will not move. I can destroy the gunpowder in those places in a week or less. The warriors can then occupy them at their leisure. After that, I can turn my attention to the Varags. That will be a more difficult campaign, but if we move boldly now, we can cripple them before the winter and finish them come spring."

"This could work," said Zarruk, "but only, as Atark says, if we move boldly. We require one *helar* to go east and another to go south. Who shall have these tasks?"

"My Lord!" said Atark suddenly. "Forgive me, but I believe the time has now come for the Kas to name a Re-Ka who will command all. We have delayed this as long as we might. We need a leader!"

Silence filled the great chamber. Then, slowly, a low murmur began which quickly grew to a loud clamor of voices. Eventually, there was a shout for silence. Atark saw Teskat whispering in Ka Battai's ear. Teskat had found a new home, it seemed, and was already spreading his poison. Battai was now the one to speak.

"And how is it that a shaman is the one to instruct the Kas in what they must do? You have grown mighty, Atark, and you think that gives you leave to order our decisions. Is that why you have kept the magic for yourself alone? To eventually rule us all? You tell us we must have a Re-Ka. Then you shall tell us who it must be. Why not dispense with this all and name yourself Re-Ka! If we protest, you can simply burn us to ashes as you have your other rivals!"

The silence returned, thicker than ever. Out of the corner of his eye, Atark saw motion and he turned his head slightly and almost laughed out loud. Thelena's slave was working her way toward him bearing his lunch basket! The woman had no clue what was happening around her. The future course of the Kaifeng was balanced on a knife's edge and she went blindly about her chores.

"Atark is here as the shaman of my tribe," said Zarruk coldly. "His place here is assured by law and by custom and surely no one else here has done more to earn it!"

"Nevertheless, a shaman's place is to advise, not dictate our policy!"

There were a few snickers at this. Shamen had *always* worked behind the scenes to influence policy! But it was true that Atark had been far more visible—and vocal—than was customary.

"It is true that Atark's role here is greater than normal," said Ka Oliark, echoing Atark's thoughts, "but let us be truthful and admit that this is not a normal situation. And let us not reject the truth in Atark's words simply because he is not a Ka. We do need a leader! We have succeeded so far because we have acted as a single army with a clear goal in front of us. We have been able to agree on a course of action. That time will soon be past. Indeed, it *is* past. We shall now need to send our warriors in many directions. Kas will not be able to meet and converse. And tasks may need to be done that are not so pleasant as looting a city." Oliark paused as there was considerable laughter. "Sometimes an unpleasant task will require doing and it will be necessary to *order* a Ka to do so—not ask and wheedle him! Only a Re-Ka can do this. I agree with Atark, it is time to choose!"

Atark breathed a sigh of relief. He and Zarruk had hoped they could count on Oliark, but they had not been certain. He glanced at Zarruk and was pleased to see him standing up. *Now for the final lance into the ox!*

"I also agree," said Zarruk. "The time has come—and none too soon. For there is one more reason we need to select the Re-Ka now. We have five *helars* and five Kas to command them. With the invitations we are sending out to our kin in the west, by spring we might well have a score of *helars*. Fifteen more *helars* and fifteen more Kas commanding them. No doubt they will be worthy men—but worthy or not, they were not here! Who broke through the mountains? We did! Who crushed the Berssian Army? We did!" Zarruk paused and took a deep breath and passed his gaze over all the assembly. *"Who took this city?"*

"We did!" shouted back every voice. "We did!"

"Yes, we did! And those who led the way should continue to do so! If we do not select a Re-Ka now, what might happen in the spring? The fifteen new Kas could decide that they wish to have a Re-Ka and select one of their own. Then we, we who led the way, would be obliged to follow those who followed. I say no to that! Let us select a Re-Ka now and let those who come later swear fealty to him! Let the leaders lead!"

A loud cheer went up. All the kas and all the noyens and all their shamen and all the watching warriors cheered. The captive women in the center huddled against each other in terror, not realizing that they were the farthest things from the minds of their captors. Thelena's slave was only a few feet away, still holding the basket and looking nervously at the cheering men. Atark smiled and took the basket from her. She bowed and then slipped away. He was in a good mood. This was all going very well. And Zarruk was behaving brilliantly. They had quarreled after the slaughter of the Varags, but they were still friends and they still agreed on what must be done. And the first step had just been accomplished. No Ka would dare oppose selecting a Re-Ka now. Battai was gnashing his teeth and cursing, but he could not oppose, and it would make no difference if he did, any vote would go against him. Atark suspected that Battai had friends among those who would come later and had hoped to delay the vote so he would have more support for his own bid, but that was not to be. They would make the selection this day.

Or perhaps this night, for it would not be a quick thing to do. Zarruk had laid the perfect groundwork for his own selection by reminding everyone that he was the first. He had led the attack on the fort and opened the pass. And he had been in the center of the attack on the Berssian Army. And, of course, Atark was his shaman. None would forget that.

Still, it could well be a very long day. Atark opened the basket and looked to see what his daughter had sent to him.

Long hours later, Atark knelt in the darkened tent and looked at the ghost.

"So, it is done? Zarruk will be the Re-Ka?"

"Yes, it took half the night, and Battai nearly drew sword on Zarruk at one point, but in the end it was done. Zarruk is the first Re-Ka in three centuries! The others all swore to him."

"Good! Good! Unity of command is essential. The stories I could tell you of the in-fighting and treachery in the army the last time we came east!"

"I believe that all the Kas will prove loyal—even Battai."

"Perhaps. But do not deceive yourself! Ambition will overcome any oath given enough time. Zarruk will need to watch his back. And so will you! I agree that the time has come to begin the instruction of the other shamen. But once you no longer hold the power yourself, there will be those who will wish your destruction."

"I am aware of that. I will be careful."

"Care is good, but precautions are even better! There are spells, simple spells, which can give you protection."

"Indeed?"

"Yes, and it is time for you to learn some of them."

It was amazing what a little bit of yelling could accomplish, thought Matt Krasner. He looked, with no small satisfaction, at the cavalry detachment that was escorting him through southern Laponia. Two dozen lancers jogged ahead and another two dozen behind. People and wagons cleared the road at their approach. Of course, officially, they were escorting the Laponian Special Emissary, but none of them would be here but for him.

Three weeks earlier he had swum his horse across the Glovina River. Not long after that, his companions had turned southeast in hopes of finding someone to report to. Matt had turned his horse northeast, instead, and ridden hard for Laponia. There was nothing more he could do in Berssia. He was quite sure Berssenburg had fallen, the King might well be dead, and the kingdom was a shambles. No meaningful resistance to the Kaifeng was going to possible in Berssia—and he was thoroughly fed up with being part of a *meaningless* resistance. The only hope lay farther east and he was going to make damn well sure that they knew what they were up against.

He'd arrived in Laponia, out of uniform, riding a Kaifeng pony, and in no mood to take any shit from anyone. Fortunately, fast riders had already arrived carrying the terrible news of the fall of Berssenburg. At least he would have no trouble convincing the Laponians about *that!* Everything had been in a panic and Matt did not waste any time trying to convince local magistrates or local officials. He had ridden straight to the capital and demanded to see the king. That had involved quite a bit of yelling, but he would not take no for an answer. His sheer persistence—and loud voice—had finally won him an audience. The fact that he could claim to have witnessed the disaster first-hand did not hurt, either.

The king of Laponia was not a strong ruler, the local dukes and princes held much of the power in the land, but that had made him all the more eager to meet this valiant cavalry officer who had fought the Kaifeng and lived to tell about it. Matt had lied shamelessly, too. In the stories he told, he'd been a major at Fort Pollentia, and a lieutenant-colonel at the great battle. His regiment had slain two thousand Kaifs in a glorious charge before being swarmed under by their endless numbers. He'd led an escape from the Kaif death-pits and killed another thousand and burned part of the camp in the process. He'd personally seen and heard the Kaifeng leader and seen the sorcerer in action. Well, that last part had been true, if only from a distance. He did not have the slightest qualms about his tall tales— anything to get these people to listen to him!

And listen they had. The Laponians had their own legends about the Kaifeng. During the great invasion of three hundred years earlier, a powerful Kaif army had gone north around the headwaters of the Glovina and ravaged Laponia. Mothers here still used the threat of the Kaifs to frighten unruly children. The younger Kingdom of Berssia might have been a rival, but they had also been a buffer against the Kaifeng. And now Matt was telling them that buffer was gone.

And the Kaifeng were coming—here.

It did not taken anything to convince the king that Laponia could not face the threat alone. The king had figured that out on his own. Matt had told them everything he knew about the Kaifeng magic, too. Not that he knew anything at all about *how* it had been done, but he could tell them plenty about its effects. The parts about the magic had created the greatest consternation in the Laponian court. Advisors and 'experts' had been brought in but none had any answer for the fireflies. Answers—and help—would be needed from farther east. An embassy was decided upon and Matt made sure that he would be a part of it. He was determined to see that the word was spread.

So now he jogged along on a splendid horse, wearing a splendid uniform. The Laponian king had made him a colonel. He wasn't exactly sure what he was a colonel of, but the uniform was very nice indeed, and his purse was full of gold. Yes, it was amazing what some yelling in the right place could accomplish.

At one time he might have felt very pleased with himself, but there was too much weighing on him. Would the other principalities realize the extent of their danger? Would they put aside their petty quarrels to face the real threat? Could any answer be found to the fireflies—or the spell that was said to have shattered Berssenburg's walls? If not, could the eastern armies be convinced to give up their muskets and cannons and return to bow and sword and lance? He knew that in Laponia they were already searching attics and basements and old town halls looking for armor and weapons. Would the others do the same? He had no answers, but he would do what he could.

His mood grew grim as he thought about it. Not so much because of the enormity of the task he had set for himself, but because of the realization that this was all he had left. The Regiment was dead, his only home had been destroyed, Chenik was dead, Kareen was a slave and hopelessly out of his reach. He was completely alone. His only purpose now was to stop the Kaifs.

How could such a huge job leave him feeling so empty?

No matter. If that was all he had left then he would embrace it totally. If it was possible to stop the Kaifs he would see that it was done!

He rode east to spread the word.

CHAPTER FIFTEEN

Captain Kostlan had been doing a great deal of shouting over the last few hours, but it did seem to be having the desired effect. *Unicorn* had clawed its way against unfavorable winds and a raging sea and was finally sliding into the sheltered waters of the great harbor of Zamerdan. Those waters were packed with vessels which had had the good fortune, or the good sense, to get here before the weather turned foul.

Jarren had no opinion concerning Captain Kostlan's sense, but apparently his luck had not been too good on this voyage. On the return trip to Erebrus, a squall had carried away some of the rigging and the ship had been forced to put in at an island to make repairs. They were two weeks late getting to Erebrus—two weeks which Jarren could have spent at the wizards' island taking more notes if he had just known. Still, Captain Kostlan had nearly decided to head straight back to Zamerdan, which would have stranded Jarren and Gez for the winter. He was very glad that had not happened. The people of Erebrus were far friendlier on the return stay, but it still would have been a terribly dull place to spend three or four months. He wanted to get back to civilization! He had so much to talk to Oto about!

And a great deal that he could not talk about. He had decided during the wait in Erebrus and the long voyage back, that he was going to have to take Weibelan into his confidence. At least to the extent of telling him that there were things he *couldn't* talk about rather than try to pretend that he simply did not know. An out and out deception just was not going to work with Oto. He was sure the old man would understand—no matter how disappointed he might be.

The ship was in the harbor now and the sea was much calmer. Most of the sails had been furled and *Unicorn* glided slowly along, looking for a place to anchor. Kostlan was cursing the fact that there were no berths left along the quays. They would have to unload their cargo into the boats and row it to shore.

"And what are the bloody princes up to now?" snarled the Captain, pointing to the arsenals. "Their warships are swaying up their topmasts and taking aboard stores! I hope to hell they aren't planning on turning the harbor into a battlefield!"

"Why else would they be doing that?" asked Jarren.

"Don't know. I can't imagine those lubbers actually trying to *go* anywhere during the winter!"

"Just so long as they don't start until we get off this tub," said Gez. Kostlan frowned at the boy.

"Well then, I suggest you get your things packed so you can get off 'this tub' as soon as we are anchored and can lower a boat." Kostlan moved away, still frowning.

"Been packed for hours," answered Gez.

"What do you plan to do now that you are home, Gez?" asked Jarren.

"Dunno. I wasn't any luckier at dice on the way back than I was on the way out. Pretty nearly broke. Guess I'll go back to carrying people's bags on the docks—not that there's much traffic this time of year." The boy paused and looked at Jarren. "Unless, of course, you'll still be needing a servant. I mean, you did save my neck and all. I could probably be persuaded to stay on."

"That would be a very good idea, Gez. I'd be happy to have you around—and I could keep a much better eye on that mouth of yours that way."

"Hey!" said Gez in outrage. "I gave you my word! I won't say nuthin' about the wizards!" The boy turned red as a dozen sets of eyes turned his way.

"That's exactly what I mean," said Jarren. "You may slip up without intending to. Less chance if you stay with me."

"Maybe. But I'm giving up a fortune, you know. The other merchant houses would pay me as much gold as I could carry for what I know."

"And one merchant house would slit your throat for doing so. You'll be safe at the University, Gez. Warm and fed and paid, too."

"Well…yeah, I guess so. Same wages?"

"I think so."

"Done!"

There was a sudden roar as the anchor was let go and the cable rushed out the hawsehole. The ship lurched ever so slightly and slowed to a halt. Almost immediately there came a cry from above. "Boat approaching! Looks important, Captain!" All eyes turned toward the shore and indeed, there was a large boat with eight oarsmen pulling hard toward them. Jarren was amazed to see that there was a flag fluttering from the stern that bore the crest of the University! He looked closer and was even more amazed to see Oto Weibelan sitting near the stern!

"Ahoy the boat!" cried Captain Kostlan.

"Ahoy *Unicorn*! Is Jarren Carabello aboard?" came the reply.

"Aye, he's here."

"Thank the gods! Can we come up?"

"Aye, why not?"

Jarren looked on in growing curiosity as the boat hooked on to the ship and several people, including Oto, scrambled up the ladder to reach the slightly pitching deck. Oto spotted him immediately and rushed to embrace him.

"Jarren! Jarren, my boy! I'm so relieved to see you!"

"Uh, it's good to see you, too, sir. But I've only been gone a few months. You act as though I've been gone for years."

"Eh? What? Oh! Of course, you couldn't possibly know, could you?"

"Know what, sir?"

One of the other men who had come aboard, a younger man than Oto with a thin, stern face, stepped forward impatiently. "Did you find them?" he demanded suddenly. "Did you find the wizards?"

Jarren stepped back in surprise. Who was this person? He was dressed very richly with an ornate golden chain around his neck. Someone important, obviously, but how did he know what Jarren had been looking for? He stared sharply at Weibelan. "What is this, Oto?" Weibelan looked embarrassed.

"Oh, Jarren, my boy, I do apologize. This is Lieter Pelacore, the Chancellor of the University! He has some very important things to ask you."

"Did you find them?" he asked again. "Out with it, man! Yes or no?"

"Sir, this is hardly the place for such a discussion," protested Jarren. He looked appealingly to Oto. What was going on here?

"Dammit!" snarled Pelacore. "You'll answer me or we'll be having this discussion in the city dungeon!"

"Lieter! Lieter!" cried Weibelan. "Patience, please! Jarren just returned and he has no idea what has been going on in his absence. And he's quite correct, you know: this isn't the proper place to be discussing this. Let's go back to the University and we can get this all settled."

Pelacore scowled ferociously and Jarren thought he was going to explode. But then he got control of himself and nodded. "Very well! Let's go! We have no time to lose!"

"We'll fetch our bags," said Jarren.

A few minutes later, they were in the boat and rowing back toward shore. "So what is going on?" asked Jarren to Weibelan.

"Bad news, my friend, very bad news. The Kaifeng have taken Berssenburg."

"What?!" Jarren exclaimed. "How can that be?"

"Who're the Kaifeng?" demanded Gez. "Where's Berssenburg?"

"The city fell a little over a month ago. Apparently the Kaifeng took two of the border forts several months before that. The Berssian Army marched out to meet them and was annihilated."

"But how is that possible? By all accounts the Kaifeng are little more than savages these days. How could they defeat a modern army and capture the capital of a great kingdom? And what does this have to do with me?"

"I know it sounds incredible, but we have confirmed the information. As for 'how'? Well, my boy, we are hoping that *you* can tell us that."

Jarren looked at him in astonishment.

Mattin Krasner frowned at all of the be-ribboned, plumed, perfumed, prancing...*fops* in the council chamber and his heart sank. What could he possible hope for from this gathering of fools? But perhaps looks were deceiving; he had to admit he probably looked pretty foppish, himself, in his Laponian colonel's outfit.

At least he was here, and perhaps something of use would be done. Certainly, little of any use had happened since he left Laponia. He had traveled through the Duchy of Nirbon and the Principality of Mundoor, to the port city of Ibeck. They had spread the word as they went and while they had generated a good deal of panic, there had been depressingly little action. Then had come word of a gathering of leaders and ambassadors in Zamerdan to discuss the crisis. A voyage on a small coaster had gotten them here yesterday, despite the worsening weather.

"Colonel? If you'd please take a seat, perhaps we can get started." Matt looked up to see one of the University officials at his elbow. He had never been to Zamerdan before, but he knew that the free city was divided into many rival factions. The University was hosting the conference as a sort of neutral ground. He spotted a seat near the center of the long table and grabbed it. One of the officials looked upset and he was certain he had ruined some pre-planned order of precedence they had in mind, but he did not give a damn. Sometimes he wondered if this whole masquerade as a colonel was going to land him in a dungeon someday.

The others started finding chairs and Matt took the opportunity to look them over. As far as he knew, there were no actual *rulers* here. No kings or princes or dukes had yet arrived—if indeed they ever planned to. Instead, there was a bewildering array of ambassadors, chancellors and ministers, along with priests, generals, admirals and more than a few he could not begin to identify. The soldiers might be of interest, but he had his doubts about the rest.

A middle-aged man went to the head of the table and called for their attention. He was dressed in rich robes and had a chain with the seal of the University on it. "My Lords, I am Lieter Pelacore, Chancellor of the University of Zamerdan. I want to thank all of you for coming here in this time of terrible crisis. It is our hope that we together can find an answer to the danger that now threatens us all.

"I am sure that you are all aware of what that threat is: our ancient enemy, the Kaifeng, have crossed the mountains and ravaged the Kingdom of Berssia. The city of Berssenburg, itself, has fallen. The Kaifeng have some new weapon of great power that has allowed them to sweep aside the armies of Berssia. The enemy now stands poised to ride east and attack the rest of us. It is up to us to decide how to respond, There are representatives here from all the major powers—with the regrettable exception of Eparo—and it is vital that we put aside our differences and act in unison to defeat this enemy." Heads around the table nodded grimly and even Matt was impressed. The man had laid out the problem and the task with commendable brevity and clarity. Now if these men could just bring themselves to act!

"We are fortunate to have with us several men who were eyewitnesses to much of this great tragedy," continued Pelacore. "First, I would like to present Brother Thaddius, who has just arrived from Berssenburg. He can appraise us of the terrible events which have taken place there." A man in priestly robes stood up. He looked to be about Matt's age, but a worn and haggard expression made him look older, probably about the way Matt had looked when he reached Laponia. This man had escaped from Berssenburg? Matt looked on with great interest.

"Uh, thank you, My Lord," said Thaddius. He was speaking in Tatni, which was the language of the church and of most scholars. Matt had been schooled in it, but had not spoken it in a long time. He had to concentrate hard to understand the man's words. Thaddius glanced around at the assembled nobles and looked uneasy. "I was sent here by the deacon of my order to plead for help. The people of the city and the surrounding countryside are being subjected to the cruelest conditions by the Kaifeng conquerors. We beg all of the East for aid."

"Brother, can you tell us of how the city fell and how you managed to escape?" asked someone from far down the table.

"I'm afraid I don't know a great deal. I am a priest of Clarabra and a healer. When the news of the Kaifeng invasion arrived, it was soon followed by a wave of people seeking refuge in the city. My order was nearly overwhelmed in caring for those who needed it. Then we were told that the army would soon go out to drive away the invader and we made preparations to receive the wounded from the expected battle. The army marched away and about a week later word came to us that it had been defeated. We could scarcely believe it. At first there was great panic, but order was restored and we were told to prepare for a siege.

"A few days later the enemy arrived outside the city. I looked at them from the tower of our chapel and there seemed to be a great many of them. Then, without warning, things began to explode. The forts around the city, ships in the river, and the great gunpowder works. The whole city shook. The enemy attacked and I feared the worst. But our brave men held the old walls of the city and drove the enemy back. We were still fearful, but it seemed as though we might be able to hold out. A week passed and the enemy got many of their men across the river and circled the city. I was not able to observe very much because there was already sickness beginning to appear in the city. Our hospital was filling and my duty kept me there.

"Then the word came that the enemy was massing for another

attack. I climbed up to the tower to watch. I could see the enemy in the open ground beyond the city and I could watch our own men running to take positions on the old walls on the west bank of the river. But then the city began to shake again, much worse than from the explosions. I did not know what was happening and could only cling to the railing in the cupola. I saw the great spire on the Temple of Hadron come crashing down and I feared the same would happen where I was. But all I could do was hang on and pray. There was great noise from all around and smoke and dust went billowing up into the sky. I could see little except a few more buildings close by falling in ruin. I don't know how long the shaking lasted. Probably not as long as it seemed, but for a few minutes at the least.

"At last it stopped and I tried to see what was happening. Smoke and dust still filled the air, but eventually enough of it blew away that I could see in some directions. It was a terrible sight. Almost all the city on the west side of the river was in ruins. Much had already burned in the first attack, but now there was scarcely a building standing. Damage on the east side was less, but still very bad. Many buildings had collapsed and fires soon started. All of the bridges, save one, across the river had fallen. I saw a great many men coming across it and was horrified to realize that they were Kaifeng. The enemy was in the city and coming toward me."

The man paused for a moment, as if reliving the moment again. "I-I realized they would be coming to the temple before long and I hurried from the tower to help prepare—both for them and for the wounded. I had no idea what to expect from the Kaifeng and feared they would slaughter everyone, even the sick in the hospital.

"They did come, but their actions were more restrained than I expected and feared. They did strip the temple of most of its valuables but they left all the people inside alone, even the women." Now the man's head fell and he shook it slowly. "They did not show such restraint elsewhere. Many people were killed and the women were subjected to terrible abuse. Some managed to flee to our temple and we clothed as many as we could in the robes of priestesses and novices to protect them, but it was only a handful. The rest were… were…" the man's voice faltered and silence filled the chamber. Matt could imagine the horror in the great city. He had seen what was done with the army's camp followers.

"How did you escape from the city, Brother?" asked someone, gently.

"It was not really difficult, My Lord. There are so many captives in the city, the Kaifeng do not watch them very closely. And they seem to hold clerics in some regard. My deacon arranged to have a horse waiting for me outside the city and I simply walked out one day and then rode off that night. I was chosen because I am a good rider. It was hard for me to leave when so many people were in need of help, but I was ordered to go and now I am here. I again plead with all of you for aid. My people have been reduced to the cruelest slavery and every sign points to the Kaifeng continuing eastward and trying to do the same to all of you."

"Do you have any knowledge of how the Kaifs defeated the Berssian Army or destroyed the city's defenses?" asked a general to Matt's right. The priest started to shake his head and Chancellor Pelacore stepped in.

"We have another witness who may be able to better supply that information. Colonel Mattin Krasner can give us an account of what has happened and fill in many of the details that I'm sure all of you want to know. Colonel? Would you oblige us?"

Matt had been fully expecting this, and he had given his 'account' so many times in the last few weeks that he scarcely had to think about it anymore. He stood up and told them the whole sad story from the initial discovery of the massacred Varag patrol to the destruction of his squadron, the capture of the fort and the annihilation of the Berssian Army. He left out his mistaken arrest for desertion and since there was only one Laponian present, he bumped his rank down to captain and major in his two battles. It was nearly an hour before he concluded with his escape from the Kaifeng and his arrival in Laponia. The assembled nobles listened with rapt attention. He gave them as much information as he possibly could about the Kaifeng's numbers and about the magic spells which had brought disaster. He did not spare them any detail on the Kaifeng depredations. He *wanted* them to be appalled and from the looks on their faces it seemed as though he was succeeding. He finally came to the end, but remained standing to answer the inevitable questions.

"You are convinced that these 'fireflies' were magical in nature, Colonel?" asked Pelacore.

"I cannot think what else they might have been, sir. During the battle, I watched them as closely as I could. They were like fireflies, except much brighter, and there was nothing there but the light.

That is to say, there was no 'fly' that was producing the light, it was just a bright point of golden light. And I was watching as one of them went after a cartridge box that was near to me. The light went right *through* the leather flap on the box. It didn't go under the flap, it just disappeared as it touched the leather and an instant later the box exploded. I'm no expert, but it seemed damned magical to me."

"Surely there can be no doubt that this was black sorcery!" exclaimed another priest. Matt was fairly sure he was the patriarch of the city. His robes were certainly elaborate enough. "The Kaifeng have made league with demons and are using the forbidden power. We must all pray to the gods that these heretics receive the same punishment as all who violate their laws." A few heads nodded, but most, like Matt, seemed to think that it was going to take far more than prayer to stop the Kaifs!

"Colonel Krasner," grunted a gray-haired and gray mustached man wearing the uniform of a Zolerhan general, "are you quite certain that these so-called 'fireflies' ignited *all* of the gunpowder in the Berssian Army? The number of them needed to do that would seem quite incredible. I don't mean to be insulting, but it is well known that the standards of discipline in the Berssian Army are...not up to the same standards as we enjoy in Zolerho. Is it possible that there were a fewer number of explosions than you suggest and that it was the resulting panic that allowed the Kaifeng to win such a huge victory? Perhaps better troops could have withstood this initial surprise and still prevailed. You, yourself, proved what superior discipline could accomplish with your gallant charge. But then you are from Navaria, as I recall."

For not intending to be insulting, the Zolerhan managed to be very insulting. The Berssian representatives made an outraged noise and Matt had to work hard to control his own anger. The Zolerhans had what was reputed to be the best and most brutally disciplined army in the entire East, and they never missed a chance to tell that to everyone.

"Sir, I can assure you that no troops—from anywhere—could have done any better in that situation," said Matt stiffly. "And I'm quite certain that the fireflies got all—or nearly all the powder. After I was captured, I was led back right through the center of where the army had been. Every single artillery caisson and ammunition wagon had blown up. Almost every body I saw had a burst and charred cartridge box on it. And the grenadiers of the Berssian

Guards were all lying dead, still in their ranks—except for the bits of them that had been blown off by their own grenades! It was not poor training or panic that had done that! Sir."

The general frowned. "So you are actually suggesting that any army we might send against the Kaifeng would meet a similar fate as the Berssians?" It was clear that the man did not believe that at all.

"Yes, General, that's exactly what I'm suggesting. If the Kaifeng can use this magic against us each time we meet them—and it seems as though they can—then a modern army using modern weapons and tactics would meet a *very* similar fate."

"But without muskets and cannons, how can we hope to fight them?" exclaimed another man, who from his dress and his accent was from Durace.

"It will be difficult, sir," said Matt. "But not impossible. Only fifty years ago half of any army's infantry was armed with pikes and not muskets. A hundred years before that, we had bowmen and cross-bowmen and no muskets at all. Our cavalry already fight with sword and lance. Surely we can learn to fight this way again if our very lives depend on it—and I can assure you that they do!"

"Crossbows would probably be best," muttered one of the other officers at the table, "Takes less training."

"We'll need armor for the infantry if they're to stand up to the Kaifeng bows," said another.

"All the forts will be worthless…"

"What about the older castles…?"

"No good with that earthquake magic they have…"

"The navies will be useless without their cannons…!"

"We'll need to find more smiths who can make armor…"

"And craftsmen who can make the crossbows…"

"Don't forget about the bolts, we'll need lots of those…"

"How long would it take to train them…?"

A dozen voices all started talking at once. Matt looked on as the conversation grew out of control. At least they were talking about what they could do! Up until now, most of the leaders he had talked to had been fixated on what would *not* work anymore. Still, there were going to be major obstacles to overcome. Probably the greatest was…

"Colonel!" One voice cut through the others. It was that Zolerhan general again. "How accurate are the figures you gave us for the Kaifeng's numbers?"

"From what I could see, there were thirty to forty thousand Kaifs fighting against us at the battle. But their numbers kept growing, sir. There were only two thousand when my squadron was destroyed. The survivors from the fort did not think there were more than three or four thousand who attacked them. During the initial raids into Berssia, it did not seem like they had more than ten thousand. While I was being marched to Berssenburg we were constantly being passed by new warriors on their way to the city. It seems as though the tribes of the Kaif are all being drawn east. If that is so, there could be a hundred thousand of them by spring. Maybe twice that number. I just don't know."

"Two hundred thousand!" exclaimed a minister.

"We can't hope to even *supply* an army half that size," said the Zolerhan grimly.

"So how can we hope to stop them if we have to use the same weapons they have? They'll just swarm us under!" A babble of angry and frightened voices filled the room. The Patriarch was insisting that prayer was what was needed. The earlier determination to do what was needed was giving way to panic.

"My Lords! My Lords, please!" cried Chancellor Pelacore from the head of the table. He kept calling for order and eventually got it. "My Lords, it seems to me that we have two options. One is to try and revamp our armies so that we can fight the Kaifeng without using gunpowder. I think that we must pursue this option in any case. To ignore it would be courting disaster."

"And what is the second option?" asked the minister from Heguria.

"The second option is to find some way to counter the Kaifeng magic." This brought a moment of surprised silence from the delegates. Then a dozen voices spoke out at once.

"How...?"

"No one knows magic anymore...!"

"Impossible...!"

Pelacore again called for order and the men finally fell silent. "My Lords, it is true that we have little knowledge of the magic the Kaifeng have used against us, but we are not entirely ignorant of it, either. By good fortune, we have Master Jarren Carabello with us here today." The Chancellor paused and Matt saw him indicating a nervous-looking young man seated next to him. Matt had assumed he was a clerk or something. "Some of you may have heard of

Master Carabello. He has been pursuing a fascinating study on the workings of magic for the past several years. I believe there is a possibility that he may be able to provide us with some means of defeating the Kaifeng magic."

Matt watched as the young man turned very pale. He whispered something to Pelacore and shook his head. Pelacore appeared to become angry. "Haven't you been listening to all this!" hissed Pelacore in a voice that all could hear. "I don't give a damn who you gave your word to! By all the gods, you'll tell them what you know!" Matt became intensely interested. An answer to the fireflies? He'd been hoping for that for months! What did this man know—and why didn't he want to talk about it?

"Is there a problem, Master Carabello?" he asked in a loud voice.

"Forgive me, Colonel," said Pelacore. "Master Carabello is proving reluctant to discuss his recent discoveries."

"Reluctant? Why?" asked Matt with growing anger. "If you have some answer, then it's your duty to tell us!"

"I…I don't have any answers," squeaked the man.

"But you found people who do, didn't you?" demanded Pelacore. "You found the wizards! Admit it, damn you!"

"I gave my word…"

"To who? You admit that you gave your word to someone. It was the wizards, wasn't it?"

"What wizards?" demanded Matt and several others simultaneously. Wizards? But there weren't any wizards anymore. Were there?

"Heretics!" exclaimed another priest. He was wearing pure white robes and had amazingly red hair and eyes that glittered with a frightening intensity. Matt did not know who he was. "We must have no dealings with them! They must be rooted out and destroyed!"

"Master Carabello has been researching magic, as I mentioned," explained Pelacore, pointedly ignoring the priest. "His research led him to believe that there were still at least a few practitioners of the magical arts alive in the east. Don't try to deny that, sir! Master Weibelan has confirmed this!" The young man turned and looked at a much older man who was sitting off to one side. The old man looked terribly embarrassed, but nodded his head.

"I'm sorry, Jarren," he said, "but you have to understand this goes far beyond personal promises or personal desires."

"Master Carabello and Master Weibelan discovered a possible location for these wizards and he set out to try and find them," continued Pelacore. "I am convinced that he did find them. But he is reluctant to reveal any more." The young man looked around the table with a terrible pleading look on his face.

"I'm sorry. Please try to understand. They are afraid of you and I gave my word not to betray them!"

"Afraid of us? Why?" demanded Matt.

"They...they aren't powerful. Not the way you probably think. They are afraid you will destroy them, or make them into slaves." He cast a terrified glance at the white-robed priest.

"Ridiculous! We need their help!" exclaimed Pelacore.

"No, we don't...!" began the priest in white, but his arm was seized by the Patriarch who silenced him.

"They won't believe you," said Carabello. "That's why they have hidden themselves."

"We know their approximate location," said Pelacore. "We can find them ourselves if we have to!"

"You won't! They've hidden themselves with their magic. You'll never find them!"

"You found them!" snarled Matt. What was the matter with this young fool? Couldn't he see what was at stake?

"They consented to talk to me! If I try to lead you back to them, they'll just stay in hiding. I'm sorry! I wish I could help, but I can't!"

"You miserable coward!" cried Matt, standing up again. "This isn't some scholarly problem to discuss over brandy! Thousands of people have died and hundreds of thousands more will die! Do you think the Kaifs are going to spare you or your precious university? The University in Berssenburg is in ruins! The master scholars' heads are on pikes outside of it! The students are yoked like oxen to harvest the crops for the Kaifs and they use the books and scrolls as tinder for their fires! When they get here, they will do the same thing!" Actually, Matt had no idea what had happened to the University of Berssenburg and he hoped Brother Thaddius would not contradict him, but it sure sounded good. And it was certainly getting through to Carabello. His already pale face was now nearly white. Matt thought he was probably getting ready to wet himself.

"So you are going to take us to your damned wizards! I swear I'll wring your neck myself if you don't!"

Jarren stared at the angry soldier, standing a few yards away, and tried to compose himself. Colonel Krasner looked to be about the

same age as he was, but he had never seen a harder or more determined man. Of course, he had heard the tale he had to tell and
Jarren could understand why the man looked hard—and angry.
How else would he look at someone he thought had the answer to a
terrible problem?

But I don't have any answers! He looked to where the white-
robed priest was barely being restrained by the City Patriarch. *Even
if I did, should I give them out?*

He still could not believe this was happening. He had come back
to Zamerdan expecting to spend a delightful winter, enjoying his
first snow and carefully poring over his notes with Oto and making
plans for books and papers and lectures. Instead, he had been
snatched off the ship, held in virtual house-arrest for two days, and
then dragged to this meeting where a group of powerful men suddenly told him they were counting on him to save the world!

But he couldn't save the world. He did not know how. He rather
doubted the magickers on the island knew either, but he could not
even ask them without betraying them and breaking his word! He'd
already lied to these men about their not being able to find the
island, but what if they went ahead and tried anyway? He could just
imagine what Stephanz would say if he came running back to
Erebrus with a fleet of ships and a batch of soldiers demanding their
aid! And Dauros would be terribly hurt and Lyni would sneer at him
and even Idira would be disappointed. He'd given them his solemn
promise not to betray them.

But surely they'll be able to see that the situation has changed!

Would they? Would they even care? Idira would, but Stephanz
and Lyni certainly would not. And what about that priest who was
shouting about heresy. The Church used to burn heretics! What
should he do? He teetered in agonizing indecision.

"Well?" snarled Colonel Krasner, menacingly.

*Maybe I should take a page from Gez's book: self-preservation
comes first!*

"I...I want to help, but I'm not sure what I can do."

"Jarren," said Oto gently, "I can understand that your word is so
important to you, but this crisis goes beyond any man's word or
honor—or even beyond the desires of the wizards. We are all in
danger and that has to take precedence. You will help us, won't
you?"

He could feel his resistance crumbling. All these men looking at him! But it was important, wasn't it? Uncounted thousands could die and cities go up in flames. He'd listened in horror to Krasner's description of what had happened to the University in Berssenburg. *Surely they didn't harm the great opera house, did they?* But he knew that they probably had. The stories he had heard from the wizards about the Battle of Soor and what had come before were enough to convince him that the Kaifeng were capable of nearly anything. What else could he do but try to help?

"I...I can take you to Erberus and probably get a message through to the wizards, but I can't promise anything beyond that!" he gasped at last. "They might not even answer!"

"Just get me there and I'll make them answer!" snarled Krasner.

"You intend to go there yourself, Colonel?" asked Chancellor Pelacore.

"I think that I must. Both because I have the most firsthand knowledge of the Kaifeng magic and...to ensure that the mission is carried out as boldly as needed." He stared at Jarren.

"I must insist that an emissary from Heguria accompany this expedition," said the minister from that country.

"And from Durace!" Within seconds, all the delegates had made commitments to send someone along.

"And the Church demands a representative as well," said the City Patriarch.

"S-so you can burn the wizards as heretics?" demanded Jarren, amazed that he had the courage to even talk. "I-I won't help you do that!"

"No one is suggesting we burn any wizards, Master Carabello," said Pelacore.

"He just did!" said Jarren, pointing at the man in white. "Not five minutes ago!"

Pelacore hesitated for a moment and the eyes in the room all turned towards where the priests were sitting. The man in white looked furious, the Patriarch was trying to calm him, and Brother Thaddius looked extremely uncomfortable. "Your Eminence," said Pelacore, "I'm aware of standing church doctrine in these matters, but I'm sure you can understand that the circumstances are different now. The fate of our civilization—and the church—might well rest on acquiring the aid of these wizards. While your request for a representative on the expedition is certainly reasonable, your man would have to agree to being nothing more than an observer."

The priest in white was about to spring up when the Patriarch held him back again. "Very well, Chancellor," he said. "Brother Dominak, here, represents the Church's Council of Purity, but I agree that he is not the proper representative at this time. Who would you find acceptable?"

"How about Brother Thaddius?" asked Colonel Krasner. "He can certainly appreciate the seriousness of the situation as well as anyone."

"That would be acceptable to me," said the Patriarch, although it was clearly not to the liking of Brother Dominak. "Brother Thaddius, would you be willing to make this voyage?"

"Yes, Your Eminence. I will accept whatever task you charge me with."

"Very well, I think this is an excellent plan," said Pelacore. "If we present a plea from all the civilized lands in a united effort, these wizards must surely give us aid." Jarren was not so sure, but he kept his mouth shut. He sagged in his chair. It was all out of his hands now and he felt a bit of relief, but considerable guilt, too. No matter how he—or these people—might try to rationalize it, he had broken his word. The wizards would never—ever—trust him again.

"So then," continued Pelacore, "Colonel Krasner shall be put in command of the expedition. The Princes of Zamardan will each contribute a ship. Representatives from each of the principalities— and the Church--will go along. Meanwhile, the rest of us can conclude agreements for future military cooperation against the Kaifeng. Even if we do find an answer to the enemy magic, we will still have a terrible war to fight come spring."

"Thank you, Chancellor," said Krasner. "I believe that we must make plans to depart as quickly as possible. The weather will be working against us and only get worse as the year wanes." He walked over to Jarren. "Master Carabello, shall we get to work?"

"This is Erebrus," said Carabello, pointing to a sea chart. "The wizards' boat picked me up here and it took about twelve hours to reach the island." Matt craned his head to look over the man's shoulder.

"How fast was the boat?" asked the commodore of the squadron. He was one of the Princes of Zamardan's men, but Matt wasn't exactly sure which one. How he had been selected to lead the squadron of five warships, Matt didn't know.

"I'm not really sure," said Carabello. "It seemed very fast to me, but I am no seaman."

"Faster than the *Unicorn*?"

"Perhaps. But then it was smaller and lower to the water. It may have just seemed to be going faster."

"And you really have no idea what direction you were sailing?" The Commodore's question seemed to indicate what he thought of any man who did not know what direction he was sailing.

"Generally north, I think. When the sun rose, it was to our right. Of course, we could have been going in any direction before then. I'm sorry, but I wasn't really paying attention."

"What about the voyage back?"

"It was very cloudy and rainy. I could not see where the sun was."

"Well," snorted the Commodore, "If we assume this magical boat was not doing over eight knots, then this island could be almost anywhere within a hundred miles of Erberus. Probably off to the north, but it could be anywhere in a fairly large arc."

"You are not going to just search for it are you?" asked Carabello. "We will try to contact the wizards first, won't we?"

"We will," said Matt. "But if they don't answer—and right quick— we shall have to go looking for them. Magic concealment or not. Correct, Commodore?" Matt was in nominal command of the expedition, but the Commodore was in charge of the ships. Matt would have to be careful how he dealt with the man. He was still somewhat amazed at the authority he had somehow come to have. But he had come barging in here trying to get people to do what he wanted, and it was only just that they would expect him to do a part of the job. And he would. The idea of finding these wizards and getting an answer to the fireflies was consuming him. He had a vision of the Kaifs charging down on him and the army, just behind a cloud of fireflies—and then the fireflies not working! It was a lovely image.

But to make that happen he was going to have to find the wizards and to find them he was going to need the help of this Carabello person. Matt was trying not to dislike him. He kept telling himself that the man wasn't a soldier and could not be expected to act or think like a soldier. It wasn't really helping. He had acted like a coward in the meeting and Matt could not really forgive that. Not with what was at stake. Not with what others had already sacrificed. Well, Master Carabello was going to give his all—even if it killed him!

"When can we be ready to sail, Commodore?" asked Matt.

"The day after tomorrow. I know you are eager to be away, but we still have provisioning to do on all the ships. We may be out here half the winter and I won't be caught short on supplies."

"I understand. Very good, we'll be ready." He turned to Carabello.

"Get your things packed. And pack what you'll need. We aren't coming back without your wizards!"

CHAPTER SIXTEEN

Colonel Mattin Krasner clung to the rail as the ship heeled again. The bow dug into a gray-green wave and sent spray flying the length of the ship. Were it not for his oilskin jacket, he would have been soaked to the skin. He was very nearly soaked to the skin even with the jacket. And he was cold. The wind was out of the northwest and it carried the rumor of winter with it.

It would be drier and warmer in the stern castle, but Matt could not stand to be in there any longer. The Commodore expected to sight the island the town of Erberus was located on today and Matt wanted to be on deck when it happened. There was no practical reason for it, he knew, but three weeks at sea and the enforced idleness that it had entailed was wearing heavily on him. Lately, any delay at all—in anything he was doing—seemed to send him into a rage. He wasn't sure why, but something kept telling him that time was short. Waste not a moment. Spring was months away and it seemed unlikely that the Kaifeng could do much during the winter. Berssia had hard winters. Perhaps it was just his impatience to be doing something—anything.

What is Kareen doing right now? The lack of activity on shipboard had allowed him to think about his sister far too often. He could do absolutely nothing to help her and worrying about her did no good at all—but he couldn't help it. Thelena had said that she would protect Kareen, but what did that mean? Matt had nearly forgotten that Thelena was herself a Kaifeng. When he first saw her outside the pen, he had assumed that she was a slave like all the other women who had been captured. He realized now that he was probably wrong. Thelena had somehow been re-absorbed into the Kaifeng society and she had Kareen with her. But she was protecting her now. From what? From rape? He doubted it. From torture or death? Probably. He supposed that was all he could hope for: That Kareen would be spared the harshest sort of treatment—as long as she cooperated. Matt had no illusions about what 'cooperation' meant for a slave of the Kaifeng. *It's still better than her being dead.* He really did mean that. When he had read Thelena's message he had wept with joy and relief—even knowing full well that Kareen was probably warming some Kaif's bed. He was very glad she was still alive. If he'd learned one thing in the Kaif death pen, it was that the living could still have hope, while the dead had none at all.

As long as he and Kareen were still alive there was some hope they would see each other again. She was all he had left and he wanted to see her very much. And the only way that had any hope of happening was if he could find some way of beating the Kaifeng magic. Maybe that was why he was so impatient.

He turned slightly as Carabello staggered onto the deck and went to the nearby rail. He didn't vomit, but he looked like he wanted to. The young scholar did not seem very comfortable at sea. He did well enough usually, but any time the wind or waves changed their rhythm it would send him to the rail. Matt was trying his best not to dislike the man. His seeming cowardice had, apparently, been sparked by some misplaced sense of personal honor, so maybe he wasn't quite the coward that he appeared to be. And Matt had to admit that he had been as cooperative as you could ask for on this voyage. Once he had overcome his initial reluctance to talk, he had hardly shut up. The dinners the Commodore held had been dominated by Carabello's talk of the wizards. Some of it had not interested Matt a great deal, but other parts had fascinated him. If he could just keep the scholar properly focused, he might prove quite useful after all.

Carabello stood back from the rail and then caught sight of Matt. He jumped slightly in surprise. The man was nervous around Matt, but considering the circumstances under which they met, perhaps he should not hold that against him, either.

"It's all right, Master Carabello," said Matt, speaking, loudly against the wind, "I don't bite. Or not usually, anyway."

"H-hello, C-colonel. How are you today?" stuttered Carabello.

"Cold. Wet. But anxious to reach this island. We should get there today."

"Yes, that's what the Commodore told me. But he seems very concerned about the *Wyvrn*." Matt instinctively looked astern. Only three other ships were in sight. The fourth ship of their little squadron had disappeared two nights earlier when there had been a nasty squall. It had probably just lost touch with them and would show up later, but one never knew. If it did not reappear, that could make things interesting: several of the representatives who had been sent were aboard that ship. Matt turned back to Carabello.

"Master Carabello, I'd like to apologize for threatening to wring your neck back there during the council. I was a bit distraught at the time. I realize you had reasons for your seeming reluctance to help us. And since we shall be working together closely, I'd prefer to be on the best terms possible."

"I-I'd like that, Colonel. And I want to apologize for being so hesitant to help. This situation took me rather by surprise."

"Yes, it's not easy to break your word. But I've come to realize that a man's *intentions* are what's important." He paused and then laughed. "I've told so many lies to reach this point, that I've lost track of them. Yet I don't regret a one. Technically, I'm still a captain, sworn to the King of Berssia, and yet I'm acting as a Laponian colonel, on a Zamerdanian ship, representing a council of a score of different principalities. If I'd stuck strictly to the letter of my oath, I'd be floundering around in Berssia doing no good whatsoever."

"Still," said Carabello nervously, "if a man's word isn't worth anything, how are we to trust one another? There need to be some rules that everyone can abide by."

Matt frowned. He was neither inclined nor equipped to engage this man in a debate on ethics and morality. But avoiding the issue was not going to solve anything, either. "I suppose it comes down to a matter of degrees," he said slowly, still clinging to the ship's rail. "What promise are you making and to who? What are the circumstances that cause you to break it? If you promise someone that you will meet them at a certain time for dinner, but on the way there see a child trapped in a burning building, do you ignore the child to avoid breaking your promise?"

"No, of course not."

"No, the person's life is more important than some trivial meeting. And yet you break a promise to save the life and no one thinks less of you for it. Quite the contrary, you become a hero."

"These circumstances are not quite the same."

"No, I suppose not. They are worse. Frankly, I cannot see why these wizards fear being killed or enslaved, but even if the threat was a valid one, I wouldn't hesitate in tracking them down. You say there are a few hundred people on that island. I've seen a hundred times that number slain in a single hour, Master Carabello. Enough blood spilled to float this squadron! And there have been far more than a few hundred reduced to the cruelest slavery—including my own sister."

"Gods!" exclaimed Carabello. "I had no idea. I'm sorry, Colonel!"

"She's just one," said Matt sadly. "But in my way of thinking, any sacrifice is worth making in order to stop the Kaifeng. The safety of the wizards matters no more than your word, sir. There's a child in a burning building and I have no intention of ignoring it."

"I...I never thought about it in such a fashion. My personal honor seems like a trivial thing in comparison, doesn't it?"

"Yours, mine, anyone's. I hope we can secure the cooperation of your wizards peacefully. But be warned, sir, I *will* have their cooperation! And if I have to make their fears come true by killing some and enslaving the rest, I will do so." Carabello looked very pale again and Matt did not think the tossing seas were the cause.

"I will do whatever I can to secure their cooperation, Colonel."

"Good. That would certainly be best—for everyone's sake."

Jarren swallowed nervously and was relieved when Colonel Krasner moved away to another part of the rail and paid him no more attention. The soldier made him nervous, especially when he was in a mood like this. He took a deep breath and tried to settle himself down. Surprisingly, his seasickness was gone for the moment. They were supposed to reach Erebrus today and he was not looking forward to it. He kept hoping that something—some minor mishap with the ships--would happen to spare him the shame of returning under these circumstances, but in spite of some very nasty weather, the ships had gone on, day after day.

He heard the cabin door slam shut behind him and he turned to see Brother Thaddius coming out on deck. He smiled; against all expectation, the young priest was the most agreeable traveling companion he could have asked for. The man was bright and courteous and interested in seemingly everything. They had had several very enjoyable conversations. There was a darker side to the man, too, of course. He had gone through some of the same trials as Colonel Krasner and seen the same horrors. That could not be entirely hidden and there were moments when he would suddenly stop in the middle of a conversation and seem to be staring at something he did not want to see.

"Good morning, Thad," said Jarren.

"Good morning, Jarren. The weather seems a bit calmer today."

"Yes, a bit. We should reach the island today."

"So I understand. How long do you think it will take to contact the wizards?"

"I don't know. They certainly found out I was there quickly enough on my first trip, but I have no idea how they will respond to the arrival of this armada."

"I suppose they have some reason to be wary of us. It is true that magic-users have been badly treated at some times and places in the past. The Church, in particular, has not been their friend. I'm wondering if, perhaps, I should put off my priestly robes and pretend to be something other than what I am."

Jarren stared at the man he was starting to consider a friend and was not sure what to say. "Y-you are not really going to accuse the wizards of heresy are you, Thad?"

"I'm not here to pass judgement on anyone. My instructions are simply to observe and report back to my superiors."

"And what will they do?"

"I don't know. I am far too junior to be privy to their counsel."

Jarren was silent for a few minutes, digesting that. "I have been doing some reading on Church doctrine," he said at last. "I got a few books from the University library and brought them along. I can understand how the Keridian Revelation came about with the disasters that took place with the magic after the Battle of Soor, but surely it is time for that to be reevaluated, don't you think?"

Thaddius frowned and shook his head. "It's not my place to try and tell the Church what its policies should be."

"But I've explained to you what happened after Soor. How the lake of magic was stirred to a tempest. It wasn't Divine Wrath that caused all of those mishaps afterwards. With care, that sort of mistake can be avoided in the future. Magic could be a huge benefit to mankind."

"You are a very learned man, Jarren, far more learned than I. And you are a man of science. Perhaps you don't see how…disturbing some of the things you have said would be to a man of faith."

"What do you mean?"

The ship took a sudden heel to the left and they both had to cling to the rail until it righted itself. Thaddius regained his footing and stared hard at Jarren. "If I were to accept your version of things,

Jarren, then the gods have no place in this universe. Magic is just a 'natural phenomena' governed by physical laws—as are the winds and the tides and lightning and earthquakes. I can't deny the truth of some of what you and your colleagues have discovered, but I cannot accept a world with no room for the gods."

"I never...!" blurted out Jarren and then stopped himself. Had he? Had he suggested the gods did not exist? He thought back to a long conversation he had had with Thaddius two nights before. He had theorized that in ancient times men had accidentally learned how to use magic in various ways and this had been taken as a sign from the gods by the simple folk who lived then. This had led to the magickers being seen as the chosen of the gods. They had become priests and priestesses and religions had grown up around them. Men who could work fire magic had become priests of the fire god, healers the healing god and so on. It had all seemed very logical to Jarren and there were fragmentary records from those times that even supported that view. But what did that say about the gods? With a shock, Jarren realized that he had consigned the gods to the realm of myth. Stories and legends made up to explain the phenomena of magic—and wind and weather. No wonder Thad was upset!

"I'm sorry, Thad, I never meant to insult your beliefs."

"I know you didn't, Jarren. But there are those in the Church who would not be quite so charitable as I. A century ago you would have been burned for that pleasant chat we had last night. Even now there are those who would object very strongly to your views. Very strongly."

"But what do you think?"

"I don't know. Doctrine says that long ago the gods granted special powers to their priests and priestesses. When the first wizards appeared they were heretics who had tried to steal the blessed power of the gods by making league with demons. After Soor, the gods decided that magic was too dreadful a power for any mortal to wield and what you describe as 'the storm on the lake' was their way of taking away the power from priest and heretic alike. Now, since the gods no longer bless mortals with their power, anyone using magic must be consorting with demons and hence, a heretic. Now you tell me that the power is there for anyone with the talent to use. That neither god nor demon is involved. What am I supposed to think?"

Jarren looked out on the gray sea and realized he had been a fool.

He had thought that a nicely reasoned and logical argument would be enough to convince anyone of his position. Now he saw that simply wasn't so. Beliefs had little to do with facts or logic. Thaddius seemed a reasonable man and not prone to fanaticism. But there were others who would be. Like that Brother Dominak in the council... A new thought struck him.

"Thad, I can't claim to have all the answers. But my belief is that the world is here for us to make of it what we can. If the gods created it as you believe then they created all of it—including magic. We breathe the air they made and drink the water. We eat the plants and animals they have put here. We mine metal and forge it into tools. We even take their chemicals and make fearsome things like gunpowder which can kill thousands. If magic is a part of the world, why should it be forbidden to us when nothing else is?"

Thaddius was silent now and his brow furrowed in thought. "Perhaps the magic is too powerful. Too powerful for mortals. If a man misuses gunpowder he can cause some small measure of harm, but I have seem what magic can do in the wrong hands, Jarren!"

"If that's the case, why haven't the gods put a stop to it?"

"I don't know. The gods don't tell me their plans."

"Perhaps the wizards we seek will be the tool the gods use to stop the Kaifeng. Perhaps we are supposed to find them and bring back their aid."

Thaddius laughed sourly. "That argument could be used by anyone to justify nearly anything, Jarren. Stick to science. I don't think philosophy is your strong point!"

"Perhaps not. But I believe that much good can come from magic, too. You serve Clarabra, the goddess of healing, Thaddius. You will be amazed at the things Lady Idira can do! No one can call healing the sick or curing the injured evil!"

Thaddius slowly nodded his head. "Yes, that is the hardest part of your argument to refute, Jarren. I and my brothers and sisters work so hard to save people from illness and injury. And so often we fail. If there was another way to help..."

"There is! Just wait and see!"

"Very well, I shall."

Atark pulled his cloak more tightly around himself and tried not to shiver. The wind was biting and there were even a few flakes of snow swirling around in it. The season was not that late and it might well get warm again, but clearly real winter was not that far off. He was frustrated. They had accomplished a great deal, but it was becoming clear that the task would remain undone until spring. They had seized three towns to the east of Berssenberg with little trouble. Most of the enemy had fled before they even arrived. It had only been a matter of securing booty and rounding up slaves who had not run fast enough.

Sadly, the campaign against the Varags was not going so well. Not only had the Varags shown more spirit, but there had been far more of them than Atark had realized. The vermin infested the whole region between the Pedeff River and the Sea of Latouz. Atark and the Ka Oliark's *helar* had burned a hundred villages and towns, but there seemed to be no end to them. Still, the Varags had only tried one pitched battle and they had been crushed. The Varags were good horsemen, but they had adopted the Easterners' gunpowder weapons completely and Atarks's magic had stripped them of those. Then, against the Kaifeng bows, they had had no chance. Since then, they had tried to flee.

But while the Varags may have been distant kin to the Kaifeng, they had given up the nomadic ways of the plains and now built houses and planted crops—neither of which could be packed up and moved. With the coming of winter, most of the Varags had tried to defend their towns and villages—with disastrous results. The Kaifeng had descended on each in turn—sometimes three or four in a single day—and each had been destroyed. Atark robbed them of their gunpowder and the warriors had done the rest. The males—all of the males—had been slaughtered, their heads set in neat stacks, and all the women had been herded north. The lands for a hundred leagues behind them were utterly deserted except for the miserable columns of slaves heading for Berssenburg—and the corpses of those who could not stand the pace.

But as much as he might desire otherwise, there were going to be Varags who survived to see the spring. And perhaps for far longer than that. Rumors had it that some of the enemy were fleeing south, all the way to the land of Omak and asking to take service with the ruler there. Zarruk would not permit a pursuit across the border—at least not yet—and Atark had to reluctantly agree. The day might come when Omak would fall to the Kaifeng, but for now their business was to the east.

Or it would be after today. Just ahead was a sizable Varag town. It was packed with refugees who had fled here before the Kaifeng. Oliark's warriors were massing for the attack and Atark would smooth the way for them.

"All is ready," said Oliark.

"How many do you think oppose us?"

"Perhaps a score of scores of fighters. Maybe four or five times as many others. They have barricaded the streets with their wagons. Turned the town into a little fortress."

"We have dealt with fortresses before."

"Yes, and we'll deal with this one now."

Atark nodded. Only about half of Oliark's *helar* was here. The rest were out scouting or escorting the slaves and herds. But even half would be more than enough. Atark glanced behind him and saw that the sacrifices were ready. Only a dozen would be needed for this. As he was about to turn away, he noticed that one of the doomed men was not a man at all. A boy of perhaps twelve summers stared at him with wide, terror-filled eyes. *Ardan would have been nearly his age now.* The thought filled him with both guilt and anger. Guilt that he and the warriors were slaughtering this boy— and thousands of others, many even younger than this one—and anger at the memory of what sent him out upon this quest in the first place. So far, he had carried out his promise to Hetman Reganar. No male of any age had been spared. Killing even the infants had bothered him, but there was something driving him on. He could scarcely understand it, but he knew that this was something he had to do. Enough, there was work to be done.

At his signal, the magic began. The sacrifices died and the spell was cast. The explosions from the town were rather feeble things compared to the battles against the Berssians. The Varags had no artillery and no great magazines to explode. Puffs of smoke, faint poppings and some shouts came from the doomed town, but that was all. Then Oliark sent forward some of his warriors. Only a single score of scores for this first attack. The rest were kept hidden in nearby gullies and behind patches of woods.

The horsemen rode to within a hundred paces of the barricades and loosed their arrows. No return fire came from the town. Without gunpowder, the Varags had no way of striking back. But the fire of the Kaifeng seemed to have little effect, either. The enemy huddled in their houses or behind the barricade. A few men fell now and again, but only a few. The warriors circled around the town, looking for targets or weak spots, but found none.

"Perhaps we shall need a bit more of your help, Mighty Shaman," said Oliark.

"Very well, tell your men to turn their arrows against the buildings and the barricades." The order was passed along and the warriors regrouped. Atark prepared a new spell.

The horsemen advanced again and raised their bows. Atark reached for the power and fashioned his spell. As the arrows were loosed, they flashed into flames. They traced fiery arcs against the gray skies and then plunged back down again. They struck log houses and thatched roofs and wooden wagons. The magical fires grew and spread instantly. Cries of alarm came from the defenders as smoke poured up from hundreds of places. Another shower of flaming arrows came down, and another and another. Soon most of the houses on the edge of the town were burning briskly. The wagons of the barricade were also on fire. Some people tried to fight the blazes, but when they showed themselves, the warriors shot them down.

The flames continued to spread, but then there was a great deal of shouting and Atark could see movement inside the town. A part of the barricade was being removed and then Varag horsemen came charging out. There were ten or fifteen score of them and they galloped out and charged the Kaifeng bowmen. The warriors did not try to stand and fight. Instead, they retreated, yelling in apparent panic. The Varags gave chase.

Atark watched impassively at the apparent rout. He had seen this done many times before and it almost always worked. The Varags were led on and on until they were in the trap. The concealed Kaifeng then came galloping out from their hiding places. They outnumbered the Varags by more than ten times. The enemy tried to turn and ride away, but a shower of arrows rained down on them and over half went down in a few heartbeats. The survivors fled back toward the town with the Kaifeng in close pursuit. Less than a score of the Varags reached the barricades and the Kaifeng were right on their heels. As the Kaifeng had hoped, the Varags were unable to close the barricade before the first of the Kaifeng forced their way through. In moments, the defense collapsed as ten scores of scores burst into the town.

Atark listened to the sounds of fighting, but they did not last long. In less than a quarter hour a rider came back to tell them that the town was theirs. Not that there was much left of the town, itself. Almost every building was afire by now. Atark and Oliark rode forward to look at their victory.

All of the prisoners had been herded into an open area on the edge of town, but even as he rode up, Atark could sense that something wasn't quite right. There was all the usual screaming and wailing going on, but the Kaifeng warriors were just sitting their horses around the perimeter. The Varags huddled in the center, old men, young boys, a few wounded fighters and women of all ages.

The orders had been very clear: all men—of any age—were to die. But the Kaifeng were just sitting there. Several glanced his way and then dropped their eyes.

"What is the matter?" he asked Oliark. The Ka looked around and then back at Atark.

"Too much blood will rust even the finest sword in time. Sometimes even the best warrior can have enough of victory." Oliark was a veteran warrior and Atark had come to respect him highly. But now the man just sat his horse, chewing on his lower lip and frowning.

Atark sat and thought about this for a long time. Finally he nodded. "Very well. We shall go. Let the gods decide if these shall survive the winter."

Oliark looked at him with an expression of relief. Then he turned to the men. "We are finished here. Form up! We ride north!"

Jarren sat in the pitching boat and his uneasiness had nothing to do with the motion. The town of Erebrus was only a few hundred yards away and it was really the last place on earth he wanted to be. There wasn't a person in sight and that did not surprise him one bit. It wasn't the cold wind or the sleet that was mixed with it that had driven the people from the streets, he was quite sure of that. No, it was the four great warships crowding their harbor which had done that.

What was he going to say to these people? They were sure to think he had betrayed them and the wizards. Were they right? Certainly he had broken his word by bringing these other people here, but was it truly a betrayal? Colonel Krasner, and everyone else, had been trying to convince him for weeks that he was doing the right thing. He had thought he believed them, but now all his doubts were returning.

"It's a tidy little place, just as you said it was," said Krasner from beside him. "It's still amazing they managed to keep the secret as long as they did."

"I wonder what's going to happen to them when this is all over?"

"It all depends on what 'all over' you're talking about."

A final pull on the oars drove the bow of the boat up onto the gravel beach. Seamen jumped out and pulled it farther up with the help of the crashing waves. After a moment the boat was stable enough for Jarren to stand up and jump out. Krasner and Gez were right with him. Jarren had managed to convince the Commodore and all of the ambassadors to stay on the ships for the moment. He was afraid that a sudden invasion by dozens of important-looking— and armed—men might frighten the villagers to the point they would just run up into the hills.

"Where first?" asked Krasner as they crunched up the beach toward the town.

"I suppose we should start with the innkeeper. I think he's the leader of these people. I'm sure he knows how to get a message to the wizards. He probably already has. I'm sure the sight of the fleet in the harbor has them all very frightened."

"Well, the sooner we get what we want, the sooner we'll be gone. Make sure they realize that, eh?"

They climbed up a set of stone steps to reach the street. The inn was only a short distance away. Jarren halfway expected to find it deserted, but to his relief the innkeeper was there along with a small crowd of townsfolk. It was obvious that their arrival had been observed because no one seemed surprised. Fearful, yes, but not surprised. Jarren felt very awkward, but Krasner towed him right up to the innkeeper.

"H-hello, you remember me, don't you?" said Jarren.

"Yes, I remember," said the innkeeper. His face was filled with anger and his voice as cold as the wind outside.

"I'm sorry for barging in on you like this, but there is a terrible crisis on the mainland. We need the help of the wizards. I know you have some way of contacting them. Could you please send them a message? I assure you that we mean no harm to you or them."

"I'm sorry, but I don't know what you are talking about."

"What? Of course you do! I want you to contact the wizards just as you did when I was here before. And if you could send a message we've prepared, I would be very grateful."

"No wizards here. You want some ale?"

"But you must send the message!" said Jarren who was both alarmed and angry. Before he could say more, Krasner stepped up to the bar. He twitched aside his long great coat, revealing his splendid uniform—and his sword.

"I'm Colonel Krasner, and my friend here has told me that you have a means of contacting the wizards. Now I don't think my friend was lying, so therefore you must be. I don't like it when people lie to me. Perhaps you'd like to give us another answer?"

The innkeeper, a man named Gethorpe, as Jarren recalled, looked nervous, but did not budge from his position. "No wizards," he said.

Krasner sighed. "My friend, you are trying my patience. I want you to understand that we are not leaving here without seeing the wizards. You also need to understand that we don't have the time to wait for you to change your mind. I'm sure you've noticed the ships sitting in your harbor? Well, the very big one is called the *Titan* and she carries thirty cannons on each side. The big cannons are twenty-four pounders. Can you imagine what a twenty-four pound cannon ball would do to your little inn here?"

Gethorpe swallowed nervously, but said nothing. As irritating as it might be, Jarren could not help but admire his courage. But Krasner went on,

"Now, I'm not going to blow your inn to flinders—at least not yet. But if I don't get the right answer out of you, the *Titan* and one of the other ships—probably *Firedrake*, she's nearly as large—are going to start using those very big cannons. They are going to start at the two ends of the town and work their way inward." He turned to the watching townsfolk. "You might want to warn the people in those houses to get out of them." The peoples' eyes got very wide and several of them dashed out of the inn. "They are going to work their way to here, my friend. And then, if I still don't have the answer I want, we are going to knock down *this* building, too." Krasner leaned forward and stared the sweating innkeeper right in the eyes.

"Make no mistake: get the wizards here, *or I'll blow this town apart around your ears!*"

You really didn't have to be so hard on them, Colonel," said Jarren on the ride back to the ship. "You scared those poor people half to death."

"It got their cooperation, that's all I care about," said the Colonel.

"Really? And if he had still refused, would you have actually carried out your threat?"

"Yes. Or at least part of it. I would have had the Commodore start blowing down the houses. Presumably the townspeople would have had the sense to get out of them so no one would have gotten hurt. Whether I would have destroyed the whole town..." The man trailed off and Jarren wasn't sure what he might have said.

"So what do we do now?"

"We wait. I was charitable and gave them three days. We wait and see if the wizards get our message."

So they waited. Nothing at all happened on the first day, except that the missing *Wyvrn* finally showed up. It looked as though nothing would happen on the second, either. At dinner, Jarren began to feel very nervous. The Commodore was discussing plans for leveling the town if it became necessary. The emotionless manner in which they talked filled him with foreboding. They would really do it! They would use their great cannons to reduce a defenseless town to rubble. Jarren began to wonder if Stephanz had been right about the Mainlanders. But no, they were only threatening this because the situation was so desperate! He had to believe that. Still, he wondered if he could convince Thaddius to intervene. Of all the people here, he knew what it was to be in a city under attack. Surely, he would side with the villagers!

Halfway through the main course, a man hurried into the cabin to report that a sail had been sighted. They all rushed up on deck and sure enough, the small ship that had carried Jarren to the wizards' island and back was just rounding the headland and coming into the harbor.

"Only five people aboard," said the Commodore, who was looking through a telescope. "They are heading for the town, rather than here."

"We'll have to meet them there," said Krasner. "Would you lower a boat for us, Commodore?"

This was quickly done and Jarren found himself heading for town again. His heart was pounding at the thought of confronting Lyni like this. The wizards' boat was already there by the time their own boat reached the shore. Jarren, Krasner and Gez walked slowly across the beach to where a cloaked figure waited for them. As they got closer, Jarren could see that it was, indeed, the young woman who had first met them. As he got closer still, he could see the look of raw fury on her face.

"Lyni," he began, "please let me explain..."

"Carabello! You miserable bastard!" she snarled. "I should have cut you up for fish bait myself!"

Thelena sat on the parapet of one of the city's few surviving walls and looked out to the south. Her father was out there. He had been gone for weeks and she missed him terribly. But he was on his way back. He would be here in a few days, if the messengers were correct.

"Thelena? What are you doing up here?" She turned and saw Kareen standing there. She was holding a beautiful fur-lined robe. "It's freezing outside! You are going to catch your death!" Kareen came over and wrapped the robe around her. It had belonged to some Berssian woman and it was wonderfully soft and warm.

"How did you know where I was?"

"One of your guards told me."

"My guards?"

"Well, your father's, but when he's not here they are yours."

"Yes, it seems so strange to have them lurking around all the time. In the old days, it was just the four of us. Now it's like our household by itself is a whole tribe."

"Your father is very important," said Kareen.

"Yes, that seems so strange, too. Before, he was a simple tribal shaman. Respected, yes, but with no real power. Now all the Kas and even the Re-Ka look to him for guidance."

"That would make you very powerful, too, it would seem to me."

"In some way, I suppose," said Thelena. "But you are right: it is very cold here. Let's go back to our tent."

"I've been thinking that one of these buildings would be a lot warmer when winter really gets here," said Kareen,

"No doubt. But my father will not live in one of them. But don't complain, at least he agreed to move the tent into the courtyard of the palace."

"True, with all the buildings around, at least it will break the wind."

They walked down the cracked steps to the rubble-strewn streets. The city did not look much better than it had when it was first taken. A few gangs of slaves had been put to work to clear the debris from the main thoroughfares, but that was about all. The Kaifeng had already taken the least damaged of the houses for their own use. If the other slaves wanted to fix up whatever houses they had been given, they were welcome to do so.

Many of the buildings were nothing but burned out shells. The smell was still strong even weeks after the fires. The skies were gray and threatened snow. It was a drab and dreary place.

They picked their way through the wreckage and soon reached one of the bigger streets. Thelena glanced behind her to see one of the guards following them. Her father insisted that Gettain assign at least one guard for her at all times. It seemed very strange to have to worry about her own people wanting to harm her.

There were a lot of people in the streets. Mostly Kaifeng, of course: there were still new tribes arriving, despite the lateness of the year, and they naturally wanted to see the conquered capital of Berssia. Impromptu markets had been set up where those who had managed to grab the loot were selling it to those who came too late. Thelena wasn't quite sure what the newcomers were using to trade, but she supposed there were certain things that were becoming rare in the city—like food. And it seemed that one of the most common forms of loot that was being sold were the city's inhabitants. Slave markets had sprung up all over the city. Thelena noted the grim look on Kareen's face as they hurried past one.

"I'm glad you were unconscious when I bought you from those Varags and didn't have to go through something like that," she whispered. "What a demeaning thing! I hope you or your father never decide to sell me."

"What a thing to say!" exclaimed Thelena. "I would never allow it!"

"I'm glad. I don't mind being your slave, but to be sold to someone else..." The woman shivered.

They crossed a small bridge over a stream that fed the Glovina and entered the section of the city near the palace. The houses were bigger here and the streets wider. Much of the nobility had lived in this quarter. Now the noyens and the Kas lived here—and the former nobles served them.

Up ahead, Thelena could see a small group of Kaifeng children. They were laughing and shouting and clustered around...what? As they got closer Kareen stiffened and a chill went through Thelena that had nothing to do with the weather. A young Berssian woman—just a girl really—was carrying a bundle of wood. Or she was trying to. The children were tripping her and pelting her with pebbles and hitting her with switches. Her face was running with tears, but she kept trying to carry the wood. From the remains of her clothes, Thelena guessed that she had once been a servant to a noble family. Now she stumbled along with a blackened eye and bare feet, despite the cold.

Suddenly Kareen gasped and Thelena realized what had caught her attention. One of the boys—a lad of seven or eight—who seemed to be leading the attack, was someone she recognized. He was a Berssian, a captive from the fort. The other children were Kaifeng, and the boy was dressed just like they were. Kareen stopped with a furious expression on her face.

"Edard Halaran!" she snapped. "You stop that at once! You should be ashamed of yourself!"

The children all jumped like they had been stung. Edard whipped around to look at Kareen. At first he looked scared, but after a moment he looked as angry as Kareen.

"How dare you speak to me like that—slave!" he said in thickly accented Kaifeng. "I am the son of Yiranar of the Hyami tribe! Keep quiet or we shall whip you, too!"

Kareen gasped and looked shocked but still angry. Before she could say any more, Thelena took her arm and shook her head. "If he's been formally adopted, then he's a free man. Hold your tongue, Kareen."

"But..."

"Edard, son of Yiranar," said Thelena. "Your behavior shames your family. Leave this poor girl to her duties. She has done nothing to deserve such treatment."

Now the boy looked less sure of himself. But another lad, a bit older and Kaifeng, came to the front of the group. He looked at her with a sneer. "And who are you to talk of shame? I know who you are! And I know that you were the Berssians' whore!"

It was Thelena's turn to gasp. Coming from the mouth of this child, the slur hurt worse than all the stares and whispers of the adults. She didn't know what to say or do.

"Berssians' whore! Berssians' whore! Berssians' whore!" the children shouted. The woman they had been tormenting took the opportunity to slip off with her wood. Thelena and Kareen backed away as the children came toward them, chanting their insults. Thelena grabbed Kareen's arm and tried to steer her down the street, but the children swarmed around them, blocking the way. Some of them were picking up stones…

"Begone, you little vipers!" roared a loud male voice. Thelena's guard came dashing up with his sword drawn and the children shrieked in fright and ran. In moments they had vanished. The man stopped next to them. "Are you all right, my lady?"

"Yes, fine," said Thelena, thoroughly shaken. "Thank you very much for your help."

"Maybe I should stay a bit closer to you in the future, my lady."

"Very well." They continued walking and a short while later arrived at the palace. Thelena and Kareen went into their tent and the guard took his position outside. The women put more wood on the small fire in the middle of the tent. Thelena took the wine skin and poured a cup for each of them. Kareen took it gratefully.

"I can't believe that happened," she whispered. "Edard always seemed like a good boy."

"He seems to have adapted very well. He's a perfect little Kaifeng now." Thelena regretted the bitterness that had slipped into her voice. Kareen noticed it immediately.

"They shouldn't have called you those things, Thelena. They were very cruel. But pay no attention to it. They're just children."

"But they were right," said Thelena and a tear rolled down her cheek. "I was the Berssians' whore."

"You were not! You had no choice! No more choice than…than I've had!"

"I could have died. That's what I could have done. That's what I should have done! Sometimes I wish you had not saved me, Kareen."

"Rubbish! Oh, what a foolish thing to say!" Kareen came over next to her and put her arms around her. "I'm so glad you are alive, Thelena. Don't ever think such things." Thelena returned the hug, but she could not stop crying.

"All the rest of them can go the Nine Hells!" said Kareen fiercely. "As long as we are friends—as long as we have each other—we can stand up to all of them!"

Thelena nodded her head and buried her face against Kareen's shoulder.

"Well, the traitor has returned and brought the jackals with him, I see!" snarled Stephanz. Jarren cringed as he stepped into the library.

He had spent so many pleasant hours here, but he knew that the next few minutes were not going to be pleasant at all. Dauros was seated in his usual chair and looking very old. Stephanz was standing off to one side. Idira was near a window and looking terribly worried. Lyni had not said a word to him on the voyage here and she excused herself as soon as she had delivered her passengers. The rest of the wizards were clustered out in the foyer. Jarren and Colonel Krasner and Brother Thaddius stood before Dauros. The dozen man 'escort' they had brought with them stood outside.

"Please, Stephanz," said Dauros. "You saw the message. They have come to us for help."

"Yes, I saw all three messages from Erebrus! The one telling us the ships had arrived, the one from them—and the one relaying their threat to destroy the town! Hardly a surprise from this sort!"

"I'm terribly sorry about all this," said Jarren. "I can't ask you to forgive me for betraying your trust, but I hope you can understand that I would not have done so if it had not been the gravest crisis."

"I can vouch for Master Carabello on that issue," said Colonel Krasner. "If it will help you think less badly of him, I should mention that I threatened to wring his neck if he did not cooperate." Jarren looked to the Colonel with gratitude. It should have made no real difference—but to him it did.

"And so now you are going to threaten to wring our necks, too, if we don't cooperate?" asked Stephanz. "How utterly typical!"

"Please, Stephanz," said Dauros again. He sounded as tired as he looked. "The information these gentlemen bring us fits perfectly with the disturbances Brother Rianzzi felt recently. Clearly, magic of the first order is being loosed far to the west. Nothing like this has happened since the Great War. They come to us looking for aid. I have to believe that they are sincere—and that it is our duty to give it to them."

"Duty? To them? When did we owe anything at all to them?"

"A duty to common decency, Stephanz. Millions of people are in peril. A whole civilization could fall to barbarism without our aid."

"Perhaps it should be allowed to fall. Let the Kaifeng wipe the slate clean! After they are gone, we can start fresh."

"The Kaifeng will be a threat to you, too," said Krasner.

"They have never been seamen. They will have no interest in our tiny island."

"Enough, Stephanz. We must try to aid them—if we can."

"That remains to be seen, as well! The level of power that Brother Rianzzi reported is far beyond the skills of any of us. How can we hope to match something like that? These people wish us to throw ourselves into the furnace along with them!"

"But where could such a magicker have come from?" asked Idira. "If the Kaifeng had such wizards for all this time, why have we not encountered them before this?"

"We cannot answer that question," replied Dauros. "But, Jarren, you said that Colonel Krasner has some information on the Kaifeng magic?"

"Yes, I do," said Krasner coming forward. "Probably not as much as you want or need, but as much as anyone on our side can know." With that, he launched into a description of what he had seen. It was similar to what he had said at the council in Zamerdan, but with less information on the military aspects and more on the magic. Jarren could see the faces of the magickers become grimmer and grimmer as the story progressed. When Krasner finished, Dauros shook his head.

"By all the gods, a necromancer. That we should live to see such a thing again in the world! Colonel, you are certain about the sacrifices?"

"I can't say that I saw them myself. But there were twenty men in the pen with us at Berssenburg who did. The Kaifs had taken two hundred of the prisoners just before they attacked the city. Twenty of them did not get 'used' but they saw the whole thing. The Kaif sorcerer had the heads of all of them lopped off as he was casting the firefly spell."

"What, exactly, is the significance of this ghastly slaughter, sir?" asked Jarren.

"There are a number of different ways to tap the energy from the 'magic lake', Jarren. The most common is for the magic user to draw the energy with the force of his own will. This is what we do here, for the most part. The amount of energy drawn depends on the strength of the magic user. Only very strong, very experienced people can draw enough power for the great spells. However, there are several way to 'cheat'. One is through the use of potions or wands or various other devices. These allow the magicker to 'store up' energy in advance and then use it when he needs it. Such potions and devices are exceedingly difficult to make.

"An easier—and totally abominable—alternative is necromancy.

All living persons have an energy bound up in them. It is magical in nature, although its exact make-up is unknown. If a person is slain in the proper fashion, a magicker can capture the energy as it leaves the dying body and use it to power his spell."

"Gods! That's horrible," exclaimed Jarren.

"More horrible than you imagine," said Dauros. "There is some evidence that such a procedure has the most terrible consequences for the souls of the slain sacrifices."

"This is obscene!" cried Idira. "We must help put a stop to it!"

"How, Idira?" said Stephanz. "Such a monster would have more power at his disposal than all of us together could produce!"

"We shall just have to try!" snapped the usually jolly woman. "For once could you try to help solve a problem instead of telling us how impossible it is?" Stephanz reared back and even Idira seemed surprised by her own outburst.

"Yes, we must try," said Dauros, frowning at both of them.

"So you will help us?" asked Jarren eagerly.

"I do not see that we have any choice."

Jarren felt a huge surge of relief. Not only would they get the help they need to save the East, but they would not have to threaten the wizards. That prospect had been hanging on him like a heavy weight. He glanced over to Stephanz. The man was clearly angry, but after a moment got control of himself.

"Very well, My Lord, you are our leader and I will abide by your decision—no matter how much I might disagree with it. How shall we proceed?"

"It seems to me," said Dauros, slowly, "that we cannot hope to match the Kaifeng magicker with brute force. We shall have to be more clever. One thing that strikes me immediately, is the fact that all the accounts indicate that there is only a single man wielding this magic. During the skirmishes before the main battle, there was no sign of any magic in use. Only when the main armies engaged did he appear. If this is so, then we may be able to take advantage of our greater numbers."

"I will remind you, My Lord, that none of us is skilled in battle magic."

"This is true. But with months to prepare, some of us might be able to learn. And even those who cannot, might still be able to perform useful service. And having said that, I think, perhaps, we should move this discussion to the hall and allow everyone to participate." The old man struggled to his feet and Stephanz and Idira helped him shuffle out into the foyer and then usher the other wizards into the great hall. Jarren was beaming, but then he noticed the grim look on Krasner's face.

"Is there something wrong, Colonel? They have agreed to help us!"

"Yes, but I'm rather alarmed by the fact that they don't seem to know what to do against this Kaif necromancer. Perhaps it was unrealistic on my part, but I had just assumed that if we managed to get their cooperation, these wizards would have an answer!"

"They'll find one, Colonel. I'm sure they will find one."

Matt followed the crowd into the large hall. Dauros explained to all the other magickers what he had decided and the task that was now facing them. Most of the people seemed to accept the decree without comment. Several seemed very eager, while others appeared reluctant or even frightened. But they all got to work on the problem. Or at least he thought they were working on it. The discussion quickly became so...well...arcane...that he could follow little of it. After a while he excused himself and saw about finding quarters and food for the men of the escort. The soldiers seemed a bit apprehensive, but once they had some food in them, and some rather nice quarters, they grew relaxed. Matt was glad he would have nothing for them to do. He was *very* glad he had managed to convince all the diplomats—except for the priest—to remain on the ships back in Erberus. Most of them had insisted on coming along, but they would have been nothing but a nuisance at this stage of things. It was the sight of the wizards' tiny little boat, more than anything else, that had convinced them to stay put. Some had wanted to follow in the warships, but most had seen the wisdom in not provoking the wizards any more than they already had. Matt was still a little uneasy about having their transportation completely outside of his control, but it all seemed to be turning out all right in the end.

He finished his arrangements with the servants and then returned to the hall where the discussion was still going on. The tall angry one, Stephanz, was still being a twit, but most of the rest were all working hard. Matt grew interested in what the Alchemist was talking about. He knew a great deal about gunpowder, it seemed, and when he spotted Matt, he drew him into the discussion on how the fireflies probably worked and measures that might be taken to defeat them.

"You say that the 'fireflies' were drawn exclusively to the gunpowder, Colonel? No other inflammables? Wood? Oil? Candles?"

"Uh, I'm not really sure, Master..."

"Hessaran."

"...Master Hesseran. The exploding gunpowder rather monopolized my attention. But I would have to guess no. The baggage train of the army—especially the camp followers—would have had little or no gunpowder in it, but plenty of oil and candles. Yet the baggage train did not burn. Or very little, and some of that could have been from the exploding ammunition wagons or the Kaifs when they looted it."

"All right then," said Hesseran, "that narrows things down a bit. Blast, I left one of my books in my laboratory. It might have some information on this type of spell. Excuse me while I get it."

"Stay, Hesseran, stay," said Stephanz. "I'll fetch it for you—assuming I can find it in all of your clutter. I'm contributing little to this. Tell me which book and give me your keys."

The tall gloomy man left and Matt felt glad. "He doesn't seem too enthusiastic about all of this," he observed.

"Stephanz's field is winds and weather. He maintains the spells concealing our island. I'm not sure what he could do to help in this situation. He probably feels a bit left out."

"So do you have some ideas how to defeat the fireflies?"

"Perhaps. One option is to try and counter the spell itself. That would be difficult. Considering its power, we probably could not interfere with the actual casting of it. However, we might be able to destroy the fireflies themselves when they get close. Unfortunately, I doubt we could get them all—or even a majority."

"Considering all of the individual weapons and cartridge boxes and caissons in the Berssian army, there must have been at least several hundred thousand of the fireflies—more," said Matt.

"Yes, and I doubt that any of us could destroy more than a few hundred, or maybe a thousand of them. Not enough. We might be able to safeguard some of the artillery, but not much more."

"That doesn't sound too good," said Matt glumly.

"No, we need some other approach, I think.," said Hessaran. "Perhaps something that would draw the fireflies away, a decoy of some sort."

"Can't you attack the Kaifeng magic user with your own magic?

Keep him too busy to even cast the firefly spell?"

The alchemist looked uneasy. "That sort of magic is not something we have given much study here. Battle magic, as it's called, is very specific, very dangerous—and not much use for anything else. We've concentrated on useful—peaceful magic here."

"Very commendable, but this crisis calls for something different."

"Yes, well, we shall try."

A bit later Stephanz returned with Hessaran's book and the man soon had his nose pressed into it. But he made no immediate discovery and Matt eventually wandered off to look over other people's shoulders. Brother Thaddius was talking animatedly with the woman called Idira. Matt wasn't sure what to make of the priest. He had a natural inclination to be sympathetic for him, considering all he had experienced, but he was worried about how the Church was going to respond to all of this. Some of them could be real fanatics. The talk went on and on. Dinner was served, but the food had to fight for space on the tables with the books and scrolls. Carabello was as deeply involved in the discussions as any of the wizards.

Evening came and the magical lights were lit. Matt noticed that the girl who had brought them here, Lyni, was standing in a corner frowning. She had been there most of the day and only moved when one of the wizards wanted something. From what Carabello had told him, she was a wizard in training or something like that. On an impulse, he walked over to her. She frowned when she saw him approach.

"Good evening," he said.

"There is little good in this evening."

"I take it that you disagree with the decision to help us?"

"Yes. We are dooming ourselves. You and your kind might well already be doomed, but I see no reason we should go aboard your sinking ship and drown, too."

"The common good might be a sufficient reason."

"If it were truly the common good, I might agree. But what you really mean is *your* good. And if by some chance we should help you defeat the Kaifeng, you will simply turn against us afterward."

"You speak as though we are entirely different peoples. And yet most of you come originally from the mainland. You were once one of us. I can tell from your accent that you come from Durace. Hesseran, there, is clearly from Heguria. Don't you feel anything for your countrymen?"

"Ha!" she spat. "My countrymen! I feel as much for them as they felt for me and my kind!"

"I don't understand. You talk about 'your kind' like you are a different race."

"No, you don't understand. And yes, we are a different race. Those with the talent for magic are different—and your kind hate them for it."

"How so? Few of us were even aware you existed before this crisis. I can't recall ever seeing or hearing about magic users being persecuted. In the old days, perhaps, but not now." He glanced at Brother Thaddius.

"Then your eyes and ears have been closed! Or perhaps you just lived in a region where all those with the talent have fled—or been killed. I can assure you that such things do happen!"

"You speak as one who has witnessed it. Have you?"

The woman was silent for a moment and her face was drawn like she was in pain. Eventually she nodded. "I've seen it. My older brother had the talent, just as I do. We lived in a little village in the mountains near the border with Eparo. Things are a little...backwards...up there. We had the talent, but, naturally, had received no training on how to use it. There were no schools anymore because all the wizards were gone." She paused and took a breath. "If an untrained person has the talent strongly he can accidentally cause things to happen. He doesn't necessarily even know he is doing it. Well, my brother, Toren, made things happen. Nothing bad. No one hurt or killed, just unexpected things. When the people figured out he was the cause they killed him. No trial, no hearings, they just beat him half to death and then the village priest ordered them to burn him alive. I was eight and I saw them do it. He had not hurt anyone and they burned him to death—just because he was different!"

Matt looked at the young woman. Her face was flushed with anger, but there were tears in her eyes. "How did you end up here?" he asked.

"I was eight when Toren died. The villagers kept a close watch on me because they suspected I might have the talent, too. So they were waiting to burn me to death when the time came. Every day I lived in terror that I might accidentally cause something to happen—even though I had no clue how—and they would burn me like my brother. But I was lucky. The wizards here go to the mainland from time to time to save people like me. Master Dauros found me. He heard the story about my brother being burned and he tracked down the village and found me. He snuck me away in the night and brought me here. So, Colonel Krasner, the only thing I feel for my countrymen is anger. Let the Kaifeng wipe them all out! It is no less than they deserve!"

"I'm sorry about your brother," said Matt. "But not everyone on the mainland are like those villagers. You can't judge them all from that one incident."

"Most of the people here have similar stories to tell," said Lyni, waving her hand to encompass the laboring wizards.

"Perhaps people fear the magic users because they are so mysterious," said Matt, quite sorry he had begun this conversation. "If they knew more about them, the fear would not be so great."

"That is what Dauros hopes. I think that he will discover he is mistaken."

"But you follow his command."

"I owe him much. My duty is to obey him."

"I see. Well, perhaps you can understand that my duty is to secure your help. Everyone I know or care about in the world has been killed or enslaved by the Kaifeng—including my own sister. I owe it to them."

The woman stared at him for a long time without saying anything. Then Dauros slowly got to his feet and announced that the discussions should cease for the night and resume in the morning. Lyni was instantly at the old man's side. Matt watched her help him from the room.

Jarren awoke in his cozy room—the same one he had been given the first time he was there—and felt refreshed. All the agonizing and worry of the past weeks were over. The wizards would help! And they did not seem to even hold the fact that he broke his word against him. A vast weight had been removed from his heart. He had slept late and was eager to get back to work. He made his way to the refectory and saw that Colonel Krasner was there with all his men, eating enthusiastically. Gez was there, too, but the boy seemed to be falling asleep again. He sat down next to Brother Thaddius and one of the servants brought him his food. It was really excellent. Flatcakes and sausage and fruit and tea. He would have thought it was some sort of celebration, except none of the wizards had appeared yet.

"Good morning, Colonel," he called out to Krasner. "A fine day."

"It will be fine if you and your friends find us some answers."

"Don't be impatient, Colonel! We have a lot of work to do. Hundreds and hundreds of books and scrolls to go through. I'm sorry, but this will probably take some time. A few weeks, I would imagine, at the least. Research like this does not yield results overnight."

"This isn't some damn school report, you know. There will be no second chance if we fail this test!"

"I know, Colonel. But we have months to prepare for the spring campaign. I have faith that we'll be ready."

"I hope so. A hell of a lot of people are coun…"

The Colonel stopped in mid-word. He was staring past him, toward the door, and Jarren whipped his head around. He gasped when he saw Stephanz and Idira and Lyni in the door. Idira was dabbing at her eyes with a handkerchief, but Lyni was weeping openly. Stephanz had an icy expression on his face that matched the lance of fear that went through Jarren's heart. He sprang to his feet and went toward the door.

"Lyni! Idira! What's the matter?"

Lyni's face took on a look of raw fury when she saw him. The tears still flowed down her cheeks, but her lips drew back in a snarl. "You! This is all your fault! You killed him, you son of a bitch!" Before he could even react, she stepped forward and slapped him across the face—hard.

He stumbled back in shock and pain. No one had hit him like that since he was a boy. The blow left his cheek stinging and tears welled up in his eyes. "What…? What did I do…?" he gobbled in confusion. Idira took hold of Lyni and pulled her back. Stephanz stepped forward.

"I have tragic news: Dauros, our revered leader, is dead."

"Dead!" squawked Jarren in disbelief.

"H-he died in the night," said Idira, shaking her head sadly.

"How?"

"He was old. His heart just stopped beating."

"It was the strain of this crisis you have thrust upon us," said Stephanz. "Had you left us in peace, he would still be alive."

"I-I'm sorry. B-but this is hardly our fault." Jarren's head was spinning. The news and the slap had rocked him to his core.

"I'm very sorry to hear this," said Colonel Krasner from behind him. "He seemed like a good man. But this does not change anything. We will still require…"

"It changes everything!" snapped Stephanz. "I am Dauros' chosen successor. I am now the leader here. I opposed this cursed 'alliance' from the start, but as Dauros' loyal subordinate, I did as he wished. But now the burden of leadership has fallen to me. I shall make the decisions—and my first shall be to dissolve any and all agreements with the Mainlanders!"

"What? You can't!" exclaimed Jarren.

"I can and I will!"

"I'm afraid I cannot allow that Master Stephanz," said Colonel Krasner. Jarren turned to look at the man. He was clearly very upset by these developments. His face was white as a sheet and he clutched at his chair as he stood there. "You will give us your help!"

"And how do you propose to make us give it to you?" sneered Stephanz.

"By force, if need be."

"Indeed? And how will you do that—when you can barely even stand up?"

Krasner reached for his sword, but he wasn't wearing it. The simple motion nearly overbalanced him and he almost fell. "What have you done to me?" he snarled. Then his eyes widened in comprehension. "Poison!" he gasped. The other men of the escort cried out and tried to rise, but several of them fell. The rest could not even get out of their chairs.

"Stephanz!" cried Idira, "What have you done?" She looked completely surprised. So did Lyni.

"Just a little something from Brother Hesseran's laboratory. Nothing harmful, I assure you. But it will suffice to prevent any unpleasant scenes."

"You bastard!" grated Krasner. He grabbed a knife off the table and staggered a few steps toward Stephanz before collapsing on the floor.

Jarren's head was spinning faster and faster. Something in the food, he realized in a daze. He had gotten here later than the others, so it had affected them first. He turned to look at Idira and Lyni. He tried to form a plea for help, but the words slipped away. He felt himself falling. Soft hands caught him and lowered him gently down. From a long way off he could hear Stephanz's voice:

"Take all of their weapons and lock them up."

CHAPTER SEVENTEEN

"Jarren, I'm terribly sorry we have to do this," said Idira from the other side of the locked door. "But Stephanz is willing to let you out of your room if you promise not to make any trouble."

"I didn't think he would accept my promises anymore," said Jarren bitterly. He could almost hear the woman blushing.

"Well, actually, he accepted *my* promise that I'd keep you from making any trouble. But I need you to promise me."

"I see. What about the others?"

"Except for Brother Thaddius they will have to stay confined. Stephanz doesn't trust them. They are all soldiers and much too dangerous to let wander around."

"Whereas I'm so weak and stupid he doesn't worry about me?"

"Oh, Jarren, I didn't mean it that way! But you don't seem like someone who would resort to violence. Will you promise me not to do anything rash? If you do, you can take the air and even make use of the library."

Jarren hesitated for a moment. He was still furious over the whole situation, but there was no real point in staying in his room for another day. "All right, I promise you, Idira."

"Good!" she said and he could hear the broad smile. "Now let's get you up to the refectory for some breakfast!"

"With or without a sleeping potion?"

"Without, this time—if you behave yourself." He heard the clinking of keys outside and a moment later the door opened. Idira was standing there with Thad and one of the larger, stronger servants. Jarren stepped through and looked around. It was amazing how everything could look exactly the same, but feel so totally different. Idira looked the same, the hallway looked the same, even the little table by the window with the vase of flowers on it looked the same. But now Idira was a jailer instead of a friend and the comfortable accommodations were now a prison.

He followed Idira down the hall, but stopped and knocked on the third door. "Colonel? This is Carabello. They are letting me and Thad out for a while. Colonel?"

"He's not in there, Jarren," said Idira. "Stephanz didn't think this was…secure enough."

"So where is he? And the others? The dungeon?"

"We don't really have a dungeon. But there is a nice suite of rooms over on the north side which only open onto an interior courtyard. We've locked all the doors and lower down food and drink from a balcony above."

"They've been there three days. They must be getting a bit… testy," said Jarren. The three days he had spent locked in his room had tried his patience sorely. He could scarcely imagine the sort of mood the soldiers would be in. Colonel Krasner was probably mad enough to chew through the rock to freedom.

"Yes, they are not happy. Perhaps you can talk to them later."

"Oh? And just what am I going to say to them? What has Stephanz decided to do with us?"

"He is not going to harm any of you, I can promise you," said Idira firmly. "I would not permit it and most of the others back me on that. I believe that Stephanz simply plans to keep you here until the weather makes sea travel impossible. Come spring he'll have to decide what to do."

"So we are to be prisoners here. The Commodore of our squadron will search for us, you realize."

"Stephanz knows that. We all had a long discussion. He does not think only five ships will be able to find us in the short time they will have before the really bad weather."

"And what about Erebrus? Once they realize we are being held prisoner, they might carry out the threat to destroy the town. I'd hate to see that."

"So would I," said Idira sincerely. "That was one of our chief worries. Stephanz is making arrangements for the townspeople to flee across the mountains to one of the other towns on the island. I hope it works."

Jarren sighed. "Stephanz seems to have thought of everything. I don't suppose there is any hope of convincing you that he's wrong?"

"He is our leader, Jarren. I'm not going to go against him just because I disagree any more than he went against Dauros when he disagreed."

Jarren just nodded. He'd been afraid that would be the prevailing attitude. Idira was the strongest supporter of helping the mainland and if even she would not oppose Stephanz, then there was no hope at all that anyone else would. They reached the refectory and had a breakfast that was not quite so grand as the one Stephanz had loaded with the sleeping potion. Jarren wasn't terribly hungry anyway. Gez, who had been trailing along silently, ate far more than he did.

"We stuck here for the winter?" he asked between mouthfuls.

"Looks that way."

"But I still get my copper a day, right?"

"I'll do what I can, Gez. The situation is a bit…uncertain."

"Great."

"How are you doing, Thad?" The priest had hardly said a word.

"Well enough considering the circumstances. Feeling a bit embarrassed, actually."

"Embarrassed? Why?"

"In my healing work I make use of a great many herbs. When we sat down to our drugged breakfast the other day, I was sure I tasted something unusual in the food. But I was not sure what it was and said nothing. And now we are in this fix."

"Hardly your fault."

"Perhaps not."

"What do you think we should do?" asked Jarren, his voice falling to a whisper.

"I don't know."

After breakfast, they wandered back to the library and were somewhat surprised to see a number of people there, poring over books. After a moment Jarren realized that they were still working on the problem of confronting the Kaifeng!

"What is this?" he demanded of Idira.

"We are free to study what we wish here, Jarren. No Lord Master has ever tried to interfere with that—unless something truly dangerous was involved, of course. Some of us still believe that the Kaifeng problem is serious enough that we should try to prepare."

"'Some of us'? Does that include you, Idira?"

"Yes, of course. I have no doubts at all."

"And yet you won't help us."

The usually jolly healer looked troubled. "If we come up with some answer that you can take with you and go, then perhaps

Stephanz would allow it. He has to realize that our concealment will eventually be lost. But I doubt he will permit any of us to go in person."

"He can't control what you study, but he can imprison you here, just like me and my friends?"

"Please, Jarren, don't start this again. It's not the same situation. If it endangers all of us, then we need to act as he directs for the common good."

"We are trying to act for the common good of a considerably larger group, Idira," said Thaddius. The woman just frowned but refused to be drawn into a debate.

"Feel free to read or talk with the others if you like, Jarren. Brother Thaddius and I are going down to my infirmary to 'talk shop' for a while. Please don't leave the library alone. I'll be back in a while." She and Thad left and Jarren stood there and watched the wizards at work. Several of them glanced up at him and then, somewhat guiltily it seemed, went back to their books. He noticed that Hesseran, the alchemist, was at one of the tables. There was an empty chair opposite him and Jarren went and sat in it.

"Good morning, Master Hesseran."

"Oh, hello, Jarren. How are you today?"

"I'm feeling fine. Your potion does not seem to have had any lasting effects."

Hesseran winced slightly. "I had nothing to do with that, Jarren," he whispered. "Stephanz took the drug from my workshop without my knowledge. I was rather angry when I found out. There are strict rules about that sort of thing."

"Stephanz seems to be willing to make his own rules," said Jarren. Unlike Hesseran, he was not whispering. A few eyes were flicking in his direction.

"He is our leader now, Jarren. Don't try and start an argument about that! The Lord Master sets the policy for our community. The rest of us can have our say, but he is the one to make the final decision. It is a good system and it has worked for centuries. He was willing to obey Dauros even though he did not agree with his actions. Now we must do the same for Stephanz."

"I see. I also see that it was extremely convenient for Stephanz that Dauros died when he did."

"Jarren!" exclaimed Hesseran. Everyone was looking at him now and there were several exclamations of protest. "What a terrible thing to say! I refuse to discuss this any further. And if you persist, I'll have to have Idira take you back to your room."

"Very well. I'm sorry. I'll behave, as I promised Idira. So what are you working on now?"

"Oh. Well, I'm still looking into all the references we have on gunpowder. It goes back quite a way, you know. Farther than I had realized. There are indications that the substance was known as much as a thousand years ago. Perhaps longer."

"Really? Interesting that it was never used as a weapon until only a few hundred years ago."

"Yes, that's true. I suppose no one realized it could be used in such a way. These references just mention that it could be used to produce a flash and smoke for festivals and entertainers."

"Perhaps when the wizards were numerous, there was no need for gunpowder as a weapon. With their fireballs and such they would have been better than cannons. And with all the magic armor and swords, the knights would not have been interested in guns. Only after Soor would the need have arisen."

"Why, that's true! I had never thought about it in those terms. When you look in the larger context, it becomes very obvious, doesn't it?" Hesseran laughed. "We are too close to our particular subjects to see the whole picture. Perhaps we need to have a scholar in our community who is not a magicker to point these things out to us."

"Well, you shall have one for the immediate future, it seems. And once the Kaifeng destroy the mainland, I'll probably have no reason to want to leave—and nowhere to go even if I wanted to." A number of the others were staring at him again and Hesseran looked uncomfortable. Jarren decided he had planted enough little seeds for one session and he took one of the books from the alchemist's pile and opened it. "Let's see what else I can find."

The day passed and Jarren was able to lose himself in his research. He found many fascinating bits of information, but nothing really relevant to the immediate problem. At the noon meal he briefly saw Lyni in the refectory. She did not look at him at all.

"She really hates me, doesn't she?" he asked Idira.

"She's very upset over Dauros' death, Jarren. He was like a father to her. Right now she's hurt and angry and probably not inclined to be very fair in her judgments. Don't worry, that will pass. You know that she was actually rather impressed with you on your first visit."

"Really? She never showed it."

"We talked a few times. Girl talk, you know," Idira giggled.

"I see," said Jarren, not really sure that he did see.

Later Idira took him and Thad to see Colonel Krasner and his men. Jarren was partly eager to see them, and partly dreading it. He feared that his 'parole' was going to make him look like a collaborator to Krasner. But there was nothing he could do about that. A servant unlocked the door to a room and they went inside. There was a large window and door opening onto a balcony at the other end. He went through and looked down into a small canyon in the rock of the island. About thirty feet below him was a courtyard, perhaps twenty feet square. Several doors and windows looked out onto it. It was enclosed on all sides and had no other exits. The rocks were quite sheer and climbing out would be impossible without special gear. There were a few soldiers lounging down there and they immediately caught sight of Jarren.

"Is Colonel Krasner down there?" he called. Stupid question, where else would he be? The men relayed the call through a door and very shortly the Colonel came out and looked up.

"Carabello? Is that you?"

"Yes, Colonel, I'm here with Brother Thaddius. Are you all right down there?"

"I suppose we are. The quarters are comfortable enough—I've certainly had worse—and the food and drink are passable. But what is going on? How long are we to be kept in this jail? I see they have let you loose."

"Only under guard, Colonel. I'm afraid they see you as a bigger threat. They have not told me when you might be let out." Jarren expected the Colonel to explode. He had a hot temper and this situation must be incredibly frustrating to him. But to his surprise, the man merely nodded.

"I see," he said. "Well, as much as I hate to say it, we are depending on you, Master Carabello. We can do nothing from in here. At least you can talk to the wizards and try to change their minds." Jarren had been afraid he would say something like that.

"Uh, Colonel?" said Idira. "You say you can do nothing, but I really must ask you to do less than the 'nothing' you are already doing. Please stop taking the baskets and rope when we send the food down. If you persist, we are going to have to just drop the baskets down from here and that will make an awful mess of the food."

"I see," said the Colonel again.

"And our carpenter asked me to tell you that if you keep scraping at the door with your spoons, he's going to have to just nail it completely shut with extra bracing and that would be an awful waste of effort on everyone's part."

"I see."

"Stephanz told me to warn you that if you make trouble he'll just order the mason to wall up the doors completely."

"Your Stephanz seems to be a man of decisive action," said Krasner. He paused and then added loudly: "You realize that he murdered Dauros, don't you?"

"Colonel!" gasped Idira. The servant twitched like he'd been stung. "I will not stand here and listen to such slander!"

"Stephanz tricked Hesseran into giving him the key to his workshop last evening, you know."

"Just to get the sleeping potion!"

"Yes, and just why would he need the sleeping potion to handle us? *Dauros was still alive at that point!*"

Idira took a step back and looked very pale. "I won't listen to any more! Jarren, we are going!"

"I'll talk to you again later, Colonel—and I'm already working on that line of reasoning." They went back into the hall. Idira looked very upset.

"I think you better go back to your room, Jarren. I'll send someone to get you for dinner."

"Very well. I shall see you later, Idira."

Matt looked up at the empty balcony for a long while before stirring. What a mess! And it was almost entirely his fault. He had allowed Dauros' cooperation to lull him into a false sense of security. It had not occurred to him that there might be a coup among the wizards—but it should have, blast it!

"So what do we do now, sir?" Matt turned and saw the escort commander standing next to him, a young lieutenant from Zamerdan named Tul Jernsen. He reminded Matt of a certain young lieutenant he had known about four years earlier.

"Well, dinner should be delivered—or dropped—down to us in an hour or so. Afterwards, we could always play some cards." In fact, he wanted to scream and pound his fists against the rock. But the men were watching him and he had to be in control of himself if he wanted to control them—or the situation.

"Sir! We have to do something!"

"We just did something, Lieutenant. We planted doubt in the enemy ranks. For right now that's about all we can do."

"We can keep working on the door. And we have a hundred feet of rope now."

"The door is not going to work: they are aware of what we are trying. Any other digging through the stone would take far too long to do any good. As for the rope..." He looked up and eyed the balcony above them. It was the only possible exit. Could they fabricate some sort of grapple that would allow them to get a rope attached up there? Maybe. The railing on the balcony was solid and did not have any convenient balusters that a weighted rope might snag. If they heaved something through the windows behind the balcony it might catch on something. But that would also make a great deal of noise when the glass broke. Someone came to check on them every hour, so anything they tried would have to be done in a shorter time than that. And if they failed, the next place Stephanz put them might not be nearly so comfortable as this.

"I shall have to think about what we can do with the rope," he said to the lieutenant.

"Hess, I think I may have found something interesting," said Jarren to the alchemist.

"Oh? What?" Hesseran did not seem terribly interested. Jarren had been working with the man for nearly a week and he seemed more distracted each day. He was afraid he was losing his enthusiasm for the project.

"Yes, it's here in a letter from a magic user in Kirast to a friend in Duma. It's nearly four hundred years old. He writes about a traveling circus that visited Kirast. Apparently, there was some fake magicker with the show who was using gunpowder to trick the locals. He had no real power, but the flashes and smoke from the gunpowder fooled the people. The writer describes what he did to expose the fraud: *'Thus I used the olde Seeker spell with a touch of fire and set the golden bees upon the rascal's powder. It caused the greatest conster-nation! But I did not realize he had so much powder with him and I near to burned down the whole tent! Recall ye how we used the Seekers to bedevil poor Franzi back in school?'* This sounds to me like the 'fireflies' that the Colonel describes!"

"It certainly does!" exclaimed Hesseran, suddenly filled with his old enthusiasm.

"But do you know what these 'Seekers' might be?"

"Yes, of course! It is a very simple spell. A tiny magical 'sprite' is created and it will look for something. They would be used to find lost items—keys, money, anything, really—and when the Seeker found it, it would give off a loud whistle. Portin! Would it be possible to substitute Fire for the Wind that makes the noise?"

"I don't see why not," said one of the other wizards, looking up from his book. "But the fire a Seeker could carry would be very weak, I would think. Hardly more than a spark."

"A spark is all that's needed to set off gunpowder!" cried Jarren.

"By the gods," said Hesseran, shaking his head. "Here we were looking for some mighty battle magic and it turns out to be a spell that any student might know!"

"But much greater in power," said the man called Portin. "A typical Seeker spell might create a few sprites at most. This spell the Kaifeng necromancer uses creates vast swarms."

"True, but if it works the same way, it lets us know what we are up against. This is a wonderful discovery, Jarren!"

"Thank you, Hess," said Jarren, extremely pleased with himself. "But can you discover a way to fight it?"

"We are certainly a lot closer to finding a way now!" The man was smiling, but suddenly his face fell.

"What's wrong?"

"What? Oh, nothing. Nothing at all. Let me do a little more reading here. Keep up the good work, Jarren." He stared at the man as he went back to his book. What was the matter? Something was going on here, that was for sure. Well, there was nothing he could do about it. He shrugged and went back to his own studies. The letter had been in a collection of correspondence he had discovered and perhaps there would be more references to the fireflies. The writer had made it sound like the trick he pulled on the fraud to be a common occurrence. He was soon oblivious to his surroundings once again.

It was late afternoon when Idira and Thad came to collect him for dinner. He was surprised to see that Hesseran was gone and that there was only one other person in the library. "Hello, Idira, Thad. Later than I thought. But we made some real progress today! Did Hess have a chance to talk to you?"

"Yes," she said quietly. "In fact, I'd like us to go and talk to him right now." Jarren looked at the healer and was surprised by her sad, almost grim, expression.

"Is something wrong?" She did not answer. Instead, she led them down a series of increasingly narrow hallways and then through a door. It led to a small balcony that overlooked a gray and angry sea. Hesseran was there. After they were through the door, Idira looked behind them and then shut it.

"What...what's going on?" asked Jarren. Hesseran looked even grimmer than Idira had.

"I'm almost wishing that Lyni *had* cut you up for fish-bait, Jarren," said Hesseran.

"Why? What have I done now?"

"You've brought chaos here is what you've done!" said the man angrily. "Things were so simple and orderly before you came. Now... now I don't know what to think."

"You can't ignore the truth, Hess. The evidence is damning and you know it."

"Please, what are you talking about?"

Idira stared at him. "You should know. What you said earlier. What your friend, the Colonel, said the other day."

"You mean about Dauros' death...and Stephanz?"

"What else?" said Hesseran angrily. "After talking to you—and hearing about the Colonel's accusation—I couldn't rest. I kept thinking about what happened and what Stephanz might have done in my laboratory besides take the sleeping potion. Finally I had to see for myself. Everyone thinks I'm a terrible slob. They are probably right in most things, but not when it comes to my chemicals and potions! I know *exactly* what I have there and no one but me has access to it."

"So? What did you do?"

"I took an inventory, of course! I've been up almost every night all week doing it."

"And what did you find?"

"Well, the missing sleeping potion, of course. But I was also missing five drams of Scodgeblume."

"I'm not familiar with that," said Jarren.

"It's a medicinal herb," explained Idira. "It can cool the blood and slow the heart. I often prescribe it for some of our older people here. But the normal dose would be an eighth of a dram!"

"What would five drams do to a person?"

"For a healthy person it would probably put them in a sickly sleep for several days—if they were lucky."

"And for an old man—like Dauros?" Jarren hated to ask, but he had to.

"It...it would slow his heart down until it stopped."

"Which is exactly how he died, as I recall. His heart just stopped beating."

"Yes," whispered Idira.

"It doesn't prove that it was the Scodgeblume or that Stephanz gave it to Dauros, Idira!" said Hesseran. "We just don't know!"

"We know enough. At least I do." She paused and sat down heavily on a stone bench and stared out at the tossing sea. "Dauros was old, but he was in good health. I had examined him myself not three days before. And Stephanz was almost rabid in his opposition to Dauros' policy. No, it all fits together. Colonel Krasner is right: Dauros was murdered—and Stephanz is the murderer."

"But...but..." stuttered Hesseran.

"You know it's true, Hess!"

"I...yes, I know." The man's shoulders drooped and he plunked down on the bench beside Idira. Jarren looked at them, exchanged glances with Thad, and sighed. Partly in relief and partly in guilt. In some ways Lyni—and Hess—were right: he was the cause of all this.

"So what do you plan to do now?" he asked.

"I don't know," said Hesseran.

"We have to do something!" said Idira. "He cannot be allowed to get away with this! I will not follow a murderer!"

"Nor will I—but others will. I mean, they will refuse to believe the evidence. Most of the older members opposed Dauros' policy to begin with. They will follow Stephanz."

"What about the younger ones?" asked Jarren.

"Maybe a few would side with us, but only a few. And Stephanz has all the servants in his pocket. He's been in charge of them for years and he's been giving some of the stronger men special treatment and flattering them for a long time. They will follow him, I'm sure."

"And those same servants have the soldiers' pistols and swords," said Idira.

"Well, that rules out both a new election or a coup," said Jarren, glumly. "Counter-coup, I suppose would be a more accurate description, but in any case, we can't pull it off."

"Then we'll leave!" said Idira suddenly.

"Leave? And go where?" asked Hesseran.

"With Jarren! To the mainland! We'll do what we were planning to do before Dauros died. We'll help them against the Kaifeng!"

"How?" said Jarren and Hesseran simultaneously.

"How would we leave? Why we'll just get in one of the boats and go! Stephanz would not dare try to stop us. We're not prisoners—or his slaves!"

"It won't be as easy as that, Idira," said Jarren. "He's not going to suffer anyone challenging his authority. He'd stop you just out of pride, if for no other reason."

"He's right, Idira," said Hesseran. "The man's ego is beyond comprehension. He will try to stop us."

Idira was silent for a few moments and then she nodded. "Yes, you are certainly correct. I wasn't thinking clearly. But we shall still leave; we'll simply have to do it in secret."

"I insist that we bring Colonel Krasner and his men," said Jarren.

"I was assuming that, Jarren," said Idira. "Getting them out of their confinement will be difficult, but not impossible. From there we can go directly to the boats."

"Who is going to sail the boat for us, Idira?" asked Hesseran. "I certainly can't. I don't think you can, either." They both looked to Jarren.

"Not I! I don't think any of the soldiers are sailors, either."

"Nor am I," said Thad. They all looked out on the roiling ocean. "We'll need someone who knows what they are doing, or we'll all end up drowned."

"Lyni," whispered Idira.

"What?" exclaimed Jarren. "She'd never agree to help us! She hates me!"

"She might agree to help—especially after she's told what killed Dauros," said Hesseran.

"She's the only one, Jarren," said Idira. "Her field is winds and weather—just like Stephanz—and she's an experienced sailor. There are only a few others on the island and I would not trust any of them."

"Well, if you really think she might help..."

"I do. If this is going to be done, we had best do it quickly.

Stephanz is still distracted trying to consolidate his power, but that won't last forever. Now let's go find her."

They found Lyni alone on another balcony, contemplating the same sea that they had been. She was dressed all in black. She looked up as they approached. Her face was sad, but it quickly became angry when she saw Jarren. "What do *you* want?" she snapped.

"Lyni, dear, we need to talk to you. It's very important," said Idira gently.

"If it concerns him or his friends or his cause, I don't want to hear about it!"

"It concerns all of us, Lyni. Him and you and all of us."

The young woman looked defiant, but did not protest when Idira sat down beside her. Hesseran stood nearby and Jarren and Thad retreated as far as the small space would allow. Idira reached out and took one of Lyni's hands.

"We've all suffered a terrible loss, but I know that you have suffered most of all. I'm terribly sorry, but I fear I shall have to increase your pain still more."

"What do you mean?"

"There is no easy way to say this, Lyni. Dauros did not die of natural causes, he was murdered."

The woman in black looked up at Idira and then ran her eyes over the rest of them. She dropped her head and nodded. "I know. Stephanz killed him."

"What?!" All four of them shouted at once.

"It's obvious, isn't it? He had everything to gain by killing him. He had the opportunity—and he took it."

"But…but, you mean you *knew*?" gobbled Jarren.

"Not until it was already done. When I found his body the next morning, when I saw the white sludge in the bottom of his cup… then I knew."

"What?" exclaimed Hesseran. "You found the Scodgeblume?"

"If that's what it was. I washed out the cup later. It's all gone now."

"I wish you had kept it, Lyni. I could have verified that that is what it was."

"It doesn't matter. I know Stephanz killed Dauros."

"But you still hold me to blame," said Jarren.

"None of this would have happened if you had not come here."

"You are not being fair, child," said Idira. "Jarren did not intend any evil when he came here. No one forced Stephanz to do what he did. Stephanz willingly chose to murder."

"To protect what he held dear."

"Does that make it right? You opposed dealing with the Mainlanders as strongly as did Stephanz. Would you have been willing to kill Dauros?"

"N-no." Lyni suddenly sobbed and buried her face in her hands. "No!" Idira gently put her other hand around the woman and pulled her close. Jarren stood there and watched Idira trying to console the younger woman. He felt extremely awkward, but at least had the good sense to say nothing at all. Eventually, Lyni's weeping stopped.

"Since you have figured it out, Lyni, what were you planning to do?" asked Hesseran. The woman sniffled and then her look of anger returned. Jarren jumped when she produced a knife from somewhere in her clothing.

"I had planned to kill Stephanz—and him!—and then jump from this balcony. But I don't suppose you will allow me to do any of that now."

"Oh, Lyni!" cried Idira. "You shouldn't even think of such things!" The healer looked horrified. Jarren felt a little horrified, himself. The way she had looked at him just then!

Lyni casually tossed the knife over the railing. "I'll think of such things until the day I die. But I don't suppose I'll ever do them. So. You four have also reached the same conclusion. What are *you* planning to do about it? Not that I really need to ask." She glared at Jarren again.

"We plan to leave," said Idira. "To go to the mainland."

"And help him?"

"That was our plan, yes."

"I don't want to be a part of that."

"Dauros wanted to be a part of that," said Jarren. "He died because he believed that was the right thing to do. You could honor his memory by carrying out his last command."

Lyni stared at him for a long time. "You fight dirty. But I should have expected that from you."

"Lyni, we need your help to reach the mainland," said Idira.

"So I surmised. Why else would you come looking for me? You need me to sail the boat and tame the winds."

"Will you help us?" asked Jarren.

The woman hesitated for a long while, but finally she nodded. "There is nothing left for me here, now. Why not? When do we go?"

"Tonight," said Jarren.

Matt watched the basket with the supper dishes being pulled up through the gently falling snow. At least they didn't have to do their own washing up. And there was even running water and an ingenious toilet system. As prisons went—and he'd been in a few in recent months—this one was by far the best—and probably the most frustrating. They had been stuck here for a week and might be stuck here for months.

No, by the gods, they would not! They were going to get out of here and they were going to get what they came for. He didn't know how, but he knew that they were going to do it! The rope seemed like the best chance. They had fashioned a grapple, of sorts, which they hoped might allow them to get up to the balcony. Unfortunately, it was what happened *after* they got to the balcony that worried Matt. In all probability, the room the balcony was attached to would be locked from the outside. If they managed to get up there, they would still be stuck. The only thing he could think to do would be to wait in ambush for the next person who came to check on them. But he had no information on the procedure. They only *saw* one person up on the balcony, but that didn't mean there weren't a dozen others who came along just in case. And even if they did get up there and then get out, they still had to find their way down to the boat and sail it out of here.

After they found Carabello and kidnapped a few of the wizards.

In Matt's mind, that was the truly tricky part of all this. There was no point in getting away if they left without what they came for. But would a single wizard be enough? Which one? Could you even kidnap a wizard if they didn't want to be kidnapped? So far, these people had not shown much in the way of magical powers, but you never knew...

They were only going to get one chance at this and Matt did not want to waste it. The grapple had been ready for three days and the men were itching to go, but Matt had held them back waiting for... what?

What was he waiting for? One night would be as good as another. It was unlikely that he would learn anything more useful by waiting.

He looked again at the snow. Before long, escape would be impossible until the Spring, anyway.

"Lieutenant?"

"Yes, sir," said Lieutenant Jernsen.

"Let the men know that we shall be leaving tonight."

"Yes, sir! When, sir?"

"As soon as they check on us again. Right after that, we'll get moving."

Jernsen eagerly went to spread the word. That took about a minute and then Matt had to keep the eager men out of sight and quiet for the next hour. There was almost an inch of snow covering the courtyard before he saw a light in the window above them. A few moments later someone leaned over the railing and held the lantern out. The swirling snowflakes glittered in the light. Then the lantern pulled back and the window went dark. Matt made them wait a while longer and then they silently filed out into the courtyard. One of the men carried the rope and the grapple. It wasn't a very good grapple, just the legs from a chair they had taken apart, roped together so that there would be a few prongs that might possibly catch on something.

"Ready? All right, just try for the balcony first. If we can avoid breaking a window, so much the better."

"Yes, sir. I'll try my best." The man swung the grapple around and around and then threw it up toward the balcony. It was far short on the first try, but the man caught the grapple as it fell and tried again. The second throw bounced off the railing of the balcony. The third try went neatly over the rail and fell on the balcony. He pulled in the rope slowly and carefully, but they all sighed when the grapple came right over the balcony and fell down to them again.

"Keep trying. This could take a while," said Matt.

"Yes, sir." The man tried again and again, but with no luck. The snow was coming down more thickly now and they were all coated in white.

"All right. This doesn't seem to be working," said Matt after a while. "I think we are going to have to take a chance and try for the window."

"Right. I'll give it a real heave this time, sir." The man hauled back and hurled the grapple like a spear. It flew up and over the railing. There was an unnervingly loud bang, but nothing that sounded like glass breaking. The man slowly pulled took up the slack and everyone restrained a cheer when it suddenly went taut. The man pulled more strongly but the rope did not move.

"Good! Larst! Your turn,"

The smallest and lightest man in the group came forward and took hold of the rope. He pulled on it and then let his whole weight hang from it. It held. He stood back and spat on his hands and then jumped up and seized the rope. Several of the taller men gave him a boost and he was soon halfway up. Then three-quarters. As they held their collective breaths, he grabbed the railing and scrambled over. Almost immediately he reappeared and waved. Then he was gone again and Matt assumed—and hoped—he was re-securing the rope to something solid. There was another short wait and then Larst was at the railing again, motioning them to climb up.

Matt let several of the others go first, and then it was his turn. Rope climbing was never something he had done much of and he felt extremely clumsy doing so. But eventually he reached the top and the men hauled him over the railing. He was sweating despite the snow, and he sat there for a moment to catch his breath.

"Door's locked, sir," said Larst. "Just another room with nothing in it at all. Heavy wood door and it won't budge."

Blast, he'd been afraid of that. He glanced around, quickly. The grapple had not actually broken the glass, so they could just let themselves back down and probably their captors would never notice. But there was no point in that. They had come this far and they could go the rest of the way!

"All right. We'll wait for the next person to come in. Maybe we can persuade them to cooperate."

So they waited. Usually someone came to check on them every hour or so, although they had noticed the checks had become less frequent in the last few days. Perhaps their captors were becoming as tired of this as they were. Matt placed his men as best he could. He wanted the next people to enter to not notice them until it was too late. Unfortunately, it was not a very large room and there were no real hiding places. He briefly toyed with the idea of sending some of the men back down to the courtyard, but dismissed it: they had to be ready to move when the time came and it would take too long to have them climb back up again. So he put the men into corners and against walls and crouched down on the balcony and waited.

It seemed like they waited for a long time. The snow was getting thicker on the balcony and he knew that he could not keep the men out there much longer. What if no one bothered to check on them tonight? Well, they could always go back down and try again tomorrow...

There was a noise outside the door and everyone suddenly stiffened. Yes, there was no doubt that there was a key being put into a lock! Matt motioned for everyone to get ready, although it was totally unnecessary: they were all ready.

There was a loud click and then the door swung open. Matt was just to one side. He cursed under his breath when he saw the lantern, it was one of those magical ones and extremely bright. They were going to sce he and men almost the moment they came inside. The person with the lantern stepped into the room and Matt immediately grabbed an arm and flung the person to a waiting soldier. He used the momentum that gave him to leap into the hallway. There were several other people there and he grabbed the closest. The first person had given a yelp which was cut off almost immediately. Then Matt suddenly had his hands full of a twisting, screeching, clawing wildcat. Several other people were crying out. Damn! There were at least five of them. His men came rushing out into the hall to try and grab them.

"Run, Idira!" cried a very familiar voice.

"Let go of me, you bastard!" snarled the woman he had hold of. Her voice sounded familiar, too.

"Wait!" he shouted. "Everyone stop!" The woman in his grasp kept struggling, but the all the others froze. "Carabello, is that you?" The lantern was in the room and it was almost completely dark in the hall. He tried to see the dark shape a few feet away.

"C-colonel? Is that you?" Yes, it was definitely Carabello.

"Yes, it's me. What the hell are you doing?" The woman stopped her frantic attempt to get loose.

"Uh, we were here to rescue you. But I guess you already took care of that."

"Well, we wouldn't have gotten far if you had not unlocked the door. Who else is with you?"

"Thaddius, Idira, Hesseran, Gez, and I think you've got Lyni, there."

"He does, and he damn well better let go! Right now!" Matt did let her go and she pulled away from him with a snort.

"All right, we are loose and all together and you even have three wizards, Master Carabello. Well done. I assume the next step is to get out of here—or did you have something else planned?"

"No...no, we were just thinking about getting down to the boat and leaving. Stephanz is too strong to attack directly, Colonel. He has loyal servants—and they have your weapons."

Matt thought about it for a moment. It seemed to make the most sense, but... "Are you three wizards going to help us? Against the Kaifeng, I mean. Have you found an answer?"

"We have made some substantial progress in finding an answer, Colonel," said Idira. "We are determined to help in any way we can."

"All right, that's as good as we are going to get, I suppose. Let's get going. Lead on." The sextet pulled themselves together. Matt saw that the first person he had grabbed was the alchemist. He picked up the lantern and did something to it so that the light became much dimmer.

"This way," he said and the large group followed.

"How did you manage this, Carabello?" whispered Matt as they went down a set of steps.

"Well, the others just realized that we were right about Stephanz murdering Dauros. Thad worked on Idira and I worked on Hess. Once it became clear what had happened, this was the only thing we could do. It wasn't hard to get the key to that room—we couldn't get the ones directly into your rooms—and then we just waited for the right moment. Seems like you did, too. I'm glad you didn't hurt anyone. That was rather frightening."

"Sorry we scared you, but it worked out. Is the boat ready?"

"I think so. Lyni took care of that. But we have several bundles of books and things that the wizards need stashed up ahead. We'll need your help carrying them."

"Not a problem. We are traveling light."

They followed Hesseran through a bewildering maze of stairs and passages. They mostly went down, but not always. Finally they came to a room in a dusty, and apparently unused section of the island. "Here," he whispered. "We need to bring these." Matt looked and he saw a number of large bundles on the floor. He directed his men to carry them. Then it was onward and downward. Several times their path took them outside and Matt could see that the snow was still falling and the wind was strong. He could hear the roar of the waves splashing against the rocks.

Finally, the sound of the water was very near and the alchemist slowed his hurried pace. "Just about there," he whispered. "This next door." They were in a small tunnel, lit only by the faint lantern. There was a maddening delay as he fumbled with the latch. Finally, Lyni came forward and pushed the door open. A gust of chill air rushed down the tunnel. They started forward onto the dock and were immediately halted by a shout.

"Stop! Who's there! Don't take another step!"

"Oh hell!" hissed the Alchemist. Matt did take another step forward and then he could see three men standing on the snow-covered dock. They were facing Carabello, Hesseran, Idira and Lyni, who had been leading the way. Matt and his men were all at the rear with the bags. Damn! He should have insisted on being in front!

"I am taking one of the boats out, Pirat," said Lyni. "I won't be needing any assistance." She took a step forward.

"I'm sorry, Miss Lyni," said the leader of the men. "Lord Stephanz has issued strict orders: no one may use any of the boats without his permission. And who are those people with you?" The man came forward a few steps and then suddenly sprang back. "The prisoners! Stay where you are!" He and the other two produced pistols and pointed them at them. They were probably their own pistols, too, dammit!

"Stand aside, Pirat," said Lyni. "I am leaving and I am taking all these gentlemen with me. Don't try to stop me."

"It's all right, Miss Lyni, you're safe now! Come over here and we'll protect you from these ruffians. Lady Idira, Master Hesseran, come over here with us!"

"You are quite mistaken about this, Pirat," said Idira, "We are not hostages, we simply wish to leave. Now do put away those silly guns and let us pass."

The man looked startled. The situation was not what he had thought and now he did not know what to do. Matt stared at the three men confronting them. They had the pistols pointed at them. The snow was still coming down, how long until they could hope for the priming to get wet? The covers were closed, but a heavy rain or snow could soon render them inoperable. Perhaps if he could stall them long enough...

"Gentlemen," he said loudly. "There are three of you, and it's true that you have three pistols. But there are nineteen of us. You could shoot down three of us, but the rest are going to beat you to death with your empty guns and throw your carcasses into the sea. Now let's be reasonable and no one needs to get hurt."

The three looked really uncomfortable now. Matt moved a little to the side so more of his men could come out of the tunnel. With a little luck, they could bluff their way out of this.

Unfortunately, Lyni chose this moment to start forward. "Pirat! You will put down that gun or I'm going to take it away from you!"

The man stepped back and raised the pistol. Suddenly Carabello was rushing forward. "Lyni! Stay back!" The man shifted his aim to Carabello and Matt found himself dashing forward, too.

There was a flash that illuminated the falling snow for a dazzling instant and then there was a loud bang. Lyni screamed, Idira screamed, Gez yelped and Carabello tumbled onto the dock and slid two yards in the snow. Matt changed his direction in mid-stride, away from the man who had fired and toward the nearest one who still had a loaded gun. The man was frozen in shock and Matt reached him unharmed. He grabbed hold of the pistol and struck the man in the face with his fist. The man fell backwards, leaving the pistol in Matt's hand. He reversed the weapon, but before he could do more, the third man aimed his pistol at him and pulled the trigger. Matt sucked in his breath and prepared to be hammered down by a one-ounce lead ball. Instead, the flint made a feeble spark and the priming failed to ignite. An instant later, the man—and the one who shot Carabello-- were swarmed under by the rest of Matt's charging men.

"Jarren!" cried Idira. "Oh gods, he's been shot!" The woman and the priest rushed to his side. Lyni and Hesseran stood there without moving. Carabello's young servant was crying.

"Come on!" shouted Matt. "We can't stay here! Get the baggage into the boat. Move!"

His men obeyed instantly and in a few seconds, all the bags were thrown into the bottom of the small ship. Then they carefully picked up Carabello and loaded him aboard. He gave off a sharp moan as they moved him, so apparently he was still alive. Probably not for very long, though, thought Matt grimly. It looked to be a belly wound and that was a guarantee of a painful death. Too bad, the scholar wasn't a bad sort. He'd even been brave—foolishly brave— right at the end.

"In the boat! Everyone!" The wizards were still standing there in shock. Matt grabbed them by their arms and hustled them aboard. The three men who had tried to stop them were senseless on the dock, but not seriously harmed. "Can you sail this thing?" he shouted into Lyni's ear. She had been the one to bring them here, she ought to be able to get them back again.

"What's going on down there?" came a shout from above. Matt looked up and saw someone in a window, far up the side of the island. He did not answer, but he shook Lyni. "Come on! Tell us what to do!"

The woman blinked and jumped and then seemed to be aware of herself again. "The ropes, cast off the ropes, someone take the tiller," she said. Matt relayed the order and the men scrambled to obey.

"Hey! Stop!" shouted the voice from above.

The ropes were untied and the boat began to rock quiet violently in the heavy sea. Lyni did something with one of the ropes and the sail unrolled itself. The wind immediately caught it and nearly threw the boat against the dock. The young wizard shouted something in a strange language and the wind veered around and drove the boat out and away from the island. Matt could hear a bell clanging frantically from behind them.

Once clear of the dock and the little inlet, the wind was much stronger and the seas mountainous. The boat climbed up the side of one wave and then slid down the other in a fashion that made Matt queasy. But Lyni was doing…something…and the waves became smaller and the wind blew them on a steady course. The island was now just a dark mass astern of them with a number of lights flickering in windows. He could not hear the bell anymore. Matt made his way to where Idira and Thaddius were with Carabello.

"How is he?" he asked.

"Still alive," said the woman. "But I'm going to have to work on him right away to save him."

"Save him? With a wound like that?" asked Matt in amazement.

"Of course, I can save him," shouted Idira against the wind. "But I need a stable platform. Lyni! Can you steady the boat down so I can work?"

"I'll try," came the reply, and Matt could hear the annoyance in her voice. "Give me a few…"

A powerful blast of wind cut off her voice and the boat lurched sharply and then almost rolled over. Matt grabbed a rope and hung on for dear life. Men shouted and Idira shrieked in alarm. Another blast, this time laden with stinging sleet hit them from the other side and again the boat nearly capsized. A wave broke over the bow, drenching them all in an instant.

"What's happening?" he shouted.

"It's Stephanz!" cried Lyni. Matt faintly saw her pointing astern—and upward. Matt looked and thought he could see a blue glow from the highest point on the island. He remembered the slender tower that was there. He also remembered that Stephanz was a master of wind and water—just like Lyni. He was up there, and apparently using his own powers against them.

The wind had been blowing them away from the island, but now it was doing just the opposite. The sail flapped and shuddered and the seas became a choppy turmoil as Lyni and Stephanz fought for control. A flash of lightning suddenly split the skies, tearing aside the darkness for a moment.

"Gods! Is he tossing lightning bolts at us, too?"

"No, neither of us did that," snarled Lyni. "But hang on, this is going to get rough!"

"*Get* rough!? What do you call this?"

She did not answer, but he soon found out. The wind seemed to be coming at them from all directions at once. Waves were colliding with each other and sending spray leaping upward and then crashing down on top of them. The bottom of the boat was soon filled and Matt shouted to his men to start bailing.

The boat leaped and bucked like an unbroken horse. Matt was amazed that the wind had not snapped off the mast or torn the sail to shreds by now. Somehow the little boat held together, but another flash of lightning revealed that the island was much closer now. Even in the dark, he could see the waves breaking against its base and sending sheets of spray into the air.

"He's trying to smash us against the rocks!" he shouted to Lyni.

"I know!"

The wind and the waves were driving them toward the island. Most of it was sheer cliffs and if the boat was thrown against them, they would be smashed to bits and drowned in the raging sea. Matt could see that Lyni was straining to do something, but he couldn't begin to say what. From time to time the wind would reverse itself and they would pull a little farther away from the threatening rocks. But then the wind would change again and they would lose all the distance and more. The island wasn't more than a quarter mile off now. He looked around desperately. Was there anything he could do? All the men were bailing frantically. Water was flying out of the boat—almost as fast as it was coming in. Idira, the alchemist, the priest and the boy were all huddled with Carabello, trying to shield him from the wind and water.

The cliffs got a little closer, but then Lyni seemed to gain some bit of control and the boat hung there, not getting closer or farther away, for long minutes. He could see the strain on her face. Was this some sort of battle of wills? Could she outlast Stephanz? For a few moments his hopes rose, but then the boat began to slip back towards the island once again. Lyni suddenly screamed.

"Stephanz! Stephanz, you bastard! Try handling *this*!"

The woman raised her arms and in a flash of lightning, Matt saw her eyes blazing. She put out her arms and the boat leaped forward—towards the rocks! The winds and waves were all moving in the same direction now—directly for the island!

"What are you doing?" cried Matt.

A huge wave picked up the boat for an instant and then passed on by. Matt clung to the rail as the wave smashed into the island. An enormous gout of spray rose up.

And up, and up…

The wind was blowing incredibly hard and it seemed to seize the spray from the wave and suck it skyward. The lightning revealed a frothing geyser shooting up the side of the island, higher and higher—right toward the tower on the top. At the last second it seemed like the wind changed and tried to blow the column of water away, but it was too late. The flying deluge smashed into the tower and exploded into a gushing torrent that completely engulfed it. The blue glow was snuffed out in an instant.

The rock wall was looming over them, now, only a hundred yards away. But Lyni cried out again and the wind shifted once more. The sail bellied out and the boat surged around and pushed through the waves—south, toward safety.

Matt let out his breath. The tempest was calmed. It was blowing a mere gale now and it seemed like the calmest of seas. The island sank rapidly behind them and then a mass of clouds seemed to obscure it completely. The lightning faded and soon the only light came from the magical lamp. Matt picked him self up and went over to Lyni. She seemed terribly tired and worn and she clung to one of the stays with a hand that looked like a claw.

"Are you all right?" he asked. She just nodded her head. "That was very impressive. You have my admiration, and my thanks." She nodded again.

"Lyni!" cried Idira. "Can you hold this steady for a bit? Jarren needs attention right away."

"Another quarter-hour and we'll be safe," she croaked. "Can he last that long?"

"I think so."

Lyni went back to whatever she was doing and Matt left her alone. He went over to where Carabello was lying. They had his tunic off and he could see the bloody rag they had pressed to his belly. He did not look good at all. He could not see how Idira expected to save him—but then he'd just seen a slender young woman throw a hundred tons of sea water four hundred feet up the side of a cliff a few moments ago, so who was he to judge?

The boat skipped over the waves for the quarter-hour that Lyni had ordained and then slowed. The wind and waves calmed in a circle perhaps a hundred feet across. Beyond that line the wind still howled and the seas heaved, but within the circle it was like a mill-pond on a windless day. Lyni staggered over to Idira.

"I can't hold this long. Work quickly."

Amazingly, Carabello opened his eyes and looked at the woman. "I'm nine-tenths of the way to being fish bait," he said through clenched teeth, "why bother for me now?"

"Shut up, you fool," snarled Lyni.

"Shut up all of you," commanded Idira. "Now, hold him down and see that he doesn't move. Jarren, I'm afraid this will hurt a bit. There's no time for the pain-killing spells."

"Go ahead."

"Hold the lamp higher, will you, Hess?" The healer began to chant. The words meant nothing to Matt, but they had a compelling rhythm to them that seemed to go right to the heart of him. It went on and on and then the woman placed her hands on either side of the wound. Matt gasped when a spout of blood gushed out. Carabello convulsed and screamed and then another gusher of blood followed the first. What was the woman doing? She was killing him!

But then the blood flow slowed to a dribble and a dark, round object squirted out and landed on Carabellow's bare chest. It was the pistol ball! Matt couldn't believe it. The woman was breathing hard now. Carabello was twitching and moaning in the hands of the men holding him. Idira pressed her hands to the wound and she and he cried out as one. Then she fell back gasping. Hesseran wiped at

the blood with a cloth and it mostly came away—and no more followed. Matt leaned closer and he could see that the wound was
closed. There was still an ugly mark, but it was sealed!

"Gods!" he gasped. "You did it!" Brother Thaddius was mumbling
something in a strange language and making odd motions with his
hands.

Idira picked herself up and touched Carabello's brow. The man
went limp. "He'll sleep now. Keep him warm. I think I'll sleep now,
too. I've not had to deal with a wound like that in many a year. Thank
you, Lyni, dear. You can set us back in motion."

"No choice," murmured the woman. "Keep her going with the
wind until dawn."

Lyni's eyes rolled up and she collapsed into Matt's startled arms.

CHAPTER EIGHTEEN

"Reaching for the Great Power is done in a fashion similar to what you do when using your lesser spells," said Atark. "But you have to immerse yourselves in the power more fully, reach deeper, find the real strength that lies beneath." He looked out on the two dozen faces staring at him from inside one of the palace's splendid chambers. Some of the faces nodded in apparent understanding, some looked blank and confused, and some looked skeptical, even hostile.

Atark was discovering that teaching was *not* something he had a talent for. His patience was probably lacking, too. He was trying to teach over a score of shamen, from as many different tribes, to use the magic he had learned. A few of them seemed to be catching on, but the rest were either surly and confrontational or simple clueless. The old graybeards were the worst. They were twenty or more years older than Atark and obviously resented being instructed by someone so much younger than they. Several of them had already left in disgust and Atark was happy to see them go.

"But how do we *do* that, Mighty Atark?" asked one of the younger ones. "I say the words of the spell and focus myself as you have taught, but I do not feel this 'great power' of which you speak."

Atark frowned. He was finding that he lacked the words to even *describe* adequately what he wanted them to do. When the Ghost taught him, there had scarcely even been a need for words. The Ghost simply showed him and he understood. Was there something happening at those times that he did not realize? He had been tempted, more than once, to bring the Ghost in here and let *it* teach these people!

But he had not. The Ghost still remained a secret from everyone but Thelena. He was extremely reluctant to reveal the source of his knowledge and he could not forget the Ghost's desire to posses the body of some young shaman. Atark had made numerous excuses to the Ghost about why he had not found a 'volunteer' but he suspected that they both realized he was never going to find one. The very idea repulsed Atark. And he feared the power the Ghost might have if he regained his strength. The Ghost was becoming angry of late and it was starting to refuse to teach him new spells. It wanted a body and Atark feared that soon it would hold further knowledge hostage to that demand.

"Can you remember how you first found the power when you were young?" asked Atark to his pupil. "How did your tribal shaman teach you to control it?"

"Why, I just felt the power. It was like the wind. I could not see it, but I could feel it blowing in my mind. My old master taught me to say the words that would make that wind do what I wanted." The man seemed surprised that anyone could ask such a question. Atark nodded. It was as good a description as he had heard. Better than what he could have come up with himself.

"Yes, that is how it is. But you need to realize that it is your mind and will that control the 'wind', not the words you speak. The wind is deaf and does not hear your words. The words are simply there to order your mind and focus your will. You need to learn to go beyond the words and grasp the power itself. The 'wind' you feel is but the prelude to a great storm that lies beneath. The real power is there. I cannot tell you how to get to the storm, you must simply try and find it yourself."

"But what of the sacrifices?" demanded another of the older ones. "You say you draw power from them. When shall you teach us to do that?"

"You must learn to grasp the Great Power first. Only then can the strength of the sacrifices be used." The man looked unconvinced. Atark bit back his anger. Did these simpletons think magic was like...like tying knots in a rope? That he could show them a few times and they would master it in an afternoon? He looked away for a moment, out the windows. Somehow, most of the glass in this room had survived the explosions and the earthquake. He could look out through that marvelously clear glass and see the winter storm raging, and yet not be touched by the biting winds. Truly there were things of value in the East beyond mere loot. When the next year came the Kaifeng would reach out to take it all. He would have to talk to Zarruk about making sure that skilled slaves were not killed or misused. What a waste to put a master glassmaker to work in the fields!

Or would it be better to simply kill them all? Knock down all the buildings and turn all of the East into grazing lands? He was not sure. There were stories from far, far to the West, from farther than any of Atark's immediate kin had ever traveled, that disturbed him. The tales told of another great civilization to the west of the Kaif. It was huge and rich and decadent—much like the East. But unlike the East, the tribes of the Kaif had conquered it—many times. The tales told of the vast riches and beautiful concubines to be had. But they also told how the conquerors quickly became soft and adopted all the customs of the conquered—until they were conquered in turn by the next wave of true Kaifeng from the plains. Atark was not sure if the tales were true. The Kaif was so vast that it would take years to travel from one end to the other. But if they were true, could the same thing happen here if they enslaved these people and lived among them as masters?

He dragged his attention back to his 'class'. "All right, shall we try it again? I shall cast the spell. You shall watch and feel what I do. Then each of you in turn shall try." Atark cleared his mind and reached for the power. Now that the image had been suggested, it did rather feel like the wind. A very gentle wind with little strength in it. But just beyond, deeper, there was a stronger wind, a wind with seemingly limitless power. He reached for it, but in trying to think of some adequate way to describe what he was doing, he nearly let it slip through his grasp. In irritation he pushed the distracting thoughts away and firmly seized it. He would only need a modest amount for this and he easily took it and molded it into a swarm of the Seekers. A golden ball the size of his fist took shape in front of him and then burst into a few hundred of the tiny glowing specks. He had given them nothing to seek, so they flitted about the room aimlessly for a while, harassing all his students, and eventually blinked out.

"There. Did you see and feel what I did? Let each of you try to do the same thing. Daret, you shall go first." He had chosen a young man in front who he knew could do the spell fairly well. The man looked nervous, but he nodded and went to work. He chanted the words to focus his mind and Atark could feel the power he was manipulating. Was he reaching through to the Great Power? It was hard to tell, the spell was weak, but not so weak as the last time Daret had tried. A gold ball the size of an egg appeared. It wavered and flickered and then strengthened again. It burst into a dozen seekers, which flitted around the room for a few heartbeats and then vanished.

"Very good!" exclaimed Atark. "Much better than last time. Did you feel the Great Power?"

"I'm not sure, Lord," gasped Daret, who was clearly rather spent by the effort. "I felt...something, but I am not exactly sure what it was."

"I think you are right on the verge of success. Keep practicing and you will succeed. Odarul, you may go next." This man did not do quite so well. After a great deal of effort, a grape-sized golden ball appeared and popped, releasing a single seeker which zipped away and was gone. The shaman seemed embarrassed.

"I am sorry, Atark," muttered the man.

"Do not be. This is not an easy thing. You will get better with more practice."

"I hope so."

He went around the chamber to each shaman and had them try to cast the spell. Some did better, some did worse. Finally, he came to a graybeard named Nurnall, the same one who had asked about the sacrifices. "You are next, Nurnall," he said. The man glared at him.

"I'm not used to being addressed like some novice, Master Atark!" snapped the man.

"Your pardon. Would you like to go next, Master Nurnall?"

"What I would like is to dispense with this nonsense and have you give us the secrets of the Great Magic! You spend days and weeks talking of 'winds' in the mind and forcing us to do these ridiculous exercises."

"It is all necessary, Master Nurnall," said Atark. This was not the first time he had clashed with Nurnall, and he was growing irritated with the man. But he was the shaman of Ka-Noyen Battai and had to be dealt with carefully. He had a great deal of power and influence and it would not do to anger him. Still, if he was to learn the magic he had to do the work...

"Why?" demanded Nurnall. "Where did you learn *your* powers? I am unaware of any great master of magic who might have taught you. I have asked many questions about you, Atark of the Gettai-Tatua. Five years ago you were a simple tribal shaman, with no more power than the rest of us. Then you and your family disappeared into the plains. Months later you returned—alone!—and were a changed man. Your powers grew and grew! How? Now you hold lonely vigils in a small tent. Why? You keep many secrets from the rest of us, Atark!"

Atark frowned and his anger blazed up. This man had been spying on him! He probably should have expected it, but he had not. And still this simpleton believed that the magic was some 'trick' that could be learned in an afternoon! It had taken Atark months and years—even with the help of the Ghost—to really master the magic he used.

"If I have secrets, then they are my own to keep, Nurnall," he said, trying hard to keep the anger out of his voice. "I am willing to teach you what I can, but you have to be patient and willing to learn. If you are not, then there is nothing I can do for you. Now, would you like to try the spell?"

"I would not!" snarled the man. He lurched to his feet. "I will not be made a fool of! Keep your secrets, Atark—if you can!" Nurnall turned and stalked off. Another of the graybeards went with him. Atark watched him go with mixed anger and relief. That one was going to make trouble. He slowly looked over his 'class'.

"Anyone else? I will teach you, but I will do it *my* way and you will cooperate! If you are not willing to do so, then leave now!"

Most of the men would not meet his gaze, but two did and after another moment they got up and left, as well. There were now twenty left. How many would there be a week from now? Personally, he wouldn't really mind if they *all* left. Teaching them was not his idea, after all. But if the teaching stopped, there would be serious repercussions with the Kas. No, he could not just quit. But this was all very tiring. He was coming to look on these sessions with a feeling of dread. And they would go on for more months. Oh well, there was nothing for it but to keep going. In a few weeks would be the mid-winter festivals and perhaps he could take a rest then.

"Very well! Shall we try it again?"

Kareen worked the pump in the Royal Kitchens and was glad to see the stream of unfrozen water gush out to fill her small bucket. Atark would not permit them to live inside the palace, but he had not forbidden her to make use of its facilities. So, rather than struggle through the shin-deep snow and chop through the ice covering some well to find water, she was in the very cozy kitchen using the convenient pump. A Kaifeng woman, probably the wife of someone very important, cried out in amazement and demanded to know how the pump worked. Kareen explained as well as she could in her sketchy Kaifeng and then stood aside to let the woman try. Most of the other women there already knew how to use the pump and laughed at her. There were a great many children in the kitchen, too, playing and laughing with the rest. It was obvious to Kareen that the Kaifeng loved their children very much. They took good care of them. After all the terrible things that the Kaifeng had done, it was easy for her to hate them, but they were just people like any other. Why did they have to fight?

Kareen looked around and sighed. The huge kitchen had four roaring fireplaces and it was very warm. The tent was so cold all the time. Snow had been built up around it, as the Kaifeng did out on the plains, and that helped some, but the fire they kept burning inside never seemed to do much good. And the winter was only halfway past! The coldest months were yet to come. She shivered in spite of the heat, which was actually making her sweat.

But she needed to get back to the tent and start preparing dinner. Atark would be there tonight and on the rare times when he did eat dinner with Thelena, he was always very prompt and expected the meal to be ready. She picked up the bucket and her heavy coat and went down the hallway. The place was full of Kaifeng, but they paid her no mind and she wove her way between them. When she entered the more formal (and cooler) areas she stopped to put her coat on. There was a large gilt-frame mirror on the marble wall across from her and she stopped in shock when she saw the strange woman looking at her from it. *Is that really me?* The face seemed familiar, in spite of the new scar on the right cheek, but the eyes… There was a tiredness and pain—and fear—in those eyes which had no place in her memory of the person she once was. That memory was of a smiling girl modeling a white, frilly wedding gown. What had ever become of that gown? Had it been burned in the fort, or had some Kaifeng woman cut it up for rags? The thought made her very sad. Phell had bought her that dress. It was gone, he was gone, the ring he had given her was gone, too. She had tried not to think about things like that, but now the memories came flooding back and she was crying. Crying did no good, she had learned that, but she could not help herself. A few people glanced in her direction as they passed, but she was just another weeping slave. The city was full of them. She finished putting on her coat and lacing it up. She wiped her nose on the sleeve and picked up the bucket again. She turned and headed for the door.

Suddenly, a strong arm grabbed her and she was pulled through a different door into a small cloakroom. Two men were there and for an instant Kareen was afraid that she would be raped again. She didn't scream—she'd learned not to scream—she just looked at the pair with fear-filled eyes. One of the men was quite old and bearded, but the other was younger. They stared at her intently, but the looks on their faces were not ones of lust.

"You are Atark's slave?" asked the younger one. He was nearly whispering, and it was hard to understand him, but she managed to figure out what he said and she nodded her head. "You live in his tent?" She nodded again. What was this all about?

The older one talked rapidly to the younger and she could not catch more than a few words. The younger one turned back to her. "Is there a *something something* in the tent?" Kareen wasn't sure what he had asked. Something in the tent, but she did not understand several of the words.

"Forgive me, lord, but I do not understand," she said. *That* phrase she knew how to say perfectly! The young one got angry and slapped her, but not terribly hard. The old one touched his shoulder and shook his head. He said some more and then the young one addressed her again.

"Is there a small..." he tapped the door and then the small table. The word he used was similar to firewood. Wood? A small wood what? The man held his hands out about a foot apart and then moved them so that one was above the other and then again so that one was in front of the other. He kept moving them and Kareen realized that he was defining a shape like a...

"Box!" she exclaimed in Berssian. "A small wood box!" The two men looked puzzled and she could see they could not understand Berssian. But they seemed to realize that she had understood the question.

"Is there one in the tent?" asked the young one urgently. A wood box? In the tent? She tried to think. There wasn't anything quite that size or shape that she could remember except for...*Atark's box!* The little box that he let no one other than Gettain touch, not even Thelena. Atark treated it like it contained precious gems. And there were times when he went to his little tent carrying the box... "Is there?" snarled the man. Kareen nodded yes.

"Can you get it? Bring it to us?"

"No!" she exclaimed. The young one grew angry again and drew a knife. Kareen gasped and pressed against the wall at her back. "Please, Lord! There are guards! Always guards!" For an instant she thought he was going to kill her, but the old one said something and shook his head again. The young one slowly put the point of the knife to her throat.

"Say nothing or you die!" he hissed. Kareen nodded her head as much as the knife would allow.

"Yes, Lord! Yes, Lord!"

The men left the room, leaving her alone. She was still clutching the bucket, although half the water had spilled. She stood there, breathing hard, for a long time. Then she pulled herself together and hurried back to the tent.

Thelena looked at the singing, dancing swarm of people in the enormous ballroom and told herself that she should be as happy as all of them. It was the Mid-Winter Festival and celebrations were going on all over the city. The Kaifeng had never seen anything like this. Usually there would be no more than a single tribe gathered together to celebrate surviving halfway through the winter. But now, countless thousands had gathered in Berssenburg and the gaiety was without bounds. The great ballroom of the royal palace was filled with the leaders and their families. Hundreds of slaves saw to it that they lacked for neither food nor drink. Musicians and jugglers and tumblers provided entertainment. Thelena should have been happy.

But she wasn't.

In spite of the crowd, there was not a person within ten feet of her. She had a tiny island of complete privacy in a sea of people. She thought she had become used to the way her people shunned her, but somehow it had never been quite so *obvious* as it was now. There were no taunts or nasty looks or whispered comments, they simply ignored her. There were a thousand people around her and she felt completely alone. Her father was off with the Kas playing politics, and she had no one to talk to.

A slave walked past with a tray full of wine goblets. Thelena grabbed one and drank deeply. She was drinking a lot more wine lately. When she had been a slave she had rarely had the chance.

Now she could have as much as she wanted. In fact, she could have as much of just about *anything* as she wanted. Gold, jewels, furs, she had but to ask Gettain, and they would appear. She could have anything. Anything but friends. Except for Kareen, she had no friends at all. Not a one. There was her father, of course. But he was often away and even when he was there he seemed more distant. She knew he was under a lot of strain with his teaching and all the politics between the Kas, but it all meant that he had little time for her.

And she was twenty years old and had no husband.

Most Kaifeng women married by age fifteen. Her mother had been working to arrange a match for her when the Varags caught them. She had actually been talking to her about prospects when the Varags rose up out of the grass. Those old prospects were all long gone now, of course, and there would be no new ones, either. Four years as a slave in a Berssian fort had seen to that. No respectable man would ever want her now. They would all know what had happened to her, and she wasn't even pretty anymore. A broken nose and missing teeth had marred whatever beauty she once had.

She took another drink from the cup and looked at the people dancing. Mostly young men and women, although a few older ones were joining in. They laughed and sang and flung each other about the floor in a traditional dance. Many of the watchers were clapping their hands in time with the music. They all looked to be having a wonderful time. She would dearly love to be out there dancing with them.

She was standing there, her mood growing blacker and blacker, when she noticed a young man a few yards away glancing at her. He was not particularly large or handsome, but he kept looking at her. She did not recognize the pattern or color of the ribbons in his braids. He must come from a distant tribe, newly arrived to the city. He saw her looking back at him and he smiled awkwardly. She was so startled, it took her several moments to gather the wits to smile back at him. He blushed and looked away, but he soon looked back and smiled again. A strange thrill went through her. No man had smiled at her like that in she could not remember how long. A very long time, she thought. Indeed, it had been a long time since any man had touched her. She had managed to avoid the men in the fort for a number of months before it fell—and there had been no one at all since then. Nearly a year since she had been with any man, she realized. Once, she had felt quite certain that she would never miss the touch of a man again, but lately she had felt…different. And that fellow over there wasn't bad looking at all.

Her daydreaming was interrupted when another man came up to the one who had been smiling at her and whispered in his ear. His eyes jerked up to stare at her and his smile vanished. His face went pale and he turned and plunged into the crowd and vanished. She stared at the spot he had occupied, holding in her anger and her tears, for a long time.

It was still early and the celebration barely started, but there was nothing that could keep her here now. With a face as rigid as stone she gave her empty cup to a slave and went back to the tent. The air in the courtyard was very cold, but there was not much wind. Snow had been banked up several feet high around the sides of the tent and the path leading to the entrance had been stamped down and then covered with some straw. Two guards sat near a roaring fire a few yards away. Thelena told them to go inside and get warm and have something to drink. They thanked her, but they did not move. She shrugged and went in the tent.

The fire had burned down and she threw some more wood on it. She sat next to it, stirring the ashes and staring into the hot coals. There was something fascinating and restful about a fire. She remembered how she loved to be put in charge of the family fire when she was little. There were times when she had pretended the fire was another pet, something she would feed and take care of. She had had a number of pets as a child, mostly ponies. She wondered what had become of the horse she had been riding when the Varags caught her. Sela had been its name, but she never saw it in the fort after her capture.

She glanced over to where Kareen was sleeping. She'd begged to be excused from serving at the celebration and Thelena had allowed it. Kareen had been acting rather oddly the last week or so. She wasn't sure what was wrong. Kareen claimed she had not been raped since the city fell, so it wasn't that. As she watched, she could see the blankets shaking.

"Are you cold, Kareen?" She wasn't sure if she was awake, but she answered immediately.

"Yes, a little. But thank you for the extra furs, Thelena. They help a lot."

"You are welcome. But there is another trick to staying warm that works very well. I've been meaning to suggest it."

"What?"

"Snuggling. Two people together will stay much warmer than one alone. I'm getting a bit chilled sitting here. Do you want to try?"

"All…all right."

Thelena noticed the slight hesitation on Kareen's part, but she crawled over anyway, found the edge of the furs and blankets and slid in next to Kareen.

"Brrr! You're cold! I think I'm getting the worst of this bargain!" she protested.

"Patience. Roll over on your side, facing away from me." Kareen did so and Thelena snuggled up against her and draped her arm across Kareen's waist. They were both fully clothed, so it took a while to feel the shared warmth but after a while Kareen sighed.

"You are right: it is warmer this way."

"It can be a little awkward until you get used to it, but it still beats waking up shivering every half-hour."

They lay like that for a while. Then Kareen stirred slightly. "Did you have fun at the festival? It still seems early and I can hear the music in the distance."

"It was too loud and too crowded and I was tired," lied Thelena. She did not fool Kareen for an instant.

"I'm sorry they were cruel to you, Thelena. People can be so awful sometimes."

"Yes."

"I've seen how they treat you. It is not fair. You did not choose to be caught by the Varags. And except for chance, you would have died—like they *expected* you to."

"That doesn't seem to matter to them."

"I've sometimes wondered how I would be treated if I ever got back to my own people," said Kareen. "There are those who would act just like your people do. They would shun me and treat me just as cruelly."

Thelena hugged herself to Kareen a little tighter. It seemed like she was the only one she could talk to anymore.

"It is so unfair," continued Kareen. "The men want their own women to be proper and chaste, but they go out and rape other men's women with hardly a thought. But if their own women are raped, that leaves them in disgrace. As if we had a choice!"

"It is unfair, but I doubt it will ever change."

"No." They were both silent for a while, but then Kareen spoke again. "Thelena? Do you think your father will ever take me to his bed?"

Thelena twitched. She had wondered the same thing herself. "Would...would you wish him to?"

"I...I don't know. I'm very afraid of your father, and I know he does not like me. But it would be the only way I could ever be more than just a slave. And...and..." she trailed off.

"You are much more than 'just a slave' to me, Kareen. You are my friend. My best friend."

Kareen took hold of her hand and squeezed. "Thank you, Thelena. Having you to talk with is the only thing that makes this bearable for me."

Thelena's thoughts turned back to the man at the festival. "Kareen? Do you ever get...lonely?" There was a long pause, but eventually she answered.

"Yes."

Thelena wasn't quite sure what she wanted to say next—or if she should say anything at all. Her own feelings were swirling around, but her affection for Kareen was growing stronger and she could not stay silent. "I...I learned about the customs of your people in the fort, and I know that our customs must seem very strange to you. But here there are always more women than men in our tribes and the men can often be away for weeks or months at a time tending the herds or on the great hunts. There is nothing wrong or unusual for the women to seek comfort with each other. I care for you a great deal, Kareen."

The woman next to her did not reply and Thelena mentally kicked herself for having said anything. Kareen certainly was aware of what she had told her, but that did not mean she would ever accept it. She came from a very different culture.

"I'm sorry, Kareen. I should not have said that." She started to move away, but Kareen seized her hand.

"Don't go. It...it's all right. I care for you, too, Thelena... but I don't think I'm ready for anything else just yet. Of course, you could always command me..."

"I would never do that!"

"I know. But for now just hold me." Thelena snuggled closer and hugged Kareen tight and closed her eyes.

"Just hold me."

Atark went out into the courtyard. The icy night air felt refreshing after the heat of the ballroom. He was looking for Thelena. He had intended to spend time with her at the festival, but there had been an endless stream of people insisting that they talk with him. By the time he had managed to deal with all of them (or most of them, there were still others waiting) Thelena had gone. Friends had told him of how the other people had snubbed her and his heart ached for his daughter. The swine! Hadn't she suffered enough? He wanted to find her. He would ask her to dance with him. They would go out on the floor together and they would dance. The others could sneer all they liked, but he would say to the whole world that he loved his daughter! The rest could all be damned!

As he neared the tent, he immediately noticed that the guards were gone, although their fire still burned brightly. That was strange, but it was very cold. Perhaps they went in the palace for a while. He silently pulled aside the tent flap and stepped inside. He looked to the spot where Thelena usually slept, but the blankets and furs there were empty. His heart sank in disappointment. Where could she be? He hoped she had not run off somewhere because of the snubbing.

He glanced over to where the slave woman was sleeping. He considered asking her if she had seen Thelena. Then he noticed that the lump in the furs was strangely large. He took a careful step closer and realized that there were two people there. Thelena and the slave? He froze in place, locked in complete indecision. They might just be trying to stay warm. It was very cold and this was a common and effective way to keep warm. Even if they were doing more than keeping warm, there was nothing whatsoever wrong with it. He told himself that, and he believed it. Or part of him did. Part of him said that it was an accepted practice among his people. He'd never encountered it personally since he and his father and grandfather had all only had a single wife, but he knew it was common in other tents. And that same part of him said that Thelena had so little chance of finding contentment in the arms of a man, why should she be denied even this?

But there was another part of him that did not want to believe it at all. That part was intensely jealous and angry. And guilty, too. His daughter should not have to turn to a Berssian slave to find comfort for her hurts! He should have been there for her when she needed him. He might not be able to give her the physical love she might want, but for everything else... It felt as though he had failed her again. The immediate impulse to pull off the furs and blankets and drag the two apart faded. Whatever was going on there, he would not pain his daughter further by visibly disapproving. But the slave definitely had to go...

He stood there for a few moments longer and then silently made his way out of the tent. The guards were still missing and that was odd. Probably inside warming themselves. He did not especially mind, but Gettain would have a fit if he found out. Atark walked back toward the doors leading to the ballroom. He still had other people he must meet and talk to and he was not in the mood.

He jerked to a halt, halfway through the doors as there was a sudden shock, like a pinprick inside his head and a shrill keening sound from behind him. He spun about and realized it was coming from his tent. An instant later he remembered the warning spells he had set. He gave a shout for his guards and then ran back to where his daughter was sleeping.

Kareen was drifting off into a warm, pleasant sleep when the noise slashed through the blankets like a knife and jarred her awake. When Thelena had first come over to her and lay down next to her and talked, she had been very tense. She knew what she had been suggesting and she had not known what might happen. But nothing had happened and snuggling had felt very warm and very nice and her apprehension had dissolved into their comforting embrace.

Now, there was a piercing shriek filling the tent and she thrashed madly to get free of the furs and blankets and Thelena's flailing limbs. She managed to sit up and look about, trying to find the source of the noise. In the red glow of the dying fire, she saw two shapes which did not belong there. They were over on the side of the tent Atark normally occupied, but neither one was Atark. One snarled a curse when it saw the two women; the other was frantically rummaging through Atark's things.

"Kill them!" snarled the second one. The first one moved to block the tent's exit and the firelight flickered off a long knife blade.

"Thelena! Watch out!" cried Kareen.

But Thelena did not need the warning. She dodged to one side as the man advanced on her and threw a blanket over him. He tore it aside in an instant, but the women used the seconds to grab up sturdy lengths of wood from the pile next to the fire. Kareen stood shoulder to shoulder with Thelena and when the man came at them again, they beat him back with a flurry of blows. A strange exhilaration filled Kareen, in spite of her fear: she had struck a Kaifeng! Hurt him, too, from the sounds of his cursing. True, she was fighting to protect her *Qoyen*, but it still felt very good. She wanted to do it again!

"Come on, you bastard!" she cried, holding the stick high.

The man advanced more warily this time. The women swung at him, but missed as he pulled back. Kareen glanced to see what the other man was doing. He still seemed to be looking for something. She also saw that there was a hole through the rear of the tent—so that was how they got in!

The man lunged again. Kareen gave him a solid whack on the shoulder, but then he slammed his elbow into her and she fell back onto the blankets with the wind knocked out of her. She saw Thelena hit the man, but then he grabbed her stick and yanked it out of her hands. He raised his dagger to strike.

"Thelena!" gasped Kareen.

But before the blade could fall, there was a bright flash and the man was engulfed in flames, filling the tent with a hellish light. Atark was standing in the door of the tent and he was burning the intruder just as Kareen had seen him do to the other man months before. The man shrieked and whirled about and then tripped and fell in a burning heap. Thelena leaped back to escape the fire. Kareen scrambled to her feet and ran to Thelena's side.

A shout from her left pulled her attention away from the burning man. The other one was standing a few yards away. He was holding Atark's wooden box out in front of him and screaming at Atark. Kareen gasped when she recognized the gray-bearded man who had questioned her two weeks earlier! He had wanted the box and now he had it! Atark stood there and a glowing fire was in his hands. It looked to Kareen that the man was trying to shield himself with the box. What could be in it that was so precious?

It seemed as though Atark was hesitating to use his magic. Was he afraid of hurting the box or its contents? The man started edging toward the hole in the tent. But then several guards crowded into the tent behind Atark. One of them had a bow and Atark barked a command. The guard, in one fluid motion, drew and fired and an arrow was suddenly in the gray-bearded man's eye.

The man didn't make a sound. He twitched and fell. The box tumbled from his hands and bounded toward the two women. Kareen yelped when the lid popped open and something bounced out. Her yelp became a shriek when a human skull, with purple fire in the eye sockets, rolled to a stop at Thelena's feet and grinned up at her.

CHAPTER NINETEEN

The warship gave one last, stomach-churning lurch and then slid past the breakwater into the harbor of Zamerdan. Jarren gave a sigh of relief and slightly loosened his death-grip on the railing. The voyage back to Zamerdan had been nearly as harrowing as the voyage back to Erebrus. Nearly. No one had fired a pistol into his belly on this voyage. He pressed one hand to where the wound had been, but could feel no pain. Idira had somehow repaired the wound completely, although there was still a faint scar on the skin. He had no experience with such things, but Colonel Krasner and Brother Thaddius and the ship's surgeon had informed him that wounds like that were almost invariably fatal. Idira, on the other hand, had told him repairing such wounds was almost routine—although she, herself, had never actually healed one.

He was very glad that Idira had been the one who was right.

"We here to stay?" asked Gez from beside him.

"For a while, I would think," answered Jarren. "The winter, anyway. And you are free to leave my service if you want to, Gez. There is nothing forcing you to stay with me."

"Ah, I'll stay on if you'll have me, mister. The pay is pretty good—and I sure can't say it's been boring!"

"Then you still have a job, Gez. Although come spring there is no telling where I might be off to."

"Spring's a long ways off. I'll worry about that when the time comes. Gods, it's cold out here!"

Jarren looked up as Idira came to the rail, with Thad trailing her like a puppy. The priest had spent nearly every waking hour talking to Idira about her healing abilities. "Zamerdan!" she exclaimed. "It has been a long, long time since I was last here. But things do not appear to have changed a great deal."

"I have never been here," said Lyni, who had come after the other two, "nor do I wish to be here now."

"Give it a chance, Lyni. There are so many interesting things to be found in any city, and Zamerdan is one of the great ones. Art, music, the theater: I missed them on our lonely island. Jarren knows all about such things, I'm sure, perhaps he could give us a tour."

"I'd be honored to," said Jarren, but Lyni simply scowled at him and moved away.

"Do you think she'll ever forgive me?"

"She's just tired," said Idira. "She spent half the voyage calming the weather and that takes a lot out of her."

"It is amazing what she can do."

"She's one of the strongest magickers to come to us in many years. She will be truly great one day."

"How about you, Idira? You must be tired, too. You spent half the voyage treating injured sailors."

"Just broken bones and cracked ribs. Common enough things for the kind of voyage we have faced, I understand. Such things don't cost me as much as healing a bullet wound, Jarren."

"I'm glad to hear that. I owe you my life, Idira. And the sailors of this ship think you are some kind of saint."

Thaddius jerked like he had been struck and Jarren realized he was treading on thin ice.

The woman snorted. "Any healer could have done those things. But then you don't have healers anymore, do you? I weep to think of all the suffering that could be avoided if there were more of us. I have talked with the ship's surgeon and while he is a worthy man, I'm appalled at the crude methods he is forced to resort to. Thaddius, here, has far more practical knowledge, but is still terribly handicapped."

"We do the best we can," said Thad, "but that seems like a mere trifle compared with your powers, Lady Idira. I am unsure what to think now."

"Surely you can see that her powers cannot have come from demons as Church doctrine would have you believe!" exclaimed Jarren.

"My heart agrees with you, Jarren, but you must understand how difficult this all is to grasp. My world has turned upside-down in the last few weeks and it will take a while to see what it all means."

"Well! I can assure you that I have not been consorting with demons!" snorted Idira. "I have a gift. Perhaps it came from the gods, but wherever it came from, I intend to make use of it."

"Maybe after we deal with the Kaifeng, you can start your school and train more healers," suggested Jarren.

"That is my hope. Indeed, I am not sure what use I shall be against the Kaifeng. There is no practical reason why I could not learn battle magic, but it goes against my every instinct to use magic to cause harm."

"We aren't asking you to use your magic to cause harm," said Colonel Krasner as he joined the group, "We're only asking that you stop the Kaif necromancer from doing harm with *his* magic."

"I'm aware of that, Colonel," said Idira. "But you leave out the significant point that if we succeed, it will allow you to kill countless thousands with your muskets and cannons. I realize that this is necessary, but don't try to tell me that my actions will do no harm."

"Very well, I won't. As long as you are willing to help, you have my thanks."

"Assuming we are able to help. We still have no real answer, you realize."

"I realize that, Idira, but you cannot go around telling that to people," said Krasner, glancing around to make sure no one could overhear them. "We must proceed as we agreed to."

Everyone looked uneasy. Jarren could feel the same thing inside him. During the entire voyage back they had been living a carefully crafted deception. The Commodore and his officers and all the ambassadors had welcomed them back to Erebrus like conquering heroes. They all assumed that the wizards had the means to stop the Kaifeng and Krasner had insisted that they do nothing to disabuse them of the notion. Not a word was said about the death of Dauros or Stephanz's coup or the imprisonment or the escape. As far as anyone was concerned, the wizards had offered help and sent their three best people to carry it out. On the one hand, Jarren could see that Krasner was correct: to tell the complete truth was to invite panic and it could well blow apart the fragile alliance that was being put together. But on the other hand, if the truth became known later the damage might be even worse.

"I certainly hope you are right about this, Colonel," said Idira.

"Hey, lying through my teeth has gotten me this far. Why quit now?"

"Battai is making trouble again, Atark," said Re-Ka Zarruk. "He insists that at least one shaman from his own tribe be taught your magic."

Atark snorted in disgust. "How quickly and conveniently he forgets that not one, but two shamen from his tribe had been learning the magic until they quit—and were then killed while robbing my tent and trying to murder my daughter!"

"Battai claims to have had no knowledge of their plans and there is no evidence to the contrary. All of the other Kas have at least one man being taught by you. Battai is worried that he will have no one that knows the magic in his own camp."

"And just what does he expect me to do about it?"

"I believe he has a young shaman he would like to include in your class."

"Wonderful. He'd be starting from scratch and have to try to catch up. Then he'll get frustrated and quit and it will all be my fault for withholding the 'great secrets'!" Atark paced back and forth in the small but extremely opulent room, which had once been the Berssian King's private council chamber.

"Well, do your best," said Zarruk, who lounged in a gilded chair only slightly more modest than the great throne itself. "How are the others coming, by the way?"

"Most are doing pretty well," admitted Atark. "All of the ones who are left can at least cast the spell to some extent. A few are actually able to make several score of the seekers."

"Several score?" said Zarruk, frowning. "That hardly seems like enough to do much good in a battle."

"No, but it is a good start. They have all they need to succeed. All it will take is more practice to produce more of them. Don't forget that it took me almost four years to build up to the strength I have now."

"That is good. When the time comes they can go out with some of the smaller columns and get battle experience. By the time the campaign starts in earnest, they will be ready. And, as we both know, the main thing is to keep the other Kas happy."

"Yes. Have you decided what our plan is to be in the Spring?"

"Only in general terms," said Zarruk. He pointed to a beautiful map, which covered one wall. "Heguria is the closest large kingdom to where we are. Since it is farther south, we could start the campaign there earlier in the year. There would be some rivers and rough terrain and forests to get past, but I hope we could get through to their capital city in a few months. After that, I'm not sure.

We could turn north into the heart of the East, or continue along the southern coastline. The map indicates a number of cities that way, too."

"What about the Varags?"

Zarruk looked at Atark and shook his head. "I'm sorry, old friend, but the Varags will have to wait for another day. They have little of value and the warriors are not going to be content with burning villages and stealing cattle when all the glittering wealth of the East lies ready to be seized. By the time we are ready to move, three-quarters of the men will be newcomers who missed out on the sack of Berssenburg, If we cannot give them new cities to plunder, the army will fall apart."

Atark frowned, but he did not argue. He had expected this answer and he knew that Zarruk was correct. And it was true: the Varags could wait for another day. After the carnage he had wreaked on them last fall, they would be cowering in whatever holes they could find. They would make no trouble. "Very well."

Zarruk leaned back in his chair, pointed again to the map and sighed. "The East is a big place, my friend, bigger than I ever supposed when we started this war. We shall not take it all in a single year, or even three, I am thinking. And even supposing we do conquer every kingdom, what then? How can anyone hope to rule such an area?"

"I would not presume to instruct my Re-Ka in matters of rulership," said Atark.

"Bah! Don't give me that! You have instructed me for nearly five years now and I am deeply grateful for every word. I will always need your advice."

"I'm honored. But, sadly, I have little advice to give. I am as new to this situation as you are. I can only suggest that we smash every army and sack every city that we can and see what happens afterwards."

Zarruk laughed long and loud. "I can tell you what will happen: we shall be crushed under the weight of our own loot! I have more wealth here already than I ever imagine existed in the entire world. What else could I possibly want?"

"Are you suggesting we stop, My Lord?"

"No, of course not, how could we? The new tribes will demand loot and if we cannot let them take it from the Easterners, they will try to take it from us. And it will only get worse. The scouts report that there are scores upon scores upon scores of tribes just beyond the mountains. As soon as the snows melt they will be coming here to join the great conquest." Zarruk paused and got up from his chair. He walked over to the lovely map and drove his knife into the center of it.

"We couldn't stop now if we wanted to."

"So, Colonel Krasner, I trust that the wizards are satisfied with their accommodations?" asked General DeSlitz.

Matt looked at the man who was now his commanding officer. He was a Zollerhan general of great prestige, not the annoying twit Matt had met at the first conference, but a real commander with a real combat record. He had been appointed to lead the combined army that was being assembled to fight the Kaifeng. So far, he had not given Matt any reason to dislike him.

"Actually, no, sir. The rooms themselves are as luxurious as anyone could want, but they tell me they need a place outside of the city where they can conduct some experiments with the fireflies. They say it would be too dangerous to work here in the city: if any of the fireflies escaped, they might do terrible damage considering all the gunpowder in the vicinity."

DeSlitz nodded. "There are a number of estates outside the city; I'll speak to the Princes about securing one for their use."

"Experiments, Colonel?" asked Brigadier Saginau, DeSlitz's chief of staff. "I'm not sure I understand."

Matt hesitated. This was getting into dangerous territory. How much could he risk telling these people? He was confident he could spin some yarn that would satisfy the immediate question, but was that the right thing to do? It was vital to keep all the kings and princes and dukes (not to mention all the people they ruled) confident in victory, but what about the generals who led the army? Matt remembered how confident the Berssian generals had been—and what that had led to. So, perhaps not the whole truth, but enough of it to keep these men properly worried.

"Sir, you have to keep in mind that these wizards are not warriors. They have lived peacefully on their little island for centuries. While they are powerful and have a great deal of knowledge, this is a crisis far different from anything they've ever dealt with. They tell me that it will take them some time—and some experimentation—to devise the proper means to deal with the Kaifeng sorcerer. I'm sure you all realize that it will not be as simple as them waving a magic wand and making the enemy vanish—in spite of what some of the people in this city might think."

The frowns and expressions of alarm from around the General's conference table told Matt that some of them had been expecting exactly that. He was relieved to see that DeSlitz was not one of them. Instead, he nodded.

"Yes, Colonel, I quite understand. At best, we can expect the wizards to neutralize the enemy magic. Fighting—and winning—the battle will be up to us!"

The men around the table nodded and Matt felt relieved. "But winning it is going to be no easy job, gentlemen," continued DeSlitz. "Creating this combined army is a task unlike anything ever attempted before. We have contingents promised from nearly every principality in the East. Only the damn Eparans are holding out."

"Why won't they help, sir?" asked Matt. The Eparans had some of the best infantry in the East. And the fact that they were a bit behind the times and still had some pikes mixed in with the musketeers would be an actual bonus in the current crisis.

"It's their bloody feud with Durace. They won't put it aside even for this."

"Don't they realize that the Kaifeng will eventually get to them if we don't stop them?"

"Oh, they realize it. Frankly, I think the bastards are counting on it. They've started a massive fortress building program in the passes through the mountains along their border. I think they're hoping the Kaifs will wipe out the Duracci but somehow leave them alone. Damn fools. But, be that as it may, we have troops coming from almost everywhere else. Or we will have when the weather turns.

"The largest single contingent will be Hegurian, of course. They are closest to Berssia and will be the first in their path come spring. They've promised 40,000 regulars and 10,000 militia. They're not the best troops, but their numbers will be useful. Durace is sending 15,000, Laponia another 10,000. We'll have a solid core of 20,000 of our own Zollerhans, probably another 20,000 from all the smaller kingdoms and duchies. There will even be about 10,000 from the cities in Ertria, although only the gods know how much use they'll be."

"What about the remains of the Berssian Army, sir?" asked Matt. He felt a little awkward asking questions that he was sure were dealt with weeks ago, but he had a lot to catch up on.

"Well, that 40,000 figure I gave for Heguria includes most of the Berssians who escaped east after the disaster at Berssenburg. As for the King and his southern army, I'm afraid we can't count on them in the Spring. After he escaped from the city, the King went south to where his army was fighting the Omaki. The last word we had tells us that he's concluded some sort of truce with the Sultan, but basically he's stuck down there for now."

"I see, sir," said Matt, somewhat relieved that he would not encounter his theoretical master any time soon.

"So, all told, we are looking at around 125,000 troops," continued DeSlitz. "While on the one hand, this is very good news—we should be able to meet the Kaifs with something approaching equal numbers—it also creates some major problems. Our army will be twice the size of anything ever seen before. Controlling it, coordinating our movements, and above all, supplying it will be enormous tasks. The planned rendezvous is in Heguria, naturally, but it is up to us to see that it all works. Now, I have assignments for each of you..."

For the next two hours the discussion went around the room as the general received reports and handed out work. Matt was impressed. The Zollerhans were also reputed to have the best-organized army in the East and he could believe it. Finally, the meeting seemed to be winding down and Matt took the opportunity to raise another issue.

"Sir?" said Matt. "There is one other thing the wizards are going to need."

"What?"

"Some privacy, sir. Ever since they arrived, they have been dragged off to one dinner or ball after another. Everyone wants to meet them and rub elbows with them. They are being run ragged. And it is worst of all with Mistress Idira. Anyone with a cough or a hangnail is coming to her to heal them. She's a kindly woman and cannot bring herself to turn them away." Matt paused and frowned. "And unfortunately, not all of the people hanging about are admirers and well-wishers. There seems to be a faction of churchmen who are not at all happy with the wizards being here."

"I know," said DeSlitz, shaking his head. "Their bloody Council of Purity" has been bending my ear, insisting we should not be using the wizards at all. Spouting nonsense about us all damning ourselves by dealing with heretics. I just told them that if they can whistle up a hundred thousand armored knights to face the Kaifs I'd be happy to dispense with the wizards. You say they've been causing more trouble?"

"Some, sir. A few small crowds have gathered from time to time to denounce the wizards. I've seen churchmen among them. So far it has not been serious, but that could change. We need to set up a picket line to keep the mobs at a distance."

"All right, I can see we need to deal with this. Very well, Colonel, you are already the official liaison to the wizards, you are now also in charge of their security. Put together a body of troops to act as their guard. Once they relocate to outside the city, it won't be so bad, but they will still need a guard in any case."

Yes, sir," said Matt. "But, sir, I was hoping for a combat command in the coming campaign. I have some scores to settle with the Kaifs, sir."

"No doubt, no doubt. But, Colonel, if you want to have a combat command, then make one! I'm authorizing you to create a Wizard's Guard. I didn't say a word about how large it should be. I leave that entirely up to you."

Matt felt a large grin forming on his face in spite of his efforts to stop it.

"Yes, sir. I'll get right on it."

"Jarren?" said Idira, "Hess asked me to come and get you. He says he's got something to show you."

"Really? What?" asked Jarren, looking up from his book.

"He didn't say, but I think he's got the seekers working."

"Wonderful!" said Jarren, springing to his feet. "Let's go!" He carefully marked his place in the book and then followed the healer out of the room he was using as his study. The estate Colonel Krasner had secured for their use was large and luxurious, if a little run-down. It was on a good-sized bit of dry land a dozen miles south of Zamerdan. The spare rooms and corridors were packed with crates full of books and scrolls from the University. He was amazed at the resources he now seemed to have at his command. Anything he asked for arrived in short order. Well, as short as possible. There were many more books and scrolls on their way from other cities that had not arrived yet. But he did have a dozen eager graduate students poring through what was on hand, looking for any reference to the seekers or gunpowder.

They went down a set of steps, through a long hall and out the back door of the sprawling building. It wasn't quite a palace, but almost. It had a number of outbuildings, too, and Hesseran had set up his workshop in one of them. As he followed the tramped-down path through the snow, he noticed that Colonel Krasner was out drilling his troops again. He looked and it seemed as though there were more of them every day. He guessed there were at least two hundred cavalrymen churning up the fields in precise patterns. A bugle call rang out and the horsemen wheeled around and headed off in a new direction. Jarren shrugged his shoulders and kept walking. It was cold and the thrill of seeing snow had worn off quickly. He was looking forward to spring—or at least he would have been except that this spring would mean war.

He glanced around and then back at Idira. "Where's Thad today?"

"In the city. He said he has to give a report to the Patriarch on what we're doing here."

"Well, I'm sure he'll make a very favorable report. He's incredibly impressed with what you can do."

"Yes, he's a good man and he's not terribly comfortable spying on us. He's every bit as dedicated to healing as I am—more, since he comes from a place where the sick and injured are a lot more common. He's seen all the suffering close up."

"It must be a bit frustrating for him to see your powers and know he can never do the things you do."

"Actually, he could do them if he had the training."

Jarren's head snapped around to stare at the woman. He stopped in his tracks. "You mean he has the power?" he asked incredulously.

"Yes, but please don't say anything to him. He'd be terribly distraught if he knew. I should not have said anything to you, Jarren, but I'm terrible at keeping secrets."

"That...that's amazing. I had heard that this 'Council of Purity' goes around screening all of the acolytes when they are young to make sure no 'heretics' get in."

Idira laughed without humor. "I did a little investigation about that. Apparently the Council goes around with some old magical staff and tests the acolytes. They hold it and if it glows the person has the power—and they burn the poor wretch. But no heretics have been found for over seventy years. You realize what that means?"

"Uh, that the people with the power are staying away from the church?"

"No! It means that their bloody staff probably burned out seventy years ago and those dolts don't realize it! They've been letting heretics into the church for seventy years." Idira grinned like it was a huge joke.

"Heavens! I don't think you should tell anyone about that, either, Idira."

"You have got that right!"

"But Thad has the power?"

"Yes. Not strongly. It would probably never manifest itself without some training, but he could do the healing spells."

"Interesting. Uh, I don't suppose that I...?"

"No, I'm afraid not, Jarren."

"Oh, well." He wasn't sure if he was disappointed or not. He resumed walking.

They reached Hesseran's workshop and opened the door—and retreated in alarm when a cloud of white smoke came billowing out. Hesseran himself followed a moment later, coughing and wiping his streaming eyes.

"Hess!" cried Idira. "Are you all right?"

"Yes, yes, I'm fine," wheezed the alchemist. "Excellent, actually."

"What happened?" asked Jarren.

"Well, I managed to recreate the spell the Kaifeng necromancer must be using—and I'm going to need some more gunpowder."

"How much did you have in there?"

"Oh, a pound or so."

"And it all went up?"

"I'm afraid so, well, nearly. I had a small amount in a bowl and the rest in a cloth bag. I created the seeker, just one, you know, and I expected it to go after what was in the bowl, being so much closer, but it went after the sack instead! Fortunately it was not tightly packed, so it just flashed rather than exploded."

"You are going to have to more careful, Hess!" cried Idira. "Are you sure you're not burned or hurt?"

"No, I'm fine. But come in, I still have the little bit in the bowl. I can show you what I did."

"Perhaps we should call Colonel Krasner over and have him watch, too. He can tell us how it compares with what he saw in the field."

"An excellent idea!" A servant was quickly sent slogging across the field to summon the colonel. Another was sent toward the distant shed where a supply of gunpowder was kept. Meanwhile, Jarren, Idira and Hesseran opened all the windows in the workshop to let the smoke out. Jarren could see the charred spot on a table where the gunpowder had been.

"Interesting that the seeker went after the larger amount of powder," said Jarren. "Do you suppose it will always do that? Maybe we could decoy the seekers with some large amounts out in front of the army."

"A possibility," said Hesseran. "But this time, I'm going to make two seekers and see if we can do something like that."

They waited and after a while Krasner came in, his boots splattered with mud to the knees. "What did you want me for?" he asked. "Aside from showing me how you almost burned the building down, I mean."

"An unfortunate accident, Colonel," said Hesseran, blushing, "but I'm sure you'll find this interesting—ah, here's the powder!" The servant arrived, out of breath, with another bag of gunpowder. Hesseran took it eagerly. "All right, I'm going to divide this up into a number of smaller portions of different sizes, and see how the seekers respond." The alchemist got out a number of pottery bowls and set them around the room. He then measured out differing amounts, carefully recording just how much gunpowder went into each.

"Do you think they might go after even individual grains of powder?" asked Jarren.

"An interesting question. I'll spread the last of this out on the table there." He shook out the bag so there was a scattering of individual grains on the wood tabletop. Then he stood back. "Where's Lyni? She needs to learn this, too."

"I saw her out walking," said Idira. "Leave her be, Hess, she still is in a lot of pain and needs time."

"We haven't *got* much time, Idira," said Krasner. The healer frowned at him and he subsided.

"All right, then," said Hesseran. "Let me show you what I've come up with. Idira, watch how I substitute Fire for Wind." The man stepped back and closed his eyes for a moment and Jarren could hear him whispering something under his breath. He glanced over to Idira and could see that she was watching intently. Could she actually 'see' Hesseran manipulating the power? After a few moments, a tiny speck of glowing light appeared in front of Hesseran. Jarren heard a sudden intake of breath from Colonel Krasner. The glow brightened and solidified in the air. It just hovered there for a moment, then it split into two glowing points of light. The lights floated in the air for one more heartbeat and then darted away. They zipped past the scattered grains of powder and each darted into a different bowl. Instantly there was a red flash and a whoosh and a gush of white smoke that rushed up to the ceiling and then spread out through the room.

They all retreated outside while the smoke cleared. "When the weather gets warmer, I think I'll be doing these experiments out-doors," said Hesseran. "Well, Colonel, did that look like what you saw the Kaifeng do?"

"Yes. Exactly," said Krasner and Jarren could see the grim look on his face. "The only difference was that the first time I noticed a bit of red smoke go up as the gold ball was forming."

"Ah, yes, you had mentioned that. There are several ways to tell a seeker what to seek. One way is to give them a 'sniff' of what they are supposed to look for. It is the simplest way, but not necessarily the best. I made their goal part of the very spell, so I did not need to burn the gunpowder as the Kaifeng apparently did. Perhaps we can take some comfort that our magic is more sophisticated—if less powerful."

"I did see how you substituted the Fire, Hess," said Idira. "Very clever."

"Do you think you can do it?"

"Let's find out."

They went back into the workshop and Hesseran examined the bowls and frowned. "Odd, they ignored the individual grains, as we expected, but while the one seeker did go after the largest amount, the other went after the bowl with only the sixth largest amount. I'm not sure what—if anything—that proves."

"We'll have to study this further," said Idira. "Here, let me try."

Idira concentrated and in short order had created a single golden seeker. It zipped off to ignite a bowl of powder.

"Hmmm, it chose the third largest amount of powder," said Hesseran and he squinted through the smoke. "No discernible pat-tern yet. Let me try with three this time."

Without waiting for the smoke to clear, Hesseran created three of the seekers and they quickly found their goals. Three more bowls whooshed into flames. The smoke was quite thick in spite of the open windows and the chill breeze they let in. Idira and Hesseran took turns casting the spell until only a single bowl of gunpowder remained.

"All right, I am going to create two seekers this time," said the alchemist. "Let's see if both of them go for the one remaining bowl, or if one of them can be tempted to go after the individual grains"

Hesseran stood back and quickly created two of the seekers. It seemed to Jarren that it was easier and quicker each time they did it. The seekers hovered for an instant and then both darted into the remaining bowl. It ignited immediately, but to Jarren's surprise, one of the seekers remained, flitting about in the cloud of smoke. It circled the room, ignoring the gunpowder on the table.

"Apparently it cannot find anything that small," said Hesseran. "Interesting. Perhaps we can..."

The seeker darted out the window.

"Where's it going?" cried Jarren.

They scrambled out of the building and looked around.

"There it is!" shouted Krasner. They all looked and there it was: a golden point of light flying across the snow-covered field with great speed. It zipped past the Colonel's startled troopers and into a small clump of woods.

"What's it doing?" demanded Jarren. "There's nothing out there except..."

Booom! A small explosion rumbled in the distance and a large white cloud boiled up out of the trees.

"The shed where we store the gunpowder," said Colonel Krasner.

All eyes turned to Hesseran.

"Oh, dear," said the alchemist.

Kareen lay back in the pool of hot water and closed her eyes. It felt so good! The Royal Baths in the palace had survived almost intact and after the Kaifeng had learned what they were and how they worked, they had ordered their slaves to keep them in operation continuously. Most of the time they were reserved for the masters, but there were times when the slaves could use them, too. She lay there and let the heat soak into her bones and drive out the chill. The winter was passing and they had had some warmer weather, but the nights were still very cold. She sighed contentedly and tried to forget about everything.

For a few minutes she succeeded.

Unfortunately, after a while her worries began to intrude. She could take some comfort in the fact that they were simply worries rather than the agonizing fears that had filled her during her first months as a slave. It still amazed her, but her fate, which had seemed too terrible to endure at first, was now almost normal. She had her chores to do and her daily routines, which filled most of her life. She even had things that she enjoyed. She was learning to cook and sew very well and could take satisfaction in some of her accomplishments. She even had fun. Thelena had been teaching her how to ride properly. Before, she could bounce along on a horse without falling off, but now she was actually learning how to ride and it was fun. She and Thelena had fun together. She wished Thelena was here with her now, but she was off with Atark somewhere.

Atark. He was her biggest worry. She still had no clue what he was going to do with her. In some ways it was so odd being a slave. With her own people a wife was, to a certain extent, the property of her husband. He could demand certain things from his wife and she had to obey. He could even be cruel and beat her and nothing would be done. But the woman still had some rights. Here, with the Kaifeng, she had no rights of any sort. Atark could take her to his bed, or he could beat her or torture her or kill her and no one would say a thing. He could sell her to some other man. She was his property and had no more rights than one of his horses. Less, really, for the Kaifeng would strongly disapprove of a man who beat or killed his horses.

It was clear to her that Atark did not like her. He did not like Easterners in general, and her role in the escape of the prisoners had made him hate her on a personal level. And he was jealous of how close she was to Thelena. She could see that in the way he would frown when he saw them together. They had done nothing more than snuggle in the tent at night, but it was obvious that Atark did not like even that. She worried that Atark would decide to kill her or sell her away. It was frightening to have no control of any sort over her life...

"Hello, Kareen."

She twitched and her eyes popped open. Teela Deseter was standing there with a silk robe wrapped around her. Her lovely red hair spilled down to her waist. "Mind if I join you?"

"Please do," said Kareen, sliding to the side in the tile bath. Teela let the robe fall away. She was far more slender than Kareen, but still a very pretty woman. She was the Re-Ka's slave and Kareen instantly saw that, unlike Atark, Teela's master had certainly taken her to his bed. There was a very obvious swelling in her abdomen.

"Teela, are you...?"

"Oh, yes," said the woman with a smile as she lowered herself into the bath. She ran her hands around the swelling. "I've got a little Kaif growing in my belly. Must have happened almost that first night."

"That's...that's..." Kareen had no clue what to say.

"Wonderful? Terrible?" asked Teela. "I wasn't sure myself at first."

"What do you think now?"

Teela seemed to draw herself up. "In the Spring I will bear the Re-Ka's child. He is happy, and therefore, so am I."

"I'm glad for you, Teela."

"Dara and Felaa are pregnant, too. Almost all our old friends are. The place is going to be overrun with babies in a few months." Teela paused and looked at Kareen's smooth stomach through the water. "I have heard that Atark never touches you. That must be hard." There was a note of smugness in Teela's voice that marred any sympathy in her words. Back in the fort they had been rivals of sorts, the two most beautiful girls in the Regiment. Now it appeared that Teela thought she had won. Her master found her attractive and had taken her and given her a child. While Kareen's master did not even bother to use her. A strange anger surged up in Kareen. "The Re-Ka can be very passionate," Teela added with a sly smile.

Kareen bit back her anger and jealousy. It would do no good to say anything back to Teela. And it could do a lot of harm. As she had said, she would bear the Re-Ka's child in a few months. That made her important. Far more important than Kareen. She did not need any more enemies. As her anger faded, her envy grew a bit. She had managed to avoid becoming pregnant thanks to an ugly, bitter root that Thelena had given her to chew. Thelena had used the same thing in the fort. Apparently it was a common herb that the local women knew about. At first she had been very grateful. The thought of bearing the child of some unknown father from her rapes had horrified her. But now... She looked at Teela's swollen belly and felt envy.

"How... how do you get along with Zarruk's wives?" she asked instead.

Some of Teela's smugness disappeared. "They are all right, I suppose. They are far more demanding than Zarruk—in bed and out—but they are kind enough. And they seem excited about the baby, too."

"What about...what's her name?...the Berssian general's mistress?"

"Ha! That slut! She's gone. She tried to use her little whoring tricks on Zarruk to get special treatment. All three of us beat the hell out of her. So he gave her away to one of the new Noyens as a gift. But she's stupid; she'll probably try the same thing with him. If she's not careful she'll find herself in a slave caravan headed west come Spring. I hope she ends up in a brothel serving a hundred men a night. It would serve her right!"

Kareen looked at Teela in shock. She was a single man's slave; what could she possibly know about serving a hundred men in a night? Well, Kareen didn't either, not a hundred, but she wouldn't wish that on anyone.

"How are you and Thelena getting along?" asked Teela suddenly. "I remember how terribly we used to treat her back in the fort." She reached out a hand and touched the scar on Kareen's cheek and then ran it down her back feeling the scars there. "I guess she got her revenge, didn't she?"

"She... she was angry at first. But that's past."

"You're lucky... I guess. The other Kaifeng women all hate her, you know. They call her 'The Berssians' Whore.'"

"That's not her fault! She had no choice!" Kareen was getting angry again.

"I know, but what difference does that make?"

Kareen got to her feet and stepped out of the bath. She grabbed a towel and walked away without another word.

"Squadron...*Halt!*" shouted Matt Krasner. The double line of horsemen reined in their mounts smartly and stood waiting for his next command. He glanced up at the watery, late-winter sun. Lyni had told him that there would be no bad weather until tomorrow. He would still have the afternoon to drill his men, so he could let up on them a bit this morning. "One hour break! See to your horses and then rest." The men made sounds of appreciation and dismounted. Matt dismounted himself and an orderly took his horse. He rounded up his officers and leading sergeant and they sat down on some chairs at the edge of the formal gardens.

"A good morning's work, gentlemen," he said. "The men are shaping up well. My compliments on your efforts."

"Thank you, sir," they said in unison.

He looked them over. They were mostly young—except for the sergeant—and eager. When General DeSlitz gave him permission to raise a 'wizards' guard', he had just announced he would be accepting recruits. Since then, men had been pouring in. So far, they were mostly lesser nobility from the Zamerdan region, but he knew the word was spreading. He already had an overstrength squadron and it would soon be necessary to split it into two. At this rate he would have a regiment by the time the campaign began—assuming he could pay for it.

The wizards seemed to have an unlimited treasury at their disposal, and as a part of them, Matt could draw upon it. He had done so shamelessly. Horses and uniforms, weapons and armor, he had placed orders with the local craftsmen for all of that and more. As long as the well did not run dry, he should be all right.

"We can expect another load of the helmets and breastplates by next week," he told the officers. "I'm still trying to see about armor for the horses."

"You really think that's going to be necessary, sir?" asked Sergeant Holmanz. Matt looked at him. He was like—and unlike—Sergeant Chenik in a lot of ways. But then, he was a sergeant and the good ones were all out of the same mold.

"If—when the wizards stop the Kaif magic, it will then come down to a stand-up fight. I want a force who can cut a swath right through the bastards. We'll have plenty of light cavalry, but not enough heavy. I want us armored so that we don't have to worry about their arrows."

"Right, sir. And you still plan to arm us with lances?"

"Yes, I do. We've got a few Laponians who know how to use them. They can train the rest."

"Yes, sir," said the sergeant. The look on his face told what he thought of the whole thing. But he was a good man. They were all good men.

"Colonel! Colonel Krasner!" shouted a young voice. Matt turned and saw Carabello's young servant running up to him.

"Yes? What is it?"

"The wizards wanted to talk to you. Can you come over?"

"All right, I'll be there shortly. The rest of you carry on." His subordinates saluted him and he returned it. Then he followed the boy.

He had been in the city yesterday, conferring with General DeSlitz and had not talked with Carabello or the wizards since the day before. Perhaps they had something good to show him; he certainly hoped so. They had been out here working for nearly a month and with precious little to show for it—beyond blowing up the gunpowder shed. He headed for their workshop, but the boy told him they were in one of the fields on the other side. As he rounded the building he saw Carabello, Thaddius and all three wizards a few hundred yards away. He slogged across the muddy field to reach them.

Hesseran was standing about a hundred yards away from the others. Idira and Lyni and Carabello and Thaddius were by a small table. When he came up to them, he saw a small bowl with a small amount of gunpowder in it.

"Ah, there you are, Colonel," said Idira. "We thought you might be interested in this."

"Indeed? What is going on?"

"A contest of sorts," she explained. "Hess is going to try and explode my gunpowder, here, and I'm going to try and stop him."

Matt's eyebrows shot up. He'd seen dozens of demonstrations of the wizards recreating the Kaif's fireflies, but this was the first time they had claimed to have any defense against them. "I'll be very interested in seeing that, Idira."

"All right, Hess, you can begin," she called out to the alchemist. He nodded and started doing whatever it was that wizards did to cast their magic. Idira seemed to be doing something, too. A few seconds later a single golden firefly appeared in front of Hesseran and an instant later came streaking toward them. Almost immediately a second firefly appeared in front of Idira. It took off in the opposite direction—straight at Hesseran's oncoming seeker.

The two fireflies met—and vanished. Matt almost expected there to be a 'pop' or a 'bang' or a flash, but there was not. They simply met and were gone. Carabello and Gez cheered and clapped their hands. "You did it, Idira!" cried Carabello.

But Hesseran wasn't done yet. Two more fireflies appeared and came toward them. Idira immediately made two of her own and all four vanished when they collided. Hesseran responded with four and Idira did as well. The next batch had ten and Idira countered them. After that, there were too many to count easily. Twenty, thirty, fifty, maybe a hundred golden fireflies and Idira matched him, fly for fly. The gunpowder lay in the bowl untouched. Matt felt a giddy exhilaration growing in him. She was doing it! She was stopping the damn things!

It went on for another few minutes. More waves of fireflies dashed each other into oblivion, but Matt noticed that the numbers were no longer growing. In fact, there might have been fewer. He could see that both wizards were getting tired. Finally Hesseran threw up his hands.

"Enough, Idira," he cried. "I call a truce!"

"Agreed!" answered the woman. Hesseran waved and walked slowly toward them. Everyone, including Matt had a huge grin on their faces.

"You did it," said Matt to all of them. "How?"

"It was Idira's idea," explained Carabello.

"Simple, really," said the healer, breathing deeply. "The seekers normally carried a bit of Wind to make a noise. The fireflies had fire substituted and were made to seek gunpowder. I thought that I could make a seeker that carried a tiny bit of water—and have it seek the fire carried by the other seekers. As you can see, it worked."

"Waterbugs, eh?" said Matt with a grin. "Very clever." But then his grin disappeared. "I don't want to sound negative, but was that all you could make at one time? The Kaifeng necromancer sent a million of the damn things against us in the battle. A few hundred waterbugs isn't going to help at all."

"Yes, we know," said Lyni a bit testily. "Each of us can make a few hundred at a time and we know that is not enough."

"We'll get better with practice," said Hesseran.

"That much better?" demanded Matt. "Enough better that you can stop a million of them?"

The others looked uneasy. "Probably not," admitted Idira. "But this is at least a start."

"I don't need to remind you that we're going to get exactly one—one!—chance at this. In about two months the army will assemble and a month or so after that we'll probably meet the Kaifeng in battle. If we lose, if that army gets wiped out, then it is the end. Aside from the fact that we'll all be dead—or slaves," he paused and looked pointedly at Lyni, who, although not terribly pretty, was still a healthy, young woman. "Aside from that, it will be the end for the East. There will never be another chance to stop them and they'll roll over everything. We need a lot better than just 'a start'!"

"We are doing our best, Colonel," said Lyni, returning his stare.

"What more can you ask?"

"They have all been working terribly hard," added Thaddius.

Before Matt could reply, Carabello broke in. "Colonel, we did find something else of interest yesterday. One of my student helpers actually found it in an old collection of..."

"What did you find?" interrupted Matt.

"Oh. Well, it was instructions for how to make containers that the seekers cannot get through."

"Really? Well that's wonderful! If we can just safeguard the powder, we won't even need those waterbugs of yours!"

"Don't get too hopeful, Colonel," said Idira. "What the instructions call for is a rather fine grade of lead crystal glass."

"Crystal? What the hell good is that going to do us? We can hardly make 70,000 crystal cartridge pouches! Or even line the artillery caissons with the stuff!"

"We know," said Hesseran. "In fact, that's exactly what that Hegurian gentleman said yesterday when I told him about it."

There was a long silence as Matt stared at him. "What Hegurian gentleman?" he asked, at last.

"The one who came here yesterday while you were in the city. He said you had given him permission to visit our facilities and ask us for a status report."

"I didn't give him—or anyone else—permission to come out here!" snarled Matt. "What did you tell him?"

"Well, pretty much anything he wanted to know. We told him what we had accomplished, demonstrated the seekers and the counter-seekers like we just did for you. Frankly, he did not seem any happier than you did. I don't think any of you realize just how difficult..."

"Gods!" groaned Matt. "You are sure he was a Hegurian?"

"Well yes, I'm from there originally, and I was quite certain he was, too. Why is that so important?"

"Because Heguria is supplying a third of the army, that's why!" exclaimed Matt. "We're going to assemble in Hegurian territory!" He turned and looked to the southwest. Heguria lay that way. It was hundreds and hundreds of miles to Heguria, but Matt was quite sure there was already a fast courier on his way there with the news that the wizards could not stop the Kaifeng magic.

"Gods," he said again. "What have you done?"

CHAPTER TWENTY

"Atark, thank you for coming so quickly," said Re-Ka Zarruk.

"I could hardly ignore the summons of my Re-Ka," said Atark. "But your message indicated that something interesting has happened."

"Yes, indeed, we have a visitor," said Zarruk with a strange grin. "An embassy from the Hegurian Empire has arrived."

"From Heguria?" asked Atark in surprise. "In this weather?"

"Yes, through the sleet and rain and mud, all the way from their capital of Zienne. The ambassador was most eager to see me."

"What does he want?"

Zarruk laughed. "For once I get to instruct you! How delightful! What would you guess he would want?"

Atark paused for a moment, puzzled, but then it became clear. "They want to buy us off?"

"Exactly! They have offered us fifty large wagons loaded with treasure if we will leave them alone this year. And another twenty wagons each year after that."

"A handsome offer. Are you going to accept it?"

"Well, I'm going to discuss it with the Kas for form's sake, but I am inclined to accept."

"Why? Not that I disagree, I'm just curious about your thinking."

They were in the same conference chamber they had been in before, with the lovely map on one wall. Zarruk now got out of his chair and went over to it. "We've been hearing rumors that the eastern kingdoms have been banding together to try and fight us. They are trying to raise a huge army to match ours. That's not surprising, but we've also been hearing that they are trying to re-equip their men with bows and crossbows and pikes so they are not dependent on gunpowder. I find that a far more disturbing rumor."

"I do have other magic I can use against them," said Atark. "Between that and our own warriors we can still defeat them."

"I don't doubt it. Still, it could be very costly. This offer from the Hegurians is clearly a break in the ranks of the Easterners. I would much rather deal with them separately than together. The Hegurians would be the first in line for our conquest in the spring and apparently they don't think they can stop us, so they are trying to buy us off. If we turn them down, that will force them back into the arms of the other kingdoms and we'll have to fight them all at once."

"That would give us the opportunity to destroy them all at once," Atark pointed out.

"True, but Heguria will still be there next year." He pointed to the map. "Instead of east we can go north. We can finish off Berssia completely. Take Gira and then turn east into Laponia. By mid summer we could be in the heart of all these little principalities here. I don't think we are going to finish this in a single battle or a single campaign, my friend. There are just so many of these people. So many towns and cities; we'll be sacking the East for the next ten years. "

Atark hesitated, but then he nodded. He remembered his own short campaign against the Varags. He had destroyed village after village, but there always seemed to be more. And once the Varags had realized that there would be no mercy shown them, they had no reason to ever surrender. They either fled or fought. If the Easterners were given that same choice, they would probably react in the same way. "Do you think, perhaps, we should deal with these people a little more kindly? Give them a reason to submit to us?"

"The thought had occurred to me," said Zarruk. "If they know that all they can hope for is slaughter for the men and enslavement for the women, it will give them the courage of despair. They will fight and we'll have to take every city and town by storm—and most of them have old walls just like Berssenburg did, from what I've heard. That will be a long and slow process. Perhaps if we treat those who surrender without a fight gently—but be more ruthless than ever with those who resist—it could break their will."

"As long as there is enough loot for the warriors," said Atark.

"Oh, there will be!" chuckled Zarruk. "I said 'gently', I did not mean we would not make demands of them! Gold, food, maidens, we'll want all of that and more. If they give us what we demand, we will spare their lives and not burn their town. If they resist, every male will be put to the sword, their women treated most harshly and their town left in ashes. Once that message gets across, I think resistance will crumble."

"At least after we've beaten the army they send against us. As long as that exists, they will still have hope."

"True. But they will have to come and meet us sometime, and when they do, we shall crush them."

Atark nodded. It seemed a good plan. "What about the cities that do yield to us? Will you leave a garrison to rule them, or simply return every year to demand more tribute?"

"I think in the larger cities we shall leave a garrison. There are several thousand of the older warriors who are not really up to a hard campaign anymore who I was already planning to leave here. We can do the same elsewhere. The smaller towns, we'll just come back to again later."

"So we shall lay claim to all this land? Live here and rule the inhabitants forever?"

"Why not? It is a rich, fat land, just asking to be taken."

Atark sighed. "And in time will we become too rich and too fat, my Re-Ka? There are so many more of them than there are of us. When each man has a fine house and mounds of gold and a dozen pretty concubines to attend him, will they still be willing to ride hard and fight harder?"

Zarruk laughed. "You worry too much, my friend! Taking the land will be a task of years. What comes afterwards we can worry about later!"

"I suppose you are right. We have much yet to do. So, when do we ride?"

"The weather will still be bad for some time. Another two months, I would expect. We shall have to send messengers west to tell the newcomers to meet us on our ride north rather than east. Yes, I would guess we shall begin in two months. Meanwhile, I shall send for the Hegurian ambassador. Would you like to stay while I see just how much we can squeeze out of him?"

"It would be my pleasure," said Atark.

Jarren rubbed his eyes and shifted the candle a bit to give more light. His little magical lamp was so dim now it was of little use. He wasn't sure what time it was, somewhere near dawn, he guessed. Another long, long night of digging through centuries-old tomes on subjects he would never truly be able to understand. He had thirty assistants now and he could see that several of them were asleep at their desks.

Oto Wiebelan was here, too, although he was asleep in his room. But even with the extra help, the new material was piling up faster than they could hope to go through it. Crates and boxes seemed to be arriving daily as universities and librarians from all over the East responded to his call for records dealing with magic.

He leaned back in his chair and sighed. Mountains of words, but no answers. Over a month had passed since that unpleasant scene with Colonel Krasner. Fortunately, there had not been any apparent repercussions from Hesseran's blunder with the Hegurian, but Krasner was hounding them to find some solution to the Kaifeng's magic. Unfortunately, neither Jarren, nor any of the wizards had much confidence that there *was* any answer. The three magickers had been pushing themselves unmercifully to strengthen their spells. Lyni was doing the best and she could produce several thousand of the 'waterbugs' at once. Idira and Hesseran could make a thousand or so. They kept improving, but by Jarren's estimate, they would probably not be able to make more than forty or fifty thousand by the likely date of the battle. Not enough, not nearly enough.

They'd all had to argue hard to prevent Krasner from trying to sail back to the Wizard's Island and dragging all the others back in chains. With the thirty or forty others who were there trained to create waterbugs, it would almost give them enough to stop the fireflies. But the chances of actually dragooning the other wizards seemed so slim it did not seem worth the attempt. Especially since Lyni refused to guide them back to the island. Without her help it might take months to find the place. When Krasner realized he might miss out on the spring campaign and bring back the additional help too late to do any good, he dropped the idea.

So they needed another answer. At first, Jarren had been encouraged by the discovery about the crystal. If one thing could keep the seekers out, perhaps something else could, too. Something more practical to make than lead-crystal cartridge boxes! In truth, such things would not work in any case. The seekers would probably just swarm around until the soldiers opened them to get out their ammunition. Zip-boom! No they needed something else...

A huge yawn erupted without warning. He really needed some sleep, but he was finding it difficult to rest. The knowledge that there were unread books, scrolls that had not been opened, and that in one of them could lie the answer drove him on and on. He could work for a few hours yet, but he needed a cup of hot tea. He pushed himself out of his chair and headed for the kitchen.

There was no one there, nor had he expected anyone to be. He built up the fire and put a kettle over it and waited for it to boil. While he waited, he went to the back door and opened it. The chill, pre-dawn air slapped him awake. It was frosty and very clear. The stars glittered down on him. It occurred to him that those same stars were shining on the Kaifeng hosts. In a month, or maybe two, those hosts would start to move. Killing, burning and raping their way across the landscape, they would come east. A chill went through him. For some reason it all seemed terribly real now. For months, ever since he'd first returned to Zamerdan from the Wizard's Isle, this had all seemed like a dream. Like some history book come to life. It wasn't really going to happen, was it? All of Colonel Krasner's warnings were just a fairy tale, right?

Wrong. It really was going to happen. And if they could not find a way to stop the Kaifeng, they would roll over everything. Everything. Even familiar and comfortable places like Sirenza would eventually fall. His mother and grandmother and a dozen aunts, uncles and cousins lived there. What would happen to them? Old Porfino's shop would be looted and the old man put to the sword when he tried to use his pitiful wooden club to stop them. The University would burn and Hano Beredane's head would be put on a pike. The opera house and the art museum, all gone.

And long before that, Jarren Carabello would be a rotted corpse, ridden into the dirt of some battlefield by the hooves of the Kaifeng horses. Colonel Krasner would be dead, Hesseran would be dead. Idira might survive as a slave, and Lyni...

They'd get Lyni, too. Knowing her, she would not give up without a fight and she'd probably end up killed. But if she wasn't killed, they would catch her and rape her and make her a slave. Her powers would not help her; they'd just put an iron collar around her neck and then rape her some more. The thought of Lyni as a slave filled him with horror and rage. He liked her far more than he would admit and he could not bear to think of her harmed. He knew she hated him, but he could not help how he felt about her.

We've got to stop them somehow.

The water in the kettle was boiling and he made his tea. The hot liquid drove some of the chill from him, but it could not get rid of the feeling of dread that filled him. They were running out of time.

He returned to the study and took up the book where he had left off. He finished it just as dawn was coming up, but found nothing of interest. He was seriously thinking about going to bed, but some of the students were stumbling back in now and a few had questions he needed to answer. By the time he was done with that, he was thinking about breakfast. The kitchen was full now and he was just in time to see Colonel Krasner going out the door—which was lucky: he didn't need another lecture on how desperate the situation was. But Oto was there and he took his food and sat down beside him.

"Morning, Jarren," said Wiebelan. "Another late night, I see. You can't keep pushing yourself like this, you know."

"I'll go to sleep in a bit. It's easier to concentrate at night."

"Yes, I did that, too, when I was young. Can't do it now."

"This is so frustrating," said Jarren wearily, "I used to love going through the old books. The thought that I was reading things that no one had read for centuries was thrilling. And when I would find something of interest, I would sit there and think: 'I'm the only one in the whole world who knows about this'. It was a wonderful feeling, almost god-like. But this desperate search is no fun. None at all. I can feel the time and everyone's hopes and expectations pressing in on me. I feel like a grape with all the juice squeezed out of it."

"You're tired, Jarren. Go to bed."

"Yes, I think I'll go to bed."

"Oh, did you see that package that came for you late yesterday?" asked Wiebelan.

"Package?"

"Yes, it was addressed to you personally. I noticed it, because it came from Sirenza. At first I thought it might have come from Beredane, but it's not his handwriting on the wrapping."

"Really?" asked Jarren sleepily. "Where is it?"

"On the table in the foyer."

"I'll take a look at it. Thank you." Jarren finished his breakfast and then found the package. It was a book-shaped object wrapped in many layers of paper. He picked it up and carried it up to his room. He flopped down on his bed and fumbled to untie the strings that bound it. He finally had to resort to a knife to cut them and then he tore away the paper. It was an old, leather-bound book that looked exactly like ten thousand others that were now filling the estate. The gold letters on the binding had been worn away so that he could not read them. He carefully opened the cover and saw that a new piece of paper was resting inside. He took it and squinted at it in the bright morning light that was streaming in the window. In spite of his fatigue, his face took on a huge grin.

Porfino! That old rascal! I was just thinking about him!

The note said simply: "Jarren, I thought you might find this of interest. Look at page 289. Porfino."

Jarren set the paper aside and turned the pages to the title. *Practical Magical Alchemy, by Gheradin.* The name meant nothing to him, but he shrugged and turned to page 289 as Porfino had instructed. He began to read...

What follows is a description of a spell I devised at the behest of a merchant who deals in fireworks. The man came to plead with me for help. It seemed that his main customers were traveling circuses and his goods were constantly being imperiled by...

Jarren's eyes widened in amazement and every trace of fatigue vanished. "Hess! Idira! Lyni!"

His bellow roused the entire household.

"I'm afraid it has been confirmed," said General DeSlitz, grimly, "Heguria has formally withdrawn from the alliance. Their troops will not be joining us and we cannot rendezvous in their territory as we had planned."

Several of the officers around the conference table gasped in alarm, but Matt simply winced. He'd been fearing this for weeks, ever since he'd heard what Hesseran had to say.

"But, that's crazy!" exclaimed one of the staff officers. "They're committing suicide!"

"No," said DeSlitz. "They have concluded an agreement with the Kaifeng. In exchange for a huge tribute the Kaifs will leave them alone—for now."

"Those traitorous bastards!" snarled General Saginau. "Leaving the rest of us in the lurch!"

"Yes. We shall be losing nearly 50,000 troops, more, really, since it's unlikely any of the Ertrian troops will be able to reach us in time now, and we'll have to completely redraw our plans for the rendez-vous and supply."

"But why did they do it?" demanded another officer."

DeSlitz turned his piercing gaze on Matt and he realized that all of his lies had finally come home to roost. "I think Colonel Krasner can probably answer that question better than I can."

Matt cleared his throat nervously and glanced at the other officers. "I would imagine it is because the Hegurians believe that the wizards have *not yet* discovered a way to counter the Kaifeng magic. Sir."

To say that pandemonium broke out in the room would not have been accurate. These were all military men and had a certain amount of self-discipline. Still, the number of dropped jaws and cries of surprise was fairly impressive. Matt forced his face to immobility and simply watched.

"What...what do you mean they can't counter it? They promised they could!" exclaimed Saginau.

"They promised they would work on finding the proper solution, General," countered Matt. "They *are* working, working very hard, and they still have hope."

"Hope? Hope! We need more than just hope!"

"Yes, I must agree," said General DeSlitz. "Colonel, do not attempt to play clever with me. I recall your earlier statements very clearly, and I have accounts of what you and the wizards said both here and aboard the ships bringing you back. There is not the slightest doubt that you and they have deliberately misled us about their abilities. This entire alliance was created based on the assumption that some counter to the Kaifeng magic could be found. Do you have any explanation?"

"Yes, sir. I will admit that I lied to all of you. Deliberately and with forethought." There were growls of anger from around the table, but Matt pushed on. "As for my explanation, well, you said it yourself, General: the whole alliance depended on it."

"But you admit they don't have an answer!" cried Saginau. "When word of this gets out, the alliance will fall apart!"

"And if I had told you the whole truth from the start, the alliance never would have been formed in the first place!" snapped Matt. "Then what would have happened? Everyone would have run around like headless chickens and we would have still been squawking when the Kaifs rolled over us. The alliance is absolutely essential and I was not going to say anything that might have imperiled it! Sir."

"You had no right to make such a decision yourself!"

"Just a moment, General," said DeSlitz, putting up a hand. "You could be right about that, but Colonel Krasner makes an excellent point, too. The alliance is absolutely vital. No individual kingdom or duchy can hope to fight the Kaifs on their own. Our only hope is the combined army. If he had told the truth, it might well have collapsed immediately, just as he says. He couldn't—and we can't—allow that to happen."

"But…but how can we hope to win against the Kaif magic, sir?"

"We'll do it the way we were planning to before the wizards arrived. Send out the word to get the craftsmen back to work on the bows and crossbows and pikes! We won't rule out our gunpowder until it is certain the wizards aren't going to succeed, but we will have to make plans that assume they will fail. We are soldiers, damn it, and we will fight no matter what weapons we end up using!"

"But won't that give away the secret, sir?"

"We'll just tell everyone we are taking no chances and want to have the other weapons available. They'll suspect, they'll worry, but as long as we act like we still expect to win, they'll go along with it. They'll go along with it because we're their only hope and they know it. That places a great deal of responsibility on each and every one of us, gentlemen. But see to your duty and we'll get through this."

The men around the table seemed to relax, ever so slightly. Matt could see they were still shaken, but hopefully they would do their jobs.

"Colonel Krasner," continued DeSlitz, and Matt snapped back to attention. "If you were a Zollerhan officer, I'd have you cashiered for this. While I can, perhaps, understand your actions, that does not mean I'm happy with them. You deliberately withheld information from me, your commanding officer. I'm very tempted to relieve you of your command."

"That is your privilege, sir. Just so long as I get a chance to fight. I'll go as a common trooper if I have to."

DeSiltz frowned and rubbed at his ear. "Still, the wizards seem to like you and to remove you now would raise too many questions with the aristocracy who are used to seeing you. I'm afraid we shall have to continue your policy of deception with them. And I suppose that if your wizards don't succeed, then it doesn't really matter who the liaison is, does it? Very well, keep your job—but I'm assigning one of my aides to act as *my* liaison. I'll expect him to keep me completely informed of what's happening—and I expect you to give him full access to the wizards."

"Yes, sir. Thank you, sir."

"Now, before we go on, I would like a full accounting from you on what, if anything, the wizards *are* able to do—and how that Hegurian bastard managed to find out all the things I could not!"

"Yes, sir," said Matt. He was relieved that this was all out in the open now—and it had not gone as badly as he had feared. He proceeded to tell the general about the 'waterbugs' and the lead crystal firefly barrier. As he expected, neither one terribly impressed the man.

"Well, I'm a bit relieved that there has been *some* progress—however small. I agree that the crystal probably isn't a practical solution, but we'll put out a call for glassmakers anyway. We might be able to safeguard some powder, although it remains uncertain if that will do any good. But tell me, Colonel, in your opinion, is there any hope at all for some new discovery? Something might really make a difference?"

"I don't know, sir. They are all working terribly hard. Realistically, we have, at most, three months before we're likely to meet the Kaifs. Whether they can come up with anything in that time, I just don't..."

There was a knock on the conference room door that interrupted him. A servant poked his head in. "Excuse, me, My Lords, but Master Carabello is here and wishes to speak with Colonel Krasner. He says it is most urgent." Matt's eyebrows shot up. Carabello here? What could be that important? For a moment his hopes rose, but then he reflected that he was probably here to report that Hesseran had accidentally blown up the whole estate this time. Matt looked to General DeSlitz who simply nodded.

"Send him in," said Matt to the servant. A moment later, Carabello entered. He was smiling, which was good, although he seemed a bit intimidated by all the uniformed officers who were now staring at him. Matt noticed that the man was splattered with mud and was clutching a large leather valise in his hands. Had he found something?

"Ah, Master Carabello," said General DeSlitz, "Welcome to our little meeting. I understand you have something urgent to report? Please have a seat and tell us about it."

Carabello glanced over to Matt and looked uncertain. Matt just waved him to a chair. "Yes, please sit down, Jarren. And don't worry: *we have no secrets* from the General." Carabello's eyes widened and he swallowed nervously and did as he was told. He fumbled around with the leather case and carefully drew out an old book.

"I found something very interesting today. I think it might be the answer we've been looking for."

The silence that answered clearly startled Carabello. Obviously he was expecting something a bit more enthusiastic.

"Hopefully not more lead crystal cartridge boxes," muttered one of the officers.

"Uh, no, no, not that at all," He began flipping through the pages of the book until he found what he was looking for. "Here it is. This was written by an alchemist about forty years before the Battle of Soor. Now, wc had already learned about how fake magickers used gunpowder to fool unknowing people, and how the seekers could be used to expose the frauds. But in addition to those frauds, there were also legitimate users of gunpowder. Fireworks makers, in particular, used it and had a perfect right to pursue their avocation. But naturally, their wares were just as vulnerable to the seekers as..."

"Master Carabello," interrupted Matt, "could you please get to the point?"

"What? Oh, I'm sorry. Well, to summarize: The legitimate users of gunpowder didn't want their powder to be exploded accidentally by seekers sent against someone else. This alchemist, apparently devised a means to make gunpowder immune to the seekers."

"What!?" cried a dozen voices simultaneously.

"The author provides an unusually detailed description of the spell. Much of it means nothing to a non-magicker, like me, but the wizards seem very excited by this. They seem to think they can recreate the spell."

"That's wonderful!" exclaimed General Saginau. He was echoed by several others. General DeSlitz was not quite so enthusiastic.

"How long will it take to do that, Master Carabello? And then how much powder can they treat and how long would that take? We don't have a great deal of time remaining before the Kaifs come east."

"I realize that, sir. The wizards are very hopeful that they can devise the spell quickly. Apparently it is a variation on another spell that Idira already knows and that will help. So, perhaps a month to perfect the spell, itself. As for how much powder they can treat, we won't know that until they have the spell working. I'm sorry I can't be more specific, but this is not an exact science. At least not yet."

"I see. Well, this is still the best news I've heard all day. You have my congratulations, Master Carabello. Please keep me informed of the wizards' progress on this." He turned back to the assembled officers. "But we shall proceed as I outlined earlier. Training with the non-gunpowder weapons will proceed as quickly as they are available. The fact that our troops are still scattered all over the East complicates this, too. I don't plan to relocate our headquarters for another month at least, so our couriers are going to be kept very busy.

"Let's get to work, gentlemen!"

Thelena stood on the balcony overlooking the great audience chamber and stared down at her father. He looked tired, but then he almost always looked tired these days. He was working far too hard. Between teaching his students and attending to the seemingly endless political crises, he never had enough time to rest. She had tried to convince him to slow down, but he had simply smiled and told her there would be time for rest later. She hoped he was right, but for the moment, things looked to be busier than ever.

The preparations for the spring campaign were in full swing. The snows were nearly gone and it looked like they would be getting mostly rain from now on. With the thaw, the roads were all mud, but the Kaifeng did not depend on wagons, so that was not a major problem. But they did depend on horses, and horses needed to be fed. There was no possibility of carrying fodder along for a half-million animals, so the army and the families and the herds could not move until the new year's grass had grown enough to feed the horses. The locals said it would probably be another month, although some fresh green shoots were coming up already.

So they would ride north. Just three days ago a huge wagon train had arrived from Heguria laden with tribute. They had been forced to hitch twenty large horses to each wagon to drag them through the mud, but they had arrived. The Hegurian ambassador had groveled before Zarruk and begged him to leave his people in peace. Zarruk had accepted the gift and would abide by the agreement—for now. The ceremony had been impressive and the gifts given out lavish. There was now an incredibly elaborate, gold and diamond chandelier hanging in their tent. Thelena had no clue how they would ever manage to transport it when they moved.

There had been other arrivals, too. More tribes were braving the mud and scarce grazing lands to arrive in the city. They did not want to miss out on the loot this year. Enough had arrived to form a new *helar* and elect a new Ka. The man was down there now, swearing loyalty to Zarruk. Atark was standing in his usual spot to Zarruk's right and witnessing the proceedings. As part of the ceremony, her father worked some magic and sent fireballs streaking into one of the fireplaces. It was strictly to overawe the new Ka and convince him that the tales he had heard were true. Even from this distance she could see that the magic had had the desired effect. The Ka's eyes were wide and he bowed more deeply than ever.

Thelena's brow furrowed. For some reason it bothered her that her father would use his magic in such a cavalier fashion. He had been doing more and more of that lately. Perhaps it was because he was no longer the only one who could work the magic now. Some of his students were becoming quite good. Did her father feel the need to continually show that his was the greater power? Or was there some other reason? In her mind's eye she could see the skull of Ransurr grinning up at her with the eyes glowing purple. In spite of her eavesdropping, she had never actually seen the skull before, and now she could not get the image out of her head.

Or the voice.

There had been a faint voice in her head when she stared at the skull. It had been calling to her, telling her to pick up the skull, hold it to her. It had promised her power and happiness. A loving husband and healthy children. It could give that all to her if she wanted it enough—if she would submit to him. All of that had flashed through her mind in an instant and it only took her an instant more to realize that it was all a lie. She had stepped away and allowed her father to retrieve the skull and put it back in its box. The wood box was now in a much larger and heavier chest with a very strong lock on it. But the inches of thick oak could not seal in the voice. Ever since that night she had heard Ransurr whispering to her. Tempting her, pleading with her. Not all the time. Not every night. But he was there.

And he wanted her.

It was a hunger deeper and more terrible than she had found in the most sadistic and lust-crazed Varag. Ransurr did not just want her body for a few hours' pleasure. He wanted her body and her soul—permanently. But he would never have it. Thelena knew exactly what it meant to be a slave and on some instinctive level she knew that to submit to the Ghost would mean a slavery more complete and more terrible than anything mortal chains and whips could inflict. No, she was not tempted and she was certain the Ghost could do her no harm if she did not let it.

But what about her father?

Clearly, the Ghost had not taken control of her father as it wanted to take her. If it had, it would no longer be in the skull and demanding her own body. No, that was not the danger. But what sort of influence did the Ghost have over her father? She had noticed from that very first night—the night he had burned Gerrik to death—that he was harder and more violent than she remembered him. Well, she was harder than he probably remembered her, too. They had both been hardened by life's cruelties. They both had good reason to crave revenge.

But her thirst for vengeance had been sated very quickly. The sight of Kareen, unconscious at her feet, with the blood from her mangled back spattered on her hand and dress hem had sated it completely. The sight of five hundred headless bodies and the anguished howls of their doomed souls had purged any remaining hunger to hit back at her tormentors. She had enough of revenge.

But her father clearly had not. He had ignored her pleas about the sacrifices and had continued to take them. She had heard the plans for the coming campaign and knew that it could be far crueler than what had already taken place. If the enemy resisted—and they would—they would pay for it in a terrible fashion. She found it hard to believe that it was her own father so calmly discussing mass impalements and mass rapes. Was it really him she was hearing, or was it some echo of Ransurr?

She looked down and saw that the ceremony was nearly finished. She knew that the end of it would include Re-Ka Zarruk embracing his new vassal and then presenting him gifts. One of the gifts would include a naked and terrified slave girl, wrapped in chains and laid at his feet. Thelena had no desire to see that. She turned and made her way back to her tent.

The last soaring note of the symphony died away and the huge audience broke into cheers. Jarren shuddered with delight. The performance had been magnificent and the selection from among his favorites. He glanced to his right and saw Idira with a warm smile on her face that almost countered the dark circles under her eyes. Dark circles under the eyes were standard issue for everyone.

They had all been working 18-hour days for months. Jarren had decided they needed a night off.

"Oh, that was lovely," Idira sighed. "It has been so long since I've heard anything like that. Thank you for bringing us here, Jarren."

"You are very welcome. Consider it a going-away present. We won't have the chance to do this again for quite a while." The woman's smile faded slightly. In just two days they would be taking ship for Laponia. The army was starting to gather and they had to be there. He looked past Idira to where Thaddius and Hesseran and Lyni were sitting. The Alchemist had appeared to enjoy the concert, too, but he could not quite decipher the expression on the young woman's face.

"Did you enjoy the music, Lyni?" he dared to ask. She looked over at him and her expression became troubled.

"I…I've never heard anything like that before. My village was poor and far from any town. After that I went to the Island. This was… beautiful."

"You see, Lyni?" said Idira. "Civilization does have a few redeeming qualities after all."

"Maybe it does," she admitted. "But we'll soon be leaving it behind—the good and the bad."

The audience was filing out of the concert hall. Jarren had secured a private box and they were all here incognito. If it had been known that The Wizards were here, they never would have been left alone. They waited until the crowd was nearly gone and then left the box and went down a rear stair. Jarren looked out the back door and was relieved to see only their carriage waiting for them with a small cavalry escort. It was raining rather hard, so there were few people about on the streets. They quickly crossed the short distance to the carriage and got inside. He was surprised to see Colonel Krasner and Lieutenant Prinz already there. Putting seven people in the coach was a bit of a squeeze, but Jarren didn't mind when he found himself sitting next to Lyni. Was she wearing perfume?

"I trust you all had a nice time?" asked Krasner after the coach had lurched into motion.

"Yes, very much," said Idira and Hesseran together. Lyni and Thad just nodded.

"I was hoping to let everyone relax a bit, tonight, Colonel," said Jarren.

"Well, I'm sorry to interrupt your evening out, but General

DeSlitz wants a fresh report on your progress. It's been a month since you discovered the 'immunizing' spell. Do you have it working?"

"Yes," said Idira, Hesseran, Lyni and Jarren in unison.

"Just 'yes'?" asked Krasner his eyebrows rising in surprise. "No 'buts' or other qualifiers? You can protect the gunpowder?"

"Yes," said Jarren. "We ran a series of tests today and it works. That's one reason we are out celebrating."

"It was quite tricky to do, in spite of the instructions we had," said Hesseran. "Before we found that, I had been experimenting with ways of preventing the fireflies from igniting the gunpowder, but that was just not working. Anything that would stop the fireflies also prevented the gunpowder from being ignited at all. We assumed that gunpowder that would not burn wouldn't be of much use to you."

"A good assumption. But you found something that does work?"

"Yes. As we've explained before, the seekers that the Kaifeng are using were originally devised to find things. Lost items, but also things that had been stolen. In fact, that was probably its most common use: tracking down stolen goods. Jewelry primarily, I believe. Obviously you couldn't send out seekers to look for stolen coins, because they'd just go after the nearest coins they could find—whether they were stolen or not. But unique items like jewelry could be found and returned."

"Fascinating," said Krasner in a patient voice. "But what does that have to do with gunpowder?"

"Ah," said Idira, taking up the explanation, "sadly—or perhaps I should say fortunately—not all magickers were completely law-abiding. Some used their powers for bad purposes. Apparently the thieves guilds in some of the larger cities were upset that seekers could be used to track them down, so they hired magickers to find a way to defeat the seekers. They devised a spell that could be cast on an object that would prevent any seeker from finding it. The alchemist who wrote that book used a variation on that spell to protect the gunpowder."

"And it works? You've tested it?"

"Yes, we have. All day today we worked with it. We even borrowed a pistol and some cartridges. After the spell was cast, the seekers could not find the cartridges and we could still load and fire the pistol using them."

Krasner relaxed and leaned back in his seat. "Thank the gods!" he whispered. "And thank all of you, too," he added in a louder voice.

"You are welcome," said Idira. "We are happy we could help."

"Excuse me, my lady," said Lieutenant Prinz. "How long will it take for you to safeguard the army's powder supply?" It was one of the few times that Prinz had spoken since he had appeared as Krasner's aide some weeks earlier.

"Oh, well, I'm not really sure," said Idira.

"We just perfected the spell, you have to realize," said Hesseran. "But as a rough guess, I'd say each of us could probably treat three or four pounds of powder a day—we have to work with small batches, you understand. Lyni probably more. So, say a dozen pounds a day for the three of us. If we still have two months as you hope, then we could probably have, what? Seven or eight hundred pounds treated. That will be enough, won't it?"

Krasner's face had gone white. "Seven or eight hundred *pounds*?" he choked.

"Yes, quite a lot, isn't it?" chuckled Hesseran. "Make quite a bang if that all went off at once!"

"Master Hesseran, Mistress Idira," said Krasner gravely, "I don't want to deride your accomplishment, but you are badly out of your reckoning. We are going to have at least fifty-thousand infantry in the army. They will use up eight hundred pounds of gunpowder *with one volley!* That doesn't even consider the artillery! You are going to have to do better—a lot better—than that!"

"Oh dear," said Hesseran.

"We'll do our best, Colonel," said Lyni, "But there are limits to our strength."

"They've been working themselves to death as it is," said Jarren angrily. "You can't ask the impossible of them!"

Krasner was visibly struggling to hold his temper. After a moment he was in control of himself. "All right, all right. Do what you can. We may end up with a core of the army that has guns and powder and the rest with spears and bows. If we do, so be it. We're still far better off than we were a few months ago."

"I hope the General sees it that way," said Lieutenant Prinz.

"None of us have any choice, Lieutenant."

The passengers of the coach fell silent. They passed over some rough paving and they were shaken back and forth a bit. Jarren was extremely aware of Lyni's warm arm pressed against his. She had enjoyed the concert, he was certain of that. They had worked together a lot in the last two months and she hardly ever snarled at him anymore. Did she still hate him?

"This does not appear to be the way back to the estate," she said suddenly. Jarren looked out the coach window and saw that she was right.

"Where are we going, Colonel?" he demanded.

"To the harbor. Our ship is waiting."

"What? We weren't scheduled to leave for another two days!"

"Change of plans. We've received word from a spy." Krasner paused and ran his gaze over the other passengers.

"The Kaifs are on the move."

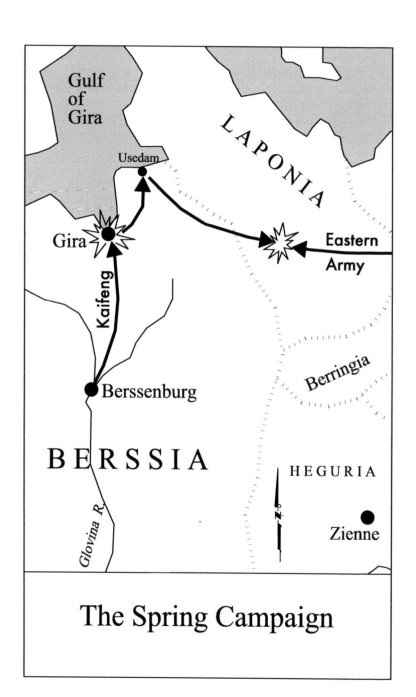

The Spring Campaign

CHAPTER TWENTY-ONE

Kareen sat on her horse next to Thelena and looked through the shattered gate of the city and cringed. She had thought the sack of Berssenburg had been bad, but now she realized that Berssenberg had been nothing, nothing at all. The city of Gira, the great northern port of Berssia, lay before her and it had been... butchered. She didn't have any other word for it. It was like a cow or a pig or a sheep that had been cut open. The entrails and blood lay scattered on the ground and the meat was being cut up into slices.

A huge mound of severed heads lay next to the gate. It was easily fifteen feet high. Kareen could not guess how many had died to make that pile. But she knew it was not the only such pile in the city. And it was not the only—or the worst--example of the Kaifengs' cruelty. A line of stakes marched away in either direction, curling around the walls of the city. A body had been impaled on each one. Most of them were already dead, but a few still twitched or moaned in the last paroxysm of agony. Kareen could scarcely imagine how much those victims must have suffered. It could take days for them to die.

A shrill scream made her jerk her head around. A hundred yards away a man—no, it was just a boy—came dashing through one of the many openings in the walls. Several mounted Kaifeng warriors were in hot pursuit. The boy shrieked and ran, but one of the warriors had a rope and expertly lassoed the Berssian, bringing him to the ground. A small crowd of Kaifeng on foot came into view through the same gap and Kareen gasped when she saw they were carrying a long pole. They weren't actually going to...?

Her stomach heaved when she realized that they were. She was too far away to see anything, but the boy's shrieks became more and more desperate and finally rose into a terrible cry of pain. A few moments later another pole was added to the grisly fence surrounding the city. The body on this one flopped about and wailed without hope.

Kareen tore her eyes away and sobbed. "Why? Why are they

doing this?"

"The city refused to surrender," said Thelena. "They are being made an example of."

"He was just a boy!"

"Zarruk has decreed that all the males—all of them—are to die. That one must have been hiding somewhere. They are burning the city now and the fires will drive out the last survivors and they will be killed."

"Gods, how can anyone be so cruel?"

"I'll make no excuses, Kareen. It sickens me, too. But the leaders hope that this example will persuade the rest of the East to surrender without a fight. If they do, then maybe the rest will be spared this horror."

"They will kill all the men? The boys, too?"

"Even babies. Yes, that is the command."

"What...what about the women?" Kareen knew they would be enslaved, but what else might have been ordered to punish Gira?

"As you'd expect: rape and more rape. There are five times as many warriors now as when Berssenburg fell—and this is a smaller city—so I'm quite sure each and every woman and girl has been quite thoroughly...punished for the city's resistance." Kareen could hear the bitterness in Thelena's voice. "Those that survived will be slaves, of course."

Kareen just shook her head and her tears fell and splattered on her saddle. "Did they spare anyone? Anyone at all?"

"Oh yes; that was part of the plan, after all: someone has to spread the word about the consequences of resistance. All of the priests and priestesses from the temples were not harmed. They were given horses and sent east."

"Well, that's something, I suppose."

Thelena gave a bitter laugh. "No, it wasn't. Don't think any of those clerics were really spared."

"What... what did they do?" asked Kareen in horrid anticipation.

"They were witnesses while all the male nobility was forced to watch their sons being impaled and their wives and daughters being raped and beaten to death—before they were impaled themselves. Most of those clerics probably wish they were dead, too."

Just at the moment Kareen was wishing the same thing. This was all like some vision of the hells...

Thelena kneed her horse into motion and started through the gate. Kareen did not know why Thelena was going in here, or why she had agreed to go along, but she and their guard detachment followed. It was just as bad inside as out. Most of the bodies that those stacked heads belonged to were inside the walls. A thick cloud of smoke was rising from the city's western quarter. By tomorrow all the city was to be burned.

"I've been thinking a great deal about what is happening, Kareen," said Thelena. She spoke in Berssian and none of the guards could understand that tongue. "I thought about it when I was a slave and I thought about it during the sack of Berssenburg." She motioned to the carnage around them. "This seems evil to you; it would seem evil to most people. But it is not the Kaifeng or the Berssians who are evil: the real evil is *power*, Kareen. Power is where the evil comes from. Years ago, back before my father discovered the magic, the Berssians and their Varag vassals had the power. They had the guns and the cannons and my people could not match them. They could come out onto the plains and kill and burn and torture. My mother and brother died and I was beaten and raped. I would have died, too, but for your kindness.

"Were the Varags evil? Were the Berssian generals who set them on us evil? I don't think so—even after all that I've suffered, I don't think so. They weren't evil, but they had the power and the power is what's evil. They did those things *because they could!* There was nothing to restrain them, so they did what they did because they could. Power, Kareen, unrestrained power is the great evil." Kareen stared at her friend wide-eyed. She'd never seen her like this before.

"And now we have the power. My father's magic gives the Kaifeng the power. He has made the East's guns and cannons useless and the unrestrained power lies in our hands. *Gira died because we could make it die.* No other reason! And unless the East submits, all those other cities will die, too. I weep for them—and I weep for my own people. The power will consume them as surely as it will your people. We are all utterly damned."

"Gods...gods, oh, Thelena I'm going to be sick. Please let me go back to the tent."

"Go. Take one of the guards with you. The warriors' blood is still up and they might go after you."

Kareen nodded and turned her horse and galloped back toward camp.

Thelena watched Kareen ride off. A large part of her wanted to follow, but she was looking for someone and apparently he was in the city. She turned around to face forward and put her horse in motion again. She probably should not have said what she did to Kareen, but it had been building up inside her for days now and it needed to get out—and Kareen was the one person she could safely say it to. Damnation. The whole of the Kaifeng were on the road to damnation. But who was really leading that march? She intended to find out.

By the time she had ridden a block, she regretted her decision to come into the city. She should just wait until later to find the man she was looking for. She knew it was going to be bad once the city refused to surrender, but this was far worse than she had feared. Headless bodies were everywhere. For once, the old cliché about the streets running with blood was actually true. Small streams of dark red flowed down the cobblestone streets to collect in pools.

She had known it was going to be bad. The great army had set out from Berssenburg with six *helars*, over fifty thousand warriors. It had only been about three hundred miles from Berssenburg to Gira, a distance that could have been covered in five days by the warriors, but it had actually taken over three weeks. The families and herds were following and they could not travel so fast. More importantly, there was a constant influx of new tribes who were pouring through the mountain passes. Hardly a day went by when a new *helar* was not formed. New *helars* meant new Kas. These had to be elected by the noyens and they then had to swear loyalty to Zarruk. All of this held the army's progress down to little more than fifteen miles a day. There were twenty *helars* now, over one hundred and fifty thousand warriors. It made an incredible sight, but most of those warriors were eager for loot and slaves.

And the land had been empty.

Towns and villages were abandoned and deserted when the scouts entered. Little of value was left behind. A few unlucky people had been caught, but only a few. Depending on the mood of the men who caught them, these people had been killed or enslaved or just driven east to spread panic. Few of the newcomers even saw any of them. They grew more frustrated with each passing day. By the time they reached Gira, they were ready to take the loot and the women they had been promised. Some of them had ridden a thousand miles or more to be here and they were determined to take what they had been promised.

They had taken it from Gira.

The city never had a chance. When the army was still a week away, Atark had ridden north with a single *helar* and come upon the city by surprise. He had used his magic to destroy their gunpowder and then to burn all the ships in the harbor. The city was sealed. No one could get out. But they refused to surrender. So they had waited until the main army arrived and then Atark threw down the city's walls as he had done at Berssenburg and the warriors had stormed in. The slaughter and rape had gone on for three days.

As she went down the street, there was a steady stream of warriors heading the other way. All had some sort of loot piled on their horses, but the luckiest ones had a new slave, either lying limply across the saddle in front of him, or stumbling along behind on a tether. There had only been enough women to provide one warrior in four with a slave, so there were still plenty of men looking eagerly forward to the sack of the next city.

She reached a broad square and turned down another street. The archduke's palace was that way and she would find the man she sought there. It was said that the Archduke had refused to abandon his city and had died during the fighting. His bravery had spared the female members of his family from the fate of the other noble ladies. His oldest daughter had been taken by Zarruk to replace the general's mistress, and his wife and the other daughters had been given out to the new Kas. Thelena wasn't sure what sort of message that would send to the rest of the East.

The buildings here were mostly intact. Her father had used a lesser spell to breach the city's walls and there was less damage inside. Of course, all of this would be burned when the time came. Her father had spoken of using another, far more powerful earth-shaking spell before they left to complete the destruction. She would have to be sure she was miles away before that happened. In Berssenburg she had acquired a supply of the poppy juice and she had used it this time when her father took the sacrifices. It had helped a great deal, but she hated the sick, disoriented feeling it produced. She didn't want to use any more unless she really had to.

As she neared the Archduke's palace, she saw where the new

sacrifices were being held. She had not been quite truthful when she told Kareen that all the men had been killed. Well, maybe she had been: these men were dead, too. They just had not been killed yet. Dead and damned. She shook her head. In spite of her pleas, her father was still using the sacrifices to fuel his magic. She reflected that if people really understood what the fate of the sacrifices was, the whole terror campaign Zarruk was waging would not have been needed. The threat of being condemned to an eternity of bodiless wandering would be enough to break any resistance.

Or maybe to stiffen it. She wasn't really sure what would happen if the Easterners understood. Perhaps they would surrender to avoid that fate, but perhaps they would fight to the death to avoid it in another fashion. It was pointless to speculate, in any case: no one really understood but her.

They reached the palace and a few inquiries confirmed the man she sought was there. Many men were bustling about dragging loot out of the building before, it too, was burned. She looked with sadness on the marvelous art and architecture that would soon be rubble. Inside it was even busier. Boxes and bags of loot stood in the foyer. A dozen women, roped together, huddled in a corner, weeping. She went past them without sparing them a glance and down one of the side corridors. She heard voices ahead and stopped hesitantly outside the door of a large room. Inside were eight men. One was a warrior, probably one of the Noyens from his dress, but the other seven clearly were not. Six of the seven were plainly dressed in tunics and trousers, but all had large copper medallions on chains around their necks. They were loremasters, the keepers of the history of the Kaifeng. The warrior was reciting his exploits in the fall of Gira and the men were committing it to memory. Unlike the Easterners, the Kaifeng kept no written histories—kept very few written records of any kind, although many men could read and write. Carrying libraries of books and scrolls across the plains would have been impractical. Instead, men gifted with terrific memories kept the tales in their heads and passed them from generation to generation by word of mouth.

Thelena's attention was drawn to the eighth man in the room. He was very old, with a long white beard and heavy robes. A gold medallion hung about his neck and the weight of it seemed to be bowing him to the floor. He was Vardeen, the chief loremaster. When Thelena heard that he was here, she knew she had to speak with him.

But she hesitated to intrude. This was not a place for women, in any case. After listening for a few moments, it appeared that the warrior was finished and one of the younger loremasters was reciting back what he had heard. Thelena took the opportunity to send in one of her guards to request an audience with Vardeen. To her surprise and relief, Vardeen nodded immediately and got up with unexpected agility. But one of the other loremasters was immediately at his side and as the pair came out of the room, Thelena could see that the old man was blind. As he approached, Thelena made a deep bow, even though the man could not see her.

"Hail Vardeen, loremaster of our people," she said formally. "I thank you for consenting to speak with me."

"Well met, Thelena, daughter of Atark, son of Ardak, son of Ardan," said the old man with a rich, strong voice, and he smiled. "How may I serve you?"

"I have a question to ask you about the far past. But…but I would wish to speak with you in private."

"As you wish. Ulari, is there somewhere we can go?"

"I believe there is a small room down the hall, Lord," said the other man. They went the direction he indicated and found the room. The younger loremaster found a spot for Vardeen to sit and then stepped back. "Will you be all right here, Lord?"

"Yes, quite. Now leave us, please." The man bowed and then shut the door after him. Thelena stood there uncertainly.

"Sit, my dear, sit," said the old man. Thelena did so, bur still could not bring herself to ask her question. "You may speak, Thelena, daughter of Atark the Great, I will not bite, I promise."

"My lord, do you know of a man named Ransurr?" she blurted suddenly.

The old man frowned. "The name does not immediately bring any memories to mind. Can you tell me anything more that might help?"

"He… he was a mighty shaman from long ago, Lord. I think he fought in the Great Battle."

"Ah. Well, let me think for a bit." Vardeen closed his eyes and presently began to hum to himself. Thelena sat patiently. A long time passed. A quarter hour, perhaps a half hour and the man just sat there. Were it not for the humming she might have thought he had fallen asleep.

She was trying to nerve herself to say something when the old loremaster's eyes opened. They were filmed over with white, but they seemed to be staring right at her. "Ransurr," he said. "How did you hear his name, my dear?"

"I just heard the name and was curious."

"You do not lie well, Thelena, Daughter of Atark, but I will not press you further. You are correct. Ransurr was a shaman who fought in the Great Battle. I am afraid I have little more to tell you."

Thelena sighed in disappointment, but Vardeen went on. "All that I can remember comes from an old ballad. In part, it goes like this:

The warriors gathered, row upon row,
And rode to the East to throw back the Foe.
And with them the shamen, mighty with power,
Their spells they prepared for the deadly hour.

Hadjnar and Glartus, Tlernan and Yarloles,
E'en blood-soaked Ransurr, Drinker of Souls.

Vardeen stopped his chanting and his blind gaze seemed even more piercing. "I'm afraid that's all there is," he said.

Thelena stood up and bowed. "Thank you, Lord. It is more than enough."

"Are you all right, Lyni?" asked Jarren. The young woman had her head down on a table next to a small keg of gunpowder. They were in a house in Northern Laponia near where General DeSlitz had made his headquarters. After a moment, Lyni stirred and sat upright.

"What? Oh, it's you."

"Are you all right?" Jarren asked again.

"Just resting my eyes for a moment," said Lyni. "I'm all right."

"Maybe you should sleep for a while."

"What? With Colonel Krasner cracking the whip over us? Not a chance! Sometimes I think Stephanz was right: you have made us into slaves."

"You can walk away and leave any time you want, Lyni. I would make sure no one tried to stop you."

"Ha! Like you'd ever stand up to Colonel Krasner."

"For you I would."

Lyni looked at him for a long time. Jarren wondered what she was thinking. "You know, I believe you might," she said at last. "Jarren, are you in love with me or something?"

He was so startled by the question that before he could stop himself, his mouth told the truth. "I think maybe I am." He immediately blushed red.

Lyni snorted. "Well, then, you're stupider than I thought. How could you possibly love me after the way I've been treating you?"

"Y-you have not treated me badly."

"I've treated you like shit, Jarren Carabello! From the night I had you pulled out of the water until now. I've treated you like shit and yet you say you are in love with me."

"You are an amazing person, Lyni. You are strong and smart and brave and beautiful…" Lyni snorted, but Jarren pressed ahead, "…and I care for you. I'm not sure if that is love, but that is how I feel."

The woman opened her mouth as if she were going to say something else, but then she apparently changed her mind, and closed it again and just stared at him. "You are amazing, too, Jarren," she said after a while. "Just when I think you can't possibly be any more trouble than you already are—you do something like this."

"I'm sorry for all the trouble I've caused you. I never meant you—or anyone else—any harm."

"I know," Lyni sighed. "You are not a bad sort, I suppose. But trouble seems to follow you." She was silent for a few moments and then spoke again. "So how am I supposed to feel about this?"

Jarren wasn't sure what to say. This was not the sort of conversation he had any experience with. At least she had not slapped him or driven him off. "I don't know. How do you feel about it?"

"Right now? I feel tired. That's the only thing I've felt for weeks. Ask me again when this is all over."

"Very well, I shall. But maybe you really should go to bed, Lyni."

"In a bit. I just want to finish off this barrel." Jarren looked inside and saw that there were a few pounds left.

"This will take you another hour at least," he protested.

"More like two, but I want to get it done. It will be twenty pounds for the day and that's the best I've managed."

"That's very good. Hess and Idira have scarcely been able to do fifteen—although you are all getting stronger."

"Yes, but it's not enough. What's the total up to now?"

"Around twenty-five hundred pounds, I think."

"Three whole volleys for the infantry—and nothing for the cannons. We're not going to make it, Jarren. We'll never have enough—not in the time we have left."

"Some of the soldiers will have to fight without guns, I suppose. But we still have a chance."

"Not much of one. Not against the army that is headed this way."

"And yet you refuse to give up."

"I heard what that priest had to say about Gira, Jarren, just like everyone else. I know what's at stake. I know what's going to happen to us...what's going to happen to me. I just want to hurt them as badly as possible before the end."

Jarren was surprised at her words. She had always seemed to be the most reluctant and cynical of allies. But she had changed recently. He'd noticed it that night after the concert. She had really liked that, he was sure. She had worked very hard since then, spending long hours treating the gunpowder, after the others had fallen asleep from exhaustion. And when the priest from Gira told his tale, she had been crying by the end of it, too.

"We have not lost yet, Lyni."

"Not yet."

Jarren wasn't sure what else to say, but just then the door opened and Colonel Krasner came in, his perpetually muddy boots thumping across the floor. Jarren and Lyni looked at him in curiosity and apprehension.

"Go to bed, both of you," he said. Lyni snorted and Jarren tried to wipe the guilty look off his face. Krasner did not notice. "I mean it. Get some sleep. The army will be marching out tomorrow."

"So soon?" said Jarren. "I thought we would have at least another week."

"General's orders. He's picked where he wants to meet the Kaifs and we need to get there first. Depending on what they do, we probably have three or four weeks yet, but we have to get moving. We can't march nearly as fast as they can ride."

"Colonel, I cannot do my work in a lurching wagon," said Lyni. "This is going to seriously cut back on our production."

"No it won't. We've thought of that. We've rigged up three of the ambulances with beds. They have good springs on those things so it should not be too bad. You can sleep during the day while the army marches and then work at night when we are camped."

"Colonel!" said Jarren, "They're being worked to death as it is! You can't ask that of them, too!"

"Yes, he can, Jarren," said Lyni. "He can ask it, and we can try to comply. Maybe we can do enough so there'll be ten rounds per man."

"Thank you, Lyni," said Krasner. "No matter what happens, you can all be damn proud of yourselves. Now get to bed." He nodded to her and went out.

After a moment Lyni laughed. In spite of himself, Jarren was smiling, too. "Well, he did say 'bed', singular, but I'm afraid I'm going to have to beg off sharing one with you, Jarren," said Lyni.

"O-of course!" blurted Jarren with a start. "We...we aren't anywhere near that stage yet—if we ever will be." He was blushing now.

Lyni got up and to his complete amazement came over and kissed him lightly on the cheek. "You are a good man, Jarren. Trouble on two legs, but still a good man. Now good-night."

He watched her go out. He put out the special lantern. It was like the kind they used in a ship's magazines to avoid the risk of explosions. Then he sat there in the dark a long time before he got up to go to his own bed. As he left the tent, the almost bumped into someone and jumped back in surprise.

"Oh! Who's that? Thad?" He thought he recognized the shape of the priest.

"Uh, yes, it's me. Sorry I startled you." He sounded pretty startled himself. "I, uh, I was looking for you."

"Well, you found me. What do you want?"

"I had just learned that the army will be marching soon. I wanted you to know."

"Colonel Krasner just told us. I'm heading off for bed. Are you still coming with us?"

"Yes. My superiors want me to stay with you." Jarren tried to see the man's face in the darkness. Thad seemed very nervous. In fact, he'd seemed very jumpy for days.

"And just what do your superiors think about all this?"

"There is a great deal of uncertainty," answered Thaddius, slowly. "Some are convinced that we must use any means to stop the Kaifeng. Others feel...differently."

"How about you? What's your opinion?"

"I'm still not sure. I have prayed and prayed for guidance, but so far the gods have not answered me."

"Surely you can see we have to do something. We can't just let the

Kaifeng overrun everything."

"Yes, I know. But I am still not sure what the proper action is. This is very...difficult."

"Maybe. It's clear enough to me. It's even clearer that I need some sleep. Good night, Thad."

Matt looked at the endless line of men and horses and wagons and cannons stretching out of sight in each direction and told himself that it was going to be different this time. This army might look like the last army he was a part of, but it was not the same. Aside from being over twice the size, there was no bravado, no confidence based on ignorance. These men knew what they were facing and knew they were marching toward the decisive moment of their lives. The stories of the priests from Gira had gone through the ranks like a wildfire. A few men had quailed and there had been a rash of desertions over the following days. Matt suspected they were family men who felt compelled to try to get their families out of harm's way. But most men had become more determined than ever. This time they knew about the fireflies, knew what to expect, and would be facing the enemy with open eyes.

There were actually a lot of other differences between this army and the Army of Berssia, too, if you knew what to look for. First, this wasn't just one army, but dozens. There were contingents here from almost every kingdom, duchy, principality and electorate in the East. The bulk of them were from the major powers like Zollerho, Durace and Laponia, of course, but there were also troops from Nirbon, Mundoor, Tirragon, Pollico, Taratan and a dozen others. Some of those situated along the likely invasion route had made contributions that rivaled the larger nations. On the other hand, Barringia, which lay uncomfortably between Heguria and Berssia, had sent only a token force, keeping the rest to watch its own borders. So, the mixture of uniforms in this army was truly dazzling. Blue-coated Laponian lancers with their peculiar five-sided, flat-topped shakos shared the road with Gerritican irregular sharpshooters in sheepskin jackets and every sort of hat imaginable. Pollican grenadiers with jackets that were more gold braid than cloth marched alongside mix-matched companies of volunteers from the waterfront at Zamerdan. Every conceivable type of cannon could be found in the artillery train. No army like this had ever been seen before.

There were other differences, too. For perhaps the first time in history, there was a major army which had no huge mass of camp-followers tagging along. The fate of those who had followed the Berssian Army to its destruction had convinced the men to send their women home. A few had followed anyway, but these were determined to act as nurses rather than bed-warmers. The whole mood of the army was unlike anything Matt had witnessed. They were here to fight—all of them.

That wasn't to say that the army did not have a huge train of wagons following it, it did. But these were filled with supplies to feed the enormous host. They also carried the other weapons the army would probably be forced to use. Wagons filled with crossbows, pikes, halberds, helmets and other bits of armor lurched along behind each regiment. Everyone was hoping they would not be needed, but with each passing day it seemed more likely that they would.

Matt looked over his own regiment, for the Wizards' Guard was indeed a regiment now. Eight hundred armored lancers took up a third of a mile of road. The flood of volunteers had filled out the regiment in an amazingly short time. If they had stayed in camp for another few weeks, it might have grown beyond regimental size. But it was a fine command. The men were all enthusiastic and many had prior military experience. He'd managed to get a good set of officers and NCOs in place and they had handled the training. In truth, Matt was learning a great deal himself. He'd never commanded even a squadron before, let alone a regiment.

The regiment was divided into four squadrons and on the march there was an ambulance in the gap between each of the squadrons. Inside those three ambulances, the wizards were sleeping. Or at least trying to sleep. He could not imagine they were getting much with all the noise and dust and the shaking of their vehicles. Or maybe they were; as exhausted as they all were, they probably passed out the moment they lay down. It certainly wasn't easy to rouse them once the army stopped each day.

But in another week or two, it would be all over—one way or another. Or maybe a little longer at the snail's pace the army was moving. The roads in northern Laponia were neither good nor numerous. Whenever possible, a large army would try to move on several parallel roads, but in these regions it was seldom possible. Seventy-thousand men took up a huge amount of road. Usually, the head of the column would start out, march ten or twelve miles and then halt to make camp—and the tail of the column had not even started marching yet. It was slow and frustrating.

It was a few hours after noon and the vanguard was already pulling off the road. It would be tempting to keep marching as long as there was daylight, but if they did, the tail of the army would never catch up. Mile by mile they crawled across the landscape. The only good thing was that Matt's regiment had absolute priority on the road. His cavalry and their ambulances could usually cover the whole day's march in four or five hours. That gave the wizards a lot of time to work.

A mounted orderly came galloping back along the column and came up to Matt. He saluted, pointed out the spot where his regiment was to camp and then told Matt that the general wanted to see him. Matt passed on the camping orders to his subordinates and then followed the orderly to the General's headquarters.

They had to detour around a cluster of priests who were setting up their own camp. The army had a large number of the clerics with it, but Matt did not know what use they were going to be. He had no problem with asking the gods for help, but he was quite sure that the gods sided with the army that had the biggest regiments and most firepower. As he passed the priests he noticed Brother Thaddius talking with some of the others. He had decided he liked Thad and was glad he was here. He seemed a reasonable man and those were in short supply.

DeSlitz was usually up near the head of the column and today was no exception. There were always scouts coming in and the General wanted to get their reports as soon as possible. Matt rode through the camps of the advance guard to a cluster of tents set on a little hill. He dismounted and turned his horse over to a groom and then went into the General's tent.

"Ah, Krasner, good to see you," said Deslitz when he saw him. "How is your command?"

"Excellent, sir. Eager to kill some Kaifs."

"Good, good, they'll get their chance, I'm sure. And how are the wizards progressing?"

"They are working as hard as possible, sir. We are up to about five thousand pounds of powder now. I'm still sending it all to the cartridge makers. Are you planning on using any of it for the artillery?"

"Yes, that was one of the things I wanted to talk to you about. As you know, we have managed to get a number of lead crystal boxes made. They've been tested and they will keep out the fireflies. Right now, we have twenty-five of them and they can hold about ten powder charges each. I'm going to put one with each of twenty-five of our batteries. They can hold reserve ammunition we can use once all the fireflies have expended themselves. But we are going to need enough immunized powder for at least three shots per gun. That will be another twenty-five hundred pounds. Can they do it?"

"That depends on how much time they have, sir."

"Well, we have a bit of luck on that—although luck might not be the right word. It appears that the Kaifs aren't coming right for us. They've turned north to take Usedam and that should slow them down for a few days at least. We should reach the position I've chosen in another four days. I would guess the enemy will be upon us in another week or so after that."

"Eleven days," said Matt. "That's almost two hundred and thirty pounds a day. They can't do it, sir. Lyni is able to do almost fifty pounds a day now and the other two over thirty, but that's all. They might be able to do a thousand pounds or so, but the poor wretches are ready to collapse as it is right now."

DeSlitz frowned but then nodded. "All right, have them do what they can. We may have to cut back the number of guns we put on the line."

"Yes, sir."

"All right. But there is something else I wanted to talk to you about."

"Sir?"

"You've done a really excellent job organizing and training your regiment. The reports I've gotten from Lieutenant Prinz and what I've seen with my own eyes have been most impressive."

"Thank you, sir."

"But I have a bit of a problem and I was hoping you might help me out with it."

"Certainly, sir, whatever I can do."

"Good. As you know, we've had a hell of a time putting this army together, what with all the different nationalities and old feuds and hatreds getting in the way. Well, to get to the point, the regiment of heavy horse we have from Mundoor is refusing to take orders from their Nirbonian brigade commander. I've decided the best thing to do is to assign them to you."

Matt looked at his general in astonishment. "To me, sir? What do you mean?"

DeSlitz just grinned. "Would you be willing to take a crack at commanding a brigade?"

Atark looked at the rows and rows of dark trees on either side of the road and shivered. This was probably the most unnerving thing he had ever gone through in his life. It was so closed in! He could not see more than a hundred yards in any direction and in most places he could see less than fifty. The huge trees overhung the road and with the spring leaves coming out, he could not even see the sky! He looked around and saw the men of his guard muttering to themselves and looking anxiously about them. Clearly they were just as unsettled as he was. This was no place for a Kaifeng to be. There were no forests out on the plains, at least nothing to compare with this one.

"Gods! How much longer are going to be stuck in hellspawned place?" snarled one the men.

"We should be through before nightfall," said Atark.

"Thank the gods for that! I can't imagine being out here at night!"

"All those piled up behind us will be, though," said another man.

"Well, the gods have mercy on them!"

Atark fully agreed with the man. As near as he could tell, the forest was almost thirty miles wide at the point the road pierced it and this night, all thirty miles of it would be packed with warriors and herds. It would make far more sense to advance on a broad front rather than along this single road, but that would have meant going through the forest itself, and the men had refused. He could not blame them.

Still, it was going to slow them down tremendously. It would probably take four entire days to push everyone through this tiny funnel. The whole campaign was going more slowly than he had hoped, but it was still going well. The destruction of Gira seemed to be having the desired effect, too. Five days ago the small port city of Usedam had surrendered to Zarruk. It was obvious that most of the richer inhabitants had fled by sea before the army arrived, but those who were left had piled up an impressive mound of loot outside the walls, along with a thousand young women, roped together and wailing their despair. The warriors, sated with the excesses at Gira, had been in a charitable mood. The city was not burned, nor any of its citizens killed—but they had taken the loot and the women. Zarruk left a small garrison behind and the rest of the army had moved on.

Atark looked ahead and saw Zarruk and his escort waiting in a wider space along the road. When Atark came abreast he started forward and rode alongside. "Hail Zarruk!" said Atark. "My men wonder when we shall be free of these cursed trees."

"They are depressing, aren't they?" replied Zarruk who did not seem nearly as bothered by the woods as Atark. "A dark and gloomy land, this is. I can see why few people live here. Unfortunately, I understand that there are many such places in the East"

"Hopefully, we can avoid most of them."

"We shall try, but there is no way to avoid this one. To go around would take weeks and require us to cross the river over yonder at least twice. In any case, the enemy lies ahead of us along this route."

"Indeed? Are they near?"

"Not so near, but our scouts have spotted the head of their army. Considering the delay this narrow road is costing us, I'd imagine we shall meet them in a week or so."

"Are there many of them?"

"It is hard to say. Our scouts only saw the vanguard, but the rumors we have wrung from a few captives indicates that this is their main army."

"Excellent! We can finish this at a blow. If we crush them, the rest will not dare to oppose us. City after city will surrender."

"That is to be hoped. We will conquer this land as quickly as we can ride from city to city."

Atark felt a thrill go through him. All the long years of work and training were coming down to a single day perhaps a week away. Victory! The East could be well and truly crushed. And then? What will happen then?

"I wish I knew, my friend," said Zarruk. Atark started and then realized he had said that last question out loud.

"Well, first things first. We have a battle to win."

Jarren sat on his horse and watched the army preparing for battle. It was still two or three days away, but the amount of activity was breathtaking. Jarren was not a soldier and knew little about strategy or tactics, but even he could see why General DeSlizt had chosen this spot to fight the battle. The left of the army was firmly anchored on the Telensee River and then its line ran along a four-mile ridge with its right on a dense forest that ran up into the hills. They could not be flanked and the enemy would have to come straight at them.

The infantry and artillery were laying out their battle positions along the ridge and then forming their camps a few hundred yards to the rear. White canvas tents in neat rows were springing up like mushrooms after a rain. This was the first time the whole army had been this closely packed and it made a fantastic spectacle of martial strength. Jarren could not imagine how such a force could possibly be beaten.

But he knew it could be beaten. The Kaifeng magic could beat them. His exhilaration at the sight of the army faded, to be replaced with dread. If they were beaten, would it be his fault? He knew that he had done a lot. He had found the wizards and done as much as anyone to bring them here and convince them to help. He'd discovered several of the most important clues in how to counter the seekers. But had he done enough? Was there some simpler, more effective answer in one of those books he'd never had the time to get to? Was the answer waiting in some scroll that he'd passed up because he was too tired? Had his getting one extra hour of sleep meant the doom of everything he held dear? It was a ridiculous notion, but he could not put it out of his head. *Have I done enough?* Truly, he'd felt pretty useless for the last month. Ever since they left Zamerdan, really. He had been able to do very little additional research since leaving the estate. His only real function since then was seeing that the wizards had everything they needed to do their work. Somehow, that did not seem like enough.

The sun dipped behind the hills to the west. Bugles rang out announcing the evening meal. He went back to his tent and ate a quiet meal with Gez. Unlike everyone else, Gez seemed to be having a wonderful time. It was all a great adventure to him. Jarren supposed that he would have felt the same way when he was that age. By the time he finished it was quite dark. He got up and made his way to the tent where Lyni and the others were working. He wanted to make sure they had all eaten. Sometimes they forgot. He also wanted to see Lyni because…well, just because he wanted to see her.

He walked past the guards and into the dimly lit tent. Lyni and Hess and Idira were all there, working away. He did spot a few plates with half-eaten food scattered about, so apparently they did have supper. Jarren watched as they cast their spells. He wished he could get some inkling of what they were doing!

"Hello, Jarren," said Idira as she finished her batch of powder and leaned back with a sigh.

"How are you doing?"

"Tired. More tired than I ever would have believed possible."

"Just a few more days. Hang on for a few more days."

"We will," said Lyni finishing her own spell. She picked up a heaping bowl of powder and dumped it into a sack. She tied it shut and added it to a pile of other sacks. It was a large pile.

"Wow, how much have you done today?"

"A little over a hundred pounds, I think."

"That's wonderful! You are getting better and better!"

"Yes, I'm a bit surprised, myself."

"It is surprising," said Hesseran who also leaned back with a sigh. "I'm beginning to see how the Kaifeng sorcerer has managed those great spells. He must have pushed and pushed himself for years the way we are pushing ourselves now. I've never gone through anything like this and I'm amazed at how quickly our strength has grown. We are immunizing three or four times as much powder as I had expected."

"Practice makes perfect, I guess," said Idira. "Maybe we just let ourselves get soft sitting back on the Island. If we really exerted ourselves, we might have achieved so much more."

"Well, you have achieved a lot. With what you have here, we'll have nearly twenty rounds per man and four rounds per cannon. That's a lot more than we had hoped. We'll be able to fight a pitched battle and probably won't need the older weapons at all."

"Well, just be careful with it," said Lyni, indicating the stacks of powder behind her. "We can't make much more if you squander this."

"Don't worry, all the finished cartridges are under guard in four different locations. We're treating it like gold."

"It's worth more than any gold."

"Indeed it is."

"Well, I was just coming by to make sure you had all eaten. I'll let you work and be back later..."

He turned as the flap opened and several people walked into the tent. All four of them cried out in alarm when they saw that one of the people was carrying an ordinary lantern.

"Get out of here, you fool!" snarled Lyni. "Do you want to blow us all to bits?!"

"Quiet!" snapped one of the intruders. There were five of them, all were wearing dark, hooded cloaks, and Jarren rocked back when he saw that two of them were holding pistols. "Quiet or you'll be shot!"

"Who are you? What do you want?" demanded Jarren in a quieter voice.

"We are the servants of the gods! We are here to cleanse this den of heresy!" the man who had spoken stepped forward with the lantern and threw back his cloak. A shock of flaming red hair crowned his head and Jarren realized he had seen this man before.

"Brother Dominak!" The priest from the Church's Council of Purity had an expression of triumph on his face. "W-what are you going to do?"

"We are going to destroy all of this demon-tainted powder and save the East!"

"Are you crazy? Without the powder the Kaifs will wipe us out! It's our only chance!" Jarren looked around frantically. What had happened to the guards?

"No!" said the priest. "If we use this powder it will be our damnation. The gods have decreed that man shall not use magic. If we break that commandment to try and save ourselves we shall be punished, just as the heretics were punished three hundred years ago!"

"That's insane!" cried Hesseran. "The Kaifeng are using magic, why don't the gods punish them?"

"They will, in time. But the gods are using the Kaifeng to test us. If we give in to the temptation of heresy in our desire to save ourselves, then we deserve to be swept away. No, we shall destroy this powder—and all the rest—and fight with sword and bow. If we pass this test, the gods will deal with the Kaifeng!" The man's eyes glittered in the faint light and with a chill Jarren knew there was not the slightest hope of reasoning with him.

"Bind them!" commanded Dominak. "They shall be consumed in the flames along with their heresy!" The two men with pistols pointed them menacingly, while a third came forward bearing shackles. Jarren was mustering his courage to resist when the fifth man suddenly spoke.

"What are you doing? You said no one was to be harmed! Only the powder was to be destroyed!"

Jarren gasped. He knew that voice!

"Thaddius?" exclaimed Idira in astonishment. "Oh Thad, how could you?"

There was no doubt that it was the priest he had counted as his friend. How could he have betrayed them like this?

"Don't interfere, Brother Thaddius!" commanded Dominak. "You have sided with the gods up to now—don't stumble at the end. The heretics must die!" One of the other men shifted slightly so he could cover Thaddius with his pistol as well as the others. The man with the shackles came forward. They were going to bind them here and blow them all up with the powder! Jarren looked for a weapon, any weapon...

Suddenly, the tent flap opened and in trotted Gez. "Hey, Boss, you gonna need any—holy shit!"

The men with the pistols turned for a moment and in that instant Lyni moved. Out of the corner of his eye, Jarren saw the young woman move and a second later one of the men with pistols gurgled out a scream and clutched at the knife sticking in his throat. The other man immediately raised his pistol and pointed it at her.

"No!" cried two voices in unison. One was Jarren's and in despair he knew he could not possibly intervene like he had on the dock. He was too far away! But the other voice belonged to Thaddius and he grabbed the man's wrist and wrenched the pistol upward. There was a flash and a bang as it went off and Jarren tensed as he expected the powder in the tent to explode.

It didn't, but the people in it seemed to. Suddenly everyone was shouting and screaming and scrambling. Gez grabbed the pistol from where the first man had dropped it and skipped away under one of the tables. The man with the shackles dropped them and went after Gez, but was tackled by Hess and Lyni. Thaddius was wrestling with the other one. Jarren found himself opposite Dominak. The man's face was twisted with rage, but he raised up the lantern.

"So be it! Let the fire consume us all—and save the world!" he screamed. Then he hurled the lantern toward the stacked bags of gunpowder.

Jarren leaped.

He flung himself to the side, into the path of the lantern. It bounced off his outflung hands and hit him right in the chest. He hugged it to him as he crashed to the ground. The lantern shattered with the impact, driving shards of glass into him, but he put his full weight down on it anyway to try and snuff the flame. Another pain and a hiss and smell of burned flesh told him he had succeeded.

"Bastard!" snarled Dominak "Fool! Traitor!" He snatched a small mace off his belt and took a step toward one of the safety lanterns. Jarren started to struggle to his feet.

Suddenly there were more shouts and Dominak whirled to meet a new rush of men into the tent. Colonel Krasner! Jarren watched, gape-mouthed, as the soldier thrust his sword through Dominak's body. The priest stood there for a moment. The mace slipped from his hand and then he crumpled to the ground.

"What in all the Nine Hells is going on?" snarled Krasner. There were other soldiers with him and they had subdued the remaining priests.

"The powder!" gasped Jarren. "They are trying to destroy the powder!"

"Gods!" Krasner started snapping out orders and his men began rushing off. But before they had gone ten paces, there was a loud explosion in the distance and Jarren groaned. They were too late!

Without really thinking, Jarren was running out of the tent with most of the others. In the light from the campfires he could see a cloud of smoke rising skyward. That was one of the ammunition storage areas. But there were three others still left. He started running toward the nearest one. Guards were with him and he ran as fast as he could.

He was halfway there when another explosion shook the ground. No, the bloody fools were killing them all! He ran faster. There! The tent was just ahead! He was nearly there! But he pulled up short when two men with lanterns emerged. They looked up in shock when the crowd of soldiers confronted them.

"Stay back!" cried one of them. "Stay back or we'll blow you up!"

"Get away from the tent!" commanded Krasner. "Step aside or you'll be shot!"

"We are willing to die! Stay back or you will die, too!"

"Don't do it, Luis!" gasped Thaddius and he came up. "This is wrong! Dominak was wrong! This is not the will of the gods!"

The man's face was twisted in surprise and anger. "Traitor! You are damned, Thaddius! Now watch how the Faithful can serve their gods!" the men turned and went back into the tent.

"Luis! Don't!" Thaddius darted forward and Jarren found himself doing the same.

"Get down, you damn fool!" shouted Krasner. Something tripped him up and Jarren fell with someone on top of him. Helplessly, he watched Thaddius run toward the tent. An instant later the priest was outlined by a brilliant flash and then vanished in flame and smoke.

"Thad!" screamed Jarren, but his cry was lost in the roar of the explosion.

The impact stunned him and his eyes were filled with smoke, but he struggled wildly to get out from under the person holding him down. After a few moments he was let up and saw that it had been Krasner on top of him. The man had a large wood splinter sticking out of his shoulder, but he did not even seem to notice.

"Bloody hell," hissed the Colonel.

They both got up and walked slowly forward through the smoke. They found Thaddius a few yards away. The man's limbs were twisted in strange ways and he was horribly burned. Jarren knelt down and to his amazement he saw that the priest was still alive.

"Send for Idira!" he exclaimed. "Bring the healer!"

While he waited anxiously, someone ran up to say that the last tent with the powder had been saved. Jarren hardly heard him—or cared.

"Why, Thad? Why did you do it?" he moaned. He wasn't expecting any answer, but Thaddius opened his eyes.

"B-brother Dominak can be very...persuasive," he mumbled. "B-but I can see now that he was wrong. I should have listened to you, Jarren. I'm sorry."

"Hang on, Thad! Idira will be here soon. She can help you."

"T-too late..."

The healer arrived a moment later, but despite her efforts, it was clear that she was not going to be able to save him. Too many things were hurt too badly. Idira tried anyway and she was weeping while she worked. She had been even closer friends with Thad than Jarren.

"I-idira," gasped Thaddius.

"What? What is it?"

"Don't give up on the school. The school for healers. Not everyone is like Dominak. Show the world what you can do. P-promise me."

"I promise, Thad. I promise."

"I'm sorry, Idira. I didn't want this to happen."

Then he died.

Jarren stared for a moment and then stumbled off into the night.

"Master Carabello?" Jarren looked up to see an officer on horseback a few yards away.

"Yes?"

"The General is having a conference at his headquarters. He wants you to be there."

"Now?"

"Yes, if you'd follow me, sir."

With a sigh he got to his feet and mounted his horse. He had gotten almost no sleep the night before. He was still in shock over what had happened and he had spent most of the day staring at the flowing river. The officer led the way and Jarren followed awkwardly. In spite of several weeks of riding, he wasn't much of a horseman. Fortunately it was not far. When he got there he saw a number of high ranking officers there as well and Lyni, Hess and Idira. He was a little surprised they were not still working. With the loss of nearly three-quarters of the powder they had redoubled their efforts, but everyone knew it was not going to be enough. He dismounted and went over to Lyni. She looked ghastly, but he realized she had probably just woken up from her ambulance bed.

"Hi," he said. "How are you doing?"

"Tired. What's this all about?"

"Not sure. Some pre-battle conference, I suppose." After a short wait, they were all ushered under a large canvas awning. There were chairs and several small tables. Jarren found himself sitting between Lyni and Colonel Krasner. A moment later, General DeSlitz came to the front. All the officers got to their feet and Jarren did likewise.

"Be seated, gentlemen. We have a lot to go over, so I'll get right to it. Our scouts report that the enemy is about forty miles away. They have been moving slowly—at least for them—but they could be here as early as tomorrow if they decide to leave their herds behind. I'm hoping we won't have to fight them until the day after tomorrow, or possibly the next day if we are lucky. But we have gotten to this natural choke-point and if they want to get past us, they will have to fight. If we had let them get beyond here, our job would have been that much more difficult.

"So much for the good news. The bad news is that the enemy is coming at us with two hundred thousand warriors." A silent gasp went up from the assembly. This was even more than they had feared. They were outnumbered nearly three-to-one.

"Unfortunately, we are fairly confident those numbers are correct. We had a scouting party that was able to watch them coming out of the forest and get a very good count. So, we have quite a job before us. One other bit of bad news is that for the first time our scouting parties have encountered fireflies. Only in small numbers, but it is a bit of a surprise."

"The Kaifeng sorcerer had evidently been training other magickers," said Hesseran. "I suppose that is to be expected. But evidently they are not too powerful. I don't think it will effect our plans, General."

"I hope you are correct. But now we come down to the last throw. We need to make our final plans and dispositions. As you are all aware, because of the recent disaster, we do not have enough treated gunpowder to arm everyone. Right now we have approximately two-hundred and fifty thousand musket cartridges that are safe to use. By tomorrow noon, we must have all the untreated cartridges collected and sent to the rear. Make sure your officers and NCOs search the men carefully! A lot of them are going to be tempted to hide extra rounds in their pockets or knapsacks and we can't have that. No explosions in our ranks!

"Now, as for how we use the rounds we have. If we could guarantee that each shot would kill one Kaif, we actually do have enough ammunition," DeSlitz paused as the officers chuckled grimly. Even Jarren realized that in a typical battle it took dozens or even hundreds of shots for each casualty they inflicted. "But since we can't, we don't. With what we have, we can give about ten thousand infantry twenty-five rounds per man. That will give us a solid core. The rest of the infantry will have to use the pikes and crossbows. We have about twelve thousand crossbows. So, to summarize, we will have ten thousand with muskets, twelve thousand with crossbows and slightly over thirty thousand with pikes. We hope to be able to supply a hundred and fifty cannon with five or six shots each. The cavalry will have no powder at all."

"Who will get the powder, General?" asked an officer Jarren did not recognize.

"We will give the powder to our best musket men."

A low murmur, almost a growl, went through the assembly. "Meaning your Zollehan's will get it all, I assume?" asked the same officer. He seemed angry.

"Zolleran infantry are acknowledged to be the best musket men in the world, sir," said DeSlitz stiffly. "We need to make every shot count."

"I must protest, sir!" said another man, springing to his feet. "You know perfectly well that the rest of the army has had little chance to practice with those crossbows. And against the Kaif horse archers, the pikemen will be useless! If our men know they are just to be sacrificed so your own troops can have enough powder, there will be a mutiny!" A dozen other voices were raised to support the man.

"Uh, oh," said Krasner loudly enough for Jarren to hear him. Angry voices rang out right and left. DeSlitz was slowly turning red. It went on for several minutes and half the men were on their feet. Finally, one of the general's aides shouted for quiet and eventually got it. DeSlitz was clearly angry, but in control of himself.

"Gentlemen, please. I realize this is difficult for you, but I can see no other way. The ammunition we have would only provide four or five rounds for each man if we distributed it equally. The Kaifs are going to see that their magic did not work and they will advance far more carefully than they did in earlier battles. They will use bows from long range and our men will quickly use up their ammunition to little use, because we all know they will not hold their fire long if they are being shot at. Then what will they do? Try to swap muskets for crossbows? Or will they just try to charge with the bayonet, break our ranks and end up shot or ridden down by the Kaifs? No, our only hope is to match the Kaif bows with crossbows and some cannon fire and try to draw them in on our musketeers—close enough that they can really hurt them."

"And in the meanwhile, the poor sods stuck with the pikes will be slaughtered while unable to strike back," said a general in Laponian uniform. "How long can they stand under that, General? If your infantry are so damn good, give *them* the pikes and let *them* die in their ranks!" There were more growls of agreement. The argument began again.

Jarren sat uneasily in his chair and saw the alliance falling apart before his eyes. On the one hand he could see DeSlitz's point, but he could certainly understand the reluctance of the other officers! He was amazed that DeSlitz had waited until the last minute to spring this on them. But then perhaps if he had told them earlier, the army would have fallen apart earlier. At least now, everyone was already where he wanted them. He just had to keep them here. Or maybe the loss of the powder had just stunned him to the point he wasn't thinking clearly. Jarren knew that he hadn't been thinking very clearly lately. The treachery had shaken him to his core.

Not all the officers were arguing. All the cavalry commanders had known they would have no powder and did not protest. A few were even smirking. Colonel Krasner had no expression at all that Jarren could read.

But what could be done? There was no hope of any significant amounts of new powder. Lyni and the others might be able to make a few hundred more pounds if they had the time, but that would all go to the artillery anyway. If only they had saved the other powder! Jarren had relived the moment a thousand times in his head. Somehow he should have seen what was coming. He should have been able to stop Dominak somehow! It was stupid, but he couldn't help but feel like this was all his fault. But what was done was done. They still had to find a way to win with what they had. It was so frustrating: two hundred and fifty thousand rounds seemed like a huge number...

"It is a shame we cannot somehow get the Kaifeng to come very close before our men fire, Colonel," he said to Krasner. "You could do a lot more damage that way, couldn't you?"

"Oh yes, if we could get them to come up to thirty paces before we fired we could do a hell of a lot of damage. But they won't come that close when they see the fireflies didn't do anything. They'll hang back and pepper us with arrows. And two hundred and fifty thousand rounds might seem like a lot, but those bastards probably have about five *million* arrows with them. We can't win a shooting match."

"I see." Jarren fell silent again while the argument raged. If the enemy came very close they could hurt them even with only five rounds per man. But the enemy would not come close if they saw that the fireflies had not exploded all their powder. But if the men did carry untreated powder, they would all blow up, so it would not matter if the enemy did come close. It was like one of those conundrums the philosophers liked to play with...

"It is a shame we cannot make the enemy think the fireflies did work and convince them to charge," he mused. He did not say it loudly, but Colonel Krasner heard him. His head whipped around and he stared at him wide-eyed. An instant later he broke into a huge grin.

"What…?" said Jarren.

Krasner reached over and ruffled Jarren't hair in a most unmilitary fashion. "Jarren! You bloody genius!"

"Huh? What…?"

But Krasner wasn't listening to him anymore. He sprang up and shouted at the top of his lungs:

"General!"

CHAPTER TWENTY-TWO

The tent Zarruk now occupied was a far cry from the simple leather abode that could barely hold all the noyens after the victory at the fort. This tent was pure silk and it had been made by fine craftsmen-slaves in Berssenburg during the winter. It seemed large enough for an entire tribe. Now, all twenty-three Kas and their retinues were seated on cushions and being waited on by dozens of lovely slaves. Atark observed the proceedings with growing impatience. The enemy army was only a few miles away. The great battle of their times would come tomorrow. Plans had to be made! But instead of plans, Zarruk was receiving petitions from the people while the Kas ate and drank.

"Great Re-Ka," said a man, bowing his head down to the rich carpet, "I come to you seeking aid for the poor people of my clan."

"What aid do you seek? And how is that there are poor in the midst of so much wealth?"

"In our haste to come here and take service with you and join in the great conquest, most of our herd animals died. In the midst of plenty, some of my people face starvation."

"How can this be? Did you not receive a proper share of the treasure taken at Gira and Usedam?"

"Yes, Lord, but the gold of this land is… is not any good!"

"What do you mean?" demanded Zarruk. "Is it gold or is it not?"

"It seems to be gold, Lord. It feels and looks and tastes like gold, but it not worth as much as the gold back on the plains! I cannot explain it, but a small gold coin could buy a fine horse and saddle there, or a dozen cattle. The same amount of gold from this land will scarcely buy a half-starved goat! We have more gold than we ever dreamed of, Lord, and yet we starve!"

Zarruk looked over to Atark and raised his eyebrows and shook his head. It was true that with gold plentiful and cattle in demand, the price had gone up many-fold. Everyone had noticed it, but no one knew what to do about it. And this simpleton from the plains thought it was the gold which was at fault! Atark nearly laughed out loud. But if Kaifeng were in danger of starving, then it was no laughing matter. Zarruk pondered the question for a few moments and then spoke:

"Let those who are truly in need see my chief retainer and he will provide for them from my own herds. But let this be a lesson to all! This land is rich and fat—and not just with gold and slaves. Let the warriors gather cattle instead of gold if their families are hungry! Let not our greed blind us to our empty stomachs!"

"Thank you, Lord! Thank you!" babbled the man as he was escorted out.

Atark shook his head. Still, this had been the most interesting petition all afternoon. Almost all the others had been disputes over loot, especially the women slaves. When a half-dozen men enjoyed a freshly caught slave for a night, in the morning it was hard to remember who had first caught her and thus had claim. That sort of argument far too often led to bloodshed before the Re-Ka was ever asked to judge.

"My Lord," whispered Atark to Zarruk, "We must make our plans for the morrow!"

Zarruk nodded and instructed the head of his guard to turn away all the rest of the petitioners after the next one was finished. There were cries of disappointment from outside, but all inside the tent ignored them. At least until they heard a guard shouting: "Tomorrow! Tomorrow, you damn fools! By this time tomorrow you'll have so many riches and slaves even you will have nothing to bitch about!" Everyone in the tent laughed at that.

"My lords, it is time to discuss our plans for tomorrow. The great battle is upon us and with victory, the entire East will lie helpless before us."

"It seems to me, Great Re-Ka, that we have little need for plans," said Ka-Noyen Ferache. "The enemy is in front of us as before. They draw themselves up as before. And when Atark works his magic, we shall crush them as before!" All the Kas cheered.

"What you say is true, my lord," said Ka-noyen Oliark, "but it concerns me. Are the enemy such fools that they will let another army be destroyed? Surely they have heard what became of the Army of Berssia. Do they not realize what Mighty Atark—and our other shamen—can do to them and their weapons? Are they fools—

or are we? Are we overlooking something here? Do our enemies have plans we are unaware of?"

Oliark's words caused a great deal of muttering, but Atark had wondered those same things himself. Battai was next to speak.

"Our scouts report the enemy has the same muskets and cannons as before. Our shamen have used the magic against the enemy patrols with success. There seems to be no truth to the tales we heard of the enemy using older weapons. And even if they were true, what of it? We are three to their one. If they try to match us with sword and bow we shall crush them anyway."

"And yet our scouts also report that the enemy once occupied a position some miles to the west of here," replied Oliark. "A strong position it was, too. And yet they fell back before us to where they are now and it is not as strong. Their line is twice as long and the ridge neither as high or as steep. Why would they do this?"

"Because they are afraid of us, of course!" laughed Battai. Some of the other Kas laughed, too, but Atark frowned. Why *had* they fallen back? Surely they would want to defend as short a line as possible. It would allow them to concentrate their men and restrict the mobility of the Kaifeng. But they had fallen back, leaving abandoned campfires and a few fresh graves and three spots which appeared to have suffered large explosions... He feared that Oliark was correct and that the enemy was up to something. But what?

"It is well that we show some caution," said Zarruk. "But there is little choice but for us to attack them where they are. To the right is a river with no fords for many miles. To the left is a thick forest where the enemy has many skilled men waiting in ambush. Our own warriors will not enter there. It is clear that we cannot turn the enemy without a great deal of effort. We must attack and destroy them as we did with the Army of Berssia."

"They have planted pointed stakes to protect their cannon," observed another Ka. "But our scouts made a foray earlier today and confirmed that there are no pits or traps hidden in the grass in front of their lines to trip our horses. It is like they are inviting us to ride over them."

"It does not matter," said Battai, who had been drinking heavily. "When our shamen destroy their powder the cannons will be useless. We shall ride down their infantry and slaughter them all."

"We must be wary of their cavalry," said Ferache. "Their scouts only carried a small bit of powder and were little troubled by our shamen's magic. If their heavy cavalry carries none, then there could be a serious battle."

"We outnumber their cavalry nearly ten-to-one!" said Battai, "Let them come!"

"Very well," said Oliark. "I council caution, but I agree with the Re-Ka that there is little else we can do but attack. How shall we order our warriors?"

A chorus of voices came up from the Kas, each demanding a place of honor in the battle formation. It went on for some time before Zarruk cut them off.

"There is room for five *helars* in the front line," he said. "The five *helars* who were at Berssenburg have earned the right to be there. But I will yield the place of my own personal *helar* to another. I have gathered enough glory for a lifetime. Let one Ka be chosen by lot to fill my place. I and my warriors will stand in reserve and watch the rest of you fight."

There was a general clamor of approval from the Kas. It was a good and just solution. Atark was personally happy that Zarruk would not be in the forefront of the attack. He was far too important to risk.

"And when shall we attack, Great Re-Ka?"

Zarruk grinned. "Oh, I would think mid-morning is the proper time. We all know how much Atark hates to get up early."

Jarren looked across the dark valley at the campfires of the enemy. There were far more of them than there were stars in the sky. "It's pretty, isn't it?" he asked Lyni, who was standing a yard away. "If they were not our enemies I would say that it is beautiful."

"It's terrifying," said Lyni. She glanced over her shoulder at the fires of their own army. While there were far too many to count, there were not nearly as many as in the Kaifeng camp.

"I did not think you were ever afraid. I know that I am. I've never been in a battle before."

"Of course you have. Twice now. You've even been shot. By the way, thank you for being so brave and stupid then. Pirat never would have shot me on the dock, but I suppose you didn't know that. So thank you."

"You are welcome—I think."

Lyni chuckled but then became serious again. "I am afraid. I think our plan gives us a chance to win, but so much could go wrong."

"A great deal will depend on you, Lyni. You really should be resting to regain your strength."

"I will have the strength. The weather tomorrow will be calm and I will have no difficulty doing what I need to. A storm will come tomorrow night, but everyone thinks the Kaifs will attack tomorrow. No, I can do my assigned role, but I fear what will come after that. In spite of everything, we could still lose. What then?"

"I suppose we fight as long as we possibly can," said Jarren, not too happy to be talking about this.

"We fight and we die. It seems like a very simple plan. Why does the thought worry me so much?"

"It would scare anyone. But try not to worry. I'll be right here, too and I'll..." Without thinking, Jarren patted at his side and then snatched his hand away and then blushed. Lyni noticed immediately.

"What have you got there?" she asked, moving closer and staring.

"Oh, nothing..."

"Don't give me that! What have you got under your cloak?" Lyni came closer and seized his arm with surprising strength. She pulled aside his cloak, revealing the sword that was hanging there.

"Jarren, what is that?" she demanded.

"What does it look like?"

"It looks like a sword. Why are you carrying it?"

"To fight—if necessary. There will be a battle tomorrow, you know! Everyone thinks I'm such a weakling, but I will not just stand around and be butchered. I'll fight to defend myself—and I'll fight to protect you."

Lyni laughed. She suddenly produced a long dagger from under her own cloak. She spun the blade and then snatched it expertly out of the air. "I can protect myself if it comes to that, Jarren." She paused and he could see her eyes glinting in the light of the fires. "But thank you for wanting to protect me. You are a very sweet man."

"Thank you, Lyni."

The woman turned and looked at the endless Kaifeng camp. "We shall probably die tomorrow, Jarren," she whispered. "I have no intention of being taken alive if we lose, but intentions count for little in a situation like this. Anything might happen to thwart my intentions. It is still possible I'll be taken."

"I'll stand by you..."

"I know, and I appreciate it. But your intentions count for no more than mine." She paused and turned back to face him. "I've never been with a man, Jarren. I was a bit smitten with Stephanz once, until I realized what a fool he was, but I've never had a lover. But if I had to give up my maidenhead and had the choice of having the Kaifs take it by force, or of giving it to someone I care about, well, I'd choose the latter."

Jarren gasped slightly. Was she actually suggesting...?

"Jarren, your mouth is open," said Lyni. "Close it and come along. The bunk in my wagon is big enough for two." She reached out and took his hand. In a daze, he followed her. He was acutely aware of the touch of her hand. It was like Peretski's apparatus at the university for creating static electricity.

As they got near the camp, he hesitated. "Perhaps your wagon is not the best idea..."

"Why not?"

"Well, those springs they have. If we were... From outside it might be rather... obvious."

Lyni laughed. "Always the scientist! But I suppose you are right. Where then?"

"My tent is large enough..."

"What about Gez?"

"I'll find an errand that will keep him busy for a while."

"More than a while, I hope! All right. Lead on, Master Carabello!"

Thelena was roused from a deep sleep by the sound of Kareen moaning. Even though the warmer weather did not require them to snuggle anymore, they still slept very close together, and a sudden kick brought Thelena fully awake. Kareen was thrashing about in her blankets.

"Kareen? What's wrong?" She reached out to touch her.

"Matt!" Kareen shouted and sat bolt upright. *"Matt! No!"*

"Kareen! You're dreaming! Wake up!" Thelena grabbed her by the arms and shook her gently. For a moment she resisted, but then she came awake. She looked at Thelena in confusion and then clung to her, sobbing softly.

"It was just a dream, it was just a dream," soothed Thelena.

"Oh! Oh, what a nightmare!" she gasped. "I...I saw Matt. He was wearing armor like an old knight. He was on an armored horse leading hundreds and thousands of other men. He had a bright gold helmet with a big red plume. He looked so gallant and brave. And then...and then he dissolved in flames! He and all the others burned up!"

"It was just a dream," said Thelena. She rocked her slowly back and forth and stroked her hair.

"It was so real," she whispered. "I've never had a dream that seemed so real." Kareen pulled away from Thelena and stared into the darkness. "He's there. He's over there across the valley with the other army."

"You don't know that..."

"He's there! You know him: if he did get away, can you imagine him being anywhere else right now?"

"No..."

"He's there. And tomorrow he will be in the battle." Kareen turned and looked to the spot where Atark usually slept. "And tomorrow, your father is going to kill him."

"Hush, Kareen, hush! Go back to sleep."

But she would not go back to sleep and Thelena held her until dawn.

Matt was up before the first light. He sat on a gun carriage and looked out across the valley at the Kaifeng camp. The sky to the east was turning blue, but the west was still in darkness. A few of the brighter stars were still visible, and many campfires could be seen.

Is Kareen over there? He'd dreamed of his sister during the night and the image was still fresh in his mind. She had been dressed in Kaifeng fashion, but she was struggling wildly in the grasp of strong arms. She had seemed terrified. If he knew exactly where she was, it almost seemed like he could walk across the valley and just bring her back with him. But the Kaifeng camp was enormous. There would be no hope of finding one girl in all that.

The light grew and the enemy tents took on a pink glow. There were so many of them. Two hundred thousand warriors, the scouts said. But that would just be the able bodied men. The Kaifs traveled with their herds and families—and their slaves. There could be a half-dozen others for every warrior. The amazing thought struck Matt that he might be staring at the largest city in the entire world. A city of canvas and leather. He came from a world where the cities were made of stone and bricks and wood. But if this day went against them, all the stone and brick and wood cities might be reduced to rubble and ashes and then only cities of leather and canvas would remain.

A few whispered orders close at hand dragged his attention away from the enemy camp. There were hundreds of men at work just beyond the line of stacked muskets. They had been out here for an hour or more, working by the starlight. Now they were finishing their tasks and moving back toward their camps. >From where Matt was sitting, he could just make out what they had been doing. Hundreds—thousands—of small packages had been left in neat rows just beyond the muskets. Each was a bit larger than a man's fist and each was wrapped in a piece of oilcloth to keep the heavy morning dew from soaking them. They could not afford to let *these* packages get wet! Matt could see them easily enough, but from any distance they would be hidden by the tall grass.

The clank of a pick and shovel from behind him showed that not everyone was done working. He looked over his shoulder and saw the artillerymen working to pack dirt around the edges of a series of shallow holes they had dug in the ground. The holes were about three feet square and four feet deep, with the dirt around the edge rising up another three feet or so. Farther to the rear were much larger holes with the dirt parapets rising nearly six feet high.

As he watched, the first rays of sunlight peeked over the distant trees and sparkled off the bayonets of the stacked weapons. The glittering line stretched away for over three miles in each direction. To the south it ran down the ridge until it met the river. To the north it went up the ridge to where the forest began. It was almost seven miles from end to end. This was far longer than any usual line of battle and, contrary to every accepted tactical doctrine, there was only a single line of those stacked muskets. Granted, when the men actually fell in, that single line of battle would be three ranks deep, but there were no reserves. Normally, an army would array itself with two or even three lines of battle. The second and third lines would provide reserves to plug gaps, launch counterattacks, or relieve front line regiments who had used up their ammunition.

That was not going to happen today. There would be no extended firefights and hopefully no gaps in the line or need for counterattacks or relief. No, if things went as Matt hoped, the battle would be decided in the first five minutes. That was why they had fallen back to this position from where they had been: it was long enough to put all the infantry on the front line. It let them bring every single musket to bear.

There were thirty batteries of artillery spaced along the line. Each one was fronted with sharpened wood stakes, making the more distant ones look like bristly hedgehogs. Projectiles were piled up beside each gun: round shot, grape shot and canister. Small wooden chests to the rear held the treated gunpowder. Even farther to the rear, set in other small holes, were the crystal chests with the reserve ammunition. Two of the chests had cracked on the journey here, so only twenty-three of the batteries had one.

The army actually did have some reserves. A dozen small regiments of infantry were scattered along the line. Each man in those regiments had two rounds of ammunition. They were there as a last resort. And there was the cavalry. All of the cavalry was in reserve. The light cavalry on the flanks and the heavier stuff distributed at points along the line. Matt's own brigade was immediately behind the center.

Bugles and drums welcomed the dawn and called the men to morning roll-call and then breakfast. Matt got up from his seat and walked slowly back toward his own headquarters. The sixteen hundred men of his brigade were all up and about by the time he got there—although he doubted many of them had gotten much sleep last night. Everyone was aware of what would happen today. The camps had been strangely quiet. No singing or joking. No gambling; not even much drinking. And the chaplains had been doing a lot of business. Each man was preparing for the battle in his own way. He reached his tent and saw his servants and staff laying out the breakfast.

"Morning, gentlemen," he said as cheerily as he could. "Eat hearty, we're going to have a very busy day."

Atark groaned as he came awake. It had been a late night and the morning was here all too soon, although from the light, it was several hours past dawn. Thelena and the slave were busy making breakfast, but his daughter smiled when she saw him.

"Good morning, Father. Did you sleep well?"

"Well enough, I suppose." It was a lie. He had not slept well at all and he felt very tired. There had been many strange dreams and as he sat there, one came back to him. It had been from five years ago when the Varags had attacked them. Or it seemed that way. Some things were the same: the pain of a knife entering him, his daughter's scream. But other things were different: Shelena and Ardan were not there, nor, for that matter, were there any Varags to be seen. Just the pain and the scream and then he was looking at his daughter lying on the ground. She had blood on her face and was apparently hurt badly—or dead.

He shook his head to clear the disturbing image and accepted a small cup of *yetchi* mixed with water from Thelena. "The battle will be today?" she asked.

"Yes. Probably before noon. Are you going to stay and use the poppy juice, or ride to the rear?"

"I…I think I will stay. I'd have to work my way through the entire camp to get to the rear. They are packed in terribly tight behind us. No, I'll stay and take the juice."

Atark nodded and then looked closely at his daughter. She had said nothing, but he could sense her disapproval. "I know you don't like me taking the sacrifices, Thelena. It disturbs me, as well. But it is necessary. And after today, after we crush the enemy, perhaps there will be no need to take more in the future. When we win today, the entire East will be prostrate before us. Then we can have peace."

"I pray the gods you are right, Father. I grow so sick of blood and death."

"Yes." He said no more and ate a few bites of the breakfast the women had prepared. The slave woman was becoming quite a good cook. He had never gone through with his plan to dispose of her; there were always so many other things demanding his attention. Still, it needed to be done. His daughter was getting far too close to the slave. If other people noticed, it could have ugly repercussions. Perhaps after this battle he would seek out a slave merchant and sell the woman. Perhaps this very day while his daughter was senseless from the poppy juice. Yes, that could work.

His stomach was still queasy from the night before, and in spite of the good food, he could not eat much. He embraced his daughter and left the tent. Outside, his guards shouted greetings to him when they saw him. They were eager for the battle, even though they would not actually be involved in the fighting. Many of them were carefully sharpening their bronze swords. Atark had commissioned more of the weapons over the winter and now all his men had them. Six hundred sacrifices had been ordered for the day's battle and he was certain the executions would go off smoothly.

Truth to tell, his guard embarrassed him a bit. There were nearly a thousand of them now and they all seemed fanatically loyal. They boasted in front of the other warriors that their lord did all the real fighting now and that often sparked quarrels. He knew some of the Kas viewed his guard with great suspicion—no shaman ever had such a thing before. Hopefully, if this battle did prove to be the end of real resistance he could cut back on the size of the guard— although how he could pick the men to let go, he did not know.

Gettain came up to him and bowed. "Good morning, Lord! The army is already beginning to gather. A few hours and they shall be ready."

"What of the enemy?" he asked. His camp was near the forefront of the army and he could see their lines from here. There did not appear to be any change from the day before.

"They are still in place, Lord. Ripe for the slaughter!"

"Very well. Assemble the men and bring the sacrifices forward. It would not do to keep the Re-Ka waiting on this day of victory."

Thelena looked after her father as he left the tent. She was worried about him again. He drove himself so hard. How long could he keep it up? She turned and looked at Kareen washing the breakfast dishes. She was worried about her, too. The nightmare had clearly disturbed her badly. But could it really be true? Was Matt over on the other side of the valley? It was all too likely that he was. The rumors said that the whole East had gathered to oppose them. Why wouldn't Matt be there, too? And if he was, he would probably die today. The thought made Thelena very sad. They had gone to so much effort, expended so much fear and pain, to save him the first time. There would be no hope of doing it again—even if he survived the battle.

She just hoped that if he was there, he would die quickly and painlessly and that Kareen would never find the body. If Matt was buried in some nameless grave then Kareen could cling to the hope that he still lived. Thelena did not want to see Kareen hurt any more.

They spent the next hour in chores around the tent, but they could hear the sounds of the army gathering for battle. Horns and shouts, the clank of weapons, the whinnying of horses and the thunder of hooves filled the air. Thelena could see Kareen getting tenser and tenser. She hoped the woman would not do something stupid. Thelena went out of the tent for a moment to see what was happening. The army was spread out before her and the enemy was on the far ridge. She could see the platform her father would use for the magic, although he was not on it yet. She shuddered when she saw the sacrifices already in position. It would soon be time. She went back into the tent.

She found a small leather bag and took out a glass container that had an amber liquid inside. She poured a glass of wine and then put a few drops of the liquid in it. "Kareen, I'm taking this now. Would... would you like to have a little? It might help you to relax."

"No thank you, Thelena," said Kareen, but she would not meet her eyes.

She looked at her for a few moments and then drained the glass, grimacing at the bitter taste. The drink took a little while to take effect and she settled herself into a comfortable position on the cushions. Slowly, a warm haze began to grip her. Then she realized that Kareen was gone. A sudden panic shot through her. "Kareen!" she shouted. She struggled to get up, but her limbs felt like lead. "Kareen!" An instant later Kareen was there.

"Thelena! What's wrong?"

"Oh, Kareen. I...I thought you'd gone off somewhere."

"I was just emptying the wash water. Are you all right?"

"I was afraid you were going to...going to..."

"Do something stupid? Like try to stop your father?" Thelena nodded numbly. The drug was working now and it was hard to think.

"There's nothing I can do, Thelena," said Kareen and she could see that her face was streaked with tears. "There are six hundred guards around your father now. Besides, I promised you I would be a good slave. I still owe you for two lives. I can't ask for any more." Thelena made a huge effort and held out her arms. Kareen knelt down beside her and hugged her.

The world was spinning around and going dark, but Thelena could still feel Kareen's warm embrace. She felt very safe and content.

"I love you, Kareen," she whispered. It was so faint in her own ears she wondered if she had really said it at all, or if Kareen had heard her. But the grip on her tightened and she heard a voice whispering back.

"I love you, too, Thelena."

The bugles rang and the drums rolled and the bands played. Sergeants shouted and the men scrambled into their ranks next to the stacked muskets. Once those same sergeants were satisfied that the ranks were really straight and that the interval between the ranks was really correct, the officers took over and had the stacks of muskets disassembled and the weapons passed back to their owners. The muskets were now closely inspected both by the privates and their sergeants. They had already been inspected once in the morning and any rust caused by the dew had been buffed away. Now they were inspected again. The flints were all new, of course, but each man was required to cock and fire the empty weapon to prove the flint would spark properly. They could not afford misfires today! There would be some—a lot actually—but everything possible was done to keep the number low.

Finally, the order to load was given. Each musketeer reached back to his right hip and opened the flap on his leather cartridge pouch. The rear and middle rank men each had six of the precious rounds; the front rank men only had two. The men took a round and brought it up to their mouths and bit off the part of the paper-wrapped cartridge that contained the bullet. Then they brought their musket up to the 'prime' position, opened the pan cover, and sprinkled a little of the very special gunpowder into the pan and then closed the cover again. From there, they set the butt of the musket between their feet. They poured the rest of the powder down the barrel and stuffed the paper in afterwards. They leaned forward and spat out the round, lead bullets they had been holding in their mouths into the muzzles of the weapons. Then it was out with the ramrods, ram the bullets firmly down the barrels and put the ramrods back into their holders. The muskets came back up to the shoulder and they were loaded and ready to fire. A good man could do it all in twenty seconds. One of those machine-like Zollerhans could do it in fifteen. This time, all took far longer than that to load these first, special rounds; no rushing, no mistakes—not today! One more command was barked out along the line and the musket butts came back down to the ground and the men stood at ease in their ranks. The artillery crews were busy, too. They loaded a round of solid shot on top of a charge of untreated gunpowder and then stood aside.

Matt watched it all from horseback, at the front of his brigade, a hundred yards behind the center of the line. The army had been waiting uneasily all morning for the Kaifs to attack. Hours had dragged by and nothing much happened. The men lounged by their weapons and talked. From time to time men would get permission to run back to the sinks to answer the call of nature. That had happened a lot this morning. Nerves.

But now the enemy was massing. Seemingly endless lines of horsemen were pouring out of the camps and forming ragged lines about a mile away. Matt was relieved to see that the enemy line was just as long as their own. Seven miles from end to end. He could not even see the far portions of the enemy line from where he was, but he knew they were there. His biggest fear had been that they would all mass against one portion of the line and leave half the men with nothing to shoot at. The extremely extended nature of the deployment would not allow any rapid changes to meet the unexpected. He knew they were counting heavily on the enemy acting exactly as they wanted him to and that was dangerous.

But they simply had no choice.

He looked back over his own troopers. They were arranged in columns of companies, the regiments standing side by side. They were going to need a narrow front to pass through the infantry lines to get at the enemy. Matt hoped that it would be a case of them going after the enemy rather than vice-versa. If the Kaifs broke through the infantry and caught him like this it would not be good.

A small group of chaplains marched past chanting their prayers. They seemed very subdued and Matt did not doubt that their 'escort' had something to do with that. After the treachery with the powder, the priests had all been put under a close watch. Matt knew that only a small group of fanatics had been responsible and that most had known nothing about it and would have opposed it if they had, but they were all now paying for the insanity of their fellows. And considering how easily the guards on the powder tents had been drawn away by men in priests' robes, a close watch was essential. They had not liked it, but no one had been any mood to take further chances. They could live with the restrictions—or leave. Some had.

But now everything looked to be ready. As soon as the fireflies were spotted the cavalry would dismount so as to better control their horses. Things were going to get very noisy around here.

Matt looked at Lieutenant Prinz and nodded. He'd become rather fond of the young man, but he was no replacement for Sergeant Chenik. He found himself missing the big, gruff sergeant terribly. He would have really liked to see what was about to happen. It would have appealed to his rather warped sense of humor. Well, maybe he was watching from somewhere.

"It's payback time, Sergeant," he whispered.

Atark came down off his little platform when he saw Re-Ka Zarruk and his escort approaching. "Hail, Mighty Zarruk!" he said and bowed. "All is ready here. Give the command to proceed and I shall obey!"

"Save the flowery talk, my old friend," said Zarruk with a grin. "Today we shall finish this at a blow."

"As you say, Lord, but I am still uneasy about the enemy's seeming stupidity. They stand there with their guns just as before. Surely they realize what we shall do."

"Yes, it does seem strange, but perhaps they really are stupid. In any case, we shall wait for your magic to explode their powder before we start forward. If there is some trickery, we can wait and then approach more carefully."

Atark nodded. What Zarruk said was true. There were really only two possible outcomes that he could see: Either the enemy had powder, in which case the magic would explode it and leave them helpless and stunned, or they did not have powder, in which case the army would approach more cautiously. There was no third choice that he could see. He was tempted to send out a few of the seekers as a test to see what would happen, but it was too late for that. The warriors were in position and ready to attack. There was far too much danger that even a few explosions up on the ridge would send the eager men galloping forward before all was ready. No, they would have go as they had planned. The sacrifices were ready and so were the other shamen. Twenty of them stood to the sides and each would add as many seekers to the swarm as they could. It would not be many, since none of them could yet call upon the sacrifices for strength, but their presence and contributions would be important for reasons of pride. Atark was rather proud, himself, of the job he had done teaching them.

"You can begin when you are ready, Atark," said Zarruk. He held out his hand and Atark took it. "Good luck, my friend."

"Good luck to you, Zarruk—not that you shall need any. I am very relieved that you are with the reserves this time."

"Ha! You sound like one of my wives! But enough of this! We shall stand ready for your magic." Zarruk turned and galloped off.

"I shall see you at the top, my friend," said Atark.

"Something's happening," said Lyni. "I can feel a magicker at work." Jarren was standing next to her on a small platform that had been built so she could see over the ranks of troops who were standing about fifty yards in front of them. It was high enough that they could see all the way to the ends of the long, long battle line. Jarren waved to an officer who was holding a large signal flag. He started waving it frantically and there was a stir among the troops as they made their final preparations.

"Yes," said Lyni, "he's over there, starting to cast the spell." Jarren looked at Lyni. The previous night had held delights more...*delightful*...than he'd ever imagined. He was tired and he knew she must be exhausted after the long weeks of work—plus the exertions of a few hours ago. But she looked ready to do what she had to. Jarren knew what *he* had to do: protect Lyni, no matter what. He glanced at Gez. The boy had found a sword of his own and looked at the enemy horde with goggling eyes.

"I'm gonna expect a bonus for this," he squeaked.

"Here it comes," said Lyni. She sounded confident, but Jarren saw her eyes get larger and larger and her face go pale.

"What's wrong?"

"By all the gods!" she hissed. "What power! I've never felt anything like this—and no, I'm not talking about you from last night, you lunk!" In spite of the dire situation, Jarren snorted. "There! Look!" shouted Lyni.

Jarren looked across the valley to the other little platform that looked rather like their own. They had spotted it early in the morning and they were certain that was where the Kaifeng necromancer would do his work. Telescopes had revealed the line of forked stakes stuck into the ground behind the platform. There was no doubt what they were for, either. Now, Jarren could see a ball of golden light appear over the platform. It looked like what Lyni and Idira and Hess had been able to make—only a hundred times larger. He wasn't sure, but he thought he saw a number of smaller balls to either side.

"There is more than one magicker," said Lyni, "but the others are of no concern. Get ready!" As he watched, the large ball exploded into a huge swarm of seekers, which immediately came toward them.

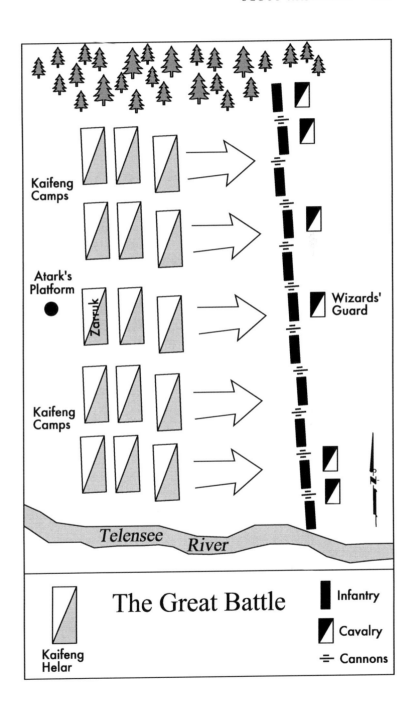

Kaifeng Camps

Atark's Platform

Zarruk

Kaifeng Camps

Wizards' Guard

Telensee River

The Great Battle

Kaifeng Helar

Infantry

Cavalry

Cannons

"I'm ready," said Jarren, who could do absolutely nothing, "Are you?"

"Yes. Now don't distract me."

Jarren shut up and watched the seekers come. They spread out into a vast cloud across the front of the army. If they all traveled at the same speed, they would reach the center of the line—right where they were—before anywhere else. Closer and closer. Was this really going to work? He was holding his breath. The infantry in front of them held their breath, too—but they also held their ground.

The seekers were here. The whole front of the army erupted in flame and smoke as the hidden packages of untreated cartridges exploded. An instant later, the cannons discharged in a long salvo that ran down the line in each direction, following the powder train of cartridges. Immediately behind the batteries, larger explosions blasted upwards out of the holes where the untreated limber ammunition had been placed. Bits of wood from the limber chests flew skyward. Finally, massive detonations from the 'ammunition wagons' shook the ground to the rear as geysers of red flame and white smoke billowed into the air. A few of the fireflies continued to circle about, but Idira and Hess, a mile north and south of here, were sending out the waterbugs as fast as they could make them. Shortly, Jarren could not see any more fireflies.

The instant the powder ignited, the men began to scream and shriek at the top of their lungs—just as they had been instructed to. For they were all completely unharmed. The special powder in their pouches and in their muskets had not gone off. It had worked! The untreated powder had safely flashed in front of them, or exploded behind them in deep holes where the blasts could hurt no one. Jarren saw the artillery crews dash to their guns, roll them back into firing position and start to reload.

Jarren's ears were ringing, but he could still hear Lyni chanting something from beside him. He looked and saw her intense expression of concentration. Now it was time for *her* magic! Lyni was a student of winds and waves. There were no waves here to control, but today she needed only the wind. Jarren could not feel it, but the wind was collecting the smoke from the explosions. All the clouds from the limber chests and ammunition wagons she sent floating upward, out of the way and clearly--and spectacularly--visible from where the Kaifeng were massed. The rest—all the smoke from the planted cartridges and discharged cannon—she gathered into a long thin cloud that stayed close to the ground and moved out until it was fifty yards away from the front rank of the infantry. A curtain of smoke, a hundred feet high and twenty yards thick and seven miles long hung in front of the army—and waited.

The men continued to scream, but with less conviction. The strange white wall stilled their voices. They had been told what was going to happen, but being told about a miracle and actually *seeing* one were two, very different, things. And above their waning cries came a new sound; two new sounds: There was the high pitched yells of the Kaifeng warriors...

...and there was the sound of hooves.

Lots of hooves. Lots and lots of hooves. Nearly a million of them. All pounding the ground at once. It was like the roar of the ocean in a terrible storm. It was coming closer and closer. The men could hear it and some took a step back. Sergeants and officers swatted them back into line.

"Stand fast, you dogs!" shouted a hundred sergeants in a dozen different languages up and down the line. "If you run you're a dead man. If the Kaifs don't kill you, I will!" Jarren watched from the platform and clutched the railing with white-knuckled hands.

The officers called the men to attention. "Front rank, kneel!" came the command. The leading rank of men went to one knee. "Battalion, make ready!" The men made a half turn to the right and brought their muskets across their bodies, pointing the muzzles ahead at a forty-five degree angle. They brought the hammers back to half-cock.

Still the noise grew. The thunder of the hooves drowned out the cries of the Kaifs. Jarren could not believe it. The ground was actually shaking. The vibrations traveled up through the supports of the platform, through his own legs and seemed to collect inside his chest. But nothing could be seen through the curtain of smoke, nothing at all.

"Wait for it! I'll have the balls of any man who fires without an order!" snarled an officer close to them.

Louder, closer. Jarren's heart was in his throat as he tried to see through the smoke. He wanted to shout, to scream. Every instinct in his body was telling him to run; find a hole and cower down in it until this terrible storm passed him by. Instead, he stood next to the woman he loved and stared into the smoke.

There! A horseman emerged from the cloud, almost directly in front of him! Then another. Dozens, hundreds more appeared almost immediately, scattered all along the line of smoke. The men with the fastest horses burst through the smoke at a full gallop...

...and saw what was waiting for them.

Even from over a hundred yards away Jarren could see the shock on their faces. They had galloped wildly forward expecting to find what they had found before: a stunned and disordered mass of men, helpless and ready to be slaughtered. Instead, they found solid ranks of steady infantry.

"Rear rank, present!" the order ran down the line. The third rank of infantry brought their muskets up to their shoulders and pointed them straight at the oncoming horsemen. They pulled the hammers back to full-cock.

The Kaifs hauled back on their reins, trying to stop or turn before they ran into the unwavering wall of flesh and steel in front of them. But more riders were emerging from the smoke. More and more and more. Men shouted and horses protested as they tried to stop their headlong rush toward death. The infantry officers waited a few more heartbeats, carefully judging the narrowing distance. Waiting for just the right moment to...

"*Rear rank—FIRE!*"

Along the vast, seven-mile front of the army a rippling, roaring, tearing volley crashed out. Since the timing and distances varied enormously, it was not a single, precise detonation; instead it lasted for fifteen or twenty seconds from start to finish as regiment after regiment let loose its fire. Sixteen thousand fingers squeezed sixteen thousand triggers. Hammers fell and flints struck steel. Priming flashed and sixteen thousand one-ounce lead musket balls were flung out to slam into the flesh of horses and men. White smoke obscured the target for an instant, but it could not blot out the sound. The battle cries of Kaifeng warriors and the thunder of hooves were drowned out by the screams of stricken men and animals.

Lyni shouted something at Jarren's side and the smoke from the volleys was whisked away, straight up.

"Rear rank, load! Center rank, present!"

"*Fire!*"

Another impossibly long volley rippled along the line. It started before the first had even finished and another hail of lead death lashed out. At this range, against a target like this, it was literally impossible to miss. Every ball was bound to hit a target. Some of the horses and some of the men were probably hit many times, while others escaped for the moment, but the whole front of the Kaifeng charge came crashing down in a tangle of dying men and dying horses.

"Battery—Fire!"

The reloaded cannons now added to the incredible din. Loads of canister on top of a solid round shot tore through the packed enemy. The canister shattered into hundreds of musket balls, taking down dozens of men at a single shot, while the solid iron cannon balls tore through rank after rank, mangling the animals and their riders in the most horrible fashion.

"Center rank, load! Front rank, present!"

"Fire!"

More death leapt from the lines, but more and more Kaifeng continued to emerge from the wall of smoke. The front of their charge was now just a mass of dead and dying flesh. Those who had come behind could neither go forward through the kicking and screaming horses who were down, nor could they go back against the press of their unsuspecting fellows.

"Rear rank, ready! Present!"

"Fire!"

The rear rank was reloaded now and fired again. They had four shots left. Still the winds whisked away the smoke from the guns, giving a clear view of the targets; still the deadly wall concealed what was happening from the oncoming Kaifs; still the muskets and cannons roared out to claim more victims. Horses fell and riders struggled free, only to be felled by the next merciless blast. No one had gotten to within twenty paces of the battle line. In a narrow space, thirty yards wide and seven miles long, Death reigned.

A hand clutched at him and Jarren turned to see Lyni there. She was shouting at him, shouting as loudly as she could, but he could hear nothing at all above the roar of the guns. He put his ear right by her mouth and she screamed again. "I can't hold it any longer!" Her face was streaked with sweat and she nearly collapsed in his arms. He looked at her and then looked back to the slaughter. The smoke from the guns was no longer flying upward as it had been, and the wall of smoke suddenly began to drift away. At first it stayed in an almost solid mass and it was like the greatest curtain on the greatest stage in the world going up.

Jarren held Lyni and watched the spectacle. The fire was slower now. The kneeling front rank could not reload easily from that position and had fired only once, then they set the butts of their muskets on the ground and presented a solid hedge of bayonets to the enemy. With only two ranks firing, a few of the Kaifs somehow fought their way through the carnage and came forward. But their horses could not be forced through the wall of bayonets and the warriors waved their swords in frustration until the next volley brought them down.

Three of the six rounds per man had been fired. The rear rank brought their weapons up and fired off the fourth. The artillery was daring to break the untreated powder out of their crystal boxes. Jarren could not even guess how many dead were piled up in front of the line, but there were still huge numbers of the enemy milling about just beyond. Arrows started to fly out of that mass. Most flew too long and others were short. A few found their mark and here and there along the line a man would go down. But the bow fire was wild and disorganized as all the warriors and horses swirled in a confused mob. The shots were the acts of desperate men who could neither go forward nor back. And the guns continued to roar; the men wielding them began to cheer a wild, animal yell; those of the enemy closest to the line were chopped down by an invisible scythe.

The rear rank was loading its last round now. If the fire faltered, what would happen? If the Kaifs regained their order they could rain arrows down on them and the army would be as helpless to reply as the Kaifs were now...

"Look!" screamed Lyni in his ear. "Look!"

Jarren looked. At first he could not see what she meant, but then the smoke cleared a little and he saw: Kaifs galloping away.

Those to the rear were finally realizing what had happened to those in front. They could see the dead, see the unbroken lines of the enemy, see what the round shot crashing through the entire army was doing. They had been told the magic would clear the way; that the enemy would not be able to fight back. The veterans of last year had gloated and boasted and today they led the way to show the newcomers how it was done.

But the veterans had lied.

The enemy's fire weapons still worked—and worked horribly.

And the veterans were dying. Smoke and fire and terrible, terrible noise had devoured the leading *helars*. Now Death was beginning to gnaw at those who followed. Lies! All lies! Those farthest to the rear turned their horses and galloped away. A shout of *treason!* was heard and in moments a thousand other voices had taken up the cry.

"They're running!" screamed Lyni. "They're running!"

Brigadier Mattin Krasner was terribly frustrated. He couldn't see what was going on! From his reserve position all he could see was the backs of the infantry and smoke. Lots and lots of smoke. From time to time the smoke cleared enough that he could see Kaif horsemen going down and when the nearby artillery fired he could see bits of men and horses flung up into the air. But that wasn't enough, dammit! He desperately wanted to ride forward so he could see, but he had to stay with his command. That lucky bastard, Carabello, was up on that platform. *He* could see!

But the mere fact that he could not see anything told him that the plan was working. The infantry and artillery were blasting away at something and not a single Kaif had made it through the lines. A few arrows came soaring over and plunged to the ground, but that was all. The battle line was solid and steady and continued to fire.

But not for much longer. Their ammunition was nearly gone. If something didn't happen soon...

"They're running! The Kaifs are running!"

Matt didn't know where the shout came from, but it pierced through the noise and was quickly taken up by many others. Running? The enemy was running?

The infantry stopped firing. He didn't *think* they had fired off every shot they had, but he could have been wrong. Were they out of bullets—or targets?

He was again suppressing the urge to go forward, himself, when a courier came galloping up to him. A very young lieutenant with a wild expression reined in his horse and didn't even bother to salute. "They Kaifs are falling back! You are ordered to attack at once!"

The boy had also forgotten to say just who had sent the order, but right now Matt did not give a damn. "Prinz! Go up to the infantry and have them clear a path for us!"

"Yes, sir!" His aide galloped off.

Matt had remained mounted throughout the battle, but his

troopers were still on foot. Now he ordered them to mount. An orderly handed Matt his helmet. It was an absurdly elaborate gold-plated monstrosity with a huge red plume. His officers had given it to him as a gift and he had not been able to refuse it. He turned in his saddle and shouted as loudly as he could. "Forward, at the walk—*March!*"

CHAPTER TWENTY-THREE

Atark knew something was amiss almost from the moment the army started forward. True, his own spell had gone off flawlessly and the seekers had dashed ahead to find the enemy's powder. It was also true that the seekers had found powder atop that ridge a mile away. Explosions had roared out and huge clouds of smoke had billowed up. He could even hear the faint screams from behind that smoke. But even as the horns of the Kaifeng blared out the order to attack, Atark had felt the enemy magicker.

He was so startled that for a moment he wasn't sure what was happening. He recognized the sensation of magic being worked, but he wasn't sure of where it was coming from. He looked to the other shamen around him, but they were all just watching the warriors go forward; exhausted by their own exertions. So where…?

From the enemy. There was someone working magic in the enemy army! It was a terrible shock: up until that moment there had not been any hint that the Easterners still had the magic. Atark could not immediately see what magic was being worked, and whatever it was was not terribly powerful, but a shudder of fear went through him. A trick! He feared that the enemy was trying to trick them somehow!

"Gettain!" he had cried, and the commander of his guard was there immediately.

"Yes, Lord?"

"Get a messenger to Zarruk! Tell him to call back the warriors! Some treachery is afoot!"

Gettain had obeyed instantly, but from the look on his face, Atark knew it was too late. Zarruk was with his *helar*, hundreds of paces away. The warriors of the other *helars* were trotting forward and already far ahead.

And there was no signal to call them back.

No one had thought there would be any need, so no signal had been arranged. Not that any of the warriors would likely have heeded it in any case. Not with the enemy army wrapped in smoke and screaming in terror.

But there was no signal and it was far too late to call the warriors back. They had gone from a trot to the gallop and charged up the hill into the smoke.

Into the smoke.

From out of that wall of white haze had come the roar of muskets and cannons and the scream of men. Muskets and cannons were firing! Somehow their powder had survived! But how? Cannon balls came out of that cloud, too, cutting through the lines of warriors still charging forward. The men had gone in and in and in...

Arark had stood on his platform, watching in frozen shock and anger. What was happening? The smoke refused to drift away and reveal what was behind. Magic was at work. It seemed to go on and on forever: The terrible noise of the guns and the screams of men and horses. But at last the feel of the magic stopped and now the smoke began to disperse.

It revealed the wreck of the army—the ruin of his dreams.

At first he could not see a great deal, but he could clearly see that huge mounds of bodies had been heaped up on the crest of the ridge. Then he could see that the enemy line was unbroken and continued to vomit flame and death.

And he could see Kaifeng warriors fleeing in panic.

Along with the cries of fear he could hear men shouting about treason and betrayal. Atark groaned. Four of the five _helars_ who had been at Berssenburg were in the forefront of the attack. They were the ones who had seen the magic work. And they were the ones who were now dead. The others had only heard the stories. True, they had seen the earth-shaking spell used at Gira, but they had not seen an army destroyed by magic. All they had were the stories. Now they thought the stories had been lies. A trick. Betrayal. No matter that it made no sense that those who had told the lies were the first to die: they had been betrayed. Cannon balls had torn apart their friends and splattered the survivors with bloody entrails. No, this was shameless betrayal!

As he watched, the whole swirling mass of the mighty army unraveled into a mob of terrified, angry, fleeing men. It tumbled away from the unbroken enemy and came galloping back the way it had come. Except for Zarruk's _helar_, the invincible army had become a pack of fugitives.

Trumpets rang out from the ridge and Atark could see that the enemy was not content with the carnage it had already inflicted. The ranks of infantry were opening up in spots. Men were dashing forward to drag away some of the piled corpses and clear a route forward for their own cavalry. On both flanks and at several points along the line, horsemen were emerging. Closest to where he stood a large body of them were coming forward. The sun glinted off polished armor and lances. Heavy, armored cavalry. As he watched, they picked their way through the mangled dead and began to deploy into a line. There looked to be several thousand of them.

A blast of horns yanked his attention to closer at hand. Zarruk's *helar* was forming itself to charge and Atark groaned again. *No! Zarruk, you fool!* He had the only organized body of warriors left and he was about to charge uphill against a heavily armored foe! He could almost see his friend's face: twisted with rage and shame at the ruin of his grand army, thirsting to strike some effective blow against the treacherous foe; a target presents itself and without thinking he orders the attack! Fool! And as impetuous as the move was, he was ordering it too late. If he had gone forward the instant the enemy appeared he might have succeeded in striking them before they were fully deployed. But he had to wait until the fleeing rabble of the other *helars* were past. He had a half-mile to cover and by the time he did so, the enemy would be formed and ready to fight. Ruin and more ruin!

Was there any way he could stop him? No. It was too late—again. He could see Zarruk's bright red banner leading the way. But was there anything he could do to help? The seekers were of no use. Somehow the enemy had found a way to defeat them and this cavalry probably carried no firearms anyway. What else could he do? He could toss a few fireballs into the enemy ranks, but it would do little good. Burning up a half dozen men was all he could hope for and that would not stop them.

But he had another fire spell that the Ghost had taught him.

It would create a vast, rolling wall of flame that would incinerate everything in its path. It could burn up all that enemy cavalry and go on to blast through the center of the infantry line. It would not kill all of the enemy, only a small fraction of them, but it might be enough. It would halt their counter-attack, punch a hole in the center of their lines, demoralize their troops, and it might—it just might—be enough to rally the Kaifeng. If they could just be made to stop and collect their wits, they could still win the battle! Yes!

But he would need power for the spell. A great deal of power.

"Gettain!" he shouted. "I will need more sacrifices! Quickly, man!"

"Yes, Lord, but the holding pen is a mile or more to the rear. It will take time to fetch them."

"What!?"

"I am sorry, Lord, but one of the new Kas demanded the spot we had wanted to use for his own camp. I saw no harm in it, so I moved the pen for the sacrifices farther back."

"Fool! I need them now! I cannot wait or all will be lost!"

"I can send men on horses..."

"No! It will be too late!" Atark hesitated for a moment and his eyes darted across the rows of tents and pavilions only a few hundred yards to the rear.

"Gettain! Take your men and scour those tents for any slave you can find. Any slave! I care not who she belongs to! Get them and bring them here!"

"At once, Lord!" Gettain began shouting to the guards who had been standing idle since they killed the sacrifices. He turned to run off himself, but Atark grabbed his arm. His fury against the East was boiling in his veins.

"Gettain! The slave who is in my tent: Bring her, too."

"Forward, at the trot—*March!*" Matt shouted the order and the trumpeters echoed it immediately. Sixteen hundred horsemen kicked their horses into motion and started down the long slope to meet the enemy. The Wizard's Guard made up the first two ranks and then there was a thirty pace gap and the 1st Mundoorian Heavy Horse followed. The four hundred horsemen in each rank took up nearly five hundred yards of front and the heavily armored cavalry rumbled down the ridge like an iron avalanche.

Matt had been gnashing his teeth at the delay in deploying. The Kaifs were fleeing for their lives and they had to keep after them or they would rally and then there would be all nine hells to pay. But there was no choice. The masses of dead and dying in front of the infantry had to be cleared out before his own cavalry could pass through. Not all of them, of course, but enough that he could get past. It had been done very quickly, all things considered, but every passing minute was a lost opportunity. It did not make it any easier that the light cavalry on the flanks was already in hot pursuit. Perhaps the enemy dead weren't as thick over there, or they had managed to get around the ends of the lines, or perhaps the light cavalry didn't give a damn about attacking in a formed body. Whatever, they were already hacking down the Kaif stragglers and Matt was not.

But as the last of his companies came onto line he saw that he had something far better than stragglers to fight. A large body of Kaif cavalry was coming up the hill toward him. They were not running, they were attacking! Good! And judging from the number of banners flying above the enemy ranks, there might well be some important leaders coming his way. Even better! In spite of the gut-wrenching slaughter he had seen as he came forward, he had not struck a blow yet. He dearly wanted to strike a blow!

And here was his chance. The enemy was four hundred yards away and already starting to gallop. Damn fools, even their sturdy ponies would be nearly blown by the time they came up this hill. He would not make the same mistake.

"Keep your ranks!" he shouted. "Forward at the canter!"

They picked up the pace and the distance closed rapidly. The Kaifs were losing whatever formation they might have had and were coming on willy-nilly. They shouted war cries in their heathen language. Matt wanted to kill them all.

"Gira!" he screamed. "Remember Gira!"

"Gira! Gira!" shouted the men. Matt wanted to shout 'Remember Fort Pollentia', or 'Remember that awful battle we never gave a name', or 'Remember Berssenburg', but none of those would do. Everyone here would remember Gira.

"Gira! Gira!"

They were at a hundred yards and the men brought down their lances. Matt did likewise. There was a big Kaif right in front of him and he was carrying some sort of standard that was bright red. A perfect target. He shifted his lance slightly.

Twenty yards, ten. The enemy were here on foam-flecked horses. But the Wizards' Guard never broke out of a canter. Their ranks were as straight and as solid as if on parade. Each man knee to knee with his comrade on either side. The Kaifs were met by an impenetrable wall of iron and lance points.

The opposing sides slammed into each other with a shout and a crash, but for the Kaifs it was like throwing snowballs at a boulder rolling down a hill. They were simply batted aside or crushed underneath. Matt's lance caught the man with the standard full in the chest and killed him instantly. Unfortunately, it also broke his lance in two. He snatched out his sword and slashed madly at anyone close enough to reach as he thundered past. Most of his men had similar success and the whole front of the Kaif charge was wiped out in a heartbeat. A few Kaifs survived and somehow managed to break through the front rank—only to be lanced by the second.

Another line of Kaifs was hacked down, and another. Matt's brigade sliced its way through the enemy. But slowly the charge was grinding to a stop. There were just too many Kaifs in front of them. There had probably been six or eight thousand of them to start and they simply could not all be shoved aside.

Matt's horse slammed into a Kaifeng pony and even though the smaller horse was pushed back, it could not go far because of the press behind it. It couldn't even fall down, so great was the crush. Matt slashed at another man and he tumbled off his saddle. Anyone unhorsed in this mess was sure to be trampled to death. A heavy blow struck him from the left, but it bounced off his armored shoulder piece. He twisted and shoved the point of his sword into the man's throat. The Kaifs wore no armor and they did not know how to fight the metal-clad behemoths who had crashed down on them.

Now the press was lessening. Matt could see the rear of the Kaif formation peeling off. They were going for their flanks, but there was nothing he could do about that. Matt used his spurs and his horse lurched into motion again. Suddenly he was face to face with a very large and powerful man. He was dressed richly and had a golden circlet on his brow. Matt didn't know who he was, but he was determined to kill him.

It might not be easy. The man was strong and seemed to be filled with a fury that matched his own. The Kaif's curved scimitar darted about like a striking snake. In consternation, Matt realized his opponent was a far more skilled swordsman than he was. The Kaif struck him several times, but the armor turned aside the blows. Even with the armor, he received a painful wound in his thigh and a bloody gash along the side of his face. None of his own strokes were getting through at all—and he was getting tired.

Boom! Boom! Boom!

All of the firing had stopped a quarter hour earlier, so these new reports came as a complete surprise. Matt dared to glance backwards in time to see smoke billowing out from the nearest battery. A moment later two dozen of the Kaifs who had been massing on his flank were smashed to pulp. The man he was fighting was even more startled and his horse reared. Matt saw his chance. His sword crashed down on the Kaif's head and sliced all the way through to his jaw. The golden circlet bounced away in two pieces.

He wrenched his sword loose as the body fell out of the saddle. He screamed a battle cry and looked for new enemies to fight. But the Kaifs had had enough. The cannon shots through their ranks and the fall of their leader and the seemingly-impervious armor of their foes were just too much. They turned their horses and tried to flee. A good number of them were not able get away and were hacked down from behind, but the rest galloped off as fast as they could.

"Reform! Reform!" shouted Matt. They had to keep moving. Don't let the enemy rest or recover! He looked beyond the retreating foe and saw a man on a wooden platform a half-mile away. Yes. Yes! There was his target!

"Form up, Lads! Our job's not done yet!"

Thelena's head hurt and she was so terribly sleepy. She had heard faint screams in her sleep, but now there was another scream. It was much louder and very close; it cut through to her consciousness.

Kareen was screaming.

Her eyes snapped open.

Kareen was a few feet away, shrieking and fighting madly with— Gettain! Why? What was wrong? She was so confused!

"Thelena! Thelena, help!" Kareen scratched Gettain on the face and the large man responded with a cuff that knocked the woman senseless. He had a rope and he tied Kareen's hands behind her back.

"Today you will, die, you Berssian bitch!" snarled Gettain.

"What? What are you doing?" gasped Thelena trying to understand.

"Your father's orders, my lady. She's needed for the sacrifice."

"No! Stop!" The horror that coursed through her cleared some of the fog from her head, but when she reached out, she ended up sprawling on the carpet. "Gettain! Stop! I command you!"

But when she pushed herself up, Gettain and Kareen were gone.

"No! *No!*" she screamed. She howled. *"Noooo!"*

"Kareen! Kareen, no, no *no!*"

She couldn't catch her breath. The tent was spinning around her. This had to be a nightmare. A mistake. It couldn't be true. Her father wouldn't...

Yes. He would. He had always hated Kareen and he would do it.

"No! Father! Don't! Please!" she sobbed.

She tried to stand up but she couldn't. She crawled a few feet, then caught her hand on something and fell, banging her face on a low table and cutting her lip. The pain seemed to help. The fog lifted a little bit and she could taste the blood in her mouth. She had to get up! But her arms and legs were numb and tingly and had no strength in them. She had to get up or Kareen would die and be damned.

She forced herself not to panic. She took a series of deep breaths and then started to crawl again. She went over to the cooking implements and found a long knife. The handle seemed cold and hard and very real in the foggy world that surrounded her. More breathing and then she crawled to the center pole of the tent. She grabbed it and painfully pulled herself upright. Her legs felt like they belonged to someone else. Another few breaths and she let go.

"I'm coming! I'm coming, Kareen!"

She staggered out of the tent to find her friend.

"Hurry! Hurry!" snarled Atark. "Get them ready!"

His guardsmen were dragging the slaves into position. Four or five hundred terrified, screaming women fought madly, but uselessly as they were bound to the forked stakes in the ground. The bodies and severed heads of the previous sacrifices lying there told the women exactly what was going to happen to them. They shrieked and wailed and begged for mercy, but all to no avail. Atark's men had become immune to such pleadings—even though they had never done this to women before. Even so, some were clearly disturbed—especially since some of the women were obviously pregnant.

Atark, himself, felt sick at the thought, but there simply was no choice! He whipped around to face the enemy and saw that they were coming on. Zarruk's *helar* had been scattered. His red banner had fallen and Atark had no doubt that his oldest friend was dead. Zarruk never would have retreated and if he was not retreating he was dead. He banished all doubts from his mind. The enemy was a half-mile away and coming directly toward him. The spell would burn them all! It would burn some of the fleeing warriors, too, but the cowards deserved no less!

He turned to look at the sacrifices. They were all nearly in place. He recognized some of them: Women taken in the very first battle at the fort. Almost all of them would belong to the men of Zarruk's *helar*, but those men were all probably dead now, so it did not matter. Directly behind his platform he saw Gettain dragging Thelena's slave into position. The woman had blood on her face and was fighting frantically. But then she stopped and looked past Atark at the fleeing army and her expression of fear turned to one of triumph. "You've lost!" she screamed at him in passable Kaifeng. "You can kill me, kill all of us, but you've lost, you bastard!" Gettain struck her across the face and she fell. He quickly bound her to the stake. Atark looked up and down the line of sacrifices. *We haven't lost yet, you bitch!* The men all had their swords and lifted them to indicate they were ready. Atark raised his own hands and reached for the power.

"Very well! Begin!"

Kareen was surrounded by screams. The high pitched shrieks of women filled her ears, her mind, and her soul. She had never heard anything like it. This wasn't the scream of women being captured, or women being raped. This was the scream of women being slaughtered.

She was one of the ones who was screaming. Her brief bit of defiance had evaporated when she found herself bound to a blood-soaked stake and looking into the eyes of a severed head only a few feet away. She was going to die and from the terrifying hints Thelena had given her, this would be the most awful death anyone could ever die. She screamed and she struggled, but it did no good at all. The fork of the stake was sticky with the blood of the last victim and the rope held her tightly and she couldn't get away.

Gettain was standing over her with his bronze sword raised. He saw her looking up at him, but his only expression was hate. She had no idea why he hated her, but she knew that he did.

And he was going to kill her.

The screams took on a new and even more urgent tone and Kareen twisted around as much as the restraint would allow. All she could see was the backs of a line of executioners stretching away and the bodies of the women they would soon kill, kneeling and thrashing on the ground. There was no hope left. She closed her eyes and prayed to the gods. She prayed that Matt would be safe and that

Thelena would not suffer too much. She prayed that the gods would take her soul in spite of what was about to happen.

And she prayed for victory.

She had seen the Kaifeng army fleeing in panic. She had glimpsed the unbroken army of the Easterners on the far ridge. Victory seemed at hand and she prayed for it.

But what was Atark doing? He was casting some new spell and her own life would help power it. What terrible magic was he doing now? She could feel a growing heat on her face and in spite of her terror, she opened her eyes. Atark was a few yards away on his low platform. His back was to her and he had his arms raised over his head. Above his arms was a vast ball of red fire. It was growing larger and larger and she could feel the intense heat of it. He was going to burn the Easterners! Burn Matt! She choked off a sob and shut her eyes again.

She could hear Death getting closer. It was marching toward her from both sides. As each executioner's blade finished its lethal task, the next one would begin to fall. The screams of the victims peaked just before being cut off forever. She could hear it getting nearer and nearer. The heat on her face continued to grow and Death was nearly here. Just a few moments more...

Then a heavy blow hit her head and for an instant she thought she was dead. But no, her head was still attached to the rest of her. Had Gettain bungled his stroke somehow? And the other screams were still going on, still coming closer, it wasn't her turn yet! Her eyes popped open and she was stunned to see Gettain's face staring up at her instead of the poor wretch who had been there before. His eyes were wide with surprise and there was a knife sticking out of his neck. Blood was still running out of the wound. What was happening?

She twisted around and saw someone standing next to her. *Thelena!* Her friend was standing there looking as surprised and as stunned as Gettain. She was literally reeling from side to side. How could she even stand with the drug she had taken—and with the pain from all the sacrifices so near at hand? But she was here! She was trying to save her!

"Thelena!" she shouted. "Cut me free!"

The woman looked down and seemed to see her at last. She collapsed to her knees and then slowly—oh so slowly!—reached out and pulled the knife from Gettain's neck. Then with growing urgency she started sawing at the rope binding Kareen to the post. It seemed to take forever and the screams were very, very close now. All the executioners had their backs to them so they could see what the others were doing and time their death-strokes appropriately, but how long until someone noticed what was going on?

The rope around her neck loosened and Kareen pulled back and she was free! "Quick! My hands!" She twisted around and Thelena went to work on the ropes holding her wrists. A moment later and they were loose, too.

"Come on, Thelena! We have to get away! We have to..." A terrible need to run, to get away from the screams was filling her. But there was a growing noise off to her left that pulled her eyes that way in spite of herself.

From where she knelt she could look right under Atark's platform. She could look underneath and see the open field beyond. That field was filled with a solid line of horsemen, perhaps three hundred yards away. They were trotting right towards her at a steady pace and the noise was the noise from their hooves. It was loud enough to compete with the dwindling screams of the sacrifices. The sunlight was glinting off their armor and their banners were flying so bravely. In front, right in the center, was a man leading them. His helmet gleamed gold and he had a huge red plume...

"Matt!" she gasped. The image from her dream came back to her like a hammer blow and in a flash she knew that was her brother.

And Atark was about to burn him to ashes.

"No!" she cried and without another thought she snatched the knife out of Thelena's hand and surged to her feet.

She went straight for the platform where Atark's spell was swelling to completion. None of the guards could possibly reach her in time!

But then she was pulled up short and she heard Thelena's voice: "No! Kareen! He's my father!" She looked back to see Thelena clutching to the hem of her skirt. Her face was twisted in pain.

That pain shot through Kareen's heart like an arrow, but she would not be stopped! She tore her skirt loose and lunged forward again. She reached the steps to the platform, but a hand seized her ankle and tripped her. She fell a few feet behind Atark. The heat of the fire was scorching her now but she threw herself forward again. Thelena was sobbing and she wouldn't let go!

Crying in fear and frustration Kareen turned around in time to see the last woman's head fall to the ground. She was out of time! She made one more frantic lunge and slashed at Atark.

She moaned in despair when the stroke was short of his back. All she succeeded in doing was driving the blade into the calf of his right leg.

The blade, the cold, iron blade.

Kareen had one instant to believe that she had failed…and then a wave of white fire, brighter than the sun, sprang from the knife and washed over her.

Atark had heard the screams and shouts from behind him, but he had refused to pay any heed to them…until the knife entered his flesh.

Then, just as it had five years before when the Varag dagger pierced his belly, he felt all the power, all the tremendous power he had collected sucked away from him. The power was gone, the mighty fireball was gone and his strength was gone. He slumped to the platform, utterly drained.

There was noise all around him. Screams and shouts and the growing thunder of hooves. But he was so weak he could not stand. Then someone grabbed him and hauled him to his feet.

"Lord! Lord! You must cast the spell and save us!" In a daze he looked and saw that it was Hobart, Gettain's second in command. What was he doing here? Then he remembered: The battle, the charging cavalry. He looked out and saw them, only a few hundred yards away.

"Cast the spell, Lord!"

"I…I can't. It's too late." The man's face went white, but he was a brave one and he nodded.

"All right! We must get you away!" He turned and shouted. "Bring horses for Mighty Atark! The rest of you, form a line! Hold off the enemy!"

Some men might have quailed at such an order, but these were the Shaman's Guard. They charged forward to put themselves between Atark and the oncoming horsemen, bronze swords raised in defiance. Hobart half carried him to the edge of the platform. Atark looked down.

Thelena was lying there! His daughter was lying senseless on the ground, a woman's skirt clutched in one hand. And a few feet away was the Berssian slave woman who had so plagued him. She was lying there, her legs bare and with a scorched and twisted knife in one hand. Her whole arm was blackened and charred and the cloth of her blouse was smoldering. Her face was burned and her hair nearly singed off. Now he understood. A rage started to build in him. She had ruined everything! If she wasn't already dead, she must now die for certain!

But the horses were here and they were starting to hustle him onto one. There was no time... his daughter.

"Wait! Wait," he croaked. "My daughter! Bring my daughter!" One of the guards scooped up Thelena and leaped onto the back of another horse. In a moment they were riding away, leaving the Berssian slave behind.

Atark was fading. He had never felt so weary. But he had a tiny bit of strength left and he clutched at Hobart, who was riding beside him.

"Take me to the tent! We must get the box!"

Matt had been quite certain he was going to die.

They had smashed through the Kaifs, reformed and then advanced again. The man on the platform was still there and Matt was certain he was the necromancer. If they could just kill him the war would be won! But as they got closer the man began to do something. A bright ball of fire began to grow over his head. More fireflies? What for? But no, this ball was red, not gold. It was something different.

Something different and something deadly, he was quite sure. And it was almost certainly going to be coming straight at him. He quickened the pace, but the horses were tired and carrying a lot of weight and they just could not go faster than a canter. They closed the distance, but not quickly enough. Whatever the Kaif was doing, they were not going to get there in time to stop him. The men in his brigade were crying out in alarm, but they didn't stop. The gods bless them, they did not stop!

But then, the red ball of fire vanished and there was a brilliant white flash. The man slumped down. A cheer went up from his men and then they began to chant:

"Gira! Gira! Gira!"

They were only two hundred yards away and he could see men moving on the platform. Were they trying to get the necromancer to safety? No! They had to kill the bastard! But then a ragged mob of

men on foot came charging past the platform. They were all screaming and waving swords. Matt looked in astonishment as they came
on. It was the bravest—and stupidest—thing he'd ever seen.
Disorganized infantry charging armored heavy cavalry?

But brave or stupid, a few moments later the men crashed into
them, yelling like banshees. It was a slaughter. The crazy fools were
wielding bronze swords! The soft metal bent and cracked against
tempered steel and Matt's cavalry just rode the lunatics down. But
the mad charge had caused his troopers to slow and by the time they
had hacked their way through, the platform was empty. A minute
later he reached it and called a halt.

The Kaifeng camp stretched out before him. Thousands and
thousands of tents, hundreds of thousands of animals—and the gods
only knew how many fleeing Kaifs. From where they were, Matt
could see that the light cavalry was already into the camp and clouds
of thick black smoke were starting to go up. The heavy regiments
from the other brigades were coming up, too. The battle seemed
won.

A victory, but not yet a complete one. For all of the ghastly
slaughter back up on the ridge Matt doubted that they had actually
killed more than fifty-thousand of the enemy. The Kaifs still outnumbered them at least two to one. If they were allowed to rally, it
could get sticky...

"Oh gods!" groaned a man at his side. Matt looked down and his
stomach heaved. Hundreds of severed heads and the bodies they
belonged to were scattered on each side of the platform The sacrifices. Matt had never actually seen this before, but the men in the
pen back at Berssenburg had. Their stories had haunted his night-
mares since then. And now here it was in reality...

But many of the sacrifices were women...

He had not expected this. Neither had any of his men. Some of
them were vomiting as they stood there. The fury began to build in
him again. It had gripped him during the fight, but it had faded.
Now it was growing again. The bastards! The heathen bastards! That
anyone could do this! Hundreds of helpless women and they had
slaughtered them! He wanted to look away, but he forced himself to
look. He wanted to remember this! He looked back and forth and he
suddenly spotted one woman who had not been beheaded. She was
lying, face-up, at the foot of the platform. But it looked like she was
dead anyway. Her face and arm were badly burned. What had the

Kaif bastards done to her?

He continued to stare. She was dressed like a Kaif, but there was something familiar about her...

"K-Kareen?" No, it was impossible. But without thinking, he slid off his horse and went over to her.

"Kareen!"

It was his sister. It really was her! With trembling hands he knelt down and grasped her. Was she still alive? He couldn't tell.

"Sir? Sir? The brigade is reformed, sir." said Lieutenant Prinz. "Shall we attack?" Matt scarcely heard him. He was searching frantically for any sign of life. He wasn't sure. Maybe...

"Sir? Shall we attack, sir?"

He looked up and saw dozens of faces looking at him and he became aware that he was crying.

"Sir?"

"Yes. Yes, attack at once. But I'm remaining here. Major Dermont, take charge and attack. Push them, Major! Push the murdering scum! But Lieutenant, send a rider back and find Lady Idira. Find the healer and bring her here as soon as she can come. Hurry!"

"Yes, sir!" cried his officers. In a moment the bugles sounded and the brigade began to move off—into the Kaifeng camp. The thunder of the hooves faded and Matt was left there with his sister.

CHAPTER TWENTY-FOUR

Jarren Carabello held Lyni's hand and looked out on the Field of Victory.

It wasn't a pretty sight.

Two days had passed since the fight, and even though the storm Lyni had predicted had come and washed away most of the blood, the burial of the bodies had scarcely begun. Thousands of people were laboring in the fields below them to dig trenches and drag the mangled remains of men and horses off to fill them. Nearly all the workers were Kaifeng prisoners and nearly all of them were women or boys. Soldiers made a perimeter around them, but since they were burying their own dead, they did not have to do much to get them to work.

All of the Eastern dead, a mercifully small number, had already been buried, but the Kaifeng bodies were so numerous the job would take many days—and they were already starting to bloat and stink. If the job seemed bad now it would be far worse in a few days. None of the smell was reaching them where they stood and Jarren wondered if Lyni was shaping the wind to keep it that way.

He glanced at the woman beside him and wondered other things, too. They had spent one night together and it had been marvelous. They had both been too tired to do anything since then, but he wondered if they ever would again. Did Lyni really feel anything for him, or had it just been the instincts of two people convinced they would soon die? He gave her hand a little squeeze and he was pleased that she returned it. Now she was looking at him.

"Well, contrary to all my expectations, we are still alive and free, Jarren Carabello," she said. "This creates unexpected complications to our lives."

"Do… do you regret what we did the other night?"

"Regret? No, not at all. It was very nice. But what do we do now?"

"I care for you, Lyni. I would like us to remain together."

"Together? How? As co-workers? Friends? Lovers? Man and wife?"

"I would be happy with any of those."

"But which would you *prefer*?"

Jarren blushed. "My wishes have to take into account your wishes. I won't force you to…"

Lyni snorted. "Jarren, you'll never *force* me to do anything. Trick, coerce, persuade, maybe, but never force."

"Good. But I still need to know what you want."

Now it was Lyni's turn to blush. "I'm not sure what I want yet. But in spite of all logic, I do care for you."

"All right. But let me know when you figure it out, will you?"

"Yes." They fell silent and just held hands. Jarren looked out on the ruins of the Kaifeng camp. The rout had been so complete that the enemy had been able to carry off very little of their goods. Many of the tents had burned and there were immense mounds of plunder. It was a measure of the fury of the Eastern soldiers that they had not even paused to loot, but had continued the pursuit as long as their horses and feet had been able to move. Most of the army was now many miles away, the Kaifeng even farther. All the reports indicated that the enemy was scattered and fleeing in many different directions. It would be hard to keep following them under those circumstances, but it appeared that the threat was largely passed. The Kaifeng invasion was stopped.

"What's going to happen to them?" asked Lyni, indicating the prisoners.

"I'm not sure. I think the General is going to try and arrange an exchange for all of the slaves the Kaifeng are still holding." Many thousands of the slaves had escaped when the Kaifeng were routed, but many more had been carried along in the flight. Some had managed to escape since then, but there was no doubt that many Eastern women were still held in slavery.

"What if the Kaifeng don't agree? What happens to these people then?"

"I don't know…"

"Slavery for them? Rape and punishment at the hands of the victor? An eye for an eye? A rape for a rape, Jarren? Where does it end?"

"I don't know."

"It has to end, Jarren Carabello. When this mess all started I did some reading on the whole conflict between East and West. It has gone on a very long time, a thousand years or more. One side gets an advantage and hurts the other. The other then takes revenge. Back and forth, on and on. Just because we seem to have the upper hand now, it might not always be that way. Only a year ago, the whole East thought like that and look what's happened."

"What can be done?"

"I think I will have a little talk with the General. It is time for someone to say: 'Vengeance might be the just thing, but this time we are going to do the *smart* thing.' Try to end this cycle of revenge."

"It would be worth a try, I guess."

"Yes it would. And the General certainly owes me a favor!"

"He does. We all do. You and Hess and Idira."

"And you, too, Jarren. None of us would have been here except for your stubborn stupidity."

"Why, thank you, Lyni. It's very sweet of you to say so."

"I mean it. Every word."

They stood there a moment longer and then, in unspoken but mutual consent, turned and walked back to their camp. Most of the army was still gone, pursuing the Kaifeng, but the camp was nearly as large as it had been before. The wounded and the escaped slaves made up for the soldiers who had left. Women bustled about everywhere, in sharp contrast to what had been before. Jarren wondered what was going to happen to *these* women? For the most part, their men were dead and their homes destroyed. They had been slaves to the Kaif warriors. What future did they have? The thought struck him, that some of the slaves the Kaifs held might not want to come back…

They reached a small cluster of tents arranged under a large tree and saw Hesseran sitting with Colonel—Brigadier—Krasner. Both men rose when they approached. Hess looked tired but happy. Krasner looked tired and happy—but worried, too. They all exchanged greetings and then sat down while a servant brought them tea. Gez was a few yards away practicing with his sword like the old veteran that he was.

"How is your sister today?" asked Lyni. Krasner's look of worry strengthened, and he glanced toward the tent where his sister was being tended.

"Idira says that she will live, but she is still unconscious. Her injuries were very serious."

"I'm amazed she's alive at all!" said Hesseran. "You do realize what she did, don't you?"

"No, not really."

"She saved your life and your whole brigade is what she did! Maybe all of us!"

"What are you talking about?" demanded Krasner clearly very puzzled. Jarren had a glimmer of what Hess meant, but the Alchemist continued.

"Well, from your description of what went on just before you found her, it's quite clear what happened. The Kaifeng magicker was in the midst of casting a spell—a very powerful spell, too! I could feel it clearly from where I was, two miles away, and it was enormously powerful. But the spell was never cast. It was cut off just before completion. There are several ways such a thing can happen, but the easiest is to touch the magicker with cold iron. Iron won't affect a spell after it's cast, but during the casting process it will suck away the magicker's power like a sponge. From the nature of your sister's burns and the half-melted knife she was holding, it is quite evident that she stabbed the Kaifeng necromancer as he was casting the spell. The power drained away through the knife—and her. Like I said: I'm amazed she survived."

"Gods!" hissed Krasner. "I didn't realize..."

"She's a hero," said Lyni. "I look forward to meeting her."

"That's really fascinating, Hess," said Jarren. "It might lead me to believe that magical energy is similar to electricity in some ways. Blast, where is my notebook?"

Everyone laughed, even Krasner. "Always the scientist, Jarren!"

"I try. That is what I am, after all. Once this is all over I truly hope to be able to return to my research."

"I'm sure you'll be able to do that, eventually," said Krasner. "What about the rest of you? What are your plans?"

"Immunize gunpowder," said Lyni and Hess in unison. They simultaneously grimaced and rolled their eyes. Krasner laughed again.

"Well, I'm afraid we'll need you to do that for a while yet. We used up nearly all we had in the battle. Our pursuit is operating almost entirely on bluff. If the Kaifs manage to rally themselves we'll be in need of a lot more—unless, of course, Kareen managed to kill the Kaif necromancer..." he trailed off.

"We can't assume that," said Hesseran, "so we'll need to work you up a whole new supply."

Lyni frowned. "Sometimes I think that maybe Stephanz was right about you mainlanders making us into slaves."

"That's not going to happen," said Jarren firmly. "I won't allow it."

"Good intentions are fine, Jarren," said Lyni, "but they rarely count for much."

"Then we shall have to safeguard our rights ourselves," said Hesseran sternly. "We have something these people need. Something they need very badly. Once the immediate crisis is past, we have the power to demand our rights, Lyni."

"What are you suggesting?" asked Lyni.

"They need the immunized gunpowder. They need it in large amounts, they will need it for years to come, and right now we are the only ones who can make it. That gives us a great deal of bargaining power to get what we want."

"And just what do you want, Master Alchemist?" asked Krasner. "Money? Power? Property? Titles of nobility?"

"Possibly. Maybe some or all of that. But mostly I want control over my own life. I will *not* be locked away in an armory somewhere with a monthly quota of powder to treat!"

"Damn right," said Lyni.

"I don't think you will have to worry about that," said Krasner. "After all, you are heroes now. People are going to want to see you and talk to you and considering that there are only three of you, no one's going to stand for you being locked away out of sight."

"Hopefully not. We shall certainly fight any attempts to control us. And don't expect us to provide you with powder so you can track down and exterminate all the Kaifeng. Once they've been driven back where they belong, we'll give you enough to defend the passes, but that's all."

Krasner frowned for a moment, but then he shrugged. "That's all outside my control. But, in any case, my original question about your plans was really about after things quiet down and you are free to do what you want. What then?"

"I'm not really sure," said Hesseran. "Idira is determined to make a school to teach healers. In memory of poor Thad, if for no other reason. She's not going to compromise on that."

"Nor should she," said Krasner, nodding. "After what she has shown people here, everyone is going to be demanding more healers."

"I suppose the logical thing to do it to set up a school for magickers in general. Teach all of the arts."

"That would be wonderful, Hess!" exclaimed Jarren. "Perhaps I could set up a parallel school for the study of the scientific aspects of magic. I've known for quite some time that the success of my studies was going to depend on consulting with the real practitioners. I know that there are several cities in Ertria, where I come from, who would welcome such a university."

"I suppose that could be done. And you have already more than proved your worth as a researcher, Jarren. We could all benefit."

"Just how are we going to pay for something like this?" asked Lyni, ever the practical one.

"That, you don't have to worry about," said Krasner. "All the wealth we took in the Kaifeng camps is legal plunder and shares will be given out based by rank. All four of you will rank as major generals for the distribution. None of you will lack for money."

Gez was suddenly right there. "What about me? What's my share gonna be?"

Krasner laughed. "I suppose we could justify a lieutenancy for you, Gez. Even that should work out to more money than you can fritter away easily."

"What about the original owners of all that wealth?" asked Jarren.

"Who cares?" said Gez, grinning.

"Most of them are dead. Finding the rightful owners for the rest would be nearly impossible. Fortunes of war, you know."

"That hardly seems fair," said Lyni. "What about all the freed slave women? They will be in great need. They should be provided for."

Krasner frowned but then nodded. "I'll talk to the General. Perhaps something can be done."

"Something damn well *better* be done! In fact, I have a few other matters to discuss with the General."

"Gods help him," whispered Jarren.

They all looked up as Idira joined them. Krasner jumped to his feet. "How is she, Idira?"

"She's waking up. I think you should be there." Idira looked incredibly tired. She had been healing the wounded almost non-stop since the battle. Krasner took her by the arm and accompanied her into the tent.

Kareen was struggling up out of a deep, dark hole. It seemed like she could hear countless voices screaming faintly all around her. She had been climbing for hours and hours but she never seemed to get anywhere. The screams bothered her enormously. They reminded her of something that Thelena had told her about. Something terrible. Was she dead? Had she been sacrificed to Atark's magic? Was she doomed to flounder in this endless blackness for all eternity? The thought gave strength to her struggles and she clawed desperately at the hole.

Then, after a measureless time, she thought she saw light above her. She pulled and pulled herself up, toward the light. *Thelena? Thelena, are you up there? Help me get out, Thelena!*

"Kareen? Kareen? Wake up, honey." She heard a woman's voice. It was close, very close. The light was close, too. After a while she realized it was just on the other side of her eyelids. With a terrible effort, she opened them and let the light in. Her eyes were open, but everything was just a blur.

"Thelena?" she whispered.

"No, honey, my name is Idira. But here's someone you know."

One shadowy shape moved aside and was replaced by another. She blinked and blinked and tried to focus.

"Kareen?" The voice sounded familiar. Damn, she wished her eyes were working!

"Who...? M-Matt?"

"Yes, it's me, Sis. How are you feeling?"

"Matt! Oh gods, you're alive!"

"You are, too."

"Am I? Really?"

"I think so. Let me check." The shape came closer and she felt his arms going around her In spite of pain in her right arm she hugged him back. Her tears were flowing and they seemed to be clearing her vision a bit. She could see him now. It was really him. She clutched him tight and the tears flowed and flowed. She held him for a long time, but finally he pulled back and they looked at each other.

"Good to see you, Sis."

"Good to see you, Big Brother. How did I get here? And where's here?"

"You're in our camp. I found you and brought you here. Lady Idira has been tending your wounds." Kareen looked to the side and saw a fat, jolly-looking woman who was smiling at her. In spite of the smile she looked terribly tired.

"Thelena? Is Thelena here?"

Matt looked puzzled. "No. Was she with you? When you...when you...?"

A stab of fear went through her. "She was there with me. Right with me. Did you look for her?"

"Yes, we searched all around for anyone who might have been alive. When I found you, there was no one close by at all."

She breathed a little easier. "Was Atark there?"

"Who?"

"The Kaifeng Sorcerer, Thelena's father."

"Gods! Her father? No, the sorcerer got away."

"He probably took her with him. I hope she's safe."

"I could scarcely believe it when I saw her outside the pen in Berssenburg. I owe her my life."

Kareen hesitated and in that moment decided she would never tell Matt about her own role in his escape. "We both owe her our lives, Matt. She is a good woman." She shifted position slightly and winced.

"Are you hurting, Kareen?"

"Some. How bad is it?" She held up her right arm and saw that it was completely covered in bandages. It felt like there were bandages on her head and face, too. The plump woman came closer.

"You are doing fine, dear. The worst of it is your right hand. You've lost your two smallest fingers—I couldn't save those, but the rest will heal fine. And there will be no scars, except for the ones you already had. I do good work, if I do say so myself."

"Thank you," said Kareen. She looked at the oddly shaped bandages on her hand and realized why they looked odd. But only two fingers lost. A tiny price to pay for all that she had been through. "But how can you know there will be no scars? Burns almost always leave them."

"Idira isn't any ordinary healer, Kareen," said Matt. "She's a magical one."

"Magic? But..."

"Oh yes, we found some sorcerers of our own. Fought fire with fire, so to speak."

Kareen just shook her head. This was all too confusing and she was so tired. "What will happen to me now?"

"When you are well, you can go home," said the woman.

"Home? Where's home now, Big Brother?"

"Wherever you want, Sis."

She thought about it. Where would she want to go? She was free to make a choice and it felt very, very strange. She'd had a life of her own once. If she tried hard, she could remember it. Well, even then it wasn't really hers. So many things had held her in a narrow place. The fort... the regiment... Matt... Phell... suddenly she was crying.

"Kareen, what the matter?" asked Matt.

"I... oh gods. Matt, I'm sorry."

"Sorry? About what?"

"I... I broke my promise to you. I'm sorry."

"What promise?"

"The one I made the last time I saw you." She sniffled and tried to wipe her nose on her bandages. Matt looked puzzled.

"I'm sorry, Sis, with all that's been happening I don't remember what promise you made. But it's nothing to cry about."

"Yes, it is. I promised you I'd still be a virgin when I went down the aisle. I can't keep that promise now, Matt. I'm sorry." She was sobbing again.

Her brother looked stricken. But his expression wasn't one of anger or shame. It was guilt. He began to cry, too. Kareen had not seen him cry since Father died... He clutched her to him.

"It doesn't matter. It doesn't matter. Just so long as I have you back!" he hissed. "No one will care about what happened!"

Kareen held her brother and they both cried. She was so grateful that he still accepted her even after everything. But was he right about no one caring? She remembered how the Kaifeng women had shunned and snubbed Thelena. Would her own kind be any different? Probably not—if they knew...

"Let's go somewhere far away, Matt," she said. "Far, far away. Where no one knows us. Somewhere with lots of trees and near the ocean. I miss the ocean. And somewhere warm."

"Well, the wizards are thinking about a school in Ertria," said Matt, stopping his tears. "That would suit. And maybe they'll still want a Wizard's Guard. Probably will, come to think of it."

"Ertria would be fine," whispered Kareen. Suddenly she was very, very tired. The healer was at her side instantly.

"That's enough excitement for now," she soothed. "Time for you to get some more sleep, young lady."

She could feel herself fading. But she refused to go just yet. "Matt? Matt? You weren't lying to me about Thelena, were you? You didn't find her with the dead, did you? Were there any prisoners? Look for her, Matt, please? I couldn't bear it if she ended up a slave again."

"She wasn't with the dead, Kareen, I swear. And I'll look for her with the prisoners, I promise. Now you listen to the healer and go to sleep."

"Yes, yes, I need to sleep. You'll still be here when I wake up again, Matt, won't you?"

"I'll be here, Sis. Go to sleep."

"Yes…" She started drifting off, but her last thoughts were not of her brother or where they might end up living, they were of Thelena. *Where are you, my friend? Will I ever see you again or know what happened to you? I owe you everything. My friend. My very best friend…*

"All is lost," said Atark to the floating image of the Ghost. "The army is shattered. The tribes and clans go where they will. They fight and steal from each other. Zarruk is dead, Oliark and Ferache are dead, even Battai is dead. The other Kas are discredited and cannot control their men. All the veterans, all the ones who believed in me, are dead. The newcomers flee like frightened sheep and cry that they've been betrayed."

"Where are we now?" asked the Ghost.

"South of Gira. A few score of scores have attached themselves to me, but my guard was all but destroyed and I have no real authority over these men. They cling here, hoping I can work some miracle."

"Then you shall have to give them one."

"What do you mean?" Atark stared at the Ghost and tried to ignore his throbbing leg. The wound wasn't serious, but days of riding had left it very sore. He had found a little tent to use and this was his first chance to consult the Ghost since the disastrous battle was fought.

"The men have lost hope, but you must show them that all is not lost. This is but a setback. Victory can still be ours."

"But how?" demanded Atark. "The enemy have magickers of their own now. The seekers no longer can destroy their powder. True, they do not seem very strong, but not even my fire magic can win a large battle all on its own. And if their magickers grow stronger or more numerous…"

"Worry not. From what you say of their actions, these magickers are nothing. I can teach you ways to destroy them. And there are other things I can teach you that will gut their army and restore the

advantage to us—all without any warrior even striking a blow."

"How can that be?"

"You have so much to learn, Atark. The magical arts are deep and strong. There are things I can teach. I can show you how to tear the soul from a man and yet leave his body alive. What remains will be a fearless and obedient assassin who can seek out the enemy magickers, the enemy generals and leaders and slay them. Imagine a thousand such agents stalking in the enemy ranks! Or you can set loose magical plagues that no physician can cure. Decimate your enemies before you even enter their lands. There are spells that will drive your foes mad so they will slay themselves. Once you have destroyed their magickers nothing can stop these spells. There are many possibilities."

Atark was simultaneously fascinated and appalled. Such things were possible? Hope began to grow in him that the war might yet be salvaged, that his revenge upon the East might yet be fulfilled.

"But first, you must secure your leadership of those around you," said the Ghost. *"The first spell I will teach is one that can command unquestioning loyalty and obedience. You can use it on the leaders of the tribes you encounter. Once you have a solid core of followers, you can force the others to..."*

The tent flap was suddenly pulled aside and Atark jumped when he saw his daughter, Thelena, kneeling in the opening. The image of the Ghost faded somewhat in the light, but it did not disappear. "Thelena!" cried Atark. "You should not be here!"

"Neither should you, Father! This monster has poisoned your mind for too long—but it ends *now!*"

Before he could react, Thelena raised something in her fist. It was a small iron mallet they used to hammer tent pegs.

"Thelena! Don't!"

But it was too late. The hammer swept down and smashed the skull to pieces.

"No!"

Atark looked at the scattered fragments in despair and dismay. But to his amazement, the Ghost was still floating before him. The image flickered and changed color rapidly. Red, green, blue, purple, but it did not disappear.

"Bitch! Traitor!" roared the Ghost *"Too long you have worked against me, but I will have you now!"*

Thelena reared back in surprise—and then the Ghost flew

straight at her. Flew straight *into* her!

"Father!" shrieked Thelena. Her hands went to her head. "Father, help me!"

What was happening? The Ghost was inside his daughter!

"Thelena!" Atark did not know what to do, but instinctively he reached out and seized Thelena's head in his hands. Her eyes were wide with terror. He reached for the power and...what? He was not sure what he did, he was acting solely on instinct.

He could feel the Ghost's presence close by, there was a trail of sorts leading into his daughter and he launched his consciousness along it—into Thelena.

He was—elsewhere.

A gray mist surrounded him. It was like being in a dense fog. He could see nothing. Hear nothing. "Thelena!" he cried.

"Father!" He heard his daughter scream. She was close. Very close. He moved into the fog, deeper and deeper, toward his daughter's voice.

There! There she was! A ghostly image of his daughter was forming just ahead.

But she wasn't alone.

Ransurr was there. Not just the image of the disembodied head, but all of the ancient shaman, just as he had first seen him in the mound. Richly dressed and with the miniature skull on the chain around his neck.

He had Thelena.

His arms were wrapped around her and he was drawing her closer and closer. She kicked and punched and fought back desperately, but she was slowly being pulled to Ransurr.

In horror, Atark realized Ransurr was going to rape his daughter. Not some trivial penetration of her flesh, no, he wanted to ravish and defile her very soul. Take it and enslave it!

"Thelena!"

Atark rushed to his daughter's side and Ransurr looked up in surprise. Atark's fist seemed as immaterial as everything else, but he struck with every bit of strength he had. He seemed to hit *something* and Ransurr cried out in rage.

"You fool! Don't interfere! This is the only way!"

Atark struck again.

Ransurr snarled and struck back. A shock of pain worse than anything he had ever felt slammed through him. Clearly, the Ghost had managed to husband more of his power than Atark had ever suspected. But that would not stop him!

"Leave her alone!" he cried and struck again. The blow made Ransurr lose his grip on Thelena. She pulled free and lashed out, hitting Ransurr by surprise.

"You shall never have me, Drinker of Souls!" she screamed.

Ransurr fell back. Atark and his daughter attacked, side by side. Blow after blow rained down. The Ghost tried to ward them off but seemed weaker at every stroke.

"Stop! Stop! You fools! You're throwing everything away!" Ransurr drew off and held out his hands. "Atark! Atark, my old friend! Stop and think! If I am destroyed then everything is lost. The war, our revenge, everything! Give me your daughter! She will not be harmed, I swear! You will still have her, but she will have my powers and knowledge! Together we can still conquer!"

The Ghost was fading. Bits of it seemed to be peeling away and dissolving like mist. Thelena clutched at Atark.

"Die and be damned, Ransurr!" she snarled.

"Atark! Please! There is no time left! Give me your daughter!" The Ghost was fading, evaporating.

"No," gasped Atark. "No, you may not have her. Die now. Die as you should have so long ago."

The Ghost screamed. *My life! My vengeance! No!* His wail trailed away into silence. He grew fainter and fainter.

Then he was gone.

Atark turned away and embraced his daughter and...

...they were back in the little tent. Fragments of bone were scattered about and an iron mallet lay on the ground.

"Father! Father!" sobbed Thelena. She clutched him and he held her very close. After a long, long time they let go of each other. Atark looked around and felt a strange sense of loss.

"What have you done, Daughter?"

"What had to be done. It had gone too far, Father."

"But the war... our revenge on the East. I swore to your mother and your brother that the East would pay for their murder. I swore to make them pay for your pain."

"And they have paid! How many deaths, Father? How much blood? How much pain? I am avenged! I require nothing more from the East in payment for my pain! And Mother and Ardan, how much do you think they desire? If you could ask them how many deaths, how many widows and orphans would satisfy them, what would they tell you? Ask yourself the question! How many deaths would your wife want?"

Atark looked down and could not meet his daughter's eyes.

"It's enough, Father. Enough!"

After a long while he nodded. He looked up into Thelena's face. "Enough," he whispered. She moved closer and put her arms around him and wept. He could feel her tears on his cheek. He returned her embrace and held her as long as he could—until the pain in his leg became unbearable and he had to move. They sat back and looked at each other.

"What shall we do now?" he asked. "The men will expect me to lead them back to war. And what future can I give you now?"

"Then we shall go away, Father," said Thelena. "Far away. Far, far to the West, where we have never been before. Where no one knows us. Where none shall expect miracles from you. As for me, that does not matter. Let us pack up in the night and be far gone by morning. By tomorrow we shall just be another pair of people returning to the plains."

Atark thought about it and nodded. It was a good plan. With his powers, he could protect them if necessary. Once safely away, they could find a new tribe. He had learned enough useful magic that he would be welcomed almost anywhere. And Thelena? She would be his recently widowed daughter. Her husband killed in the Great War. None would question that. She would be welcome where they settled. She could find a husband to love and bear his grandchildren. Yes, yes, it was a very good plan. All the anger and all the pain which had filled him for five years seemed to flow out of him and evaporate just as the Ghost had. Enough.

"We shall leave this very night, Beloved Daughter," he said.

Thelena smiled. "We shall go back to the plains, Dearest Father. Back where we belong. Back home."

"Yes. Home. That sounds very nice." He shifted and then groaned because of his leg. Thelena took his arm and helped him out of the tent.

He left the little tent and the little wooden box and the shattered fragments of an old, old skull behind. He walked away without a backward glance.

Thelena helped her father over to the fire where the few survivors of his guard were preparing dinner. It was going to be difficult to elude them when they fled tonight, but it would have to be done and somehow she had no doubt that they would succeed. She helped her father sit and after she saw that he had food, she got up and walked away from the fire.

A strange energy was filling her. She should have been exhausted from the long retreat and from the terrifying fight with Ransurr, but instead, she could barely sit still. The prospect of seeing the plains again was thrilling. She had hated the mountains and feared the forests, but the plains! Oh, how she longed to ride them again!

She realized that a whole new life was stretching out before her, just like those plains. Endless opportunity; no boundaries. Free! She thought she had been free when she was rescued from the fort, but now she knew she had been wrong. She had only been returned to an old life—a life that was forever stained with pain and sorrow. But now, her life would be new. She could not wait to start living it.

She walked farther away and turned to look East. The setting sun made the treetops look like green flame. Kareen was over there somewhere. Miles away, but somewhere. After the mad flight from the battlefield, Hobart had told her that Kareen was dead, but she knew that wasn't true. She had been holding Kareen's ankle when she struck her father and she had felt some of that terrible jolt that had gone through her. Kareen's spirit had nearly flown then, blown away like a leaf in a gale, but Thelena had seized it and held on tight. Afterwards, she was still touching her and she knew that she was still alive—and that she would stay alive. Somehow, she could feel her life even now.

I hope you are well, my friend. I hope you are with Matt and that you are safe and happy. I shall miss you very much, but I shall keep you forever in my heart. We come from two different worlds, you and I. Our worlds touched and warred for a time and we were thrown together. It was only together that we survived that storm.

But our worlds are drifting apart again and we shall go our separate ways; you East and I West. We shall not meet again in this life. But the bonds that join us cannot be broken by men or gods or death, itself. We won't meet again in this life, but in the next? Who can know?

Good-bye, my friend. May the gods watch over you and keep you safe.

Good-bye, Kareen. Fare thee well.

THE END

STELLAR PHOENIX

Made in the USA